Keeper of

the Dream

Dawn -
Here we go
again - Enjoy!
Love, Kim

Kim Mattson

Keeper of the Dream

All Rights Reserved

Published By
Port Town Publishing
601 Belknap Street
Superior, WI 54880

Web Address:
www.porttownpublishing.bigstep.com

ISBN: 0-9725990-9-6

To the newest member of my family—
my granddaughter, Hannah,
who melts my heart...

A Note from the Author:

Not too many years ago, I visited the Black Hills area. At the time, I planned to begin a bit of research for my second novel, never guessing that the Sioux's *Paha Sapas*, the Crazy Horse Memorial, and the teeming herds of buffalo would touch my heart in such an unforgettable way. I couldn't return home to Minnesota soon enough to begin my story.

Hours of research went into *Keeper of the Dream*. I found myself drawn to the plight of the Sioux people at the end of the nineteenth century. Real life characters such as Chiefs Crazy Horse, Big Foot, and Sitting Bull grew larger in my mind. They were good men who were unfortunate enough to be caught up in the final battles of the great Plains people—misunderstood because their one goal was to continue living as their forefathers had. Actual events that took place in their lives were woven into *Keeper of the Dream*. Other characters were a product of my imagination—giving me creative license to build a story around August Moon and Cole Wilkins.

I never gave actual thought to the idea of a family trilogy. It was my wonderful publisher and editor, Jean Hackensmith, who presented the idea to me one day. In fact, she insisted that I follow *Keeper of the Spirit* and *Keeper of the Dream* with a third story that will be published in April of 2004. Thus began the idea of the *Keeper Trilogy*—three brothers, three books.

I hope you enjoy the Wilkins' family's second story and that you will be sure to read the last in the series, *Keeper of the Heart*, next year!

Kim Mattson

Publishing credits:

"An Hour on the Porch" (A short story, included in "Fourteen Pieces of Gold"
Available through Port Town Publishing

"Girls' Weekend" (A short story, included in "Sixteen Pieces of Gold"
Available through Port Town Publishing

"Keeper of the Spirit"
Available through Port Town Publishing

"Keeper of the Dream"
Available through Port Town Publishing

"Keeper of the Heart"
(Available April of 2004, by Port Town Publishing)

The great Crazy Horse fathered a child in his early years;
a daughter who did not live with him.
She was not recognized as one who carried his blood
within her veins—or so the story goes.
The rumor has been reputed throughout the years...
but what if such a thing had come to pass?

Keeper of

the Dream

Kim Mattson

Prologue

Camp Robinson, Nebraska
October, 1878

The weathered flap of the teepee rustled quietly. An old woman glanced up in anticipation from where she sat on the hard ground before the fire's dying embers. Her blurred gaze settled on the shape of a young woman, who stepped gracefully through the opening. The girl paused, allowing her brown eyes to adjust to the quiet gloom. The clamor of the outside world became muted when the buffalo hide was pulled shut by a trembling hand. Their gazes met, and each recognized the other's sorrow.

"Come, child, let us sit awhile and visit."

The younger woman moved noiselessly and lowered herself to the cool ground. Her face remained shadowed in the dim light, but the old one could feel the tangible sadness of her grandchild.

"Are you ready to travel?"

"Yes, Grandmother. I have packed my few belongings and only wait for the call to leave." The young woman sat stoically and watched as her grandmother leaned forward to reach out with the gnarled hands of the aged. The girl's slender fingers were grasped in her grandmother's frail grip, and she immediately felt a rush of pain lace through her heart at the thought of leaving this old woman.

"Grandmother...are we doing the correct thing?"

The old woman's gaze searched the beloved face before her, amazed once again at how much her granddaughter resembled her father. She carried his narrow face; his eyes, which were more brown than black; and his skin, which was of a much lighter hue than others of her kind. Her long, black hair was laced with waves, unlike the other females of her race who boasted straight, flowing locks. If ever anyone doubted that she was the offspring of the great warrior chief, Crazy Horse, they had only to search her features or look into the girl's heart to see his reflection.

The old one stared keenly at her granddaughter and squeezed the small hand once more. "My child, you must hear the words I speak. Since the white monster has come to invade our home, we have lost almost everything that is the people. We can no longer pray to the Great Spirit unless we do it in secret, for the white man's holy men try to change our words and make us non-believers. The great buffalo herds are gone and, along with them, the food that makes us strong; again because of the white man. We are forced to live a crowded life on their reservations, instead of being free and powerful as we once were."

The child saw her grandmother's tension ease when the elderly woman's bony shoulders dropped to a relaxed stance, but the old one never took her gaze from the soft velvet brown eyes before her.

"How can you question whether it is right or wrong to escape back to our sacred land? Your father was a great man. He believed in the rights of the people, the privilege to pass freely over our own lands, to live as we always have. If you do not go at the appointed time, you will most likely be destined to live under the rule of the white man. Your life as a Lakota will be gone for all time. It is your only hope." She sat back stiffly and closed her eyes, tired and spent from speaking the words.

The young woman swallowed her sorrow once more and bravely controlled her emotions. Her grandmother's actions were proof that she did not want to speak of it again. The time to say farewell was at hand. Threatening tears were blinked into submission, but the child was not ready to give up.

"Grandmother, will you not rethink your decision and come with us when we leave?"

The old Indian squaw loosened her hand from her granddaughter's tight grip and reached for a small oilskin bag. Gnarled fingers worked at the drawstring. When the sack was opened, she spoke with quiet reverence.

"Do you remember the day we placed the ashes of the fire within this?"

Her granddaughter nodded slowly and met the filmy eyes of the old one. "How could I not? It was the day I came from the mountain. The day of my vision."

"Yes. In that vision, you saw yourself as a woman helping your people...leading your people. You are your father's closest blood relative at this agency. After he was murdered, the Sioux finally accepted that you are his true daughter. They know of your vision and will no longer laugh. They know of your warrior heart, even if you are a woman. They have nowhere else to turn—the sight of you gives them hope. This is the only thing they have left. It is your destiny to travel north with your father's people as the vision has shown." She raised the bag. "These are the coals from the fire that day. Remember—they will always guide you." She slowly pulled the drawstring closed and solemnly handed the leather bag into the young woman's keeping.

The granddaughter held the pouch close to her heart with trembling fingers. Her thoughts moved to the past and the memory of quiet ridicule from her village as her grandmother repeatedly explained her heritage to the others. She had heard the story many times.

Her mother spent a brief time with Crazy Horse when he was young, and she was the result. Her mother passed to another world at a young age, and the old woman before her loved her, nourished her, and never let her forget who she was.

Days before her father was tricked into going to the agency, the great man requested her presence. He revealed what was probably his last vision. Crazy Horse had seen the truth, then acknowledged her as his blood daughter.

Her own vision from that long ago day flashed in her mind. She looked at her grandmother and wished now that she had informed her of the full extent of what she saw that day. She had only been a child of six winters, and the memory of the dream truly frightened her.

The vision had shown her the terrifying view of two worlds colliding. Even now at her youthful age, she knew her way of life and the lives of her people were coming to an end. The whites were just too many. They came to the land like the locusts on the prairie in years of no rain—and they would keep coming. The vision showed that beyond a doubt. As each day passed, she understood it more.

Why me? The day on the mountain should not have happened. The gift is something that few females possess. Her body shuddered and, once again, she felt the searing physical pain she suffered that day. She left the horrifying shriek of her own voice behind, mounted astride a horse with wings as the burning ache tore at her. The vision was a premonition of her own death.

She mentally shook away the feeling of doom, then glanced at the old woman. To tell her grandmother now of the carnage she had envisioned, of her people falling to the ground only to lie in their own blood, would serve only to deeply distress the gentle woman. The course was set. Like her great warrior father, she would lead her people and meet the Great Spirit with unflagging courage.

The call to assemble invaded their quiet safe world, and the young woman felt suddenly rushed to say farewell.

"I will miss you deeply, grandmother." She forced herself to be strong and refused to show the tears that had been never-ending since the decision was made to flee northward. A slender, trembling hand rested against her chest. "I know here in my heart that I will never set eyes on your loving face again, and the notion rips at my insides."

The old woman leaned forward and grasped her granddaughter's slender body in a final private goodbye. She inhaled the scent of the girl and committed it to memory. "I am too old to run with you. I would only hold the people back when youth and a strong will to survive is needed for this journey you must take. Go now, child, I can hear the others preparing themselves. Remember, all you must do is think of me, and you will know that I am with you. Never forget that my spirit and the spirit of your father will follow you always. We have said our goodbyes and must not give the plan away on the trail. It is done."

Batting back her tears, the younger woman rose shakily and trudged to the opening in the tent. Turning, her gaze fell once more on her grandmother, who had guided her along in her short life thus far. She paused for a moment more, raised her hand in farewell, then slipped quickly back through the slit in the teepee.

* * *

Lieutenant Beau McCabe kicked his horse into motion and galloped through the dust to the front of the two-mile long procession.

"Sergeant! What seems to be the problem here?" His mouth was set in a straight line. His piercing blue eyes had taken on the look of a harrowed commander with each passing mile as the small regiment of Cavalry soldiers moved the reluctant Sioux eastward to a more secure agency. They had traveled seventy-five miles since leaving Camp Robinson and still had quite a distance to go. Keeping the Indians together was proving to be a task he was not certain he was up to.

The sergeant half-heartedly saluted his lieutenant and shook his head in disgust. "Sir, these damn redskins are dragging their feet and tauntin' the regiment. Half the time we don't know what the hell they're sayin'. Now the old ones have refused to walk any longer. They're pointing at the supply wagons." His thick eyebrows arched along with a narrowing of his flat gray eyes. "Should I make an example out of one of them and show 'em what the hell they'll be up against if some order isn't restored?"

"Cool your heels, Sergeant." Beau spun his horse around. His gaze scanned the milling Indians. "I can't blame them in the least if they refuse to walk any further today. They haven't eaten a decent amount of food since leaving Fort Robinson."

The Indians' living conditions and food sources in the months preceding the move were not conducive to readying them for such a trek. The young lieutenant tried to reason with his commander when he was first informed of his orders to move the entire band to a secure agency closer to Missouri. The Sioux were not ready to travel, either physically or mentally, but his pleas went unnoticed. The high-ranking officials in Washington cared nothing about the conditions—they cared only about procuring safer lands for the many Americans moving westward. The poor misplaced people of the land had lived on stringy government beef and bread made from wormy flour for the last...

How long has it been? Beau was so tired that it seemed like the journey was taking forever. His mind flitted through the past years and remembered a time when his patriotic views were governed by the fledging notions of a new command.

When he first asked to be transferred to the territories to work with the Indians, never in his life did he believe he would have a hand in suppressing their great spirit and participate in the decimation of one of the greatest cultures in America. He watched them die of diseases spread by the settlers who traveled the Oregon Trail. He watched the government steal their land from beneath them. The Sioux died slowly of starvation; the promise of food, which helped lure them into the agencies, never came to pass. He saw their proud features and unending humor turn into the blank stares of a lost people with nowhere to turn. It continually disgusted him when he saw how the government treated these people—people whom they had sworn to lead to a better way of life.

Now, he was a part of the annihilation.

A loud yelp drew his attention. He reined his horse around once more, and the sight that greeted his eyes made Beau feel as if he walked through a dream. Close to a third of the Indians they were herding east had suddenly veered northward. They ran for the far off slopes of what the Sioux had named the Black Hills, their *Paha Sapas*. A gunshot rang out, and his mount started beneath him.

"Put down your weapons!" His heels dug into the sides of the horse and the animal shot forward into the line of fire. Beau waved his arms wildly to gain the attention of his troops. Unbelievably with all the commotion, his command was heard, and the men lowered their rifles.

The sergeant he addressed a moment earlier raced to his side in a cloud of dust. "Sir! Are you just gonna let them run? It's easy pickins'!"

"Control yourself, man." Beau inhaled deeply in an attempt to remain calm and held tightly to the reins of his dancing horse. "Look at the number of Indians we're escorting. Just how smart do you think it would be to keep shooting? If we incite the rest of them, we'll all be dead or they'll all be running. We're a handful compared to their numbers."

"But, sir—"

"Let them go." Beau watched as each loping step the runaways took put distance between themselves and the procession headed east. He could not blame them one bit for wanting to escape. His tired eyes took in the soldiers who raced toward him, most likely in search of an order to follow the escaping band north. "Let the poor bastards go," he repeated more to himself than to anyone else. "They must have had this planned before we ever left Camp Robinson; otherwise we would've had the whole damn group taking off."

His weary gaze turned to the remaining Indians who now seated themselves on the dusty ground. Instead of the familiar blank stares, Beau now saw pride tinged with smugness in their black eyes.

He reined his horse back in the direction of the group that headed north. The last of them topped a small butte, and he could not help but hope they would find what they were running for. His desire that they be blessed with good fortune would make no difference, though. As far as Beau knew, the escapees possessed no weapons or food, and winter was closing in quickly. Beau brought his attention back to his men with a shake of the head. They still awaited a directive.

"Gentlemen, we'll stop for the day," he called out. "Set yourselves up for the night, and then get busy handing out food to these hungry people. Use as many of the supplies as you have to. I want to make sure these people go to sleep with full stomachs tonight."

"But, sir, the food in the supply wagons—"

Beau's sidearm left his holster so quickly that it surprised even him. Sparks of anger shot from the blue depths of his eyes like flames from a kiln as he pointed the weapon at the irritating man before him.

"You have three seconds, Sergeant, to decide if I shoot you for disobeying orders, or if I put this weapon back in its holster. What's your decision?" The click of the gun's hammer thundered in the sudden silence.

The surprised man backed up hastily and, tripping over his own feet, pitched backward to the ground. Embarrassed, he jumped up, swiped at the seat of his pants with trembling hands, and never took his eyes from the lieutenant's trigger finger.

"No problem, sir. I'll get the men moving right away." He turned with an unsettled look in his eyes and barked orders to the stunned regiment, who shifted silently in the aftermath of Beau's command.

The lieutenant re-holstered the gun with a heavy sigh and dismounted. He passed an old woman and, when their eyes met, he did a double take. He could have sworn he noted a perceptible nod of approval. He walked on and looked northward for the last time.

God—I hope they find what they're looking for.

They would need help not only from his God, but from their own Great Spirit as well, if they were going to survive to see another spring.

Chapter One

Minnesota,
July, 1890

Cole Wilkins snapped the whip only inches above the ground and urged the colt into a gallop. A grin tugged at his lips when Thomas, his eight-year old nephew, squealed with delight.

The time in the paddock was a daily ritual between them. The boy would wait patiently until his uncle's chores were done, and then the two made their way to the big stable to work at saddle-breaking the younger horses.

Pulling on the long tether attached to the animal's bridle, he brought the colt to a slow walk on the beaten circular path within the paddock. Cole then handed the lead rein to Thomas and let the boy take control of the animal.

"That's it, Tom, just turn with the horse and keep the rein loose." As they walked the familiar circle, Cole listened to Thomas chatter about inconsequential happenings around the ranch. The boy was like a sponge, soaking up everything and every event of his day.

"Guess what, Uncle Cole. Katy said she would make me an apple pie today. I told her we needed to make sure to save a chunk for you."

"Thanks, Tom. What about everyone else?" His expert eyes noted the slight tightening of the lead rein as the boy rattled on. "Keep the line loose." At the tender age of eight years old, Thomas already did a good job with the horses under his uncle's tutelage. "Okay, now pick up the speed a little and get him to move into a canter. Now, back to that pie. You better make sure you save a piece for your sisters."

The boy skillfully snapped the rein and smacked his lips together to urge the young colt on. "Sara and Janie don't need no pie—they get enough treats from Mamie when you and me are out workin' these horses."

Cole simply shook his head and tried to hide his smile at the boy's inflated self-importance.

A voice called out from the direction of the main house. Cole turned at the sound and squinted into the sun to see his sister-in-law, Emma, stride across the yard. She reached the fence, then hiked her daughter, Sara, more firmly onto her hip and gave them both a wave.

"Mama! Watch me. I'm training the horse all by myself!" Thomas' chest puffed out and the smile on his face widened to crease his round, brown cheeks.

"Good job, Thomas," she called back. Emma laughed when her son adjusted his hat down onto his small forehead, sobered his expression, and mimicked his Uncle Cole.

"Horse trainin' is serious business, Mama."

"So is washing up for dinner. How about you scoot yourself back up to the house and attend to that matter, young man."

"Oh, Mama..."

Cole retrieved the lead rein from Thomas and gave him a loving pat on the shoulder before sending him on his way. "Listen to your ma and get going, pardner. Tomorrow's another day. I'll be right behind you." He watched as the boy lit out for the house.

"I'll save ya a piece of pie, Uncle Cole!" Thomas called over his shoulder.

"You do that!" Cole flashed a wide grin at Emma and pushed his hat back on his forehead. "That son of yours is like a whirlwind. Sure wish I had his energy some days."

Emma threw her head back with a laugh, then automatically tightened the grip on her small daughter when Cole poked Sara's belly to produce a giggle. She tilted her head to gaze up at him with sparkling green eyes.

"You're so good with him. If he's not talking to me about something his father did, he's telling me about one of the escapades you two shared. You'll make a great father someday."

Cole rolled his thickly lashed eyes at his sister-in-law's comment and shook his head. "I have a feeling you're going to start on me again. You can stop right there."

"Humor me." Emma's green eyes twinkled again and her dimples deepened.

"No way! I've watched you matchmake Trevor right into relationships on a monthly basis. That's not going to happen to me! You've got him walking around with big calf eyes and a tongue hanging out of his mouth every time he dates. He's starting to resemble Tyler."

A laugh bubbled from Emma's lips again as she envisioned her own husband doing just that.

Cole admired her deep auburn hair as it shone in the sun, and the memory of the first time he saw Emma danced across his brain...

She and his brother, Tyler, met in New York nearly ten years earlier, during an awful time in Tyler's life. He was still grieving after the death of his first wife and, though something sparked between Tyler and Emma from the first time the couple laid eyes on one another, he left her after a single night of passion and returned home. A few short months later, Tyler received a telegram that stated Emma was pregnant with his child. Her father insisted that she move to Minnesota and marry the father of her baby, and the ensuing 'war' between the two drove everyone on the ranch to distraction.

Tyler and Emma continued to fight their secret desire for one another until one tragic autumn day when a man from Emma's past nearly killed her and caused the miscarriage of the baby. Only then did Tyler finally realize what he had almost lost for a second time.

Now, as Cole looked at his sister-in-law, it became apparent once more what Emma had done for his eldest brother. They possessed two beautiful children, and Tyler still turned to jelly every time his wife stepped into a room. Janie, Tyler's daughter from his first marriage, worshiped the ground Emma walked across, as did everyone else on the ranch.

Once the two settled into a relationship born of love and trust, Emma began an all-out effort to marry off her husband's two very eligible brothers. She managed to quite efficiently direct both Cole and Trevor to any event in the area where she knew single young women would be in attendance. Emma never missed the opportunity to remind Cole that he had much to offer a woman. He always accepted the matchmaking with good grace and understood that Emma simply wished him to be as happy as she and Tyler...

Cole handed his dusty hat to Emma and reached for his niece. Once the toddler was settled on his shoulders, the three turned toward the ranch house.

"Now, why would I want to go and get married?" He eyed her with a raised eyebrow and a comical grin curving his lips. "Maybe you just want me out of this big, sprawling house so you and Tyler can have it all to yourself."

She slapped him playfully and shook her head. "You know I would never want you to leave. It's bad enough having Trevor on the road all the time. It seems he's never at the ranch anymore. I remember Tyler telling me once that if we were to do this business of horse breeding correctly, it would mean a lot of time away, and it seems Trevor got the brunt of all the traveling."

Emma's expression turned wistful and the playfulness of the moment disappeared. "Cole, I just want you to be happy. You have so much to give and you don't even realize it. When I first arrived in Minnesota, you embraced me without a thought and were there for me when I needed you. You never once judged me for showing up pregnant on your brother's doorstep."

Her thoughtful gaze turned to sweep the treeline behind the ranch house, and Emma became lost in her thoughts—thoughts of a terrible night two years after her arrival at the ranch, when Samuel Fontaine dragged her from the house with the intent to kill her. She shuddered, remembering the nightmarish incident and how Tyler, Trevor, and Cole came to her rescue. It was Cole who finally pulled the trigger and ended Samuel's rein of terror for good. Her mind's eye could still see him standing at the edge of the trees, lowering the smoking gun from his shoulder.

That was also the night she gave birth to Thomas; the night the first Lakota Pine's riding horse was born, thus beginning a partnership between herself and the three Wilkins men. The last eight years had not only been exciting as they watched the mares multiply and add new stock to the lines, but it was also sad when buyers frequented the ranch to bid on the horses. As foolish of a notion as it was, Emma would have preferred to never sell a one of them.

"Emma?"

"Mmmm?" She turned to look at her brother-in-law's handsome face.

"I lost you there for a moment. I appreciate the fact that you only want happiness for me, but I just haven't found what I'm looking for."

He stopped just short of telling Emma of the agitation he had experienced lately. *If she were to find out what I'm feeling, she would never stop campaigning for prospects for me.* Cole Wilkins was not becoming bored with his existence, he was thirty-one years old now and thought there should be more to his life.

Lately, there had been something pulling at him; something just slightly out of his grasp. It was a feeling as fleeting as the moment just before wakefulness when he floated in the last remnants of a dream and something tangible was just within reach. Then his eyes opened, and the dream was snatched away. He knew it was there; he just needed to discover it.

They stepped onto the front porch and turned in unison when the sound of a horse cantering through the log gates reached their ears. It was Tyler, and he was home a day earlier than expected from a horse selling expedition.

A small cry of excitement left Emma's lips as she barreled down the steps to greet her husband. Cole watched as Tyler dismounted with outstretched arms. Emma flung herself into his embrace with a smile reserved only for him, and he pulled her close and kissed the upturned lips.

Is that what I'm looking for? Someone to greet me at the end of a long day with a smiling countenance and love shining in her eyes?

The idea that his mere presence was enough to make a loved one's day brighter was something Cole had not yet encountered. Would it be enough? Is that what he needed to find?

"Hell if I know," he muttered before he, too, left the porch to greet his brother.

* * *

That same evening, the Wilkins adults retired to the library to discuss Tyler's month-long trip.

"We got a good price, Cole." Tyler seated himself on the sofa next to his wife and stretched his long legs out before him. "Pederson never even flinched when Trevor asked for seven hundred a head. He flipped the cash out of his jacket like it was pocket change. Before we left to board the train for home, he sent a message to the hotel. He wants us to deliver a couple more two-year olds before winter, sight unseen. Wish Fargo wasn't so damned far away."

"Does this mean you'll be traveling again? You've just returned home." Emma searched her husband's face with a sinking feeling in the pit of her stomach. The sale would force another separation.

"This business contact is too good to pass up, Em. Mr. Pederson is influential and plans to contact some of his associates on our behalf. It could be the break we need to become a premier horse supplier countrywide."

He saw the flash of aggravation in her gaze before his own eyes sparkled with excitement. "While I was out there, I had a chance to view a stallion whose lineage goes back to the Byerly Turk. Trevor and I had some pretty lengthy discussions with the owner, and there's a good possibility we may be able to purchase the animal. Trevor was so excited by the prospect of introducing new blood to the Lakota line that he stayed in St. Paul to look at brood mares in the event that we do decide to purchase the new stud." Tyler took one look at Emma's face and knew what was coming. If there was one thing he had learned about his wife, it was her fierce loyalty to the animals they now owned.

"And what's the matter with our present line?"

Tyler saw the stubborn set of his wife's jaw and cringed as she plowed on before he had a chance to answer.

"We've added fine, sturdy brood mares in the last two years. The foals born last year were top quality, Tyler. Every animal we've let go has the perfect temperament to be sold as a riding horse. Storm has proven himself a fine sire. Why do you feel we need a new stallion?"

Cole chuckled to himself. As far as Emma was concerned, there were no finer animals than the ones being bred on the ranch. "I agree with you that we're producing good stock, Em, but, I don't think Tyler has finished with his reasoning yet." He looked at his brother and continued. "Am I right in that assumption?"

Tyler showed no surprise at Cole's perceptiveness and nodded his head in agreement.

"I think, Emma," Cole continued, "that I know where Tyler's going with this. The Byerly Turk was a superb Arabian. All his offspring possess great speed and endurance. It's a trademark of his descendants."

"I know that," Emma replied. "But, many of those descendants are trained for the race track.   We're in the business of raising quality riding stock—" She whirled to face her husband once more. "Is that where you're going with this? Are you planning to dabble in the racing market?"

"After viewing that stallion out there, the thought did cross our minds. How do you feel about our idea now?" He lifted an eyebrow in question and waited for her response.

Emma sat dumbstruck until, slowly, a smile spread across her face as she considered the speed their animals already possessed. · Bringing in a thoroughbred to crossbreed with their own brood colts could only be a lucrative business venture for all of them. Her smile widened when she thought of Spirit of Lakota, the first foal, born the same night as Thomas. The partnership had received many offers for the mare, but Emma stood firm. Spirit would never be sold. As she thought of the filly's great speed, her excitement mounted. The notion to raise racing champions was something she had never considered, but it definitely merited some discussion.

"I see by your smile that you might be changing your mind." Tyler grinned at his wife.

"I've never given it any thought. But, if we're all in agreement that this is an angle we should pursue, I guess my vote is to branch out." She paused, then a defeated sigh escaped into the room. "Whether or not we buy a new sire though, is beside the point right now. I'm more concerned about the fact that you'll be leaving again to deliver those two other mares to Mr. Pederson."

Cole stretched his arms high above his head in a characteristically nonchalant stretch while eyeing the two seated across from him. "I'll go, Emma, and Tyler can stay here."

Her head swung in her brother-in-law's direction and her gaze widened in amazement. "But you never get involved in the delivery end of the operation. And, besides, you're in the middle of training three horses right now. How can you leave?"

"Dougan can handle things while I'm gone. He's turned into an expert with those young ones, and they seem to respond well to him. Besides, I've been a little itchy lately for a change of scenery."

"Are you sure, Cole?" The thought that Tyler might be able to stay home thrilled Emma, but she did not want her brother-in-law to leave just because she was going to miss her husband. "We all have our own roles within the business, and you never deliver the horses to potential buyers. That's Tyler and Trevor's responsibility."

Tyler shared his wife's hesitancy. "Are you sure you want to do this? Emma knows the business needs to stay viable and that we all have to do our part to make that happen."

The more the impulsive idea sank in, the more Cole knew it was what he wanted to do. The restlessness that plagued him of late was something he had never experienced before. He was always happy to remain in the vicinity of the ranch, but now the thought of 'breaking free' for a time struck a chord deep within him.

"You two act as if the boogie man might get me if I leave. I know it may be out of character for me, but the decision's made. I'll deliver the horses to Pederson, Tyler, and you can stay home and enjoy your family for once." He stood and plopped the worn cowboy hat on his head. "Enough said."

Emma and Tyler exchanged surprised glances as Cole left the room. It *was* out of character for the youngest Wilkins brother to advocate his own departure from the ranch.

Emma could not keep the smug grin from curving her lips as she moved to slip onto Tyler's lap. He greeted her with a deep kiss, then she reveled in her husband's sigh as it whispered past her ear. She snuggled in closer.

A giggle escaped Emma's lips a moment later when his low growl met her ears.

"Well...Cole's gonna be gone for awhile, and Trevor's *never* around anymore." He nuzzled her neck. "So, what do you say we head upstairs and start practicing for all the time alone we're going to have in the next few weeks?"

His tickling fingers found Emma's waist, and she jumped up with a squeal, then ran for the steps. The speed of Tyler's immediate pursuit belied the fact that he had spent a long, agonizing day atop a horse.

Chapter Two

Cole hauled back on the reins and his massive roan, Joe, paused as his master looked down the dark street. Cole's broad shoulders dropped with his heavy sigh of relief when he spied the welcoming lamp that burned in the livery stable window. Urging the horse across the small distance, the weary traveler dismounted and stretched his sore muscles. He cast a cursory glance toward the two young colts that were tethered by a lead rein to his mount, then stepped up to the open doorway and poked his head inside.

"Hello in there!" He entered the building, and a grizzled old cowboy came through a doorway to his left. By the man's expression, Cole was sure he had disturbed the old geezer's much needed slumber. The livery owner spit into the straw at his customer's feet, scratched a round, ponderous belly, and yawned loudly.

"Can I help ya?" he questioned before another stream of spittle left his lips.

Cole ignored the man's crudeness. "Yes. I'd like to board my horses for the night—" and at the thought of a clean soft bed, he quickly added "—and possibly the next. Are you able to take them?"

Cole had spent every night for the past week sleeping under the stars, and the decision to treat himself for that evening, and maybe the next, popped into his mind out of nowhere.

"How many horses ya talkin' about?"

"Four."

"It'll cost ya two dollars a head, then a buck extra for every night after. If ya want me to rub 'em down before beddin' 'em in, that'll cost ya two bits extra per horse, per night. If ya want me to feed 'em some oats that'll cost ya extra, too. Two bits a scoop—scoops' big, so three of 'em ought to take care of the four of 'em. Price might sound outrageous, but I tend my renters by myself, and ya can be assured they'll be here in the morning none the worse for wear." The man heaved a great sigh and scratched his ponderous belly again. "We gotta deal?"

Cole's head spun. He got lost in the conversation sometime after two bits a horse. Regardless, whether he was able to keep up with the old man's reply or not, he knew the charges were nothing short of highway robbery. The stable was clean, however, and the other horses being boarded looked content, so Cole simply nodded his head in agreement. The lure of a hot bath instead of a cool stream, and the thought of a comfortable mattress, helped to settle the matter in his mind. Cole stiffened almost imperceptibly when the man peered at him closely.

"Well, ya look like an honest man, but I'll have to ask ya fer a down payment of five bucks—rest due when ya pick yer critters up. If ya get it in yer head ta stay on an extra night, just stop in and let me know by noon tomorrow. I'll see that they get some grazin' time in the mornin'. Where ya headin' to?" He switched the conversation so fast that Cole nearly missed the question as he counted out five dollars.

"Fargo."

"So, what the hell ya ridin' there for? Railroad stops right here in town. Seems to me yer a lunatic if you ride, instead of railin' it."

He's blunt—I gotta give him that. The man's words took Cole back to when he informed Tyler and Emma that he wanted to travel by horse rather than by rail. They both thought he had taken leave of his senses. If he had revealed the almost overwhelming need that pushed him—no, *compelled* him—to travel overland by horse rather than by train, they would have been convinced they were right. In the end, Tyler and Emma relented, telling Cole it was his decision. When they discovered he had decided to travel alone though, the battle waged once more. Cole remained adamant in his decision, however, even when the couple enlisted Trevor's aide in talking him out of traveling cross-country. The middle Wilkins brother did not push too hard, however. For some odd reason, Trevor understood Cole's desire to be alone and simply wished him a safe journey.

Cole brought his attention back to the old man and realized he had not answered his question. He shrugged his shoulders and smiled. "I guess I haven't traveled this piece of the state yet. I wanted to see it firsthand." It was as good an answer as he could come up with on the spur of the moment.

"Guess I'll never figure out you young 'uns of today." The old man shook his head disparagingly and tapped his forehead. "Know in my head for a fact, these old bones have no yearnin' whatsoever ta be sight-seein' when there's no need. Where's them animals of yours?"

Cole retraced his steps outside, untied the lead reins, and led the four horses though the wide doorway. A low whistle from the mouth of the livery owner greeted his return.

"Some fine horse flesh ya got there, son. Don't mind tellin' ya ta watch yer back when ya get farther west. Damn Injuns are movin' again, and they wouldn't hesitate ta relieve ya of those four mounts. Damn Sioux followers of Crazy Horse. That damn warrior is long dead and they still follow his way of life. The government is tryin' ta get his people rounded up and get 'em back on the reservation." He spit another brown stream of saliva mixed with tobacco into the straw at his feet. "Hostiles they call 'em. A whole passel of 'em escaped from Camp Robinson back in '77 and headed ta Canada ta hide out with old Chief Sittin'Bull. When the Chief surrendered in '81, he brought back less than two hundred of his clan. Word has it there's a whole pack of Crazy Horse's people that split off and are travelin' between here and the Dakotas. Every time the regiments get close ta findin' 'em, they disappear like a big hand picks 'em up and deposits 'em somewhere else. When horses start disappearin', ya can be assured it's them damn hostiles at it again. Thievin' aborigines." The old man inhaled deeply, shook his balding head, and spit once more.

Cole felt the need to breathe deeply himself after listening to the stream of words that spilled from the old man's mouth. Questions jumped around in his mind, and he could not help but reply. "There hasn't been an Indian uprising in Minnesota since the sixties, and I haven't heard of even minor disruptions in recent years. Why not just let them go their own way? Why is the government so insistent on catching up with a few small bands?" As soon as the words were out of his mouth, Cole wished he could draw them back. The surprised look on the livery man's face sharpened along with a cocked eyebrow.

"Yer not an Injun lover are ya, son? Cuz I'm not afraid ta tell ya ta keep that fact ta yerself around these parts. People don't ken much to Injun lovers."

I wonder what he'd think if he knew I came from a family with no prejudices?

Mamie, their aging housekeeper, had raised him and his siblings. She was the closest thing the children had to a mother, and none of them even considered the fact that she was a freed slave. They respected her, they loved her and, when she got her dander up, they feared her wrath—despite the color of her skin. There were few Indians around his home, but those who did live in the area knew they could count on the Wilkins family if they needed help, and the natives reciprocated in kind. For years, when the ranch was the hub for the family-owned sawmill, all different nationalities of immigrant workers were hired and had free access to the Wilkins home. Never did the family judge a man by his accent.

"I guess I just haven't had much contact with them." Taking his cue from the old man, Cole promptly changed the subject. "I'll let you get the horses settled in for the night. Just have the tab added up in the morning, and don't forget to give them some oats. There'll be extra money in it for you if they're properly tended to. Where's the best place in town to get a good hot bath and a clean room?"

"Down the street on the left. Missouri Inn it's called. Helluva name for a hotel in Minnesota..." He continued to mumble to himself as Cole left the barn and strolled down the quiet street to the lighted porch on the left.

* * *

A bell tinkled over Cole's head when he opened the glass door and entered the small inn. A pleased expression lit his hazel eyes at the sight of the clean and orderly lobby before him. He crossed to the counter, paid for a room, then arranged to have a bath and a tray of food delivered as soon as possible. A moment later, he followed the clerk up the stairs and waited for him to open the door and light the lamp.

Cole realized then just how tired he actually was. The door shut behind the desk clerk, and he fell across the bed, then laid there until he heard commotion in the hallway. Three boys entered the room with buckets of steaming water and moved to fill the small tub behind the privacy screen. The clerk reappeared a few minutes later with a tray of food.

"You need anything else, sir?" he asked when he turned to his customer.

"No thanks." Cole watched the hotel entourage leave in singe file, breathed a sigh of relief when the door latch clicked, then heaved himself up from the bed.

He immediately stripped the dusty clothes from his body and moved behind the screen to ease his lean, powerfully built frame into the steaming water. He rested his head against the back of the tub, closed his eyes with a groan, and let the hot water drain the stiffness from his sore muscles. After a few moments, Cole reached to drag the small table that held the tray of food closer to the tub, picked up a piece of bread to nibble on, and released a contented sigh.

I should have ordered a bottle. Right now a good stiff drink would be welcome.

Closing his eyes again, Cole's mind wandered back to the conversation at the livery stable. *Hostiles. That's what the old man called the Indians who still roam the land between Canada and the Dakotas.* It never ceased to amaze him how that word was used in conjunction with a group of human beings who refused to be herded onto reservations.

Hell, I'm the hostile. Wasn't it the white man who used force to remove the Indians from land that was theirs in the first place?

He wished now that he had taken the time to read more of Emma's books and articles on the subject. She always seemed to have some sort of connection with the Indian culture. Not that she spoke of it often, but she was insistent about using the word *Lakota* as the new name for the ranch when they switched from logging to horse breeding. Thomas' middle name was also Lakota.

What's that all about? he wondered.

When the little filly, Spirit, was born that same night, Tyler also suggested the name *Spirit of Lakota*.

Going farther back in time, Cole remembered the day Emma seemed so mesmerized by the small, wooden statue that she bought Tyler as a Christmas gift. His dark brows furrowed. *I'm going to have to ask her about the significance of the Indian figurine when I get home.*

Cole pushed the confusing thoughts aside as he reached for the bowl of beef stew that sat on the tray beside the tub. He had eaten only a few spoonfuls when his mind returned to his earlier train of thought.

Hell, Tyler and Emma have always shared that secret little look whenever anyone mentions the Indian culture. He shook his sandy-colored head. *Yup—I'm definitely gonna have to ask her about it.*

The tepid water soon forced Cole from the tub, and he dried himself off with a clean, fluffy towel. He would have to remember this place on the return trip. He would need the break.

He slid his naked body between the sheets then, and relishing the feel of the soft mattress beneath him and the cool linens next to his skin, he fell into a deep sleep without even extinguishing the light.

* * *

Hours into the night, Cole tossed and turned in his sleep. He rolled onto his side with an unintelligible mumble, and then quickly flipped onto his back. His eyes snapped open and frantically darted about the unfamiliar surroundings. Panting as if he had just run a race, and drenched in sweat, Cole leapt from the bed. The heaving breaths slowed when he remembered renting the room.

Cole crossed to the small table that still held the tray of unfinished food and reached for a glass of water with a shaky hand. His steely eyes surveyed the room as he waited for the beat of his heart to slow, then returned to the bed and sat on the edge to stare into the semi lit room. A chill swept up his spine.

It had happened again. Cole had suffered the same reoccurring dream for months, only this time somebody else shared the nightmare. He was always riding west on Spirit, and it was always late afternoon. The direction had to be west; the sun was always in his eyes, and the land shimmered as it does just before dusk. Cole also remembered that he searched for something in the dream—something or *someone* that he never found. This was the first time though, that the nightmare continued past that point; it was the first time that he had ridden up the same small hill and did not wake before reaching the top.

Cole laid back into the pillow and tried to remember the conclusion of the dream. He could see himself on the horse, urging her upward to the summit. He could feel the urgency in his veins; the desperate need that drove him to the top of the butte and prodded him to continue on. Somehow, Cole had known that this time he would crest the bluff.

Cole's brow knitted with concentration as he struggled to envision what lay beyond the summit. Suddenly, the persona of a woman standing in the midst of the tall grass swam before his mind's eye.

Was it a woman or not? Or was it an animal? No...it was a woman—it was definitely a woman. Dark, wavy hair fluttered softly about her buckskin-clad shoulders and velvet brown eyes beckoned his very soul.

Before he was able to reach her though, he awoke in a cold sweat and she was gone.

Cole pulled the coverlet around his now-chilled body, rolled onto his side, and stared at the flame that flickered inside the lamp. *Why do I keep having the same dream?* His family was forever teasing him about his ability to know what was going on in their minds before they did themselves. He had a gift for seeing things clearly when no one else could, but this experience left him baffled. Why did he have the same dream over and over again?

Finally, Cole forced himself to let it go. He drifted back to sleep with one thought foremost in his mind. *If I have the dream again, I'm gonna make damned sure I reach the woman standing in the field.*

* * *

Morning came and Cole was up early, feeling refreshed and ready to greet the day. He glanced at his watch as he reached for the door to the hallway. *I've got until noon to decide whether to continue on or to stay over for one more night, but I'm not making that decision until I eat breakfast and check out the town.*

Pulling the door shut behind him, he strode to the staircase and followed the smell that wafted up the steps from the dining room. He paused at the front desk, flipped a coin onto the wooden surface, and grabbed a local newspaper to read while he ate.

He sat at a table situated by the window, ordered breakfast, and scanned the paper while he sipped a steaming mug of coffee. The number of articles pertaining to the Indian populace amazed him. They covered everything from supposed renegade Indian 'raids' on unsuspecting white farmers to what was happening at reservations around the States.

Where have I been these last few years? His existence was totally given to life on the ranch, and he had never felt the need to travel far from it. *But that still doesn't excuse me from being so out of touch.*

The sound of jingling spurs interrupted his thoughts and lifted his gaze from the paper before him. A tall, muscular man strode down the steps from the upper landing. Cole's gaze followed the stranger as he seated himself at a clean table across the room. The guy was dressed in buckskin pants and a cotton shirt. He placed a worn rawhide jacket on the chair next to him as he sat. There was something familiar about him...

The man asked the waitress for a menu, and the deep voice sparked a memory in Cole's brain. *Son of a bitch—I can't believe it!* He knew that voice. He observed the newcomer for a moment longer, waited until he removed his Stetson, and then knew for certain who sat across from him.

He stood and crossed the room. The stranger turned his head and looked him straight in the eye, and Cole saw the dawning of recollection cross his features.

"Cole?"

"I didn't recognize you at first, but as soon as you took your hat off and I got a good look, I knew." Cole extended his hand to meet the one offered to him. "Beau...Beau McCabe, how the hell are you? I haven't seen you since you left for your appointment at West Point. That was thirteen years ago!"

His old friend's greeting prompted a memory in Beau's mind; namely, how he tried to talk Cole into leaving Minnesota when he did. The younger Wilkins brother could not be budged at the time. His father died not long before, and Cole felt a responsibility to his siblings. It was left to them to run the family-owned lumber business north of Duluth. Beau lost contact with his friend over the years and never went back to his home state of Minnesota for any length of time. They were boys then. Now they were men; tall of stature and broad of shoulder, and they looked each other in the eye as they renewed their friendship.

"Christ, Cole, this is a surprise! It's good to see you. What are you doing in these parts? If I remember correctly, it was like pulling teeth to get you off that damn ranch of yours."

"I'm riding out to Fargo to deliver a couple of horses. My brothers and I worked our way out of the logging business and are trying our hand at horse breeding."

Beau shook his dark head of wavy hair and smiled. "I remember the three of you talking about it when we were younger. Good for you for making it happen."

Cole's gaze strayed to where the young waitress delivered a plate of food to the table he had just vacated. He failed to notice the look of promise she threw his way, however, as she emptied the remainder of the tray's contents onto the wooden surface.

Beau mentally shook his head. *He hasn't changed a bit. Never did see the ladies looking his way.*

"Grab your jacket and come sit with me. We've got some catching up to do." Cole nodded toward his table and, a few moments later, the two men were settled across the room.

The same young waitress sidled to their shared table, produced a mug of coffee for Beau, and sent another look of longing in Cole's direction. Ignoring the silent plea in her eyes, Beau quickly ordered breakfast and waved her off.

"So, I suppose you've got a wife and a whole passel of kids stowed up there in the north just waiting for you to return." He chuckled out loud when Cole shook his head with a snort.

"Not even close, Beau. Never even had a special girl; just never had the time."

As the words left his lips, Cole's thoughts countered the statement. *No, I never had a special girl, but I was with a special lady for a time*. She was not what most gentile people of society would have called a lady, though. She was a madam in ownership of her own business.

Belle Adams possessed a heart bigger than most. Their relationship lasted almost seven years and, in the end, she came in contact with the same devil from Emma's past. The confrontation was enough to make Belle leave for parts unknown and start a new life. They both knew at the time that their relationship would never amount to more than a few delightful nights wrapped in each other's arms, but Cole still thought of her often.

Belle refused to tell him where she was going. He asked her to write, but knew she would not. It was not until after she was gone that Cole realized she had also left for him. Belle always felt that her past profession would never allow her to belong in his world. It was an affront to 'decent' society. By leaving, she had released him, leaving him free to find the one woman he could be truly happy with—an event that had never come to pass.

Watching his old friend across the table now, Cole wondered in turn about Beau's life. "What about you, Beau? Married and settled down? I see by your civilian clothes that you must be done with your service years."

"The army—especially the cavalry end of it—is no way to court a woman." He shrugged his broad shoulders and leaned back in the chair. "I guess you could say I was married to the U.S. government for a time. We split up about two years ago. I went into the service as a lieutenant, and I left a lieutenant. Toward the end, I was offered a higher station, but I'd had enough."

"Why is that?"

"Too many blind bureaucrats, too many damned do-gooders that never accomplish anything. You know, when I finished at West Point and the time was right, I *asked* to be commissioned out west. I left for the Territories filled with all these grand ideas that I would make a difference. The joke was on me."

"You sound bitter," Cole stated.

His old friend leaned forward, clasped his hands before him, and closed his eyes for a second in remembrance. "I guess the only way to explain my attitude is to say it was a loss of faith on my part. I was trained at West Point to believe in our government, to uphold its traditions without questioning why something is done the way it is. At first, I was like any other young lieutenant leaving the academy." He shook his head in what Cole took to be self-deprecation. "I was filled with patriotism. I truly believed what the government said about taming the 'savages' and making this great country a safe place to live; a place where you can be whatever you want to be. I wanted to be a part of that history. But I came to realize that the government, through its military, was slowly killing a culture that had been in existence far longer than 'civilized man' had. Squeezing the Indians out of everything they have ever known is a terrible thing to watch, not to mention participate in; especially when it's done a little at a time. It's a slow death for them, and I was ashamed to be a part of it anymore."

Both men sat in silence and reflected on the spoken words for a moment until Beau again broke the tense quiet. "I guess that makes me an Indian lover in some people's eyes."

Cole let out a small, half-hearted laugh and eyed his friend. "You know, that's the second time in the last twenty-four hours I've heard those two words—*Indian lover*. Last night, an old man at the livery asked me if I was one, simply because I questioned why the government couldn't just let the last of the roving bands go their own way—."

His words were interrupted when Beau's breakfast plate was placed before the other man on the clean wooden surface. Cole quickly thanked the hovering waitress, intent upon dismissing her, and failed to notice her exasperated sigh as she retraced her steps to the kitchen. Cole learned forward, dipped his fork into the mound of fried potatoes on his own plate, and glanced at Beau once more.

"So why is it that the army won't leave the Indians alone?"

"Because the government wants them all on reservations." Beau fought to stifle the anger that squared his shoulders. "It's as cut and dried as that. It's the way they've decided it will be, and even one Indian left to roam free of the reservations is one Indian too many. Total domain; that's the mentality of our great heads sitting in Washington—the great heads that refuse to get off their fat asses and come out here to see the defeated faces of those people. They think they can offer the Indians a treaty, and then forget it ever existed. Starve them out, take their pride, and then doom them to an existence where nothing is familiar. They tell them, 'go ahead and look at your mountains and your prairies, but don't go there or you'll be considered a hostile.'"

Beau leaned back and watched the reaction on Cole's face go from surprise, to disgust, to anger in an instant. He lowered his voice. "What's being done to the Indians can be compared to what was done to the Negroes in this country before the war. In fact, I think it's worse. After all, we didn't bring the Indians here; they were in possession of the land long before the white man arrived."

Cole pondered Beau's words and felt smaller by the minute. "I almost feel as if I should apologize to you for my being so out of touch with what's been going on all these years."

The other man shook his head and continued with his meal. "No need to apologize. Unless you've stared the problem in the face, it's easy to believe the half-truths written about it. The papers speak of ignorance, hostility, and any other negative aspect of this assimilation of the Indians and conveniently forget to mention the cowardice and betrayal of a government bent on suppressing a once proud race of people who have lost everything."

"So tell me something, Beau. I get the feeling that you haven't let it go. Somebody such as yourself; somebody who was as touched as you were by the plight of the Indian people, wouldn't just walk away. What have you been doing since you mustered out?"

"You always were good at seeing deeper into a situation than most people."

A smile touched Cole's lips at Beau's comment. It was true. He always had a sixth sense for picking out what lay just beneath the surface.

"For the last two years," Beau informed him, "I've contracted my services to the Bureau of Indian Affairs. I'm helping to round up the so called 'hostiles,' who run between Canada and the Dakotas. Since I'm working for myself, I don't have to play *exactly* by the rules the commission has set down. When I come across a group of *hostiles*, if you will, I make sure they're placed in one of the better agencies or located with their relatives. The government wants them all on the reservations so badly that they're willing to meet my demands on placement and treatment, and there are some good Indian agents out there that do work for the people. If the army doesn't meet my demands, I suddenly *lose* the group of Indians. Right now, I have a better record than any other employee of the Bureau. The government knows it, and so do those poor miscreants running for their lives." Beau's eyes lit with excitement. "It's amazing, Cole, I can stumble upon a group that I know I've never come across before, and they already know who I am. These people are so spread out, and yet they have a better communication system than the government does."

"Are you looking for Indians in this area? Is that why you're here?"

"In a roundabout way. I'm on my way back from an Indian Affairs conference that was held in St. Paul. I usually don't give them the satisfaction of showing up at their bullshit sessions, which angers them royally, but I didn't want to miss this one. Our illustrious Federal government has come up with yet another *plan* for Indian removal." He snorted his disgust. "All it will turn out to be is another means to cheat them out of their reservation lands. Slowly but surely, they'll have all the Indians in little square boxes, totally dependent on the big white hand that feeds them." A deep sigh lifted his chest. "Anyway, while at the conference, I heard about a small band that may be holed up just west of here and thought I'd check it out before heading back down to the Black Hills area." The intense interest on Cole's face told Beau that his friend shared his view of the situation. "Maybe we could travel west together for awhile. It would be a welcome change, at least for me. It gets awful lonely out on the trail. What do you think?"

Cole chuckled. "You know, I was going to find out which way you were traveling and suggest the very same thing. A little company would be welcome on my part, too. I'd never admit this to my family, but when I left home over a week ago, I was craving the solitude of a long, quiet ride. Now though, the isolation is about to drive me crazy." Cole glanced at his pocket watch before he commented further. "If you plan to leave today though, I have to get to the livery and collect my horses or I'll be charged another day's rent for nothing." He looked up in surprise when Beau threw back his head and belted out a laugh.

"I see the same old codger got you with the noon business. I've got two horses boarded at the same place. Come on—we're done eating—let's go before he empties both our pockets." He shrugged. "May as well hit the trail today."

The two men rose in anticipation of spending the next week or so together. The time would allow them not only to renew a long forgotten friendship, but would also provide companionship, at least for awhile.

As they exited the building and entered the bright, sunlit morning, Cole could not help but wonder if meeting up with Beau would help him find what he was looking for.

If not, at least I'll have some interesting conversation to share with Emma when I get home.

Chapter Three

Four days later found Cole and Beau further west and Cole much more aware of the nomadic life his friend lived on a daily basis. They had not traveled in a straight line, but rather rode the trails north and south as Beau continually watched for any sign of roving Sioux. The pace was slow and leisurely; the reason being, each man admitted aloud, that they did not look forward to the day they would part company.

Beau was a wealth of knowledge concerning the last fifty years of Indian dominance by the white man. Cole resembled a small child soaking up every detail. He asked questions, which his friend readily supplied the answers to, and had now begun to understand Beau's commitment to his present life and the reasoning for why he came to find that dedication. His companion was devoted to aiding the Indians' cause and nothing would deter him.

They stopped along the trail to rest the horses. Beau collected wood for a fire and Cole secured the two colts along side the packhorse. A campfire was started and it was not long before a tin pot of coffee boiled vigorously above the flames. A short while later, Cole poured himself a second cup and settled into the shade of a huge pine.

"When I brought my animals to the livery stable a few nights back, that old man relayed quite a story about the Indians," Cole stated as he leaned against the rough bark of the tree. "He told me about a group of Crazy Horse followers who split off from a large contingent of Sioux that were being moved eastward a few years back." He observed quietly as Beau rested against a log and stared into the fire before he glanced up to meet his friend's gaze.

"I was there."

Cole's eyes widened in surprise with Beau's words.

"I was the commanding officer who let them run. And, contrary to what the papers wrote, they didn't try to 'scalp' us first. The group just turned in an orderly fashion and hightailed it for the hills."

Cole let Beau's declaration sink in before he asked another question. "The old man also told me that a small number of the roving bands around here are some of those same people—original members of Crazy Horse's band. Is that who you're looking for now?"

Beau tossed his coffee into the dying fire and stood. "What's left of them." He strode to his horse and tightened the cinch on the worn leather saddle, his hands automatically and efficiently readying himself and the horse to leave. "There must've been about two thousand men, woman, and children who broke off that day. My best guess, figuring in the numbers that have returned to the agencies, there must be about five hundred left out there; the last of the great Sioux, still outwitting the government and building more animosity every day because of it."

Cole stood, kicked dirt over the dying embers of the small fire, and walked to the nearby stream to rinse the tin coffee pot while digesting Beau's information again. He glanced at the other man over his shoulder. "How is it that five hundred people can just disappear? You'd think a group that size would call a fair amount of attention to themselves."

"They split off in the early spring and travel in small groups of ten to twenty. That way it's easier to maintain a food supply for themselves and move about without causing attention. They only winter together in that large group. They've got one helluva hiding place, because nobody's been able to locate them yet—and the agency Indians refuse to enlighten anyone as to where they might be."

Beau finished checking the supply sacks on his packhorse and mounted a large gray gelding. "This is the best time of the year for me to catch up with a few of the smaller bands. They're so spread out that my chances of happening across them by accident increases. Once the cold season starts to close in though, I may as well forget it until spring. The Bureau thinks the Sioux winter here in the states, but I've got a hunch they cross into Canada and lose themselves in the Rockies. They disappear so completely that, to me, it's the only feasible explanation."

Cole followed suit, mounted Joe, and secured the colts' tether before he asked his old friend one final question. "Why have you dedicated yourself to this mission of yours? You seem driven somehow."

Beau clucked his horse forward, and Cole did the same. "I've asked myself that same question a time or two. I guess the best answer I can give is that it's one small way to try and make up for a huge wrong. By being in the position I was—that being my commission with the U.S. army—I aided the government in the ruination of a people that never asked us to come into their homeland in the first place. The Sioux were willing to share everything they had. Instead, I played a part in killing off their main food source, the great buffalo herds. I helped force them into giving up everything they have ever known and stood by as they were lied to at every turn. And, worst of all, I helped steal their pride."

Beau stared straight ahead, lost in thoughts of the past before speaking again. "It was about a month before we received orders to move the Indians east. I'd been working like a madman with some of the other post commanders to secure food and supplies. The damned government held up all shipments of Indian rations on the Missouri, thinking that it would be a way to get them to move." He paused for a moment, then continued.

"We heard that Crazy Horse had agreed to come in, talk with the agency heads, and maybe bring his group in. That was something Crazy Horse never wanted to do, but his people were sick of warfare, weary of being on the run, and tired of always being hungry. I was sent north with eight Cavalry companies to bring him back from his encampment. By the time we arrived, he'd taken flight and headed for the Spotted Tail Agency to find protection with his uncle. When I returned to the camp and told my commanding officer, General Crook, what transpired, I pleaded with him to let me follow the Chief and try again. I left that day with some hope. I got Crook to promise me he would meet with Crazy Horse and discuss the Chief's insistence that an alternative residence be erected on the Powder River for him and his people."

Cole sat transfixed and in total amazement of the life his friend had led up until that very moment.

Beau swiveled in the saddle. "Do you know, Cole, I actually sat and pow-wowed with the great chief? I convinced him to come back to Camp Robinson with me. I really believed Crook would live up to his promises. When we arrived at the camp, it was a sight to behold. Thousands of Indians gathered to see the great Crazy Horse. A lot of them were the last holdouts, the Indians the government had been trying to entice for months. I went directly to the office of the post commander to set up the meeting between Crook and the Chief and was told there would be no meeting. While I was gone, it was decided the government would not miss the opportunity to seize Crazy Horse, arrest him, and send him to some distant location where he couldn't cause any more trouble."

Cole shook his head. "I don't imagine you took that very well."

Beau swung his head in Cole's direction with a fiery glaze in his eyes. "They lied to me! Here, I thought I'd managed to finally be a part of the solution. What I'd actually done was maneuver Crazy Horse into government hands and right into his own death sentence. While I was arguing at the office, guards were dispatched to escort him to the jailhouse. I heard the commotion and ran outside. I'll never forget the feeling that ran through me when I saw the chief lying on the ground with blood oozing from his body. I was told later that when he realized he was being led to the jail, instead of to a meeting with Crook and the visiting General Bradley, he tried to break away. Some over-zealous guard stabbed him with a bayonet."

Beau rode quietly for a time, seeing the flashes of the past as if they had happened yesterday. "You asked me, Cole, why I'm so driven. The only thing left for the Sioux is the government reservations. I knew a lot of the people who ran from us that day. In my mind, I wished them well in the pursuit of whatever they were looking for, but it's over now. The days of the great Indian culture are a thing of the past. If I can help these last people of the land to adjust to a new life and find them a decent place to live with the least amount of outside influence, then these years will have been worth it."

"I don't think I will ever understand exactly what happened in those years of the white man encroaching on the lives of the Indians. I haven't lived it or seen it as you have. I give you a lot of credit for taking it upon yourself to help these last remaining bands as best you can."

"I'm one man, Cole, but I'll keep trying."

They rode on in silence, thinking about the directions of their respective lives. Cole was so lost in thought that Beau had to call his name twice before he reined his horse, and the three that followed, to a stop. Beau was already off his mount and motioning for him to come closer while he studied something along side the trail.

"Look here," Beau pointed to a small tree with a broken branch and an etched arrow on one of its limbs. "I think this is where we part company." The arrow was no more than an inch long. Cole would never have noticed it if Beau had not pointed it out.

"So, you think this has something to do with one of your roving bands? I never even saw it."

Beau straightened and kicked at a small tree lying across the trail. "I might have missed it too, so don't feel bad. I only started looking for it after I saw this small tree laying here. If I'm right..." He followed the limb into the tangled brush and found what he was looking for. "Come see this, Cole."

Cole followed him into the undergrowth and saw two more small branches forming an arrow at the end of the limb. "This is some sort of marker, isn't it?"

"Yup. A group came through here just recently. You can tell, because the branches haven't been broken that long; maybe three or four days. It's the way one band lets another know what direction they're traveling and where others might be located. Once I saw the tree lying across the trail, I started looking for the carvings the Indians usually leave along with it. The path isn't too obvious here, but I'm sure I'll find one that's a little easier to traverse farther south."

Both men walked back to the horses and turned to face each other. Cole extended a hand, and Beau grasped it firmly.

"I guess this is it. I hope we're not going to have to wait another thirteen years to see each other again."

Beau's face split with a grin before he clasped Cole's shoulder with his free hand. "You never know when I might be back in this area. Looks like if my Indians are traveling in the area, then I will be, too. Just keep an eye out. They're not savages, Cole, but don't back them into a corner."

"I'll remember that. And *you* remember that you're welcome at the ranch anytime. I don't know what I can do for you, but if you need anything, just send a message."

Cole stood quietly as Beau reached into his pack and withdrew a newspaper clipping that featured a photo of himself. "Here, take this. If you run into any bands, show them this and explain that you're a friend of mine. Most of these Indians speak English, so don't let them fool you into believing otherwise. Most of them know of me, so it might help you get out of a ticklish spot. If you ever need to contact me, send a telegram to the Pine Ridge Reservation headquarters in the Dakotas, or to the Bureau of Indian Affairs in St. Paul.

They'll know where I can be located. Most likely, I'll be heading to the Dakotas on this trip, though. Just keep to this trail, head west, and before you know it, you'll be in Fargo." Beau mounted his horse and reached down to take Cole's hand once more. "Take care, friend."

Cole grasped his hand firmly, nodded, and watched until Beau was out of sight before mounting his own horse again. The next week on the trail now stretched out before him, and he was already aware of the quietness that pervaded. Hopefully, he would meet up with Beau again in the future. He had enjoyed the days spent with him, the long talks, and nights by the campfire as stars shot across the sky. As he watched Beau's back disappear into the trees, his shoulders lifted with his sigh, and he sent a silent message. *I hope you find the absolution you're searching for, my friend.*

Cole followed the meandering trail through the pines and, soon, hooked onto a well-used road. Already having decided to travel back home by rail, he kicked his horse into a trot. The lead rope attached to the packhorse and prancing colts stretched tight before their gates matched Joe's. The quicker he reached Fargo, the sooner he could purchase a train ticket. With Beau gone, Cole knew he would be lonelier than ever.

* * *

Three days had passed since Cole parted ways with Beau. Being continually wary of how the overland trip affected the younger horses, he took the days at an easy pace. He wanted to ensure his charges were not road-weary when delivered to their new owner. Tyler, Emma, and Trevor depended on him to complete this transaction, and he was not about to mess it up. Thinking of the ranch brought a twinge of homesickness and a small amount of disappointment. He originally thought to find a missing part of himself on this trip. He shook his head. *I don't know what the hell I was thinking. It'll be good to be home again.*

The weather held out. In fact, the temperature rose enough that he decided to find a place to camp for the night a little earlier than normal. He had kept a close eye on the younger horses and now realized the heat was slowing their pace as the day wore on.

"Okay, Joe, a good rest and cooler temps tonight will do all of us good. Let's find a place to camp." The massive horse snorted back as if in agreement.

He left the main trail and reined Joe to a halt near a winding stream.

After a search for kindling, Cole lit a small fire, and then cared for his charges. After getting the animals settled for the evening, he pulled a small map from his saddlebag and calculated how many more days on the trail lay between him and his destination. By his reckoning, he figured he was still three to four days out of Fargo.

So much for finding myself, he mused again as he wondered how Beau handled the continually lonely days.

Cole watched the tops of small ripples break across a wider part of the stream and made a quick decision to delay his supper. His anticipation of a bath in the cool stream heightened as he quickly unpacked his gear, grabbed a bar of soap from his saddlebag, and headed back to the edge of the water. It was not long before he had shucked his clothing and dove into the murky depths, relishing the feel of the water against his skin.

There was still plenty of light left in the day and Cole stayed long in the water; first bathing, and then swimming with powerful strokes from one side of the stream to the far bank, and then back again. The feeling of exhilaration, as his body sliced through the wakes of small waves created by the breeze, was sheer enjoyment to his tired mind.

On the bank opposite his campsite, a huge, flat rock broke the water's surface. Cole swam back, pulled himself up, rolled onto his back and lay across the smooth expanse. The heat that radiated from the rock's surface soothed his bare skin. Soon, he found himself drowsily watching the clouds overhead as they skipped across the pale blue, early evening sky.

A soft breeze rustled the leaves on the branches above him. Cole closed his eyes and listened to the sound of water lapping against the grassy shore, and against the edges of the rock he was lying on. Lulled by the noise, he smiled inwardly. *Maybe I haven't given this idea of solitude a chance.* At the moment, he was enjoying himself immensely.

The horses' contented knickers filtered through his brain, and Cole imagined himself back on the ranch. In his mind, he could almost hear little Thomas asking one question after another as they worked in the paddock...

A frantic whinny broke the serene silence and startled Cole from his reverie. He bolted upright to a sitting position and watched in disbelief as someone bounded onto the packhorse and whipped the other three animals into action across the width of the stream.

"Hey! Stop right there!" Cole leapt to his feet and dove into the water without a moment's hesitation. Breaking the surface, he realized he would never get to the other side in time. He hollered out again. "Hey, you! Get away from my horses!" His corded arms pulled him powerfully through the water. Just as his feet touched the sandy bottom on the other side, he saw his gelding's backside disappear down the path and out of sight.

Cole slipped in the soft sand as he rushed forward. "Son of a bitch!" He regained his footing, raced the length of the camp spot, and let out one sharp whistle after another. His heart hammered in his ears, and he struggled to hear over its pitch. "Son of a bitch!" he swore again.

Cole let out another piercing whistle and waited anxiously to see if Joe would respond. Just as he had hoped, the pounding of hooves met his ears, and the roan reentered the clearing at a dead run. Cole jumped out of the way and yelled the horse's name when it raced by him. The animal spun to a stop, then trotted up to his master with a snort and a brisk shake of the head.

"Good boy, that's a good boy," Cole whispered as he reached out and grasped the rope that trailed from the horse's neck. He comforted the animal with light strokes to his neck and let Joe nuzzle his bare chest. "It's a damn good thing I taught you to answer to a whistle. If I hadn't, it'd be one helluva a long walk."

He glanced around the clearing and suddenly realized he was buck naked. He raced back to his clothes, hurriedly dressed, and gathered only the bare essentials. His packhorse was gone, and he was not about to load Joe down with extra weight.

"I'll be damned if I'm going to let that bastard get any farther ahead than I have to," he mumbled angrily to the silent clearing. He saddled the horse, stuffed the last of the supplies into a pack and slung it up and across Joe's back. "We'll only ride 'til dark, boy, then we'll start out again first thing in the morning."

Cole's eyes quickly searched the area for his gun. Relief washed through him when he spotted it lying in the dirt a short distance away. Luckily, it appeared that the culprit was only interested in the horses, and not his personal possessions.

"What the hell was I thinking?" he muttered to the horse. "I knew Goddamn well that there were probably thieves on the road, not to mention some of Beau's Indians."

Cole was willing to wager with anyone who would listen that the thief was an Indian. He had seen long dark hair flying in the wind just before the culprit disappeared into the trees. The fact that the bandit had also leapt onto the back of his packhorse and ridden bareback served only to add more credence to his suspicions. At the moment, if Cole's sentiments toward himself could be physically seen, his back would be flayed open.

Grabbing at the reins, he was sitting in the saddle a second later. Cole kicked Joe into a dead run and lit out in the direction of his horses.

* * *

The next day, Cole rode farther and farther from his intended destination, headed in a northerly path. He counted his blessings when Mother Nature saw fit not to add rain to his already precarious predicament. The tracks he followed remained imprinted in the dirt and, as each mile was eaten away, Cole was more certain that he tracked an Indian. No white man in his right mind would travel so deep into the wilderness. Tracks of an unshod horse were another clue. He not only watched the ground, but also kept an eye on the sun; he would be in even deeper trouble if he did not pay attention to the direction he was riding.

Cole cursed himself again. He should have known better than to let his guard down, especially after running into Beau and listening to his stories. If it was the last thing he ever did, he would get his horses back. He had no idea what he would do when he caught up with the thief, however, and decided he would cross that bridge when he came to it. *I just hope I'll only have to deal with one person and not an entire band of Beau's friends.*

He looked to the sky and his heart sank along with the sun on the horizon, knowing that every passing day would decrease his chances of catching the robber. He was definitely at a disadvantage being in an area he had never traveled before and could not help but wonder if he chased little more than a slim possibility. *But I've got to try. As long as the trail holds out, along with the rain, I can't give up.*

It was a personal issue with him now. He admitted to himself earlier that he and his brothers could easily afford the loss of revenue the two colts would bring. It was the small jab to his pride that pushed him on.

He came to a wide, shallow stream; the tracks disappeared at the water's edge. He dismounted and Joe dropped his large head to drink deeply.

Cole's alert hazel eyes searched the opposite shore as he pulled a canteen from the pack and drew a long sip himself, then knelt next to the big horse to refill it.

He should stop. Both he and the horse were tired. The tracks might continue on the other bank, or this could simply be a ploy to throw him off the trail. Sighing his frustration, the decision was made. He would cross to the other side and see if he could discover where the tracks exited the stream.

"Come on, Joe, may as well have a look before it gets dark. Then I promise we'll rest for the night." Giving the horse a pat on its rear flank, Cole mounted and urged Joe into the water. No signs of exit revealed themselves, however, when they climbed the steep bank on the far side.

Cole began a slow, methodical search upriver, but to no avail. A systematic search in the other direction, however, revealed a flattened area of grass about a quarter mile downriver from his original exit point. He jumped from the saddle and sprinted to the spot.

A whoop of joy echoed off the water's surface when he found what he was looking for. The grass was trampled and the surrounding sand still wet from the water that sloughed off the backs of the stolen animals. Examining the tracks closely, Cole's stance suddenly became more watchful. One of the sets of imprints was irregular. He had lived on the ranch long enough to discern when an animal favored an injured leg. With that realization and, the sight of wet sand, Cole knew he was not far behind the group he was trailing.

"Come on, boy, just a little longer," he spoke to Joe in a lowered voice. "I've got a hunch you'll be spending the night with your friends again."

Joe nickered softly as Cole pulled his rifle from the sheath on the saddle and led the animal quietly into the trees.

Chapter Four

Cole led Joe through a dense thicket of pines on silent feet. He stopped often to listen—alert and tuned to his surroundings. He would need the element of surprise in order to retrieve his three horses.

A soft whinny filtered through the rustling trees. Cole's stomach muscles tightened in anticipation before he dropped Joe's reins and continued alone. The horse would wait until he whistled.

Staying low and moving slowly, he followed the tracks in the small bit of twilight. His heart thumped against his ribs with each step. Suddenly, he found it was an effort to breathe normally. Around a small bend in the path, he spied the glow of a campfire and stealthily moved behind a tree to compose himself.

Slowly edging his head around the huge trunk, his eyes settled on a figure that hunkered low to the ground next to the younger of the two colts. He watched without breathing as the thief applied a poultice to the animal's right front leg. Cole squinted his eyes against the dim light to better view the tanned rawhide clothes and long, dark hair. The Indian murmured to the injured animal and patted its flank reassuringly; the horse simply stood quietly and allowed the attention.

Cole's gaze swept the clearing one more time to assure himself that the Indian was alone, then he crept softly to within mere steps of the thief. He secured a firm grip on the rifle, tightened his finger on the trigger, and aimed the barrel at the Indian's back.

"My horse have a problem?"

The thief's compact body jerked with alarm, and he turned his head slightly to look through a curtain of long hair, but did not turn or stand. He pulled a trembling hand from the colt and it dropped to his side.

"Stand up nice and slow and don't make any quick moves," Cole ground out the order as he continued to stare down the sights at the Indian's back.

The Indian murmured, but did not move. Cole inched closer and jabbed the buckskin-clad back with the barrel of his gun. "I said straighten up, and don't act like you don't understand. I know better. Now, move it." He gave another nudge with the end of the rifle and pulled back the trigger. The telltale snap of metal against metal did the trick. The Indian rose slowly until he stood straight with his back presented to his captor.

"Christ," Cole exclaimed aloud, "you're just a boy." He shook his head in amazement and muttered under his breath. "My horses were filched by a goddamn kid."

The thief was decidedly scrawny and came only to the bottom of Cole's chin. Relieved that he would not have to deal with confronting an adult Indian brave, Cole reseated the trigger and lowered the gun.

The boy's elbow jettisoned backward and rammed into Cole's abdomen before the much larger man had even thought of defending himself. He staggered back and the rifle hit the ground with a soft thump.

The boy was off and running. Cole muttered a curse under his breath, ignored the burning pain in his gut, and tore off after him. Fortunately, the young Indian brave stumbled over a protruding root a moment later. He pitched forward into the dirt and, as he attempted to scramble to his feet, Cole launched himself through the air and caught the thief around the middle with both arms. They both hit the ground, and the older man ducked to miss a flailing elbow aimed at his face.

"You little son of a bitch—" Cole's anger roared through his veins as he flipped the boy onto his back, straddled his narrow hips, and pinned his arms. Still, the wiry youngster's struggle continued.

"Knock it off, you little savage! I'm not going to hurt you—!"

Cole's words ended in a pain-filled wheeze when the struggling brave brought a knee up viciously between his legs. He clamped his lids shut over watering eyes, but still refused to relinquish his hold.

Cole opened his eyes again, and his teary gaze lowered to the heaving chest of the person beneath him—a heaving chest that was decidedly female.

"What the hell—!"

The two panting combatants locked stares—and said nothing. Cole's face mirrored his shock. The last thing he expected was to find a woman beneath him, instead of a boy.

She renewed her struggle, and Cole tightened his grip as his disbelieving eyes took in her delicate feminine features. The fire's glow illuminated smooth, youthful skin; and short breaths emitted from between full, sumptuous lips. He watched in fascination when they moved; unfortunately, she mumbled words he could not comprehend. Cole shook off his surprise.

"I hope you can understand English," he spoke slowly and evenly. "I'll let you up if you promise to stay put and quit swinging your fists and...your knees at me. I'm not going to hurt you. I just want my horses back. Do you understand?"

Jesus—I hope like hell that Beau was right about most of these Indians understanding English.

The most beautifully dark brown eyes Cole had ever seen continued to glare up at him as her full lips tightened in consternation.

"Fine—" he cocked his head in a casual manner "—we'll stay like this until I know you won't run. I told you I wouldn't hurt you, and I meant it. If I were going to do you harm, I would've done it back there, when I had the chance. I could've put a bullet in your back, but I didn't."

Her eyelids squeezed shut; long, dark lashes lay against the taut skin of her high cheekbones. He waited patiently until the thick spikes fluttered open again. She swallowed convulsively. Cole lowered his gaze to chase the quiver that ran from her jaw line and into the opening of the shapeless rawhide shirt. Tawny-colored lips parted breathlessly before him.

"I will not run."

"Ah, so you do understand. Do I have your word on that?"

Her head slowly nodded yes, and she blinked again. "I will not run."

"All right then, let's do this real slow like. I'm not in the mood to chase you all night." On blind faith, he released his grip on her arms and slowly sat back, then pushed himself to his feet and extended a hand.

The young woman glared up at him, then moved her dark stare to his outstretched hand. Ignoring it, she rolled to her knees and stood upright.

She still looks like a trapped deer ready to run. So as not to frighten her, he hooked his thumbs in the front pockets of his pants and nodded in the direction of the fire.

"Would you mind walking over there and sitting down?" *If I can keep her stationary and on her backside, she's less apt to take off...*

He tipped his head toward a fourth horse that stood in the clearing. "I see you have your own horse. I'd like to know why you felt you needed all of mine."

Her eyes, too, darted to the horse, and Cole smiled inwardly. She was measuring the distance between the animal and the spot where they stood.

"I told you," he returned calmly, "I'm not going to hurt you, so there's no need for you to run again. I just want a few answers."

He waited patiently once more until the young woman made her decision. Again, dark eyes moved between the horses and the man standing next to her. Then, with head held high, she walked stiffly to the fire and eased herself down onto the ground next to it. A small, humorous smile touched Cole's lips as he followed her across the clearing.

Her deep brown eyes widened in fright when he crossed to where his gun lay on the ground a short distance away. Cole picked up the weapon, then turned, brought his fingers to his mouth and let out a shrill whistle. Her eyes grew even rounder when, a moment later, Joe trotted into the clearing. Their gazes met and, seeing the controlled mirth in his acorn-colored eyes, she turned her head to stare at the fire.

Cole unsaddled the horse and kept her in his peripheral vision as he stowed the gear. A chuckle welled in his throat, and he could not resist a well-aimed barb that would bring her chin down a notch. "I taught him that. You might've gotten away if he wasn't so well-trained."

The young Indian woman simply squared her shoulders and continued to avert her gaze.

Cole hauled Joe's saddle over to the fire, placed it on the ground, and laid the rifle beside it. "I don't know about you, but I'm hungry. I'll fix something to eat while we talk."

"You do not need to cook for me."

He loved the sound of her voice. Her exact enunciation of each word struck a chord within him.

"I'm not—I'm cooking for me. I just thought I'd share some with you, if you're so inclined."

"I do not understand what this 'inclined' is." She glanced over her shoulder, and he read the confusion in her soft brown eyes.

"What I meant is that I'd like to share my meal with you, if you'd like to have some."

"You should have spoken such in the beginning, rather than playing with the words." She lifted her chin slightly higher. "If that is your wish, then I will eat with you."

Cole's mouth dropped open. Somehow she had managed, in just a few short words, to make it sound as if she were doing him some great favor by accepting his offer. He shook his head in bewilderment. *It doesn't matter what race a woman is—they all follow the same path.* He shrugged and went about preparing the beans, jerky, and flatbread.

The young Indian maiden watched the handsome white man from the corner of her eye. She was slightly amazed at his skill in preparing the meal and, more so, was not accustomed to being waited on. A delicate dark eyebrow lifted in surprise when he handed her a tin plate filled with steaming food, instead of backhanding her for stealing the horses. She ate slowly, belying the ravenous hunger that gnawed at her tailbone; she did not fool him, however, and he scooped more hot beans onto her tin without a word.

Cole skirted the fire again and plopped down on the ground in front of his saddle. He leaned back into the leather, tipped the Stetson back on his head, clamped strong hands behind his head, and stared at her.

His gaze made her nervous; soon she discovered that it also angered her. She had spent the last nine years on the run, caring for her own kind and helping the men of her band to make decisions that were for the good of the people. Their acceptance of her as an equal was due not only to the fact that she was the daughter of Crazy Horse, but also because their way of life had been ever-changing as the years went by. Every able body, be it male or female, was needed if the people were to survive on the run. She had fought in more than one battle and was accepted as a peer by those of her own race. It niggled at her now, however, that the stare of a mere white man—granted, a virile and incredibly strong-willed white man—could reduce her to the semblance of a child. Sitting straighter, she met his eyes with a withering glare.

"Is there something you would like to speak of? You stare at me as if you have something in your head."

Cole shrugged. "I was just wondering where you learned to speak English so well."

"Why? Do you not think my race is wise enough to speak in more than grunts?"

"Hey, don't take it so personal. It's just that you speak so clearly; you're easy to understand. I would think that wouldn't be the case, since your *race* has tried awfully hard to stay away from mine."

She tossed her long, thick black hair behind her shoulders with an abrupt shake of the head. "Better for us to stay away."

"You didn't answer my question."

"You make me think of mule." She glared at him again.

A loud guffaw burst from Cole's throat at her comment, which served only to anger her more. She spun on her bottom, presented her slim back to him, and refused to speak.

Cole stood, brushed off the back of his pants and, with another shake of the head, dug around in his saddlebag. Curiosity got the best of the young woman and she turned her head slightly as he pulled out a brown paper package. He started toward her and, consequently, she quickly snapped her head around and continued her intense perusal of the forest around them.

"Here, you want to try something? I purchased some peppermint sticks at my last stop. You're welcome to one, if you'd like. It's called candy."

"I know of it," she spat, still refusing to meet his gaze as he stooped beside her. Memory overcame good judgment, however, and, a moment later, her eyes strayed to the brown paper and the thin sticks of peppermint that lay within. A soldier once gave her this thing called candy. It was sweet and delicious—a taste that had stayed with her ever since.

"Consider it my apology for angering you," the white man continued gently. "Maybe we should start over. We haven't even properly introduced ourselves. My name is Cole Wilkins." His eyebrow arched in surprise when she suddenly spun in his direction and stared up at him with wide eyes.

"Coal...like the fire?" she whispered breathlessly.

"No, it's spelled different," he answered slowly, puzzled by her reaction. At least she was talking again though, and that was something. He held the candy toward her as a peace offering, a gentle smile teasing his lips. "Would you like a piece?"

Cole waited almost breathlessly and was tempted to heave a sigh of relief when she finally reached out a hand and selected a peppermint stick. Surprisingly, the expression that crossed her flawless features was something akin to reverence. She placed the candy in her mouth, and Cole was mesmerized as she slowly savored the sweet taste. Her free hand unconsciously fingered a small bag attached to a string around her neck. She spoke again before he could break the almost sensual silence.

"It is a strange name you have. I have never heard a white man called that before. Why would your mother name you after the fire's ashes?" She leaned forward, and he was surprised to see the genuine interest that sparked in her eyes.

Cole was at a loss for an answer; he had never given it much thought. His mind whirled as he tried to come up with an explanation to keep her talking. "I don't know. Maybe because my grandfather had the same name, and she thought I looked like him. You haven't told me your name."

The young woman stared at a distant star, suddenly lost in her own thoughts. Cole was forced to repeat the question. The slightest hint of a smile crossed her lips when she blinked back to awareness.

"Yes, you are right. We have not been properly introduced. I am August Moon."

"Why were you smiling just now?"

"It seems strange to me that I sit here speaking with you as if we were friends. I tried to steal your horses. You had a rifle to my back and could have killed me, yet you did not. All my life I have feared the white man, but for some reason, you do not frighten me. To me, that seems odd."

Cole stared at her for a moment longer, contemplated the smile that had replaced her earlier frown, then moved to sit on a tree stump a few feet from where the Indian girl sat on the ground.

"August Moon." He rolled the name off his tongue. "You thought my name seemed strange and asked why my mother would call me that. Well, your name seems a bit odd to me. I've never heard anything like it."

August Moon pulled her knees to her chest and shrugged her slender shoulders. "I was born at an agency where there were many soldiers. It was the time of year you white men call August. There was a full moon in the night sky; the type that lights up the paths in the forests. Just before my mother bore me, part of the moon was covered. When I took my first breath, my mother breathed her last. My birth frightened many of the Indians at the agency. They said I would forever carry the mark of that moon."

The young woman fell silent for a moment, and Cole waited patiently for her to speak again. Her slim fingers played with the scattered pine needles on the forest floor around her.

"The soldiers called me the little August Moon Papoose. When my grandmother tried to change my name, the people would not listen to her—even they thought I looked different from them, because of that moon." Her tone was flat and self-condemning.

She was right, Cole realized. Her hair was slightly lighter in color than others of her race. It even appeared to have waves running through its length, which was totally unheard of among the Indian people. The tresses were thick and, he was sure, soft to the touch. *I would give anything to run my fingers through it,* he mused. Upon even closer inspection, he also observed the narrowness of her face and the color of her skin—skin that was more honey-brown than red.

Where she considered her appearance, her mere existence, to be far from perfect, Cole thought she was the most beautiful women he had ever seen. Cocking his head slightly, he quickly rephrased his thoughts. *Exotic—that's the word that describes her.* Her deep brown eyes were a shade he had never encountered before, and her full tawny-colored lips moved with a sensuousness all their own when she spoke.

"What are you going to do with me?"

It took a second for Cole to comprehend that she had asked him a question and waited for an answer.

"What?"

"I am asking you what will you do with me?"

Cole shook off the almost hypnotic fascination her presence elicited in him and shrugged. "I hadn't thought about it, to be honest." He leaned forward, ignored her question, and propped his chin on a closed fist. "How is it you speak my language so well?"

Another quick jolt of surprise lifted August's eyebrows. She had tried to steal the white man's horses, yet it was as if he had totally forgotten her offense. "From the time I was a child, my people have lived on and off agency lands. Your missionaries repeatedly forced their god on us. The soldiers also made us speak your tongue, instead of our own. Some were patient and taught us the words; others would use the back of their hand if we spoke in the tongue of the Sioux. When you are a child, it is easy to find the words, rather than be beaten. It is also easier to say the words than it is to sleep at night with a hunger here." She placed her hand over a flat stomach. "If we spoke our own words, they would give our food to the dogs and laugh at us."

Cole stood to add more wood to the fire, using the movement to hide his shock. *I think I'm beginning to understand why Beau wants to help them...*

Cole had always been surrounded by familiar things—except for one night when he was just a child. He was never forced to change his ways or his thinking. He had always gone to bed with a loving hug and food to warm his belly. He was always surrounded by family and had always felt safe and secure; except for that one day—a day he would never forget...

Cole was four years old and playing outside with his brother, Trevor, when Doc Adams carriage wheeled through the front gates. He and Trevor ran to greet the old man. The doctor always arrived with a treat in his black leather bag.

On this particular day though, the old doctor jumped to the ground and hardly noticed the boys where they stood by with impish grins. Cole and Trevor fell into step on either side of him, and the old man scowled.

"Out of my way! Not today, boys."

"Come on, Doc. Come and see our new pups in the barn!" Trevor was not in the least bit intimidated.

The old man paused briefly to grab him roughly by the arm.

"Listen to me. I don't have time. I'm warning both of you boys—" his voice lowered ominously before he pointed a stern finger at a point just beneath Trevor's nose "—stay out of the house. You are not allowed to come in, do you understand? If I see either of you or Tyler underfoot, there'll be hell to pay." With that, he quickly turned, took the porch steps two at a time, and slammed the big oak door in their faces.

Cole sank down on the top step, and his chin quivered with his attempt to stifle tears. What was happening? Why was the doctor so mean? A frightened Tyler exited the house a few minutes later.

"Mama is having her baby. Doc says we have to stay out here." Those were the only words he uttered.

The three of them sat side by side on the porch, wrapped in silence until a scream pierced the air, then another and another. Cole jumped at the horrifying sound, and Tyler slid nearer to place an arm around his shoulder. Trevor flanked him on the other side.

The three boys sat huddled together until the sun slipped over the horizon; three young brothers frightened and confused about the unknown. Their mother's screams echoed across the night sky and they quickly forgot about the hunger that gnawed at their bellies—hunger generated by the fact that Mamie had not called them in for dinner.

Cole finally gave way to his fear, and the tears that rolled down his cheeks quickly turned into sobs.

"Stop it!" Tyler demanded. "Quit being a baby!"

The front door opened late into the night and their father walked out onto the wooden porch. He stared at them with a sad, distant look in his lifeless eyes. "Go to your rooms."

That was all he said. No explanations; no comforting, familiar hugs.

The boys scrambled to their feet and entered the house. They were met with deathly silence. Tyler took both Cole and Trevor by the hand and led them to his room. The three boys climbed into the same bed, frightened and alone...

It was more fear than hunger Cole had felt that night—the night his mother died giving birth to his little sister, Carrie.

One night. That's all. Just one night of being afraid of the unknown. One night of going to bed hungry.

He turned his gaze in August Moon's direction. *How many nights did she lay her head down as a child, hungry and scared, because some soldier withheld food for his own enjoyment?*

August Moon secretly watched Cole from beneath long dark lashes as he squatted beside the small fire. He was not like the white men she had ever known. Others of his kind had only one purpose in mind; to steal her way of life, and everything she held close to her heart, and destroy it. She had been abused, cheated, and harangued.

From the time she was a small child, she had never known a white man who was honest and considerate. They coerced the bands into agencies with the promise of food and clothing. The people went because they were tired; tired of being hunted down and tired of being hungry. Once inside the agencies, the lies started. The elders were tricked, then forced to sign treaties that took their land. The old and the sick were not cared for as promised; the food was not fit for animals most days, and they were forced to stifle their culture and beliefs. The missionaries insisted they become 'Christians.' It was not a word she fully understood. Regardless, the white man's explanation of *their* religion was forced into her head, and August Moon came to realize it was just another way for the people's pride and lifestyle to be taken from them.

Now, she stole horses for her band. Less than thirty souls traveled with her, and only herself and eleven braves were left to care for them. The winter just past had been hard. The band had been forced to kill and eat three of their ponies. Another animal died from injuries when it was attacked by one of the big cats that roamed the area. They needed the horses badly. The band would move to the wintering grounds in the north soon; a safe haven from the soldiers who searched for them. She and the braves worried about the old ones, who could no longer walk the paths. Even so, August would not forsake them to a certain death at one of the white man's agencies.

This man named Cole Wilkins could have killed her, but he did not. Instead, he gave her warm food and even treated her with delicious candy. He did not seem threatening in the least. It was confusing, to say the least, but not enough so to keep her from devising a plan to steal the animals once more. In order for her plan to work, however, she needed to know what he was going to do.

"You did not answer my question. What are you going to do with me?"

Cole glanced up when she spoke. Grabbing the bag of candy, he handed August Moon another stick before he relaxed on the ground across from her.

"Tell me something. Why are you out here all alone? How is it that you're not living at one of the government agencies?"

August Moon pursed her lips, and Cole hid a smile. She was getting angry with him again; it was easy to see by the square set of her jaw.

"Why do you not answer me? Why I am here is none of your business."

"Oh, I think it is. If you want your question answered, then you have to answer mine. Why are you out here all alone?" He locked stares with her and waited patiently. August Moon started to push herself up, but was halted by his sharp words. "I told you before that I don't relish the idea of having to chase you down again. So, until I get some answers, keep your backside planted in the dirt, August."

He was infuriating! August Moon dropped to the ground again, and sparks shot from the brown velvet depths of her eyes.

"My name is August *Moon*," she stated pointedly.

He shrugged his broad shoulders. "I like August. Now, answer my question. How come you're alone?"

"Why should that matter to you?" she spouted the angry words with a toss of her head.

Cole inhaled deeply and counted to ten. He was not about to tell her that he was trying to decide if he would have his throat slashed before morning when the rest of her band found them—if there was a band.

"I'm simply wondering why you felt you needed four more horses, when you've got one already."

She stared into the fire. *There is no need for me to tell him that I am traveling alone. He does not need to know that I do not plan to return to my band for another five or six nights and that no one will worry about me until then.*

On the other hand, her instincts told her that she could trust this man. He was kind and gentle, unheard of for a white man, and it appeared that he was only interested in her welfare. Still, she needed to find out what he had planned for her. Finally, she decided to be honest...to a point.

"I share the responsibility of caring for my small band. We need the horses to travel north before the snows come."

Beau was right! She's one of the Indians he's looking for and probably belongs to one of the small bands that winter in Canada. He crossed his arms over a broad chest. "Where are they now?"

"Why do you need to know that?" She pierced him with another glare.

"I'm just trying to get a handle on this whole situation, August. A friend of mine told me about the small bands of Indians that travel between here and the Dakotas. He also said that he figured you winter in Canada—probably somewhere in the Rockies. He's been looking for you."

August leapt from her sitting position and Cole followed suit just as quickly. He grabbed her arm before she had the chance to flee into the darkness.

"Let me go! I must get to my family before they are found!" She struggled against his hold and her small foot connected squarely with Cole's shin. She smiled her satisfaction at the grimace that passed quickly on his face.

"Dammit!" he gritted as he tightened his hold on her arm. "I'm tired of you beating the hell out of me, so just stop it right now! He has no idea where you are. He's headed south as we speak."

She looked up into his face and shook her head adamantly. "But you tricked me into telling about them."

"No, I didn't. I was trying to find out if I was gonna to be jumped in my sleep tonight!"

"If I am not here, then you have no worries. Now, let me go!" she shrieked into his face.

Cole inhaled deeply once more. "No. I haven't decided what I'm going to do with you yet."

That was the truth. For a reason he could not yet fathom, Cole was not ready to let her leave. "Please, August, just sit down so we can talk."

They stared at one another, neither of their gazes wavering; until, finally, August blinked.

"What do you want, Cole Wilkins? The soldiers made bargains with me. Do you wish to make a bargain with me, as well?" Her tone whispered defeat, but she raised her chin a notch in a show of pride.

His eyes widened in disbelief. *Is she offering what I think she is?* She had said it, but the look on her face told him how distasteful the act would be for her.

"What exactly are you saying, August?"

She met his gaze directly. "When my family needed something badly, the soldiers were willing to provide it...in exchange for what I or the other women of my band could give. I need the horses. Even one would help..."

Cole's stomach lurched with sickening realization. What had she endured? What had all of them endured in order to survive on the fringes of humanity? He released her arm quickly and stepped back.

"You would trade yourself for a horse?"

He watched her swallow convulsively; she reminded him of a small animal backed into a corner. Again, her chin rose a notch, a trait he was becoming all too familiar with.

"I would trade myself for the good of my family. I can do no less. Sometimes one must do what she has to in order to survive." August stepped back and, reaching for the drawstring at her waist, refused to meet his gaze as her shaking fingers worked the leather knot.

Cole stood dumfounded and was jolted from his shock only when the leather strings hung at August's side. With a slight, trembling hesitation, she moved her fingers to the soft buckskin, ready to shed the leggings, then nearly jumped out of her skin when he bounded forward and placed his palms on her forearms, staying her hands.

"What the hell are you doing?"

"I told you, I will make a bargain with you, Cole Wilkins, but you must swear to trade your horses for me."

Cole shook his head slowly, and August took the movement to mean that he would not promise her anything. Her eyes narrowed. "If you will not give me the horses, then I will not give you what you want."

"What?" He squinted at her in disbelief, then let out a heavy breath, as if someone had just punched him in the gut. "I am not making any kind of *bargain* with you—at least not the one you're talking about. Christ—!" He stepped back quickly to put distance between them, sighed deeply again, and ran a hand through his tousled hair. He looked directly into her brown eyes. "August, please; just sit down so we can talk—that's all I want to do."

Her shoulders dropped in relief when he rubbed his brow in fatigue. She would not be forced to lay with this man as he grunted over her; he would not make her feel dirty and pierce her soul with shame. She retied the drawstring of her leggings and seated herself on the hard ground again. She lifted a wary gaze when he continued.

"Before you took my horses, I rode for a time with the old friend of mine I told you about. His name is Beau McCabe." A flicker of what Cole took to be recognition crossed her smooth features. "By the look on your face, I see you've heard of him. He's not a bad person, August. He used to be a soldier, but he's not anymore. He mustered out of the Cavalry because he couldn't tolerate what the white man's government was doing to the Sioux people. His job now is to round up bands like yours for the Bureau of Indian Affairs. Beau will only bring you in if he's promised you'll be placed at the agency of your choice."

"And you believe that, Cole Wilkins?" August shook her head at his ignorance. "It always comes down to lies. I have lived it too long."

"Come on, August. You must know that he passes through this area. He hasn't gotten himself killed by renegade bands of Sioux yet, so there must be some truth in what he says." She did not look convinced. "His heart is with the Sioux. You gotta believe me when I say that. Beau is one of the few white men fighting for your rights, or at least he's trying to make the change easier for you than it normally is."

"Why are you telling me of him?"

"I want you to know he can be trusted if he finds you, August.

Unfortunately, it doesn't sound like there's anything you can do to change the future. It's pretty much been set by the U.S. Government. Beau won't force you to come in with him though; he'll just give you some options."

"We are not ready to 'go in,' as you put it." Her shoulders sagged suddenly and she moved her sad, but wise gaze to him again. Cole had the strange feeling that she peered into his soul. "Do you think I do not understand that my way of life is at its end? I have known it since I was a child. It is not time for us to give up, though. The dream is not finished yet."

"What are you talking about?"

She shook her head again and staunchly refused to answer him, and Cole sighed deeply.

A moment of silence followed, and August's shoulders drooped even lower. She stared at the ground for an interminable amount of time before bringing her gaze up to meet his again. She spoke quietly.

"Please tell me, Cole Wilkins, what are you going to do with me? I will not go to an agency, and I will not commit my people to that fate, either. You said if I meet your friend, I must trust him. Does that mean you will let me go now?"

I can't believe I'm about to say this...

Before Cole committed himself aloud, however, his thoughts returned to the decision he made a few minutes earlier. Throughout the evening, as he listened to her defensive words and thought about Beau's stories, Cole had experienced a driving need to help August and her band. The idea was irrational. Absurd and, if anyone ever found out, they would think he had taken leave of his senses. He met her dark gaze again.

"I won't give you my horses. Two of them belong to me, and I can't do without them. The other two I'm in the process of delivering to someone who purchased them. My family breeds and sells horses," he added the last in the form of an explanation. He released another sigh and voiced the words that would see him branded as a lunatic. "You probably know this area we're traveling through better than anyone, which means that you must also know where the nearest town is. I don't. In fact, I don't have a clue where I am. If you'll trust me enough to stay the night—with no strings attached—then tomorrow you can guide me out of these woods. In exchange, I'll get you some horses."

August was stunned by his words. He wanted to help her! A man she had never seen before; a man she had tried to steal from; a *white* man.

"Why would you do this?" she whispered her amazement.

Cole stood, walked to his pack and pulled out a bedroll. Retracing his steps to the fire, he handed the blanket to the woman before him. "I don't know why. I just know that if there's something I can do to help you and your people, I have to do it. It's as simple as that. Getting you the horses you need will fix your immediate problem." Cole hunkered down before her. "Look, August, I generally go about my life trying not to intrude on anybody else's business. But, the way I see it, you and your people have been done a grave injustice. Your way of life is coming to an end—you said so yourself. Whether it's over quickly or drags on for another twenty years is out of both of our hands. But, if you want to follow this course that you've chosen, then let me help. Let me get you the horses."

He watched her face closely and the emotions that flowed across it. Distrust, hesitancy and, finally, amazement. He had always heard that Indians were a stoic breed. Not so with the young woman before him. From the moment they met, her face had been a constant plane of changes.

"Where do you plan to find the ponies?" she asked almost breathlessly. "Are you going to steal them?" The question was asked so sincerely that Cole did not dare laugh.

"No," he replied with a warm glance and a shake of his head. "When you show me the way out of here, I plan to buy the horses. You just have to trust me to do it."

He rose and turned to walk away, but August jumped up to grab his arm in a gentle hold that halted his steps.

"And you would do this without asking anything in return?"

"All I ask is that, if you and your family run into Beau McCabe, you'll give him a chance to do what he can for you."

She said nothing in return, and he smiled tenderly into her astonished eyes.

"Take that bedroll and get some sleep."

She nodded slowly. *I have to take the chance...* Believing in a white man went against her grain, but there was little she could do about it at this point. Her band needed the animals to survive.

August moved to spread the bedroll by the fire, but her movements were halted by his soft words.

"Will you and my horses be here in the morning?"

She turned to face him. "I will be here. My word is my oath. You can trust me, Cole Wilkins."

"And you can trust me, August."

Chapter Five

Cole leaned wearily against the trunk of a massive jackpine. His tired gaze took in the muted light of dawn that wound its way through the previously darkened forest. An hour earlier, his eyes had closed for a short time. He awoke soon after with a wildly pounding heart; he had let his guard down.

His unruffled guise of the previous night had been an act—Cole had kept a close eye on August throughout the long dark hours. A small piece of him wanted to be assured that she would not leave quietly into the shadows, along with his horses.

Through those long hours, while he watched her sleep, Cole never once doubted his decision. *What did she or her band do to deserve the life they're now forced to lead?* Somewhere in the lengthy hours of the night, the Sioux had gained his admiration; especially the few like August, who possessed a dogged determination not to give in to those who tried to take away everything that was familiar. It did not matter that, in the end, it would prove a lost cause. Even she admitted that the Sioux's former way of life was coming to a close. Still, she would not waver in her resolve to hold onto her culture; to her very existence.

There were very few people who would understand his driving need to help her. Sifting it around in his mind during the dark hours, however, Cole came to the conclusion that he could do nothing less.

He rose, stretched the kinks from his back, and bent to retrieve an old tin pot filled with yesterday's coffee, then walked to the edge of the clearing. Cole dumped the tepid liquid into the dew-topped grass and retraced his steps. He readied the coffee pot for morning and stoked the fire, all the while keeping one eye on August's prone figure lying beneath his blanket.

Exhaustion finally overtook him, and Cole sagged to the ground, propped his head against the leather saddle, and pulled his jacket tighter around his body. Tucking his rifle close, he cast one last cursory glance in August's direction before he closed his eyes.

She gave her word. I hope she sticks to it.

* * *

August's eyes fluttered open to the new day. Bolting upright, she searched out the man who said he would help her. Cole lay with his back to her on the far side of the fire pit, which now emitted only small tendrils of smoke from the charred wood.

August knew he had kept vigil through most of the long night; she had watched him through shuttered eyes. Earlier, when he finally slept, thoughts of fleeing crossed her mind. It would have been so easy. He slept soundly. All she would have had to do was untie the horses and walk them quietly away from camp. She had given her word though—she would not run—and the thought of the badly needed horses he promised to deliver stayed in the forefront of her mind. Even though other white men had broken their promises countless times, he had not. For some odd reason, she wanted him to respect her for staying. So, she laid back, pulled the wool blanket around her slim shoulders, and succumbed to slumber once more.

* * *

An hour later, August moved quietly as she rose, folded the bedroll, and crossed the dampened grass to check the injured leg of the colt. She stooped next to the animal, ran a trained hand across his fetlock, then jumped upon the sound of his voice.

"Not planning to go anywhere, are you?"

She spun to face him with a pounding heart. "Why do you always sneak up on me? I gave you my word last night that I would not run."

"What were you doing?"

"I was checking the small one's leg. He seems to be fine this morning." Her lips drew in a straight line. "Why are you staring at me again?"

Cole was not about to tell her that when he woke and saw her near the colt, he thought she was leaving. He also kept to himself the fact that he had now memorized her face in small bits to tuck away in his mind. This might be his last day with August, depending on how close they were to a town. He would buy her horses, and she would return to another world. The last two days were something he never wanted to forget. Sending a small half-grin in her direction, he shrugged his shoulders and apologized.

"Sorry—I didn't realize I was doing that. We should eat something and pack up." He turned to go stoke the fire, but her voice stopped him.

"Will you still help me?"

He glanced over his broad shoulder to see her standing in the morning sun; small, frail, and with a look of uncertainty in her eyes.

"I said I would, didn't I?"

"You would not be the first white man to lie to me."

"Then let me be the first one to gain your trust."

Their gazes locked, and Cole acknowledged the faint nod of her head.

* * *

August led the way, and Cole followed with the colts and packhorse. She had guided him through a thick forest and across numerous streams for over four hours, and he was beginning to think she had no idea where they were.

When they reached the top of a bluff, however, and he looked out across a rolling valley and saw buildings and the semblance of a small town, a sigh of relief left his lips.

"There is your town, Cole Wilkins," August murmured softly. "Hopefully, you will find ponies to buy."

Cole nudged Joe closer to her mare, where he could better view the path that led downward toward the small village.

She stared ahead, never taking her eyes from some distant point. "I will wait here for you. I cannot go closer and take the chance of someone seeing me. If you wish, I will watch your horses until you come back."

"And what if I come back and you aren't here?"

"That is the chance you will have to take." Her words held a challenge, as did her smoky eyes when August turned her head and rested her triumphant gaze on him.

Cole leaned back in the saddle, pushed his hat back, and a smile born of respect creased his face. "You know what, August? Half the men I know don't have the gumption you do."

"You are playing with words again."

He leaned forward to rest a jacket-covered forearm on the saddle horn and looked at her intently, ignoring her last remark. "As much as I feel we've come to some sort of agreement here, I still think I need something to secure our bargain—something to make certain you'll be waiting with my animals when I get back."

"I have nothing to give."

Cole reached out to touch the small pouch nuzzled against the neckline of her deer hide shirt. She flinched, but she did not move from his reach. "I think you do. Whatever you have in that small bag means a great deal to you. I've watched you. You check continually to see if it's there. You're constantly touching it and don't even realize it."

August slapped his hand away and wrapped her fingers protectively around the oilskin bag. Since the day her grandmother bestowed her with its care, she had removed it only when bathing. The pouch was the only thing she owned that connected her to the old woman.

"I will not give it to you and take the chance of you losing it."

"Then I won't get you your horses."

They were at a stalemate. Cole nearly gave in as he watched August struggle with her emotions. He had taunted her like a small child, but before he could say anything more, August reached up to untie the string from around her neck. She handed the precious possession to him with unsteady hands.

"My father and grandmother would be ashamed of me if I forgot the needs of my people. I will be waiting when you return."

Cole gazed at the bag that lay on his gloved palm and almost gave it back to her. He felt like an oaf for blackmailing her, but the overriding need to see her again made him stuff the valued item into a saddlebag. Having the small sack in his possession would guarantee that August would wait for him.

* * *

Cole prodded Joe along the dusty street that ran through the center of the small town. His alert eyes took in the lifeless brown storefronts and the equally drab residents, who stood on wooden walkways and eyed him with suspicion. Cole simply nodded to the onlookers and steered Joe toward the town's only saloon. The tavern was a starting point; a place for him to find out where he could obtain August's horses.

He dismounted and ignored the looks he received from two grizzled men who sat in timber chairs under the rickety canopy. Cole proceeded inside and crossed to the wooden bar. Surprisingly, the airless little saloon held a number of men; men who observed him closely. A burly bartender with bulging arms and sweat-stained clothes approached.

"Can I do ya for something, stranger?"

Cole tossed three paper bills onto the sticky wooden surface before him, eyed a dirty glass, and contemplated if he really did want a drink.

"I guess I'll have a beer."

He watched the heavily built man pull a semi-clean mug from the shelf, draw him a tap, and set it down before him. Cole had already guessed what would come out of the bartender's mouth next.

"Not from around here, are ya?"

"Nope." Cole sipped at the tepid beer and casually observed his surroundings.

"Mind if I ask why you'd be passin' through this God-forsaken town? Don't see too many strangers. We're kinda set apart from the rest of the big cities."

"I'm on my way to Fargo and looking to buy some horses. Think I got turned around about two days ago and missed the main road. Where am I, anyway?"

"Son, you'd be just north of that main road. This here place we just call Miller's Creek. Ya want to go south a few miles and hook up ta the main road going through Brainerd. That road will take ya right into Fargo if you stay on it and don't get lost. Can't sees how ya would've taken a wrong turn a few days back, though. The main road is hard ta get off of." The bartender peered at Cole closely and waited to see if his patron would be forthcoming with any information.

Cole calmly sipped at his beer and eyed him back. "I was chasing a rabbit for my supper and left the main trail. Got lost, I guess."

The man behind the bar belted out a laugh. "Son, if ya can't figure out where ya are by the sun, then ya shouldn't be out rabbit huntin'! Ya got a ways ta go yet before reachin' Fargo. Yer best bet would be ta get yerself to Brainerd and jump the rail. If yer lookin' for horses, you'd be better off ta go there than purchase any of the old nags they got for sale in this town."

"Well, I'd just as soon get them here and be on my way. Don't have time to get lost in Brainerd. Know of anyone that would be willing to sell some stock?"

A fairly well dressed man stepped forward and introduced himself before the bartender could reply.

"Name's Bill Ramsey. Couldn't help but hear your conversation. If you're looking for sturdiness over beauty, I've got what you might be looking for. What're you using them for? Work or pleasure?"

Cole quickly put his thoughts in order. "I'm looking for animals that are already trained to take on a rider, good temperament, and sturdy like you said. I want to start a horse-renting business near Fargo. I need animals that are calm and can pull a wagon." *Or a travois,* he thought to himself.

Bill Ramsey nodded his head as he listened to Cole's answer. "Might have what you're looking for. When would you be needing them?"

"If it's alright with you, I'd like to see them right now. I plan to get at least on the other side of Brainerd by nightfall."

"Well then, Mr..."

"Wilkins," Cole supplied.

"Mr. Wilkins, if you'll follow me, we can head right out to my place. It's only about a mile east of here." Ramsey turned to leave.

Cole quickly downed the rest of his beer before thanking the proprietor of the saloon and leaving with the other man.

* * *

Cole purchased six horses and three mules. They were now lined up outside the town's general goods store. The appearance of a stranger in the small town was enough to collect curious spectators up and down the narrow main street.

Cole brushed off the onlookers' stares, eager to be on his way and even more eager to find August. He tightened the last of the leather straps around the belly of an aging pony, then patted the animal's shaggy flank. He had received what he thought to be a hell of a deal from Ramsey. The mules tied nearby were an afterthought, but a ride was a ride. August's band could use them to haul heavy loads; he looked forward to her reaction.

Storing the last of the supplies he purchased into a pack, Cole mounted Joe and turned the horse back in the direction he came from.

The burly saloon owner stood with his patrons in the open doorway and watched as Cole reached the edge of town and disappeared. Uproarious laughter bounced across the dusty street as they slapped each other on the back.

"Look at that dumb son of a bitch!" the bartender snorted. "I told him earlier that he'd have ta go *south* ta hook up to the main route." He glanced around at his chuckling companions with a raised eyebrow. "Anyone care ta ride out and point him in the right direction?"

The other men shook their heads and returned to the airless interior. One fellow took a last look at the departing stranger. "If he was told once and still can't figure it out, I'm not about to waste a perfectly good afternoon of drinking to chase him down. Let the idiot go."

The bartender's belly shook with laughter as he moved behind the bar again, thoughts of the stranger already gone from his mind.

* * *

August paced nervously across the small clearing she had found to hide the horses in. Her keen senses were alerted to every small snap of a twig as she waited for Cole. If it was not for the fact that he took possession of her small oilskin bag, August wondered if she would have taken his animals and simply headed north to join up with her band.

She sat on the hard ground and leaned again a tree, closed her eyes with a heavy sigh, and pictured Cole in her mind. As she thought of him, she was assailed by a pang of regret that she would not have the time to better understand him. There were few people in her short life that she had let get close to her. Not that she had gotten *close* to Cole either, but she had given him her trust, limited though it was, which was more than she had any other white man.

Why would he help me? His kindness tugs at my soul and I do not understand why—yet I trust him. He was different than most of his race; August knew beyond a doubt that Cole would return with what he had promised.

She rose to amble down an almost invisible path to the bluff above the town. *Where is he?* Her unsettled gaze searched the edges of the valley. Not seeing him anywhere, August dropped to the ground in exasperation, but still kept her eyes glued to the land below.

A movement caught her eye a few moments later. Bounding to her feet, August stared intently until she recognized the tall, muscular figure astride a horse. It was Cole. Behind him trailed a string of animals.

He did it! He's bringing back horses for me and my family! August clasped her palms together, overwhelmed by his generosity.

She raced to the hidden ponies, quickly untied them, and led the horses back out to the bluff's edge. If all the animals that followed Cole up the path were for her, the old ones in her band would be able to stay with them.

* * *

Cole anxiously watched the trail before him. He was near the base of the outcropping when August stepped closer to the edge and into his view. His heart beat erratically when he realized she was still there; she had waited for him to return. *To hell with Pederson's horses—she's still here!*

He reached the summit, jumped from Joe's back, and moved to stand before her. Reaching into his saddlebag, Cole pulled out the small, cherished pouch. Without saying a word, he stepped behind August and lifted her thick, dark tresses. His fingers brushed the soft length, and the dark, satiny strands cascaded through his fingers. Forcing himself, he tied the treasure around a slender neck, stepped back, untied the lead rope from the saddle and placed it within her clasped palms.

"Your horses, Miss August."

She looked up at him in wonder for a moment before she moved to run slender hands over the back of the animal nearest her. She repeated the same procedure with the rest of the small group, including the mules. All the while, Cole's eyes never left her slight frame. Finally done with her inspection, August turned and her brown eyes filled with forbidden tears as they met the hazel ones before her.

"You must be a very rich man to buy as many horses as you did." Her watery gaze found the ground beneath her moccasined feet.

"Not really rich—just resourceful, I'd say. Will they help—?" He noticed her tears then. "What's wrong, August? You don't seem very happy."

She stroked Joe, who had moved closer to where they stood and nudged her shoulder. "There is nothing wrong. I just have this feeling of..." She shook her head. "I cannot explain it in your words. I can never thank you enough for this grand gift—my family cannot thank you enough." She turned her shiny gaze on him again. "You do this, and yet you ask for nothing in return."

Cole stepped closer. "No, I do want something in return." His eyes traveled momentarily across the soft brown plains of her face, and his stomach lurched at the thought of any harm befalling her. "I ask that you stay safe. Last night you said the dream isn't finished. I don't know what that means, but I hope you find what you're looking for."

"Cole Wilkins, you have a great strength in your heart. I am glad our paths have crossed. If they had not, I would never know that a white man can be as honorable as one of my own."

Coming from August, Cole understood that the words were the biggest compliment she could have bestowed upon him. She began to untie the ropes that held a pack on top of one of the mules, and Cole stayed her hand. Her gaze flew to his in question.

"The supplies in the pack are yours. I've already separated mine out." His firm lips curved in a sheepish grin. "They're just a few things I thought you might need."

"I cannot take any more from you. If I—"

"Not another word, August. There's a wrapped package inside that is yours alone. The rest you can distribute among your group."

A long moment passed as she stared up at him. He watched a soft, tremulous smile appear on her tawny lips—just before she turned away. August expertly readied the horses before hoisting herself up onto her own pony. She reined her mount closer to Cole, then leaned down to press a whisper of a kiss to his cheek. His eyes widened in surprise as, once more, their gazes locked.

"My family thanks you. I thank you. Walk safely wherever you go, Cole Wilkins, and know that I will pray for your good fortune each day when the sun tops the trees. I will always think of you in a good way."

His last picture of August was that of the stoic Sioux woman leading the animals she so treasured onto a small path beneath a canopy of pines. And then she was gone.

Chapter Six

August shouldered aside the dense undergrowth from the entrance of a hidden tunnel on the edge of a distant pine-covered hill. In a matter of minutes, she would be with her small clan again, and the excitement that coursed through her body raised goose bumps on her arms. Tightening the hold on her pony's reins, her sparkling eyes darted behind her in a quick, token glance to the string of animals that she still could not believe belonged to her. She towed them along, and they followed in single file through a space barely wide enough to accommodate the width of a horse.

An expected, piercing howl of welcome cut the familiar quiet when she stepped through the opening at the other end of the passageway and into the bright sunlight. August reached up to clutch her mount's shaggy main, easily pulled herself across the animal's back, and kicked the pony into a trot. Her searching gaze finally spied Wolf as he raced down the tree-lined path in her direction.

They met on the trail. August slid from her horse's back to greet her old friend, who stood with arms akimbo and pride shining in his eyes.

"August Moon, you have returned unharmed." His eyes swept the length of her slender body, as if to confirm the words he had just spoken. His dark gaze shifted then, to the string of mules and stout, sturdy horses. "I see you were successful—even though it was foolish of you to leave without one of the braves." Wolf's pointed condemnation was tempered with a joyful turn of the lips.

He was unbearably angry when he discovered that she had slipped into the night by herself. Wolf had no doubt that August left the safety of the encampment in order to prove that she could fulfill a need of the people—and that she could do it on her own. In fact, he nearly rode out after her; in doing so, however, the band would have snickered with glee at the thought that a mere woman could turn their leader into a pining, love-sick youth.

August cocked a knee and placed a hand on her hip. "I do not need a brave to watch over me, Wolf. I am quite capable of taking care of myself and, as you can well see, I brought back the animals we will need to travel to the winter camp. I have proven myself worthy more than once." A smug grin flitted across August's lips—she loved to best him at his own game. "I can see the truth in your eyes; you are proud of me, Wolf. Why do you not admit it?" She threw out the teasing words along with an arrogant toss of the head and waited for his reply.

His black gaze moved over the soft brown skin of her face. This was a woman who held a special place in his heart. *What would she think if I told her it is not only pride I feel, but that love has also burned in my heart from the first summer we ran from the soldiers? What would she say if she knew of the times I watched the opening in the earth these last few days and prayed for her safety?*

Wolf hid his emotions with an arrogant smirk and nodded his head toward the path behind him. "Come, Little One. I do not have time to stand here and sing praises that you would lap up greedily like one of the village dogs. It is hard enough to live with your daily boasts. We will go meet the others on their way down the trail. You can brag to them of your grand deed, and they will give you the admiration you search for."

A soft laugh bubbled in August's throat when she plopped the lead rope into his upturned palm, then strode up the trail to greet the others who approached in the distance. Wolf watched her smooth gate, the high tilt of her head, and imagined what it would be like to share a life with her—a dream that would never come to pass.

August had told him repeatedly that her life was a spiritual journey. She knew that she was different and had set an exacting course over the years that she intended to follow unerringly. She would never take a man as her husband, nor would she have children as the other women of the tribe did. In turn, the life she had chosen for herself was respected and revered by the others.

Who am I to change the direction of her journey? She loves me as a brother and nothing more. Wolf was doomed to desire August from a distance. To inform her of his deepest feelings would only make her flee. Seeing her on a daily basis was better than not having her in his life at all.

Wolf continued to observe her slight form as she was pulled into a group of laughing women. He shook his head again. *Now, here I am, a prideful warrior who follows her like an old weather-beaten squaw...*

Wolf's broad shoulders dropped with a heavy sigh as he yanked on the lead rope and continued up the path.

* * *

August reached the camp amid carefree laughs and hugs of congratulation. Fires were lit immediately to begin a feast in her honor. No one member of the band would hear of her story until the entire group was assembled. While the women of the encampment began their preparations, the men joined Wolf to inspect the horses and mules August had secured for the tribe.

She was left standing alone in front of her teepee with the huge gray pack Cole had tied onto one of the mules. With surprising strength, she tackled the weight of the bag and tugged it through the open flap. Once inside, she dropped to her knees to inspect the contents. A gasp escaped her lips when the last buckle was opened and she peered inside.

An assortment of hunting knives were the first to emerge. Next came neatly folded blankets in a variety of colors she had never before encountered. A wan smile touched her lips when her hand came in contact with the next item; a wicker basket with a rounded top. Inside were a huge array of sewing needles and thick threads that would help the women of the tribe form clothes. Behind the basket came colorful pieces of cloth and combs for the women's hair. Cole had not only thought of their immediate need by providing the horses; his generosity also produced gifts that would bring happiness and pleasure. August's heart swelled with gratitude.

The last thing to materialize from the bundle was a large, brown paper wrapped package. It was tied with a string.

"He said this gift was for me..." August's anxious fingers untied the cord and pushed back the paper. She froze.

It took her a moment to recover from the shock of his generosity, then she reached out a shaky hand to caress the folded jacket that lay within the confines of the crumpled paper. The softness of the supple brown fabric and the sheer beauty of the garment itself took August's breath away. Lifting the coat with worshipful hands, she brought it close to her face, rubbed her cheek along the satiny front, and breathed in its scent. She buried her face in the soft fur that lined the collar and closed her eyes. *With a garment such as this, I will never feel the cold when the winter snows begin.*

August stood to thrust her arms into the sleeves and giggled aloud when the furry collar tickled her face. Never in her life had she owned something so beautiful. "Cole, wherever you are, know that I will cherish this forever!"

She slid her tiny hands into the front pockets and her fingers came in contact with a small wrapped parcel. Again, August rushed to rip the brown paper. The package fell open, and she sank to her knees and stared into the palms of her hands. A second passed before she brought the object closer to her eyes for examination. She had never seen a rock like the one she held, if it even was a rock. She was not sure. The stone was smooth and lightweight, flat and white. Carved into its surface was the outline of a horse. It galloped with its head and tail held high.

August turned the object slowly in her shaking palms; this gift was even more precious than the jacket she wore. *It signifies my quest to finish the dream, even if he does not understand what that dream is.*

August's lids dropped shut, and she held the small ornament to her chest. Envisioning Cole, she suddenly understood that he was a part of the dream. Their paths had crossed for a reason. *It will be up to me to find out what that reason was, even if I never see him again.* The mere thought caused a small pain to prick at her heart. *He went out of his way to make my family's life easier, even though he is a white man. He was kind and he asked for nothing in return...*

August stood and reached for a tanned strip of deer hide that hung from a wooden peg near the entrance to the teepee. Working carefully, she threaded the thin strap through a small hole drilled at the top of the white rock. Tying the ends together at the back of her neck, August tenderly adjusted the ornament until it lay next to her skin and nestled against the small bag of ashes she had gotten from her grandmother.

August busied herself for the next few minutes by piling the blankets and other gifts near the entrance to the teepee. The repetitive actions helped to keep thoughts of a certain white man at bay. She would share in her bounty after the feast later that night and wanted the gifts ready to present to her family.

She picked up the last of the folded blankets and was surprised when yet another paper-wrapped bundle slipped from between the folds. Opening it, she laughed aloud and clapped her hands in delight. Cole had not forgotten her sweet tooth. The package contained peppermint sticks and, allowing herself to enjoy one last mental picture of him, August broke off a small piece of the candy and popped it into her mouth.

* * *

The heat of the great fire carried sparks high into the air. A few seconds later, they disappeared into a dark night sky. It was late and, still, the small band celebrated August's return. Shiny new knives hung from leather thongs tied around the waists of the braves. The women continually changed the position of the tortoise shell combs in their long black hair and giggled at the outrageous comments from the men. The gifts were something the tribe was not accustomed to. Because of the presents, and the safe return of one of their own, merriment still reigned.

August huddled among the women and gossiped about happenings around the camp. She glanced up with a wide smile when Wolf approached. The other men of the band followed behind him. He stopped before her and crossed his arms over a muscular brown chest.

"Little One, it is time to tell us your story. We would like to hear how you bested a white man and made away with his goods. Stand and be heard."

August shook her head and laughed to dispel the notion. "I have told you—the knives and blankets are all gifts, Wolf. Why do you not believe me?"

"Gifts such as these from a white man?" He snorted and glanced at those gathered around him. "I ask all of you. Do you agree with me that August Moon must have fallen off her horse, hit her head, and now cannot remember the real story?" The others chuckled, then urged her to stand as they seated themselves in anticipation of the forthcoming tale.

August rose and felt the heat of the fire warm her face. The flames danced in her eyes as she moved her gaze from one face to another. She loved these people more than life itself—family members who, for one night, had forgotten the tenuous hold they had on their old way of life. The laughter-filled pleas to continue her story brought August back to the present.

"I speak the truth when I say how the white man has helped our small band. I do not think it was his intention at first. His name is Cole Wilkins, and he was very angry with me for stealing his prize horses."

"Then this Cole you speak of must have fallen on *his* head if he gave you gifts for stealing his horses. White men never were very good in the head." Wolf tapped his forehead, rolled his eyes heavenward, and the entire group hooted uproariously at the remark. When the hilarity finally died, August continued.

"I was traveling far south of here and had begun to think that my journey was a mistake. Suddenly, I heard the sound of horses through the trees. I crept quietly to a secluded campsite and found a white man readying his four animals for the night. I knew it would be best to wait until he slept—even if darkness was a long way off. He was very large, and I knew my strength could not match his in a confrontation. It was at that time that the man decided to bathe. I chose that moment to make my move. He was...in the water, and would not be able to reach shore and catch me before I could escape." August decided not to mention that, in truth, Cole's magnificent male body was stretched out on a flat rock across the river when she made her move; he was not in the water.

A raucous titter immediately spread among the women. One elderly squaw raised her arms and spread them wide.

"August Moon. You have told us that this white man was very large. If he was bathing, then I assume he was not clothed. So, are you talking about his height or something else?"

The entire tribe, save for Wolf and August, cackled loudly at the old woman's question. A few of the men slapped each other on the back at the height of their mirth. The women quieted first though, and waited eagerly for the embarrassed storyteller to answer the question. Wolf frowned upon the strange look that flitted across August's face.

She was lost in a memory—the vision of Cole shedding his clothes by the water's edge; the flex of his lean, powerful body just before he dove into the cool water. Instead of leaping from her hiding spot the moment he swam away from shore, however, August sat mesmerized by the sight of him performing his bath. When he stretched out on the rock to warm himself in the sun, she was still unable to pull her eyes from his slick male physique.

August was no stranger to the workings of the male body. As young girls, she and the other Indian maidens made a habit of creeping up on naked young men as they bathed. When she was older, she did what was necessary to gain food and clothing for her tribe—which included offering her body to the white soldiers. Until this moment though, she had not given a thought to how affected she was by the sight of Cole's nude body basking in the sun.

Someone laughed and called out for August Moon to continue with her story. Tossing her hair back, she smiled widely to cover her embarrassment and placed a brown hand on a slim hip.

"I will tell you one thing," she said to the women. "The cold water did not affect him. I know! He was lying on his back on a rock, and I could see that it did not!"

Wolf's frown deepened at her words—and at the response they brought from the others. The thought of his Little One secretly watching a naked man, and a white man as well, made his insides roil with emotions he had never experienced before. It was longing he saw on her face a few moments earlier. He was sure of it. Before he could jump up and stop the laughter, however, August held her hand high, signaling for silence.

"Let me continue!" Her dancing gaze rested on the other women. "We will have plenty of time to discuss the white man's attributes while we are doing our morning duties. To finish my story, the man rested on a rock on the far side of the stream, and I was able to untie the ropes and chase his horses from the camp. Cole possesses a well-trained mount. He whistled, and the horse turned quickly and ran back to him. That is why he was able to find me when I thought I was far ahead of him." August captured the group's eager attention once more.

"One of the colts came up lame. I was tending his injury. Cole was as quiet as one of our braves and, before I knew it, I was his prisoner." August Moon skipped the fact that Cole wrestled her to the ground and discovered she was a woman. "He made me sit and kept a gun close so I would not escape. I did not know what he was going to do with me. He forced me to answer his questions."

Wolf bounded to his feet. The anger that boiled in his veins could be seen in his burning, black eyes and pinched mouth.

"Did he also force you to succumb to his disgusting desires as the white soldiers did at the agency?"

The only sound in the meadow was the crackle of the dying fire. The tribal members waited breathlessly once more to hear her answer. August rested a gentle gaze on her old friend.

"He did not—even when I offered to barter for his ponies."

The camp exploded with chatter. Wolf jumped to stand beside her and sliced his hand through the air for quiet.

"You offered yourself?" His tight words hung in the silence.

August hesitated as she stared at those around her, then she brought her honest gaze back to Wolf's. "Yes. For the people, I would do this thing again. Cole Wilkins is not like other white men though—he would have no part in it. We spoke late into the night; he would not rest until I told him about all of us. He offered to provide ponies to replace the ones I took from him, if I would promise not to run."

Again the clearing erupted with skepticism. Why would a white man do such a thing? August spun in a circle, and her responding cry reached even those on the outskirts of the crowd.

"You must understand! Cole not only bought the horses; he purchased gifts for all of us in hope that we might enjoy even a moment of happiness! There was only one thing this white man wanted; he wanted us to stay safe and out of the path of those who would pursue us." She turned and her unsettled gaze bore into the man standing before her. "He is a kind man who would not hurt any of us."

"You speak of him as though he were a god; a savior of our people!" Wolf spat out the words, baring the emotions that raged within his body.

August was stunned by his behavior, especially when every member of the tribe stood within earshot. "Why do you not believe me?" she questioned quietly. The pain of his betrayal flashed in her dark eyes. "I have never lied to you or my people and would not start now."

"I find it hard to believe that a white man would be so generous. We have been forced to run from his kind for years, August Moon. Have you forgotten that they chase us daily and that we must always be on guard in order to keep our pitiful way of life alive?"

"I have not forgotten—that is why I offered the barter, but I tell you that he did not accept it! I speak the truth. I am sorry that you do not believe me." She hung her head in dejection.

August and Wolf spoke to one another as if they were the only two standing in the light of the dwindling flames. The rest of the band watched and listened quietly.

Wolf noted the charged silence around him. He looked at August and was suddenly overcome with guilt; he had shamed her in front of her people. It mattered not how he felt. The horses and gifts she had returned with could not be overlooked, nor could her commitment to her people. His bare chest rose with a deep, cleansing breath and, as quickly as his temper rose, it receded. Wolf spoke loudly, his voice reaching all those around him.

"I am sorry that I accused you of mistruths, Little One. I will consider the words you have spoken."

Wolf turned and walked stiffly into the darkness that surrounded the fire. The tribal members rose one by one and left the comfort of the blaze, but not before quietly thanking August one more time for the beautiful gifts.

They returned to their lodges, leaving her alone to stare into the dying embers. August closed her eyes and pictured the man she would never forget—memories of a firm jaw and gentle smile that were forever burned into her brain. A shiver rattled down her spine and, angered by the injustices in the world, she kicked at the hot ashes.

I will miss you, Cole Wilkins. May the gods smile one day and cross our paths again.

* * *

Cole stood outside the massive, yet pristine barn and shook hands with Benjamin Pederson. The man had managed to coax him into staying at the ranch, rather than renting a room in town. Pederson's ranch was located a few short miles north of Fargo and spanned the Red River banks for twenty miles. The two men had ridden across most of the ranch's fifteen thousand acres in the last week and, now, as he shook his host's hand warmly, Cole knew he would miss the elderly man's sense of humor and hospitality.

"You know, Cole, you're more than welcome to stay on a little longer. Martha and I have enjoyed your company immensely. Gets kinda lonely out here, even with the town so close."

"Thanks, Benjamin, but I need to be getting home. Even though Tyler and Trevor are there, I still have my part to do. I'd accept your offer if I was taking the train back—"

"Confound it, Cole," Benjamin interrupted, "you must be a glutton for punishment. I still don't understand why in tarnation you'd want to travel on horseback all the way back home, too. You'll be lucky not to be smacked with an August storm on the trail."

Cole's stomach lurched with the other man's choice of words.

August—in some small way, Cole knew he had already been hit by that storm. He had not stopped thinking about August since he watched her proud, straight form slip into the soft pines. Her words echoed in his brain.

I will always think of you in a good way...

Earlier that morning, Cole canceled the train tickets home, telegraphed the ranch to let them know the approximate date of his return, and purchased supplies for an overland trip. He would follow the same trail on the journey home. The reason for the decision remained a mystery, even to him, but he had not given it another thought since changing his plans.

Cole smiled suddenly. *Who are you trying to fool?* The image of August's face materialized in his brain once more. *If there's even a small chance that I might meet her on the trail again...*

"You know what I think, Cole?" Benjamin's words brought the other man back to the present with a jolt. "I'm thinking you're a little crazy in the head for wanting to callous up your butt more than it already is." He shook his head when Cole just smiled and shrugged his shoulders. "Well, son, may God keep a hand on your shoulder on the miles home. Be assured that me and Martha will pray for your safe return."

"Thank you, Benjamin. It's been wonderful getting to know you and Martha. Hopefully, I can visit again next summer with some more foals. And, don't forget, the two of you could also travel east to visit Lakota Pines. My sister-in-law would love to meet the owners of her horses." He chuckled. "Emma will want a full report on the welfare of the stock you've already purchased. She'll be happy to know that you and Martha just come short of tucking your four-legged family into bed every night."

Benjamin threw back his head with a hearty laugh and slapped Cole on the back. "Son, I'm gonna miss you." Sobering slightly, the red-cheeked elder reached out a hand once more. "Take care, Cole. Wire us when you get home."

"I'll do that, sir. Thank you for everything."

Cole adjusted Joe's reins and heaved himself onto the gelding's wide back. With one last wave, he turned his mount and cantered down the dusty lane.

Chapter Seven

As Cole left Fargo, Beau crested a ridge on the southwest end of the Pine Ridge Agency. He had ridden nonstop for eight days, crisscrossing western Minnesota in search of any small groups of renegade Indians. Each time he thought he was moving in on the Sioux, however, he came up empty handed. Once again, they outsmarted him. Frustrated, he finally decided to head west and had now finally reached his destination in the Dakotas.

A light tug on the reins halted his tired horse immediately. Beau's blue gaze scanned the agency headquarters in the valley below. He squinted his eyes and observed Indians milling around bruised and weather-beaten log buildings—hovels that emitted small puffs of smoke from their chimneys. Those Sioux who refused to completely conform had erected skin-covered tents that dotted the outer edges of the settlement.

He gave his mount a slight kick, headed him down the well-worn path, and could not help but notice how the animal moved with a little more enthusiasm than of a moment ago.

Beau patted the horse's thick neck with a gloved hand. "Just about there, boy. You and me got the same idea. Bet you're hankering for a comfortable bed and a rest, too." Beau clucked his lips together and, with very little coaxing, the animal moved into a trot.

The long days of trail life would be over soon; Beau had made a decision a few weeks back to stay on at the agency through the winter months. People talked more and more about the unrest among the Sioux when he stopped at government outposts on his trip west. Consequently, Beau thought it best to stay in the Dakotas until spring. If events began to unravel, he wanted to be nearby. He wanted to be able to speak with the Indians and discourage them from making mistakes that were bound to happen when emotions ran high.

Beau guided his mount to a house at the end of a familiar road, dismounted wearily, and tied the reins loosely around a post. Before he stepped through the pristine whitewashed gate, which looked oddly out of place amidst the dusty brown surroundings, a feminine voice called out his name. He glanced up to see a strikingly beautiful, middle-aged women exit the front door of the house. An excited smile lit her face, and she scrambled quickly down the wooden steps.

"Beau! Beau, I can't believe my eyes! You old rascal. You never even let us know you were on your way here." She rushed to her old friend and he welcomed her into his arms. Anna Gatewood squeezed him heartily for such a small, lithe woman and laughed up into his face with sparkling eyes. "Wait until Michael sees you! He was just saying the other day that he wished you weren't going to be in Minnesota for the winter."

"How is the old guy anyway?"

She elbowed him playfully and tugged him by the hand in the direction of the front porch. "What do you mean, the old guy? Michael is only six years older than you. Come on in and I'll put on a fresh pot of coffee."

Beau entered the familiar kitchen and reveled in the smell of fresh-baked bread. Jars of canned peaches sat on a shelf to his right. An immediate rush of contentment ran through him. The small house belonged to his good friend, Dr. Michael Gatewood, and was more like home to him than any other place on earth. Since leaving his service position, Beau had more or less wandered in his quest to help the Sioux, rather than set down roots at any one location.

He met Michael when they were both still in the employ of the U.S. government. Michael was a Cavalry medic and, when Beau accepted his commission, the two became fast friends. The Gatewood home became a welcome retreat from the outside world and the plight of the Sioux. It gave Beau a sense of belonging.

Beau inhaled the wonderful odors in Anna's kitchen and reminisced silently about the night that sealed his friendship with Michael...

Beau strolled past the barracks after a late night meeting with his commander, enjoying one last cigar before retiring for the evening. His easy gait halted immediately though, when muffled sounds of a scuffle emitted from one of the many storage sheds.

Deciding to investigate further, he tossed the stub of tobacco into the dust and slipped through the silvery darkness with his side arm drawn. The door to the rickety building hung open and he crept on silent feet to within inches of the opening. Beau slowly poked his head around the jamb and his eyes narrowed as they adjusted to the moonlight that dimly lit the room. A dark eyebrow lifted in surprise as he watched a shadowy form drag a seemingly unconscious body into a dark, dusky corner of the shed.

"Who goes there?" he barked.

The culprit jumped at the unexpected voice and dropped his burden. His shoulders sagged with guilt.

"I'll say it again. Speak up and name yourself." The click of the gun's hammer echoed loudly in the darkness as Beau readied his weapon.

The perpetrator stepped from the corner and into the shaft of moonlight that filtered in through the open door. Beau immediately recognized the company doctor. A sheen of perspiration covered Michael Gatewood's strong features. He held his silence though, the guilt also evident in his averted gaze. Beau stepped one more pace into the closed in heat of the shed.

"Doc? What's going on here?" His voice held a note of suspicion.

Michael's shoulders drooped further with a heavy sigh. Though his commission was equal to Beau's, the doctor had been caught in a compromising situation.

"I was moving this pile of inhumanity out of my way so I could tend to the man over there." Michael nodded first to the sergeant who lay unconscious at his feet, then at the Sioux Indian who sat with one shoulder propped against the rotted wall a short distance away. Beau glanced at the wide-eyed red man, who gripped his midsection in obvious agony.

Beau crept closer to the unconscious sergeant and dropped onto one knee. Macomb was famous for his less than humane treatment of the Indian prisoners. Beau turned and locked stares with the doctor, then shook his head and stood.

"How did the sergeant end up out cold on the floor?" He pierced the company doctor with a challenging glare.

Michael shifted uneasily and cleared his throat. His eyes darted to the face of the Indian brave, who watched him closely. Deciding it would be best to come clean, he straightened and brought his gaze back to Beau.

"I'm sorry for this mess, Lieutenant. The Indian has been locked in this shed for three days, without so much as a glass of water. And, he's had no food. I was going to slip him something to eat and drink. When I got here though, Sergeant Macomb was already *visiting*. I heard laughter, accompanied by agony-filled grunts. When I entered the shed, Macomb was so intent on kicking this man senseless that he didn't hear me." He shrugged his shoulders. "I guess I saw red. I grabbed my gun and hit him on the back of the head."

Beau's eyes swung to Macomb, and the doctor rushed to assure him of the man's medical state.

"Don't worry; he's alive. Probably'll have one helluva headache in the morning, though. Like I said, I reacted before thinking. I'm sick to death of the sergeant's harsh treatment of these people."

Michael watched the lieutenant's face closely, gauging his reaction. *There's gonna be hell to pay for this little incident.* "Lieutenant McCabe, all this Indian did was steal a few carrots from the cook's garden out back. He was only trying to procure food for his children. I don't see where that constitutes a three-day lock-up, just because the puffed up commander of this post gives the ranks full rein to treat the 'hostiles' in any way they see fit."

Michael's face blanched in the moonlight when he realized his impassioned speech could be construed as treason. The doctor straightened to his full height though, breathed in deeply, and stood his ground. "If you need to report me, I understand fully." He waited, ready to accept his fate.

Beau had already made his decision. There were few people at the fort who felt the same way he did about the poor treatment of the local Indians, not to mention the ones brought in after a forced surrender. He would follow his instincts on this one; that the Doc had more of a humane streak running through him than most.

Beau bent to grab the sergeant's limp arms and pulled him farther into the corner. He turned to Michael and noted the surprised look on the other man's face. "Do you have anything we can use to tie him up?"

An astonished Michael quickly handed him a length of twine that hung on a nail pounded into the wall beside him.

Beau met his gaze. "He didn't see who hit him, did he?"

Michael shook his head.

"Good. Let's hurry. We don't need to give this idiot the chance to wake up and report us. Christ, we'll both be shot for treason." Beau stooped to bind

Macomb's wrists, then tipped his head toward the Indian. "While I finish up here, check that poor soul's ribs, then we'll see about getting him out of here. We'll figure out a backup story later."

Beau tied the sergeant's legs and arms, and then helped Michael raise the bruised and hurt Indian to his feet. Carefully, they helped him through the doorway, checked quickly to see if anyone was within eyesight, and secreted the man into the darkness.

That was the night Michael and Beau became fast friends; their determination to see the various Indian tribes treated with dignity created a bond that had lasted for eleven years. The two men managed to improve the conditions of the Indian prisoners and, at the same time, maintain the integrity of their positions in the cavalry. The commanding officers were continually surprised by the fact that, when different roving bands were brought to the fort, it took only the lieutenant and the doctor to handle an entire group. Little did the commanders know that the reason for the uncompromising cooperation was the secreted food and supplies that 'mysteriously' made their way into the homes of the natives. The 'donations' inadvertently led the army to believe they were taming the malcontents.

The sound of Anna's voice brought Beau back to the present...

"Beau, you never did answer me," Anna spoke over her shoulder as she reached for two clean mugs. "Michael and I thought you were wintering in Minnesota. What brings you this far west?" She placed a steaming cup of coffee on the table and gestured for him to take a chair.

"When the conferences in St. Paul were finished, a lot of the men talked about going home on leave or returning to their families permanently." Beau shrugged his broad shoulders. "It hit me then that I didn't have a home to go to. Since both my parents passed away, I couldn't think of a reason to stay once I was there." His gaze swept the cozy kitchen. "This is where I want to be. You and Michael are the closest thing I have to a family."

Anna seated herself across from him at the table and reached for his hand. "Until I met Michael, I thought I would be alone forever. The three of us *are* like family, aren't we? Please, say you'll stay with us. We've got plenty of room. Michael will be so happy to have you here with him."

"Thanks for the invitation, but I'm not putting either of you out for such a long time. I'll figure out a place to stay close by."

"The hell you will," Michael called from the open doorway as he stepped into the kitchen. "Beau, it's damn good to see you after all this time." The two friends met in the middle of the room with a handshake that turned into an embrace. "If you're planning to stay put for awhile, you'll do it no other place but here."

"Mike, I'll stay down at—"

"Not another word. There's plenty of room here and you know it. Besides, I think you could be of some use this winter. Colonel Bingham is back in the area," he said as he accepted a mug of coffee from his wife. He indicated for Beau to seat himself again at the table. "He's been riding through here most of the summer and making quite a name for himself again. He follows leads from some of the agency Indians and is breaking up every little band he can find." Michael shook his head in weary resignation. "It hasn't been good for the Sioux, Beau. Bingham has cut a swath across the Dakotas and into Minnesota. He's brought in every hostile he can find, dead or alive. It doesn't matter to him. He was through here with a group of renegades a few weeks back and wouldn't even allow medical attention for those who were hurt. Says he won't waste government supplies on savages that will probably be hung anyway. The people who lived were shipped to Omaha or Florida by train."

"Jesus Christ..." The words whispered from Beau's lips. He raked his large hands through his hair and heaved a great sigh. "When is all this going to end? Wait—" he raised a palm, "—I guess I know the answer. This damn bloodshed will be over when every last one of the *hostiles* are captured and forced to live out their lives on a small patch of dry reservation land."

Michael nodded. "The government deems their coerced treaties to be a trade-off to the Indians roaming free, as their ancestors did. It's not going to end, Beau, until every last one of the Sioux are stripped of everything."

Beau brought his gaze from the surface of the table to his friend's eyes. "What's got Bingham so damned fired up now? Why is he on a crusade again?"

"The Sioux want their freedom back. More and more, they're practicing this Ghost Dance thing, and Bingham is determined to squash the movement."

"They were talking about it in St. Paul, too—said the Sioux have been working themselves into a frenzy. I wasn't ready to believe anything until I got out here and saw it for myself. The Sioux have been dancing for the last year and there haven't been any outbreaks of violence. Why do government officials think it's escalating?"

Michael lifted his shoulders in a shrug. "The Sioux are told they have to live in the small log cabins built for them and they have to farm the reservation, but they don't want to be farmers. They want to live off the land, like they used to. How are they going to do that, Beau? The buffalo are gone. The streams are fished out or the ranks have poisoned them."

Michael rubbed his forehead. "It irks the hell out of me that the government takes more and more of the promised reservation land. The Sioux end up on small plots. They're expected to grow food to supplement the almost nonexistent rations that were promised if they gave themselves up. The rations rarely materialize though, and nothing grows in this godforsaken land. The last two years the crops have failed. Because they're hungry, and because they've had enough, the courageous ones have slipped away and joined the groups running for the Canadian wintering grounds—the rest are dancing. Supposedly to bring back their dead, to make all of us whites disappear, and to bring the buffalo back. The Feds are getting damn nervous."

"I suppose Bingham is looking for political points by capturing those who escape, and then tying it into the Ghost Dance. Am I right?" Beau already knew the answer.

Michael indicated that the other man was correct with a nod of his head. "The Pine Ridge Sioux adopted the dance, and it spread over to the Rosebud Agency. Now, the settlers are crying for protection—they want the Indians rounded up."

"Just what Bingham needs to hear." Beau could only shake his head once more.

"The colonel runs routine checks between the Cheyenne River and Standing Rock. It's become his own personal vendetta to get all the groups involved. He incites the Bureau by telling them the Sioux are secretly building their forces for a massive attack. The agents, in turn, report back to Washington with accounts that have already been embellished. It's not a good situation."

"What about the agency chiefs? Have you spoken with any of them?" Beau's mind worked to store all the information for a later time.

"Not personally, but I've been told that Sitting Bull remains quiet about the Ghost Dance. He's too damn smart to get involved. I don't think he believes this is the way out for his people. But a few of the other chiefs, like Big Foot, have gotten on board."

"Where did this whole thing start? No one in St. Paul seems to know about it—not even the Federal reps who came east for the conference."

"It started in Nevada." Michael smiled up at his wife when she refilled their cups with hot coffee, then glanced at Beau again. "It's easy to understand. The Sioux have had Christianity shoved down their throats by the reservation missionaries. It's the only form of religion allowed. If any of them are caught reciting their own cultural prayers, all hell breaks loose. A man named Wovoka, a half-breed from Nevada, says the Messiah appeared to him, bringing a message for all Indians—something to the effect that Christ died for nothing the first time. Since the white race did not revere the reasons for his crucifixion, He would return a second time and save the red man. It's easy to see, Beau, how the Sioux would fall prey to something like this. Look at how their world has changed."

"So they dance?" Beau asked.

"What else are they to do? They were told to dance and hold ceremonies to attract the attention of the Messiah when He appears—supposedly sometime in the next year. Given that the Indians were coerced into signing away a valuable portion of their reservation land—land which is now occupied by whites and for which they have received nothing—they've simply lost faith in the government. They've had their fill. Being so deeply religious for all these years, I think the Indians took their spiritual values and tied them into this second coming, of sorts. They have become a people without hope—now someone has given them reason to believe that they might regain all the things they lost."

"Has there been any trouble? I mean in the form of uprisings. Do you think we're headed for some big problems?"

"I can't say for sure." Michael shrugged his shoulders and sat back in his chair again. "For as much as Bingham has prodded and poked—and raided—not one Sioux has challenged him. It's surprising as hell. It's as if they're waiting for the moment when the government, the settlers, and their current existence will suddenly disappear into thin air." The doctor rubbed his square chin, deep in thought. "How long do you think that's going to last? All it will take is one confrontation when someone—it doesn't matter which side—loses a cool head. Depending on which way it goes, it should permanently finalize our presence out here on the frontier."

Anna approached Beau and squeezed his shoulder gently. "I'm glad you're here. Stay with us, Beau. Maybe you can make it better for the Sioux. Find the stray bands before Colonel Bingham does." She shook her head. "It's been terrible. He's slaughtering them—cutting down women and children before they have a chance to surrender. He doesn't view it that way, but I've heard his men talking. They can only obey orders. At the slightest provocation, the Colonel demands that his men shoot first and ask questions later."

The small group exchanged looks of despair and wondered deep in their hearts if there was really anything anyone could do. The course was set, and the government would see that it ran to fruition. Maybe the three of them could make the situation better though, by helping the Sioux people to find the courage necessary to get past the carnage that was sure to continue.

Chapter Eight

Cole finished a quick supper of hardtack and beans, then moved to a nearby stream to swish his dirty dishes in the cool water. He rose and stretched the kinks from his back, flicked the droplets of water from the plate and utensils with a shake of the hand, then walked back to the campsite to stow them in his saddlebag. The comforting light of the small fire beckoned him, and he strolled to the flames, plopped down on the ground, and poured himself one last tin cup of coffee.

Easing back against his saddle, he crossed his legs at the ankles and gazed upward to marvel at the flashing green and blue hues that streaked across the night sky. The colors literally danced themselves into a shimmering display of slants and angles before disappearing over the horizon, only to be reborn and start the dance again directly above his head.

The iridescent evening sky, combined with the night sounds of the forest and the cooler twilight air that touched his face, gave Cole a sense of freedom like never before. He had watched the flickering illumination many times while at home, but was never so deeply affected by its beauty.

Wiggling even further into the soft leather of the saddle, Cole let his mind wander. Not surprisingly, thoughts of one person, and one person only, bounded to the forefront of his brain; a person who had dominated his thoughts for the past two weeks. *Is she seeing the same sky as me? Is she watching it at this exact same moment from somewhere close by?*

Cole was slightly south of the area where August stole the horses. How far south did her band move before heading north again and into Canada for the winter?

She had touched his life for only a few short days, yet Cole felt a small ache build in his chest whenever August's beautiful face danced into his brain. It was not a sense of loneliness; something he would normally feel when he missed someone close to him. Instead, it was a yearning derived from undiscovered emotions and experiences.

He shook his head. *Hell...I'll probably never see her again...*

He planned to send a message to Beau and let him know about his encounter with August. Cole wanted his friend to be aware of the band's presence in the area; maybe he could help make the transition into the white man's world a little easier if and when she and her small band were taken to one of the agencies.

Cole dragged a woolen blanket across his shoulders and closed his eyes, along with an audible sigh. Try as he might, images of August refused to leave his mind. Pictures of her racing across an open field on the back of her pony; portraits of her throwing back her dark hair and laughing into the wind; visions of her frightened, yet defiant gaze when she bartered herself for the well-being of her family. The images slowly gave way to a hazy apparition of August standing naked in the moonlight, with a beckoning hand held in his direction...

Cole's eyes flew open and he bolted upright, totally surprised and appalled that his thoughts had led him in the direction they did.

Christ...!

An owl hooted in the distance, breaking the rhythmic beat of the crickets and frogs that, on any other night, would have lulled him to sleep.

I'm no better than the soldiers at the fort, he berated himself. *Men who accepted what a frightened young woman offered in order that she might live another day.*

He gritted his teeth and dropped his head back onto the surface of the saddle. Only a few moments earlier, while watching the dancing colors in the sky, Cole was at peace with himself in spite of the small ache in his chest. He had helped August in her pursuit to hold close to the life of her ancestors; he was proud of his actions and willing to let it be done.

Now though, as he covered his shoulders once more and settled in for a few hours of sleep, he fervently wished for a miracle. He wanted to cross paths with her once more. Just one more time, he wanted to see her face.

* * *

The hair rose on the back of Cole's neck as he stifled the shiver that ran the length of his spine. He did not have to open his eyes to know he was not alone. His sixth sense screamed the fact silently in his head. The battle was internal—should he move quickly in an attempt to reach his gun or should he simply lie still?

Keeping his eyes closed, he chose the first option. His hand crept gingerly beneath the blanket, inching toward the rifle that lay next to his body. He tried desperately not to disturb the folds of the wool. He made contact with the cool metal barrel, then prepared himself to finger the trigger and leap up at the same time. A split second before he moved into action, a heavy object slammed his wrist firmly to the ground and held it captive.

He had lost his chance. Cole fought to jerk the hand free, but the effort proved useless. He rolled onto his back and opened his eyes.

Cole stared into the bronze face above him. The man held his hand prisoner with a mocassined foot. His heart sank when two more warriors moved into his line of vision, behind the first. Insidious fear curled within his belly.

The pressure on his wrist lessened slightly, and Cole yanked his arm free. He could do nothing but watch with a forlorn expression as his gun slid to a standstill five feet away, propelled by the other man's foot. The dull thud when the rifle impacted with the trunk of a pine tree was the only sound in the clearing.

Cole sat up slowly, careful not to make any sudden moves. His gaze traveled from one Indian to the next and, finally, to the man closest to him. They locked wooden stares. Cole held his breath, wondering what would happen next.

The warrior glared down at his captive and spoke in a monotone voice. "You are Cole Wilkins?"

Cole's eyes widened in stunned disbelief as he nodded. *How in the hell does he know my name?*

"You will stand now."

Cole scrambled to his feet. A feeling of unease curled inside his belly again, despite the fact that the warrior no longer appeared threatening.

His brow wrinkled in confusion. "How do you know my name?"

"I am Wolf. I have searched for you. You are the man who gave horses to my family."

The Indian's statement reverberated inside Cole's head. *This man must be part of August's band!*

"Yes! Yes, I gave horses to a woman named August Moon. Do you know her?"

The Indian smirked haughtily and tossed his shiny mane of black hair. "You gave horses only to get your stolen ones back. She has told me this." The other two braves chuckled quietly at the thought of a mere woman besting this white man.

Despite the precarious position Cole found himself in, his male pride refused to allow him to remain silent. "Did she also tell you how I tracked her and caught her unawares? I thought she was a young boy who'd made a stupid mistake, until I wrestled her to the ground and found out otherwise."

Wolf's knife found Cole's throat so quickly that he froze. The other two warriors stepped closer, their weapons held high.

"White man, you are wise not to move. Did you bring harm to her?" Wolf sneered ominously.

Cole swallowed convulsively and took a deep breath to clear his head. The shiny blade was icy cold against his skin. "I'm an honorable man. I would never do such a thing. Why would I have given her gifts if I did not respect her and understand what she was trying to do?"

Wolf remembered August Moon's words; she had tried to barter with this man, and he would have no part of it. As much as he hated the whites, he would have to believe this one's words as truth. Cole Wilkins could have killed August Moon, but did not. His stomach churned at the thought of how she had put herself in danger for the people.

"I could cut your throat out." Wolf watched Cole's unflinching gaze. The tall brave longed to plunge the knife deep into the neck of the man before him. Instead, Wolf's hand wavered slightly and he withdrew the sharp tip. August Moon bid him to watch over this man. He would keep her trust by doing so.

A whoosh of air escaped Cole's lungs, and he breathed in deeply once more. It seemed that Wolf respected honor along with bravado, however false it was. Cole banked on the fact that he would continue to do so. "Am I allowed to ask a question?"

The brave inclined his head slightly before crossing his arms over a massive, bare chest.

"You asked if I was Cole Wilkins, which means that you were looking for me. I'd like to know why."

"My people would not be honorable in the eyes of the Great Spirit if they accepted your gifts without giving a gift in return. We have nothing to trade but our skills. At council, we have heard that the Chippewa look to kill more whites. They are intent upon removing your kind from this land. Because they are your enemy, Cole Wilkins, they have become ours. We will see you to your home safely. We would do this thing for you, because you spared August Moon's life and gave gifts to our people."

Cole stared at the other man through large, incredulous eyes. He had genuinely thought they were going to kill him, when in actuality they were offering protection. It was hard to believe. He did not relish the idea though, of having to watch his back on the trip home.

"You don't need to ride with me. There must be other things you need to do—"

Wolf raised his hand, halting Cole's objection. "We will speak of it no more. The task has been stated." Wolf turned to his companions and spoke in the Sioux dialect.

One man slipped into the thick undergrowth that surrounded them and returned with three horses; one was the pony August rode. The three Indians then seated themselves formally around the warmth of Cole's fire and spoke to one another as if it were an everyday occurrence to be at the fire pit of a white man.

Realizing he had no choice in the matter, Cole made preparations for the long day before him.

* * *

Cole was transported into another world. He lost all fear; his wariness was gone. Anything and everything harsh he had heard about the Indians melted away into a comfortable companionship that few whites would find believable. Wolf and his friends fascinated him.

Wolf took the lead and, refusing to endanger himself or the others traveling with him, picked his way through the dense forest on the way to the white man's home, rather than riding in the open. Cole, in turn, discovered a newfound appreciation of Minnesota's natural beauty as the small group snaked its way through the thick forests of towering Norway pines, many of which were hundreds of years old.

The group traveled together for more than a week before finally entering the westernmost corner of the Wilkins' property. In that time, Cole's respect for his new companions had increased tenfold. They were not only proficient in procuring the nightly meals, but were also skilled horseman.

Cole found Wolf to be a man who possessed great integrity. His gentle and just way of handling any situation belied the awesome power found in his body and mind. It amazed Cole to think that these Indians, and others like them, were spoken of as little more than savages who were incapable of feeling sympathy or any other human emotion. The camaraderie between those in the group grew by leaps and bounds; in short, they treated him like one of their own, and Cole was loath to see the journey end the following day.

Each of the warriors was committed to their lives; lives that had remained unchanged until the white man usurped their lands and tainted their very existence. The four men visited nightly, and Cole found himself engrossed in stories of Indian ancestry, deep-seated religious beliefs and loved ones, both present and long gone. Cole easily discovered his companions were brave men who fought for their rights, for their families, and for their familiar world that was disappearing all too quickly.

August was a part of that world and that family; yet, curiously, Wolf had not mentioned her name since the first night they met. Cole itched to ask him about her; but, as the days passed, he had found neither the opportunity nor the courage. Now, however, Wolf sat alone before the fire, deftly removing the skin from a rabbit he shot earlier in the day. It might be Cole's last chance for a quiet conversation with the one man who could tell him all he needed to know.

Cole casually seated himself next to the Indian. The other man raised his dark eyes momentarily upon the white man's quiet intrusion, and then returned to the job at hand. Before Cole was able to speak a word though, the Indian brave broke the silence.

"You have something to say." It was a statement rather than a question.

Cole nodded his head. The man's astuteness never ceased to amaze him. "We've been together for many days now. I've listened as you and your friends speak of your families and of your fight for freedom. Why is it though, that you haven't spoken August's name even once?"

Wolf's heart jumped in his chest, but his outward appearance remained calm. Ever since August Moon's return, and her subsequent tale regarding this white man's virtue, he had tried to block the feelings of jealousy. She was not his and probably never would be. At one time, he was able to accept the fact that she would never take a man to her side. Now though, with that same white man seated across from him, he was not so confident.

August Moon spoke highly of him—praised his goodness. Why does this man eat at my stomach? Wolf's hands remained busy with the dead rabbit as his mind whirled in confusion. *Is it the look I see on her face every time she speaks his name?* It was an expression Wolf had never before seen on her familiar features.

Suddenly, Wolf felt threatened; somehow he knew that life would never be the same again—not since Cole Wilkins entered their world. They would all meet again someday; he knew it beyond a doubt.

He glanced furtively at the man across from him; a man who waited for his answer with baited breath. Cole said, on the night they came upon him, that he respected August Moon. It was a strange thing to say when he was white and August Moon was a Sioux. *Respect between our worlds? It can never be...*

Finally, Wolf looked up and into the face of his fear.

"Why would you think it strange that I have not spoken of her?" He struggled to keep his words calm and even.

Cole shrugged. "It's because of August that you're with me now, and yet you haven't even mentioned her. There are some things about her that I'd like to know." He rested his forearms on his knees and leaned closer to the fire. "Are you and she close?"

"Why do you not call August Moon by her full name?" Wolf's words were tinged with anger as he purposely ignored the question.

Cole hid a smile. While on the trail, he quickly discovered that Wolf had a penchant for changing the subject whenever he felt uncomfortable. If he wanted to find out anything about August, it would be best to play the man and beat him at his own game.

"You know, she asked me the same thing." He shrugged his own ignorance. "I don't know. I guess I just like the sound of it. And, at the risk of having your knife at my throat again, I also called her that because it seemed to anger her."

Wolf lifted a dark eyebrow in question, and Cole laughed.

"Hey, I wasn't above getting her dander up a little. She'd just stolen my horses, and I was entitled to a little self-satisfaction."

Wolf sat straighter and his chin came up in defiance, and Cole groaned inwardly. He had gone too far. A second later, however, a grin tugged at the corners of the Indian's mouth. "I would wager with you that she was angry, as you have said. August Moon does not like to be bested."

"I'll have to agree with you there. For the most part, she was not very happy with me during the time we spent together. I did come to realize, however, that she is honest to an extreme and devoted to the continued life of her band."

"August Moon is close to all of those she lives with."

"I gathered that, Wolf." Cole paused for a moment and, gathering his courage, plunged in feet first. "Walking Bear and Two Feathers have both spoken of their wives and children. I thought that, since you haven't mentioned a family and since you're willing to see me home safely at August's request, the two of you must have a common bond of deep friendship. It that true?"

Wolf stood quickly, reached for a stick and, with one quick jab, speared the rabbit and hung it above the flames. Keeping his eyes averted, he brushed his hands against the soft skin of his deer hide pants. For the first time since meeting the Indian brave, Cole felt sure that the other man was not completely in charge of his stalwart emotions.

"August Moon touches everyone here." Wolf placed a hand over his broad chest and finally met the understanding gaze before him. "She loves all the people with her own kind of hunger and is a friend to all. She would die for any of us. She is not like most of our women; she has a fearless heart. August Moon can be soft and womanly one minute, and fight like a warrior the next." He poked at the fire, deep in thought once more. "I once watched her face down a mountain lion in order to save a small child in our band. I could not reach her in time to help. She did not hesitate or scream, but simply pulled her knife and plunged it into the animal's heart as it leapt through the air. Not until after she knew the child was safe did she find her hands shaking and a woman's tears in her eyes."

Wolf paused momentarily, then searched out Cole's gaze once more. "Do you understand when I say she is a woman and a warrior in one? Her father was a great warrior, and August Moon carries his strength within her. We all have a deep friendship with her." He peered at the white man closely. "Why do you want to know of her?"

Cole leaned back against a tree, crossed his arms, and thought about his answer for a moment. "She's like no woman I've ever met. I understand exactly though, what you mean when you say she's soft, yet courageous like a man. I found her to be the same way. She fearlessly stole my horses, fought me like a man, and then spoke to me from the soul of a woman. The short time we were together made me want to know more of her world." He met Wolf's unflinching gaze with an equally unwavering one. "Does she have a man in her life?"

"Why do you ask a question like that?" Wolf suddenly grew angry again, and Cole guarded his words carefully. He shrugged.

"August is not a child, Wolf. In fact, she's a very beautiful woman. It just seems odd that she would be alone."

Wolf sighed and his antagonism receded. "August Moon belongs to no man and never will. It is her way. She lives for the people and is married to all of us in her heart."

Cole observed Wolf's strong features soften when he spoke of August. The brave's former words and his current expression gave away his true feelings. The truth hit Cole square in the stomach—Wolf was in love with August.

Wolf's features turned sad as he continued. "I have known August Moon from the time she was a small child. She believes that dreams are wiser than waking thoughts; her father believed the same. She will never take a man to her side."

The Indian's words hung heavily in the air between them. Each man thought of the same woman in a different way. One believed that, up to that point, August had influenced him his entire life; the other could not help but think how the short time spent with her would forever affect his future.

* * *

Dusk had settled across the treetops by the time the weary group of travelers halted. On one hand, Cole was excited at the prospect of being this close to home. In only one short hour, he would be welcomed at the front door of the ranch house. On the other hand though, he would be forced to say goodbye to the men who had protected him the past week—men whose friendship he would cherish forever. The thought saddened him; he would probably never cross paths with any of them again.

Cole quietly thanked Walking Bear and Two Feathers as Wolf stood proudly by. The white man turned to the last member of the small band then, and stretched out a hand. Wolf grasped his palm firmly, his expression solemn.

"Are you sure you won't come to the ranch, Wolf? There's nothing to fear. You could all rest well tonight and begin your journey home in the morning."

The Indian shook his head and clasped his strong hand tighter around Cole's. "We have been gone long and it is time to return to our people. They will be ready to move to our winter home soon."

Cole knew beyond a doubt that the 'home' Wolf spoke of was in Canada, even though the brave had steadfastly refused to tell him which direction August's band of fugitives would travel. Cole asked him more than once, but Wolf always avoided the answer, ever protecting his people from the white man. This time it seemed, even when a sad farewell was at hand, would be no different.

"August once told me that she would always think of me in a good way," Cole murmured. "That's how I'll always think of you, Wolf. If you ever need anything, you can come to me and I'll find a way to help. Please, don't forget that."

"Cole Wilkins, I tried not to trust you because you are a white man. I did not succeed. If only they all possessed honor such as yours. I thank you from my people." He dropped Cole's hand and mounted his horse in one fluid leap. Before the men turned their ponies to the west, however, Cole stepped up and stalled Wolf's departure.

"Please wish August well from me, and take care of her, Wolf. She's a fine woman."

The warrior held Cole's gaze for a moment and, a rare smile touching his lips, he nodded. "I will watch over her. Know that as truth. Ride safely, white man."

A kick of the heels sent the horse charging forward. Wolf never looked back.

Chapter Nine

Something was very wrong. Not a bird or squirrel called out in warning as Wolf, Walking Bear, and Two Feathers urged their ponies up the trail to the encampment. Normally, a cry of greeting would filter from the opening in the hill to the top of the trail when a member of the band returned home. Only deathly silence greeted them now.

They rounded the last bend in the trail before Wolf reined in his mount abruptly and raised a faltering hand to stop the two men behind him. The initial sense of foreboding turned to crushing horror. They sat on their ponies and stared in disbelief at the remains of their summer home. The entire encampment was razed to ground level. Pots, clothing, and bits of hide from the tepees lay strewn in all directions. Small tendrils of smoke emanated from the burnt rubble, lending evidence to the fact that the raid could not have taken place more than a day earlier.

Overpowering fear, stronger than anything he had ever experienced, curled inside Wolf's belly. He leapt from the back of his horse and raced from one smoldering pile to another as his mind struggled to ignore the bloodstained ground. Memories of camp life on the day they left to find the white man closed in from all directions. Their home was gone, his family had vanished, and Wolf's heart ached with the anguish of the moment.

An odd noise behind him caused Wolf to spin and his wide, horror-filled eyes settled on Two Feathers. The other man clutched a small twig doll that belonged to his daughter. His mouth hung open with the stunned pain of loss. The formerly fearless warrior was now doubled over in agony. He released a piercing scream that rent the silence, then dropped weakly to his knees. The grieving brave continued the piercing chant for the dead as Wolf and Walking

Bear stood numbly by.

Wolf shook himself from the suffocating shock and knelt to examine the prints in the dirt. Deeply grooved half-circles covered the entire area. His shaking fingers followed the edge of one imprint and, with dark, tortured eyes, he looked up slowly to stare at the rubble before him. His voice whispered across the short span and reached Walking Bear.

"This is not the work of another Indian band. The soldiers were here. The prints of many shod horses prove it." He shook his head slowly. "Nothing will ever be the same again."

Swallowing back the bile in his throat, Wolf circled the outer edges of the camp to search for any sign of life. He fought the uselessness of his actions—he needed to keep moving; needed to discover something that would make the awful heaviness leave his chest.

August Moon is dead! his mind screamed. The pain choked him, stole the breath from his lungs, and he could not stop his heart from crying out. *Where is she*? There were no dead anywhere; only nothingness.

He silently mourned the loss of his people, but none so much as he did the one woman he loved beyond all others. The past tripped through his mind; images of August Moon as a young girl, laughing at the antics of a squirrel or weeping with anger when she was told she could not participate in a hunt; the look of pride on her beautiful face when she shot her first deer and presented it to her people.

Wolf's devastating pain finally forced him to his knees also, and he rocked back and forth with an agony that knifed through his chest again and again. He attempted, time after time, to sing the death song for his beloved, but could not force the notes from his constricted throat.

She was gone. August Moon had been murdered, along with the rest of his family. His head sagged and he gasped for air. Wolf's mind reeled with the smell of death that surrounded him.

The three sickened men huddled on the ground, separate from one another and divided in their pain. The seconds ticked into minutes as the men swam in their sorrow. Each tried to find the courage to rise above the tantamount loss of not only family, but of everything familiar; a dream life that had disappeared into a dark nightmare. Wolf was jolted from his grief when a gentle hand squeezed his shoulder.

He raised a quivering chin and met Walking Bear's soulful eyes. Quiet words filled with grim disillusionment met his ears. "What are we to do next, Wolf? I say that we seek revenge. It does not matter who did this; it matters only that it was by the hand of the white man. I have nothing else to lose. My family is gone." His voice broke with the last statement and his tortured eyes closed momentarily. "I want to believe they are alive, but the blood on the ground tells of another story."

Wolf rose with the weariness of an aged man. The need for revenge burned bright in his heart also, and he would seek it, but not on this day.

*If only we had been here, we could have stopped the slaughter...*He found it difficult to meet Walking Bear's sad gaze when a raging guilt burned in his mind. "I also feel the need for revenge, but there can be no retaliation until we find the graves of our people. We will make sure we leave no one behind. We must do this thing before any decisions can be made."

Wolf's gaze sought out his other heartbroken friend, who still sat frozen in pain on the hard ground. He walked to him and reached out a shaky hand to touch the man's back. "Two Feathers. Come. We will search for our family before night falls." The two braves helped the desolate man to his feet. He still clutched his daughter's toy in his arms...

* * *

The three disheartened warriors searched the area in and around their former home until twilight darkened the forest, their efforts revealing nothing but the scattered remains of the encampment. The pieces of their former life were strewn down the paths that once carried the laughter of their people. Each man pushed the pain of destruction into the furthest corners of their mind and concentrated on where they would go from here.

Revenge was the only recourse. It raged strong in all three hearts. To think of anything else; of the world that was taken from them, of the loved ones lost, would crush their spirits completely at a stage when their grief was still in its infancy.

No words were spoken as they moved away from the wreckage of their summer home and collapsed near the fringes of the encampment. Being within the boundaries of their former home was still too painful to bear. They sat; three aching, devastated men who had lost everything. The hushed tones of their voices were muffled in the tall grass.

"We leave when the sun comes up." Two Feathers' words were not voiced as an order, but rather as the words of an inconsolable husband and father who could no longer tolerate the sight of his once comforting surroundings. Trembling hands still stroked his daughter's small doll.

Walking Bear stared blankly at his companions, his grief mirroring the horror and sadness he saw in the faces of the other two men. "We have not spoken of the direction. Do we travel to the Paha Sapas and seek our revenge with the strength of the mountains within us? We must decide."

Wolf's eyes sagged closed and his square chin dropped as he struggled to block the vision of August Moon that insisted upon invading his thoughts. His two Sioux brothers would abide by whatever he said; he was their leader.

What is the right thing to do? He was the one who had guided the band these past years, the one who made a decision when it was needed. Since riding through the hole in the hill, however, he had not been able to think clearly.

Should they go north, find their relatives and wait for the snows to melt before seeking the enemy? Or would including the others in on their personal revenge get them all killed? Would the Sioux even fight the white man any longer? They were so few now compared to their former numbers. He drew in a deep breath of air and looked at his friends.

"Whatever happens, we must stay together. If we part, we may never find each other again. Revenge will honor the ones who have gone before us, but I see us passing on to another world, as well. The white man will kill us. I know this here." Wolf touched his chest. "They will kill us when they get the chance, just as they killed our families."

Walking Bear nodded in resigned agreement. He would be proud to leave this world—if it was done with honor. "What is left in our hearts, except revenge? They have taken everything. I say we should not wait."

"Then it is decided—"

The sudden grasp of Two Feathers' hand halted Wolf's words. He looked from the other man's white fingers, as they firmly gripped his arm, to where his other hand pointed across the grassy meadow. Wolf spun quickly and his dark eyes searched for the cause of his friend's distress.

The moonlight revealed a figure in the distance; a figure that sagged against a tree trunk at the edge of the clearing. All three men jumped to their feet simultaneously and, before a word could be uttered, a voice from the dead reached out to touch them.

"Wolf..."

"August Moon!" He raced across the distance between them with renewed joy in his heart. *She is alive!*

August Moon collapsed into the soft grass a split-second later.

"August Moon!"

Her shouted name shattered the silence once more as Wolf ran headlong across the meadow. Two Feathers and Walking Bear followed. Wolf dropped to his knees beside August and clasped her to his chest. It was not a dream. The warm body in his arms proved that she was alive. His trembling hands pushed the hair from her face, and he looked into the eyes of the woman he loved more than life itself.

"You are alive...August Moon, you are alive." Shameless tears of joy wet his brown cheeks. He had hope now; hope that not all was lost. "We have searched and could not find anyone. We thought you were all killed, and now you are here..."

She rolled her head slowly until it rested against his bronze chest. *I am not alone anymore...*The thought was foremost in her mind; she was not lost in the dark by herself.

The soldiers failed to see her when she lay motionless in the deep grass. Eventually, they left by way of wagons, filled with the dead bodies of her clan. Hurt and bleeding, August dragged herself from the site of the massacre and the eerie silence that settled like a shroud around her. She hid for endless hours in an animal's lair, floating in and out of unconsciousness. The fear of another night within the sinister darkness though, and the need for water, had finally driven her back to the encampment. She watched the flames from across the field, hoping against hope that other members of the band had lived through the raid.

"Wolf..."

"Where are the others, August Moon?"

Wolf's question formed in her mind, and sadness welled within her. She tipped her head until she could see into his eyes.

"They were all lost, save..." She held his arm in a weak grasp and struggled to sit straighter. Her face contorted with pain and a raspy gasp escaped her lips.

"What is wrong, Little One? Where are you hurt?"

"My...leg..." The words trailed off as the merciful blackness that had become so much a part of her world engulfed her once again.

* * *

Familiar voices echoed in August's head and she tried valiantly to open her eyes. The searing pain in her upper leg was excruciating but, ignoring the discomfort, she concentrated on the words that floated around her.

"She cannot travel that far. I will stay here with her."

"But it is you who said we must stay together."

"That was before we knew August Moon was still alive. You have seen her leg. She will never survive the trip to the hills. I will stay."

"Then we will all travel together to the winter camp; it is closer. I have always respected your words, Wolf, but Two Feathers and I have discussed it. If you will not go with us to the Black Hills, then we will remain together and seek our revenge when the snow melts."

It was obvious that vengeance was uppermost in his brothers' hearts, but Wolf would not sacrifice August Moon's life by forcing her to succumb to the long trip. The Spirit of Death had returned her to him; he would not chance losing her to his clutches again.

"You must go...to the hills...we must..." August's breathless words reached their ears as she flailed weakly to gain their attention. The light blanket that covered her felt like a leaden weight on her chest, and heat engulfed her body; it did not come from the warm flames of a fire, however, but from deep within her upper thigh.

Wolf was at her side immediately. He touched her forehead and felt the heat that radiated from her skin. Her fever had worsened. He took a damp rag and tenderly wiped her brow.

"The trip will be too hard for you, Little One. We will stay here until your leg heals."

Wolf had removed the bullet lodged in August Moon's upper thigh while she was unconscious. If the piece of metal had been left in her leg, the wound would have festered, allowing the poison to spread throughout her body. The infection would have killed her, finishing what the soldiers set out to do. Two Feathers prepared a medicinal poultice, but still the fever raged out of control.

"No..." She clutched his hand weakly. "You must find Fawn and Whitecloud. The soldiers have them."

Two Feathers' head snapped in her direction and he scrambled to her side.

"Fawn is alive?" His question was filled with hope. "My woman is alive? And Whitecloud? What happened to them?"

"The soldiers came without warning." A sob clogged her throat and August fought to regain control of her emotions. It took considerable effort to force the nightmare away and focus on her words. Whitecloud and Fawn's lives depended on it. "There was screaming...the guns kept shooting and our people fell everywhere. There was so much blood..." August swallowed to wet her parched throat. Wolf lifted a rawhide bag filled with water and brought it to her lips.

August coughed and swallowed down waves of nausea when the cool liquid hit her stomach. "I thought everyone was dead. I felt the pain in my leg and could do no more to help anyone. The soldiers did not know I was still alive. I lay by the edge of the trees where I fell and...three soldiers came out of the forest with Fawn and Whitecloud. Whitecloud held Little Fawn in his arms. She was dead." Her eyes searched for Two Feathers'. His renewed pain blazed from the depth of his soul. "I am sorry..."

Two Feathers pushed aside the renewed agony that ripped through his gut at the thought of his daughter's death. He needed to think of his wife now. Fawn—she might not be lost to him after all. "Do you know where they took my wife? Did you hear anything?"

August fought to recall everything that happened during the raid. She grabbed Wolf's arm. "Your father knew I was still alive. He looked at me when the soldiers marched them past, and I saw his eyes. His stare ordered me to stay down. I could do nothing for them but remain dead in the soldiers' eyes. They said Pine Ridge. They will go there. You will go there." Her gaze moved from one man to the next. "You will all go there. You will go without me, because I will slow you down."

Wolf held August closer and clasped her feverish hand. "We will not leave you here to die. How did you escape, Little One?"

"They took our dead in the wagons. I rolled into the tall grass and lay still. They did not find me." She closed her eyes and, from the very depths of her soul, summoned the nerve to speak aloud. "Wolf...when I was a child, I dreamed of my death. The time is here. The pain is different, but all else is the same." She squeezed his hand, drawing the courage she so desperately needed. "Let me die, as it was meant to be. Your father is waiting somewhere for you. Fawn will need

Two Feathers by her side. I can do no more in this world." Her voice faded, and the three brave's dark gazes met.

"We must do something to free them from the soldiers." Two Feather's voice was adamant as his gaze penetrated their leader. The flat look of pain in his eyes was gone; they now shined with renewed hope that his wife was still alive. "We cannot think of the winter camp—if we are to ever find Fawn and Whitecloud, we must go now."

Wolf battled his emotions. His father waited for him to come. He could do no less than try to find him and set him free; Two Feathers' wife was with him. *But how can I leave August Moon? She will never survive the trip—and I cannot leave her here to die.* He sat back on his haunches and, with anxious determination hardening his jaw, made a decision. He gently laid the feverish woman back on the blanket and tucked another around her slim shoulders. His resolute gaze met hers.

"I have to try and find my father, but I will not leave you here to die."

"You must leave me." Her plea came as an urgent sob now. "If you do not go soon, the chance of finding them will be lost."

"No!" The one word cut through the night air. He would not allow her to give up her life; not even to save the life of his father. His searching gaze found his friends' once more. The determination in their eyes told him that they would travel to Pine Ridge even if he did not accompany them. But how could he expect them to find his father if he was not willing to try and do the same?

Wolf poured cool water onto the rag in his hand and laid it on August's brow. "Sleep, Little One, and let me worry about what to do. We will speak of it no more tonight." He stood then, and nodded at the two men who awaited his answer, beckoning them to follow. They moved away from the spot where August lay in heated slumber once more.

"I will travel with you." Wolf heaved a great sigh, but his next words were decisive. "First though, we must bring August Moon to the white man, Cole Wilkins. If she survives the trip, maybe the white man's medicine will help her. It might be the only chance she has."

"Do you think he can be trusted with her life?" Walking Bear's doubt was revealed in his tone of voice. Cole had seemed friendly enough when they were traveling to his home, but that did not mean he would help them now.

"It is the only thing we can do. The white man said if we ever needed help, we could go to him. August will not live if she stays here on her own, and she cannot make the long trip to the hills. Do we do this?"

In a small part of his heart, Wolf hoped they would disagree. He had known instinctively, deep within his soul, that he and Cole would meet again. The thought was nothing short of unnerving.

Chapter Ten

"What's wrong, Cole?" Emma stood at the opening of the stall, her arms crossed, a slender eyebrow raised, and a slim hip leaning against the swinging door.

Cole shrugged his broad shoulders in answer to his sister-in-law's question and concentrated on the pitchfork in his hands. *What the hell is wrong with me?* He stabbed the pitchfork viciously into the pile of straw. *Whatever it is, it damn well better give way soon.*

The agitation he had been experiencing lately was unlike anything he had ever felt before. Since his return a few short weeks back, sleep had become an intangible thing, food did not even look good and, most confusing of all, he could not keep August and the days spent with her from his mind. His frazzled brain wondered constantly if she, Wolf, and the rest of the small band were on their way to Canada.

The Sioux had made a huge impact on his life in the few days he spent with them. He had always been content to just stay close to home before. Now, however, he found himself short on patience more often than not, and the everyday routine had become a drudge. A yearning gnawed at his insides now; a yearning to explore the far horizon. Ranch life did not appeal to him as it once had. Finally admitting the source of his aggravation, Cole realized the need originated during the time spent with August. His eyes had been opened to something more; something far beyond the norm.

"Come here and sit down," Emma insisted in a voice that was somehow soothing. "You look like you're going to stab that pitchfork right through the stable wall."

Cole pursed his lips, set the pitchfork against the slatted wall of the stall, and turned to face her with a wry smile curving his lips. "You're not going to let it go until I listen to what you have to say. Right?"

The telltale hand on her hip and the familiar stubborn set of Emma's jaw assured him of the truth of his own words. "You know I have your best interests at heart." Her curly head nodded in the direction of the wooden bench outside the enclosure. "What do you say we sit down and have a heart to heart? Talking has always helped in the past."

Cole's gaze moved to the hard surface, then back to his sister-in-law's slight form. The two sat on the bench many times over the last few years, surrounded by the familiar smells of the barn. He would talk and she would listen; eventually she would help him sort out his problem. If this conversation followed the same course, there was a very strong likelihood he would feel better when it was over.

Emma plopped down on the bench and patted the spot beside her. Cole sighed heavily and moved to join her.

"Are you thinking of August and her family?" Emma cut to the chase. "You told us about them that first night you arrived home, but haven't said a word since."

Cole shrugged his shoulders again. "I sort of just stored it away, I guess. I think about them a lot when I'm alone." He glanced up at Emma and shook his sandy-brown head. "How in the hell did you figure out what was bothering me anyway?"

"Woman's intuition." A soft eyebrow lifted along with her smug grin as she waited for him to continue.

Cole rested his head against the wall behind them and stared at the rough cut ceiling timbers above. He expelled the breath from his lungs and turned his gaze to rest on Emma again. "I can't think of much else. Being with them was like living another life. By the time I got home, it was as if I was one of them. They made me feel like I belonged, Em."

"And you don't feel like you belong here?"

"I don't know. I did once..." Cole heaved another sigh. "The Sioux people are totally different than the way they're portrayed in the papers. They have the same feelings as we do. They have a fierce love for their families, they're hard workers, and they've managed to live in harmony with the land far better than the white man ever dreamed of. They take nothing for granted, Em, and are grateful for the world around them."

"I understand that, Cole, but that doesn't explain why you've been quieter than usual lately—more or less unapproachable. This can't go on. Even the children see the difference. Thomas asked me the other day if he did something to upset you."

Cole's chin dropped to his chest, and he closed his eyes with a guilty sigh. "I'd never intentionally do anything to hurt Thomas. I'll talk to him and let him know he's done nothing wrong."

"And then what are you going to do?"

"What do you mean?" He glanced up in surprise.

"You've been miserable, Cole. We can all see it. More than likely, you'll never run into August or the rest of them again. You do realize that, don't you?"

Not willing to admit it aloud, Cole simply shrugged again as Emma continued.

"You can't keep living like this, Cole. I can't tell if you're sad or if you've just become bored with all of us."

Cole belted out a rare laugh at her statement. "Bored? With this group? I hardly think so." He rose from the bench, grabbed the pitchfork again, and began to spread clean straw on the floor of the stall. "I telegraphed Beau to let him know about my encounter with August, and then followed up with a letter. Hopefully, if he crosses paths with her and her family, he'll be able to do something for them. I asked him to let me know if that happens."

He glanced over his shoulder at his brother's wife and made a quick decision. He stopped pitching hay, balanced an elbow on the end of the wooden handle, and peered at Emma. "Can I tell you something—just between the two of us?"

She nodded. "Of course."

"I think I might head out west next spring to visit Beau."

Emma's green eyes widened in surprise. "Why?"

"Honestly, Em, I don't know. Hell, I may change my mind before spring, so don't say anything to Tyler or Trevor. I have to give it some thought and don't need them badgering me about it all winter." His shoulders lifted again in feigned nonchalance. "It was great to see Beau again. We used to be good friends. He has such purpose to his life now, and his cause is something I've become interested in. I want to stay in contact with him and see where it goes. Can you understand that?"

Emma stood and moved to give him a hug. "Of course I can. If it's something you feel strongly about, then you should do it." She stepped back, leaving a hand on his arm. "You've given your entire life to this family, Cole. The business has benefited because of your hard work. Don't feel guilty about wanting something more." She tilted her head and voiced her thoughts out loud. "This need of yours doesn't stem from the fact that you hope to see August again, does it? If that's the reason behind this sudden urge to 'get away,' then you must realize that the chances of finding her are little to none." Her hand found his arm again. "Whatever you decide to do, Cole, just be careful. I don't want to see you hurt." She shook her head slowly. "And, if you do decide to leave, I hope it's what's meant to be—for you."

As he listened to her words, Cole hoped the same thing himself.

* * *

Wolf's mocassined feet tread silently across the soft, dew-covered grass that surrounded the Wilkins' homestead. The moonlight illuminated his large body in a silvery light, casting the ghostly figure into a shadow as he crept from one building to another. The rough-hewn timbers of a magnificent barn pricked his skin as he flattened himself against the wall in an attempt to stay hidden.

Wolf paused and breathed deeply to control the erratic beat of his heart. The black eyes of his ancestry searched the darkness, and he listened closely to the night sounds around him. He was uncertain what kind of a reception he would receive and, cautious to a fault, hoped mightily that Cole had been honest in his promise to help.

He had left a feverish August with Walking Bear and Two Feathers at the top of a bluff on the outskirts of the homestead. He would not risk his brothers' lives when it was his choice to bring August to the ranch.

The overland trip to Cole's home was longer than usual, in deference to the sickness she carried within her. Over and over, as they crossed the miles, Wolf's mind baulked against the decision to ask the white man to look after August while he traveled west to rescue his father and Two Feathers' wife. It irked Wolf to know that, whether he wanted to leave her or not, the choice had been taken from him.

Over the course of the last few days, August's condition had worsened.

Her fever raged on and her leg remained swollen and an ugly red. She floated in and out of awareness and, at times, did not respond to any of them. She needed a medicine man—her life depended on Cole finding one.

Light from a gas lantern spilled through the open doorway of one of the larger buildings. Wolf slithered behind the slatted barrier and hid in the shadows. He had seen Cole enter the building only a few minutes earlier; he was certain of it. Up until that point, he had no idea how he was going to make contact with the white man. Wolf simply knew that with the sickness inside August, he could not wait until morning to obtain help.

Now, the opportunity to speak to Cole without alerting others had presented itself. With the courage of his people flowing in his veins, Wolf stepped through the open doorway and into the light.

Cole stood with an arm hooked casually over the edge of a stall, facing away from the entrance to the barn. The Indian opened his mouth to speak, then nearly bolted back through the doorway when another man exited the small enclosure and stopped in his tracks. He stared wide-eyed at the intruder.

Tyler Wilkins grabbed his brother's arm and, reading the other man's surprised expression, Cole knew they were not alone. He whirled and his own gaze settled on the brave who stood just within the lantern's light.

"Wolf—" He took a slow, shocked step forward.

The two men sized each other up. A thousand questions raced through Cole's mind as Wolf silently questioned the white man's honesty once more.

"Wolf—what are you doing here?"

The Indian's dark gaze left Cole's and settled warily on the man who stood beside him. Could he be trusted? Not only his life, but August's, depended on it. Wolf stood proudly before them, a red man in a white man's world, ready to plead for the life of someone he loved.

"Cole Wilkins. You stated you would help me if ever I was in need."

"What happened?" Cole's immediate concern echoed in the silence as he took another step toward the other man.

"When we left you, my Sioux brothers and I returned home. But our home was no more." Wolf battled the instant pain that sprang into his eyes. "Our people were gone. Soldiers raided our camp. They killed all but three."

Cole's heart constricted. Was she dead—dead by the hands of his own race? His hardy complexion paled. "August?" He waited for the answer to hit him squarely in the gut.

Wolf shook his head and, misunderstanding the movement, Cole hung his head. "How...did she die?"

Wolf shook his head again, abruptly this time. "No, she is alive. August Moon is alive."

Uncontrolled relief flooded Cole's body.

"She hid in the tall grass. The soldiers did not see her. August Moon watched them imprison my father and Two Feathers' woman. They were the only other members of my band that were left alive. The soldiers have taken them away."

It was Cole's turn to shake his head. "I don't understand, Wolf. Why are you here? What do you need?" Cole took another step forward. "I told you to come to me for help if you needed it, and I'll stand by that, but I really don't know what I can do."

"You must help the woman."

"Woman? Are you talking about August?"

"She has sickness in her. I do not have a medicine man." His hands raised in supplication. "The soldiers' guns have hurt her. You will take her and keep her until she is well. I cannot make her well."

Cole's mind reeled and he breathed deeply to clear it.

"Is the woman with you?" Tyler stepped forward now, to stand near his brother. "We can help."

Wolf's body sagged with relief. Cole had not lied to them. The white men would help. August needed medical attention soon or she would not live through the night. "She is in the forest with my brothers, who watch over her."

Tyler glanced from one man to the other in quick decision. "Cole, you hook up the buckboard and go with Wolf. I'll send one of the stable hands to fetch Steve and Carrie." He turned to face the warrior standing before him. "We know of a doctor that will come immediately to help the woman. Take Cole to her. I'll make sure things are ready here."

"Your doctor, he is a white man?" As much as Wolf needed their assistance, he was still loath to turn August over into their hands without assuring her safety.

"He's our sister's husband," Cole replied impatiently. He was anxious now to see—and touch—the woman he thought was lost to him forever; a woman who, according to Wolf, was seriously ill. He started toward the Indian again. "Now, we've wasted enough time. You said August is hurt, which means that we need to get her back to the ranch."

"Wait." Wolf held up his palm, halting Cole in his tracks. "Can I trust your doctor? Will he look past August Moon's red skin and treat her well, or will he bring the soldiers to take her away?"

Cole paused before the other man and laid a comforting hand on his shoulder. "She'll be safe. You'll all be safe. On that, I swear my life. What happened to your family members will not happen here. You've got to trust me."

"Cole speaks the truth," Tyler added. "No one will know you're here. I'll send someone for the doctor now. You go with Cole."

Wolf's dark eyes moved from one man to the other and something deep inside him finally warmed. They could be trusted. The look of genuine sincerity on their faces was proof enough. *It was right to bring August here.* Concern for his beloved heated him further and spurred him to action. "Let us go."

Tyler hurried from the building as Cole led a stocky, well-built Morgan from the stable. He grabbed a harness, tossed it over the animal's wide back, and hitched the horse to a wagon that sat just outside the barn. He threw straw into the back and covered it with blankets, then both men leapt onto the hard driver's seat. Wolf pointed the way, and the buckboard bounced its way through the log gate.

* * *

"Why do the others refuse to save me from the bitter cold?" August cried out. She limped through the deep snow, shivered with the fierceness of the cold Canadian wind, and stopped before yet another teepee. The warmth would reach her if they would only allow her to go inside. She had shared the white man's gifts with her people; now they closed the flaps of their lodges when she begged entrance. She stole horses for them to reach their winter home, but for some reason, had been shunned by the ones she loved.

Weak, nauseous, and devoid of strength, August collapsed to the blanket of white and shuddered uncontrollably. The extreme cold wound its icy tentacles into her bones; death was close at hand.

The blackness was far better than the cold she experienced now. In the dark, she was warm. She prayed for the darkness. A pain worse than she had ever encountered snaked its way from her knee to the base of her back. She lay shivering, too weak to protest the terrible ache and the cold any longer. Frigid waves of agony washed through her, as did rejection by the people she loved. She was going to die alone in the snow, frightened beyond belief.

A low moan escaped her frozen lips as she fought the sob that built inside her...

Two Feathers moved closer when August moaned, and his fearful eyes met Walking Bear's over her shuddering body. Though the fever raged hotter, her trembling limbs were covered with raised bumps. He tucked the blanket tighter around her body; he could do nothing else.

"She is worse."

Walking Bear nodded in agreement and reached for his water sack. "The fever is eating her. I think it wins. It has been too many days." He forced liquid between her dry, colorless lips and prayed she would swallow instead of choking it back up. Both men watched her throat move and listened to the now familiar hoarse cough as water dribbled from the corner of her mouth.

Walking Bear rose and grabbed his rifle in frustration. "I will check once more to see if Wolf has returned."

Two Feathers felt his own loss rip through him again when the other man disappeared into the dark. He was able to keep the pain at arm's length when the others were with him. When alone, however, he felt the ache of grief rear up and, again, mourned the death of his daughter. He pictured her small brown face with the crooked smile that was always in place. Swallowing back the huge sadness, he pushed his agony to the back of a weary mind and tended August. He hoped she would not be among the final numbers of the dead. There had already been enough.

They were all that remained, and possibly Fawn and Wolf's father. Once August Moon was settled with the white man, Two Feathers would not rest until he found his wife. He prayed for her safety; he would be unable to stand against the devastation any longer if he should find her dead.

No! She will be alive! I will take her and flee farther than the winter camp and never come back to this land again! The soldiers had proven what they would do to those who did not conform—no longer would he stay just a step ahead. *Fawn, I will find you, and we will leave for the place where friends say there are no white men; only the big moose and enough deer and birds to forever feed the two of us.* He would travel far from his sacred land if that is what it took to assure them a peaceful life.

His solemn thoughts were interrupted when the sound of a high, sharp whistle echoed through the tall pines. Two Feather's head snapped up with the answering call. Wolf had returned. Two Feathers alert gaze watched warily as a light bobbed eerily through the trees. *The white man must be with him...*

The three men entered the small clearing, and Cole raised the gas lantern to take in his surroundings. August lay on the ground a short distance away, and he rushed to drop to his knees beside her.

Cole touched her cheek tenderly, and then moved his hand to her feverish brow. Trembling fingers brushed sticky, damp strands of hair from her heated temple. He glanced over his shoulder at Wolf and, when the other man nodded his permission, Cole pushed the blanket aside to check August's injury. The Indian had told him of her precarious condition on the ride to the clearing, but nothing prepared him for the serious state he now found her in.

"Christ almighty..." Cole gasped, then swore again under his breath.

The leg, from knee to hip, was swollen and, even in the dim light of the lamp, he could see the angry streaks that trailed like small red rivers across her skin from the oozing bullet hole.

Wolf hunkered next to Cole. His gaze met the white man's before he reached out to touch August's brow as Cole had done. He shook his dark head fearfully. "The fever worsens. Can your medicine man help her?"

"He'll try his best. Let's get her in the wagon and back to the ranch."

Cole moved to gather her close, but Wolf stayed his hand and gently lifted August's limp body into his own arms and carried her down the path to the waiting wagon. His actions were a statement of dominance—a declaration; it was he who controlled the life of the woman, and not the white man.

Cole held his silence as he followed behind. They reached the wagon and he hooked the lantern on a lamp peg, jumped into the back, and readied the blankets over the bed of straw. He would not question Wolf's possessiveness; a possessiveness that was evident to all who stood in the circle of light emanating from the lamp.

Cole turned in the wagon bed and caught the expression on Wolf's face as he looked down at the woman in his embrace. A mixture of love and fear mingled with abject loss as he slowly raised his arms and handed August into the white man's keeping.

Cole clasped her burning body to his chest, and an overwhelming desire to protect and shelter combined with a sense of completeness. The result was a feeling like nothing Cole had ever experienced.

The white man and the Sioux said nothing to one another as they tucked the blanket securely around August's trembling body. Neither was willing to tread upon the other's ownership where she was concerned. Each was acutely aware of the other's sentiments, however, but did not act on the knowledge or voice it aloud. They had a common goal; to help August recover, and that was enough for now.

Still holding his silence, Wolf settled himself beside August on the bed of hay. Cole, in turn, hopped onto the driver's seat, snapped the reins, and turned the buckboard back in the direction of the house.

* * *

Lights blazed from every window when the wagon passed through the front gate and approached the house. Cole's heart thundered with relief; Steve and Carrie's horses were tied to the front porch railing. The front door of the house flew open a moment later and Steve hurried down the steps before the buckboard had even pulled to a stop. Cole jumped from the seat and met him at the back of the conveyance.

Wolf's immediate concern for August's safety etched his hard features again as, one after another, Cole's family members surrounded the wagon. Two Feathers and Walking Bear, who sat astride mounts just behind the wagon, nervously ran their hands over the old Winchester rifles they carried.

Cole noticed the movement and, fearing that the slightest provocation would turn the rescue into a small gun battle, he raised his hands in a plea. "Two Feathers and Walking Bear, these people are my family and they're here to help. Please, put down the guns." He indicated the blond-haired Steven, who stood beside him. "This man is a doctor. He will help August. Don't be frightened."

The two hesitant Indians looked to Wolf for confirmation. Cole spun in the dirt to face August's self-appointed protector.

"Please, let's just get her inside. She needs help, Wolf, and she needs it *now*. No one here will harm her or you. You've got to trust me."

The proud Indian brave rose slowly in the back of the wagon. His sharp gaze darted to the silent family members gathered nearby, then back to the man Cole said was a doctor. His unwavering stare settled on Steven.

"You will not harm her? You can make her well?"

Steven stepped forward, with Carrie at his side. "I'll do my best. You can trust me, and you can also trust my wife. We'll do everything in our power to help her. Please, bring her inside." He turned to the agitated men behind Wolf, who sat astride their horses with guns raised. "You're all welcome here. While I tend to the woman, Emma," he nodded at his sister-in-law, "will get you some food. She'll also show you a place where you can rest."

Wolf just continued to stare at the doctor and his companions with a wary expression and, finally, Cole had had enough. August was near dying and they were all standing at a stalemate, trying to decide who was trustworthy and who was not. "Wolf, dammit—I gave you my word. Are you willing to risk August's life because you doubt our intentions? We're not like the soldiers and never will be. Didn't the time we spent together prove that?" He turned to Two Feathers and Walking Bear. "Put down your guns and come inside."

Wolf hesitated for a moment more, and then nodded his head to his two companions. A collective sigh of relief from Cole's family, where they stood in the yard, broke another ensuing silence. There had been enough bloodshed, the Indian decided. Cole had proven himself more than once to be an honorable man. He must remember that. The brave gathered August into his arms and followed the white man into the house.

* * *

August lay pale and fragile beneath the covers. Her weak body was finally still; the trembling had stopped. Cole watched as his brother-in-law packed his medical supplies into the worn leather bag, then moved his gaze to Wolf.

The Indian sat on a padded bench near the massive bed. He had not moved or spoken in the last six hours. Now, as the sun broke over the tops of the towering pines, he still sat motionless and stared blindly at the woman in the bed.

Steve and Carrie had worked tirelessly throughout the night as Cole, Emma, and Tyler hauled bucket after bucket of hot steaming water up the long staircase. They returned to the kitchen when the pails of liquid cooled and replaced them with boiling water that Mamie kept heated on the iron cook stove. The skin around the open wound in August's thigh burned an even brighter shade of red now; a result of the continuous steaming poultices that Steve applied to the injury. He never let up; if the poison that spread in streaks away from the wound was not drawn out, saving August's life, let alone her leg, would be almost an impossibility.

"What do you think, Steve?" Cole spoke quietly across the length of the bed.

"I don't know." The doctor shook his head in answer to Cole's question. "The infection is worse than anything I've ever encountered. It'll be a good day or so before we can tell if it's turning the other way. Her fever is high, but I'm loath to try and bring it down completely. It might be what her body needs to kill the poison—if it doesn't kill her first." He snapped his bag shut, crossed to the table to wash his hands one last time, and spoke tiredly over his shoulder. "When Carrie comes back up, I'm going to let her take over for awhile. We're going to have to take shifts for the next couple of days and keep the hot compresses on the wound."

Steve's gaze followed Wolf when he rose from the wooden bench and crossed to the bed. The Indian's frightened eyes never left August's face. He sat beside her and began the quiet chant of his ancestors.

Carrie and Emma entered with more steaming buckets of water and stopped short at the Indian cadence. Wolf's life song continued quietly even as Cole lifted the bucket from his sister's hand, retrieved more bandages, and tended August's leg. Steve hauled two other pails across the room, placed them by the bed, and left with Emma.

Cole continued to place hot poultices on the oozing wound for the next half-hour. He had just dipped the rag in the last pail of hot water when the Indian's singing stopped abruptly.

Wolf glanced up with gratitude shining in his black eyes. "There is a difference within her. Her skin still burns, but she rests easier. Can you tell?"

Cole leaned forward to touch August's brow. The high fever still worried him, but as he listened to her breathing, he detected a slight change for the better. *She's not struggling as she was earlier.* He allowed himself a hesitant smile in Wolf's direction.

"I think you might be right." He motioned for his sister. "What do you think, Carrie?"

She moved closer to the bed, slowly moved her hands over August's forehead, then laid her palm on the other woman's chest to time her respirations. She checked the wound once more before she turned to the two men. "She's still not out of the woods by any means, but you're right. She is breathing easier. Steve and I won't rest easy though, until we have another day of improvement." Carrie straightened and, with a weary sigh, placed her hands on the lower part of her back. She stretched before swinging her gaze to the creaking bedroom door.

Emma entered the room bearing a cloth-covered tray. She crossed to a round table next to the bench where Wolf had been sitting and, setting down her burden, pulled back the napkin to uncover a plate of food. With gentle hands, she coaxed the Indian back to the bench, then sat down beside him.

"Wolf, you've eaten nothing since arriving here last night. Please, eat this." She held out the food. "You must be hungry." She spoke quietly with a soft smile on her lips; a smile that was just for him. Wolf remained motionless, however, and Emma laid her hand gently on his shoulder. "You've had such a long night. Nothing would please me more than if you would just try to eat a little."

The big man looked into the sparkling green eyes of the woman next to him. Compassion and true gentleness filled the green depths.

Emma did not see his long dark hair or the color of his skin. What she saw was a man who was sick with worry over the woman he loved—a man who had not left her side to eat or drink. She communicated that to him with yet another gentle smile.

"Please, take this and make me feel better." She held up the bowl filled with hot stew. "Your two friends told me about the journey you'll be taking to find your father and Two Feather's wife. How will you do that without the strength that food and rest will bring you? It's important that you be prepared for your long trip." She prodded him with her softly spoken words and waited for him to respond.

Cole watched in amazement when Wolf took the plate from Emma's hand, picked up the spoon, and began to eat slowly. Cole had been trying all night to get the man to eat and to rest, but Wolf would have none of it. Now the brave obeyed his sister-in-law like a well-behaved child. *She always has such a special way about her.*

The Indian finished eating and handed the plate to Emma and, again, Cole watched in amazement when she talked Wolf into going downstairs to speak with Two Feathers and Walking Bear. Emma followed him out.

Cole just shook his head, then turned to help Carrie change the dressing on August's leg. The task complete, his sister left the room with the bag of soiled bandages and informed him that she would be back after a bite to eat and a small rest.

Suddenly, he was alone with her, and all Cole could do was stare. August was again within arm's reach, and he could not believe his good fortune...if she survived. He dragged a chair closer to the bed, sat, and studied her features; features that, up until the night before, were only a vision in his mind.

She was there, in his home; because of the circumstances though, and he was not quite sure if he should be thankful or not. The selfish side of him was elated, however juvenile the notion was. August had left a gaping hole in his life when they parted weeks ago—a chasm that he was only just beginning to recognize. She made him think about the part of his life that was empty; a void that he had never thought to see filled. When he was with her though, he felt more alive and complete than ever before.

She was there, however, because she was gravely hurt.

"You're going to be fine, August," he whispered. He reached out to push a wayward strand of dark hair back from her feverish brow. "What did you endure that day?"

His stomach lurched at the thought. Wolf had spoken little through the night, but what he did say was enough to make Cole sick. He mentally shook the image of the slaughter from his mind. She was there by the hand of fate, and he would do all he could to help her. He would put his emotions aside—at least for the moment.

Cole's gaze shifted back to her face, and his eyes widened when he realized she was awake and staring back at him. Though he could still see the fevered flush of her skin, she looked at him through clear, but confused eyes.

"Cole?" she mumbled in a hushed tone. Her bloodshot gaze moved slowly about the room, from the chintz curtains billowing slowly out from the slightly open window, to the finely hewn furniture. Her eyes followed a path to the closed door that led to the hallway, and then back to the tenderly smiling face of the man she thought never to see again. "Where am I? Are we dead?"

He scooted forward and gently took her feverish hand in his. "No, August, we're both very much alive and, for that, I'm grateful. You were hurt badly. Wolf brought you to my home. I'm so happy you've finally awakened. You gave all of us quite a scare."

"But...why would Wolf bring me here? What happened?" As quickly as the question left her lips, the past events that led August back to the white man crashed into her mind. Her confused expression turned to one of heartrending loss. A low wail emitted from her open mouth.

Cole grasped her hand tighter, and she squeezed her lids shut.

"I remember...I remember..." her words trailed away as another sob caught in her throat.

Cole sat silently, willing his strength to reach her, and letting her find the time to take it all in. He watched her lips move and, finally, she opened her eyes to stare sadly into the tender ones above her.

"How did I get here?"

"You were shot in the leg, and the wound became badly infected. Wolf brought you here in the hope that I could find a doctor to help bring down the fever and fight the infection that's been raging inside you. He found you after the raid."

Her head lolled against the soft down pillow and small tears inched their way across her flushed cheeks. "They are all gone...the soldiers killed all of them." Her eyes flew open again a second later. "Whitecloud and Fawn! I must tell Wolf. We must leave to find them!" She tried weakly to free her hand from his grip and rise from the bed, but Cole gently pressed her back into the soft pillow.

"He knows, August. You told him of it when he first found you."

"We must go!" She struggled against his hold.

Cole did not have the heart to tell her that Wolf would leave the ranch without her. The one thing he was sure of at the moment was that she would not take the news well. "Let me go find him. He's been worried about you and will be glad to see that you're awake."

Cole stood then, and left the room. Wolf should be the one to tell August that she would be left behind. It was his decision, and Cole was wary of taking any more from the man. He had lost enough; they had all lost enough.

* * *

Wolf crossed the room with joy in his heart. "You are awake, Little

One." He knelt on the floor and gently reached out to touch the thickness of her hair. "I am thankful you are back with us."

She pulled him close and managed to hold him tightly, despite her weakened state. It was the first time Wolf could ever remember August holding him so intimately, and he breathed in the familiar scent of her hair. The warrior battled with his heart. Now was not the time to tell her of his love.

"Your father and Fawn are alive," she whispered into the crook of his neck. "Cole said you know this. We must prepare to leave and find them." August grabbed his hand and a shudder ran through her petite body as he sat back. "We never had a chance. They came on us before the camp woke for the day. I tried to help, but there was nothing I could do. There were too many soldiers. I am sorry I could not help them."

Reliving the smell; the acrid gunpowder and the scent of fresh blood splattered everywhere, was enough to cause another shudder. The raid was the most horrific day in her short life thus far; but, still, she berated herself quietly for not having done more. "I'm so sorry..."

"There was nothing you could have done to make it better. Know that, Little One. Do not blame yourself. If there is any blame to be laid, it is with I for not being there."

August tipped her head back to search his familiar features. "You would have been killed, along with Two Feathers and Walking Bear. The soldiers would have made sure."

"We can not look back, August. It is done."

"But what of Whitecloud and Fawn? Surely we are going to search for them?"

His eyes moved over the soft skin of her face before pulling her close again. Wolf's chin dropped to rest on the top of her head, and he could not help himself as he slowly rubbed his jaw against the thick mantle of her hair. The heat of her fever still radiated from her touch.

"Listen to what I say. We will search for them, but you will not be by our side." His arms tightened around her, muting her immediate struggles. "I brought you to Cole, Little One. I knew you would die if I took you with us to the Paha Sapas. Your injury would have surely taken your life if I had not done this thing. It was the white man's medicine that brought you back to me. It will be many days though, before you are ready to ride and we cannot wait. The trail will be lost to us."

August shook her head against his chest and Wolf fought the urge to carry her from the ranch at that very moment. He closed his eyes against the vision of an uncertain future and sighed deeply with the ache that pierced his confidence. "Do not make this hard for me, Little One. You will stay here with Cole and his family. He is willing to do this." At those words, another aching twinge coiled within his belly.

August fought against his hold again, but he would not release her. "Do not leave me, Wolf. I can help!" The plea came from her heart. "You would leave me with the whites? How can you do this? You will be foolish and the soldiers will kill you!"

There was desperation in her words now, and they cut him to the very soul.

Wolf was torn. Leaving her with the white man frightened him beyond belief. There was more to Cole's interest in August than he let on. It was more than the concern of one friend for another; Wolf felt it deep within his heart. By leaving her, he might change the course of both their lives. Taking her with him, however, might cause her death yet—and he would not risk it. August did not realize the depths of her injury. She would never make the journey west, and they could not wait any longer.

A despondent sigh escaped his lips. So many things had changed. Wolf was a lost soul; one who was no longer in control of his life—a life that directed him now, instead of the other way around—and he could do nothing but follow its dictates.

The fight left August and she ceased her struggle. The years spent within the small circle of their lives had allowed her to know Wolf better than most, and she acknowledged the fact the he would never change his mind. She did not have the strength to plead with him any longer. He would leave her with the white man, as he said he would do.

A limp hand dropped to the soft quilt that covered both her and an unfamiliar bed. All she could do now was to memorize the feel of Wolf's broad chest against her cheek and the safety she felt within his arms until they were all together again.

Chapter Eleven

"I will not accept a white man's help!" Wolf's refusal reverberated across the kitchen. "There are too many of you that cannot be trusted. My brothers and I will go to our homeland. We will free my father and Two Feathers' wife, return for August, and never be seen again."

Cole swallowed his exasperation. "How many times are we going to argue about this, Wolf?"

"Until you stop harassing me." A dark brow arched above his angry eyes. "You are becoming a nuisance with your silly ideas."

Cole checked his frustration and dropped onto a chair. "It makes perfect sense to let my friend help you. I don't know why I can't make you see that."

"It makes no sense."

Cole eyed the Indian warily as he paced across the confines of the kitchen like a caged animal. He cursed under his breath and tried again. "Wolf, I wouldn't send you to someone that can't be trusted. You'll never find your father on your own. Beau's got connections—he'll be able to trace their whereabouts without anyone being the wiser."

"You are wrong, white man." Wolf pointed a rigid finger at Cole and lowered his voice. "I have traveled the land many times. I will succeed where you would fail. We will find the last two members of our family without your help—"

"I am not willing to take that chance." Two Feathers stood in the doorway and pierced Wolf with a look of defiance. "If you want to be foolish and risk your father's life, then so be it. I will not risk Fawn's. I will do anything to release her from the soldiers." His expression became bolder. "Your stubbornness will end in the death of my wife. I do not care about your misplaced pride or the soldiers—I care only to find Fawn—and I will do it with the help of Cole's friend if that is what I must do."

Cole bounded from his chair, jumped between the two Sioux warriors, and halted Wolf's angry flight across the room to where Two Feathers stood his ground. He placed a staying hand against the heaving chest of the angry brave, his mind racing to find a way to diffuse the sudden tense situation. "Wolf, you have every right to be distrustful. The past years can't be forgotten, and I don't blame you for how you feel." Cole pressed on when a hint of confusion flashed in the dark eyes before him. "The chances of finding Fawn and Whitecloud are slim to none without Beau's help. Two Feathers is willing to trust him with Fawn's life, and that should be enough to convince you. You two are brothers— don't fight each other."

The argument was the first the two braves had ever experienced between them. Two Feathers stared across the arm of the white man and would not back down. "I will not wait much longer to leave in search of my wife. August is safe here and will live—Fawn may not be so fortunate if I do not reach her soon."

Cole watched Wolf closely as the conflicting emotions in his dark eyes deepened. "Beau will help you. I'll even ride along, if that's what it takes for you to gain his trust." Cole watched the Indian's stance soften and again, quickly took advantage of the situation. "We can leave immediately."

A clock ticked loudly on the windowsill as Wolf stared back at the white man and, once more, wrestled the sickening sensation in his gut that plagued him daily. *If he travels with us, he will not be here with August Moon...* The thought created contradicting emotions within his heart. He could not shake the idea that leaving her with Cole would forever haunt him—would forever change his life. *Yet, I do not trust any other with her safety.* His inner battle continued. *My father waits—Fawn waits...*In another life, answers always came easily for him. The changes were all too confusing.

Wolf's shoulders sagged in acceptance and Two Feathers drew in a calming breath. He would not speak of it, but understood his friend's fear all too well. *He loves August Moon, but will not admit it aloud to anyone—not even himself—and does not want to leave her with the white man.* The reasons behind the fear though, eluded Two Feathers. But, no matter, Fawn came first. Wolf would have to resolve his own conflict. August Moon now had a safe place to wait until they returned for her.

"I do not want to fight with you, my brother. We need to do this thing together," Two Feathers quietly urged. "Listen to Cole—he has not let us down. We trust him. Let us trust his friend to do what is best. The soldiers have taken all we know. Do not let them take your father and my wife. Every day we wait will take them further from us."

Wolf's haunted eyes darted from one man to the other. The decision was made, whether he wanted it to be or not. He had no choice but to follow the course they spoke of. He nodded hesitantly and met Cole's gaze. "Contact your friend, but you will not ride with us." He met Two Feathers' hopeful gaze. "We leave shortly."

Wolf turned to walk stiffly from the room then, in search of one last quiet moment with the woman he would soon leave.

* * *

Miles away at Pine Ridge, Beau, Michael, and Anna were seated around the kitchen table for the nightly meal. The comfortable quiet of the September evening was broken, however, by the thunder of galloping hooves just outside the house. The group bounded up from the table, raced across the cozy kitchen, and hurried out onto the front porch.

Colonel Bingham's regiment charged past on their way to the main headquarters at the end of the lane, leaving billowing clouds of thick dust in their wake. The road weary brigade instantly attracted onlookers as the colonel dismounted and strutted to the office door. His men slumped in their saddles to await his return, totally ignoring the haggard and frightened Sioux woman and aging warrior who accompanied them.

"What do you think, Beau?" Michael glanced warily at his friend, then back in the direction of the office. "Bingham was out for nearly a month. Looks like he's placing a report."

Beau was already heading down the steps toward the open gate at the end of the front walk. "Let's go check it out. I have a sinking feeling that it's not going to be good."

Michael recognized the anxious look in Anna's eyes and squeezed her hand. "We'll be right back. Hopefully, it's not as bad as Beau thinks."

A wan smile touched her lips as Anna watched her husband fall into step beside his friend. With a heavy sigh, she retraced her steps into the house, hoping against hope that Bingham had not brought back the only two survivors of an attack.

Beau's stomach churned as he strode toward the solemn group of waiting soldiers, singling out the Sioux prisoners with his sharp gaze. "I can't believe Bingham spent two weeks in pursuit of the two he has with him. I don't know, Mike. I've seen quite a few companies come in after a raid, and this looks all too familiar."

Michael's jaw simply tightened in response.

They stepped up onto the wooden walkway and passed the cavalry group. Not one of the soldiers met Beau's questioning gaze, and he now played out the possible raid in his mind because of the regiment's reaction to his presence.

The two men crossed the threshold and walked stiffly, and uninvited, into the office. The colonel was perched on a chair tipped back against the wall. The door slammed and Bingham glanced up with a pompous expression on his face. His arrogant brow arched above cold gray eyes.

"Well, well, well, if it isn't Beau McCabe. I heard you had returned. What?" He raised his hands as if in question, took a quick look around the office, and brought his calculating gaze back to the man before him. "No Indians to save in Minnesota?"

*You cocky bastard...*It took all of Beau's reserve, and the restraining hand of his friend, to keep him from leaping across the room and punching the arrogant commander in the teeth.

Beau had never served under Bingham and was glad for the unintentional insight on the part of some higher-ranking official. The man was not well respected within the cavalry circle, or among the men he governed, but he possessed friends in high places. That fact alone had allowed the man to steadily climb through the ranks with misplaced confidence. The Colonel did his best to decimate the Indians, and he would let no one stop him. As a result, the papers in the east named him as one of the great Frontier Indian Fighters.

Beau's steely gaze darted to Harold Landers, the Bureau of Indian Affairs agency representative, as he rose from behind the oak desk and tugged nervously at the wrinkled collar of his stained shirt. The disheveled man never said a word, but his discomfort widened his eyes.

"You look suddenly ill, Landers." Beau's cheek quivered with suppressed anger.

The cool September evening did not suppress the beads of perspiration that broke out across the agent's forehead. Averting his gaze, Harold pulled a sweat-stained handkerchief from the back pocket of his saggy pants and dabbed at the shiny expanse. Bingham had already briefed him about the military raid that took place a few short weeks earlier, skimming through the report as if the lives of a band of 'hostiles' meant nothing. Landers knew Beau would not take it well.

"I'm waiting for an answer to my question, McCabe."

Anger sparked in Beau's eyes when his heated gaze swiveled back to Bingham. Once more, he felt the pressure of Michael's hand and breathed deeply to clear the red haze.

"It's my choice, *Colonel*," Beau replied in a clipped tone, "to help place the Sioux—whether I do it here or in Minnesota."

Bingham rolled the chair forward with his body, stood, and ignored Beau and Michael as if they had suddenly left the room. His bored gaze settled on the sweating agent. "You've got my report, Landers."

Harold wiped his flabby neck with the hanky, balled the dirty cloth in his palms, and swabbed his forehead once more. He chanced a furtive look in Beau's direction. *McCabe looks ready to explode...*The agent's anxious gaze swung back to Bingham. "Sir, I will need a written report before you leave Pine Ridge."

Bingham slid his gloves on finger by finger. "You'll have my written report in the morning. Then I'll be leaving for Fort Robinson. I've got two prisoners who'll need transport south—I won't be taking them with me. Set it up, and I'll sign off on them in the morning." Ignoring the other two men once again, Bingham started for the door. He had taken only two steps when Beau moved to block his exit. He pierced the Colonel with a withering gaze.

"What happened out there?"

The Colonel's mouth pursed with practiced tedium. "That's none of your concern anymore. The prisoners are mine, and I'll take care of placing them."

"What prisoners?" Beau snorted. "The bruised Indian woman I saw on a horse out there and the old man with her? They must have put up quite a battle if it took an entire regiment to haul them in."

Beau wanted a reaction; to somehow strike a chord. Remorse would do nicely. Even antagonism would be better than the total boredom he now read on the man's face. Beau did not care what response he elicited; he just wanted something. "You must be losing your touch, Bingham."

"Kiss my ass, McCabe," the other man sneered back. "Alright—you want to know what happened? The rest of the band was killed when they put up a fight."

Beau's face paled to an ashen white, prompting the self-righteous grin that tugged at Bingham's mouth.

"You understand the rules that govern us," the colonel replied easily. "If the hostiles resist, you shoot first and ask questions later. Those two out there resisted right up until the last minute. They're lucky to be alive."

"That's bullshit, and you know it! None of the wandering bands number more than thirty or forty at most, and probably half or more are women, children and old men. Your regiment is double that size. You never gave them a chance, did you?" Beau felt the bile rise in his throat. With Bingham, the end result was always the same. "Did you bother to fly a white flag and try to speak with them?"

"Of course we did. It was total resistance from the start. *And*, I'll remind you that *I* have been given full authorization by the United States government to make whatever decision I feel necessary during a conflict. Step aside, McCabe, before I have you arrested for interfering with a U.S. military officer and his command."

"You make me sick..." Beau started for the other man, but Michael stepped up and grabbed his friend's arm once more.

"Come on, Beau. It's not worth it. Let's go back to the house."

Another arrogant smile curled Bingham's lips. "You would do well to listen to your friend, McCabe, and just stay out of my way. You'll never best me. You're a civilian now, who can't see what the future will bring." He stepped around Beau, opened the door, and exited the building.

"That son of a bitch..." Beau's words escaped in a hiss. He turned to Harold who dropped heavily into the wobbly chair behind the desk. "Where did this all happen? If it's close by, Michael and I can ride out there and check the area for any survivors who might be hurt and in hiding."

Harold was still sweating profusely and wiped his brow as he shook his head. "Bingham's been on the trail for almost a month. The raid took place two weeks ago, somewhere across the border in Minnesota. It's far and too late to find anyone alive."

* * *

August tightened a blanket around her shoulders as she sat on the front porch swing and stared blankly across the yard. Her velvet brown eyes finally settled on a break in the huge pines. Three weeks prior, the remaining members of her family slipped into the forest and disappeared from her life. She had swallowed back feelings of desertion then, and did so again now. *But Wolf made the right decision when he left me behind*, her gentler side argued. *I would have only slowed their journey.*

August had left the confines of the house for the first time only a few short hours earlier. She desperately needed the fresh air to help clear her mind and to fight the now-familiar panic that overwhelmed her. She clutched her hands in her lap and blinked back threatening tears. *What will my life be like if Wolf tempts fate and never returns for me?* The thought frightened her beyond belief.

What will Cole do with me if I am left behind? She rested her elbows on her knees and pressed her fingers to her temples. She knew the answer. He would allow her to stay in his home for a few more weeks perhaps, then would grow tired of her self-indulgent behavior, put her on a horse, and send her away.

August became decidedly obstinate and standoffish after Wolf left, which should have caused Cole to retaliate in kind. For some odd reason though, he was even more accommodating and supportive. Even when she threw an entire tray of food on the beautiful bees waxed floor in her room, he calmly and quietly cleaned it up without so much as a harsh word. It was then that she realized the many things he had done for her and the members of her clan. *How long will his generosity last before he sends me from his home in disgust?*

Before he left the ranch, Wolf informed her that Cole made contact with a friend at the Pine Ridge Agency—the same man he spoke of when he and August first met. Beau McCabe would assist in their efforts to find the imprisoned Fawn and Whitecloud. Her three friends left the premises with additional packhorses laden with food and ammunition and extra blankets to keep them warm—all because of Cole's generosity.

Embarrassment heated her cheeks when she thought about how childishly she behaved during that first week. She was angry with Wolf for leaving her behind, and had taken out her ire on a wonderful family; a family who cared for her willingly and unselfishly.

Cole, in particular, went out of his way to help. She had asked his forgiveness on that long ago day when she threw her well-prepared dinner on the floor, and he only grinned and asked if she would like another plate of food.

He is like this day after day. He never becomes angry with me—even when I ignore him because of the way he makes me feel. Cole possesses a strange way of knowing that I need to see him and he finds me—at the exact moment I fervently hoped he would.

More often than not of late, thoughts of Cole flitted across the back of her mind during her waking hours; in fact, he rarely left her thoughts even in the shadows of her dreams. The reasons why were something she contemplated long and hard as each day passed. Their relationship, if it could be called that, was a mystery; the differences in their cultures could not be ignored; his continued kindness was almost unnerving; it all combined to baffle August.

The other members of his family walked into her room almost as frequently as he, and yet all she felt then were joy and happiness at being so accepted. *But let Cole walk through that door and my heart pounds harder and breathing is more difficult.*

Consequently, she became upset with herself because of her heated reaction to his presence and picked an argument. He, on the other hand, would simply shake off her words and act as if they never left her mouth. Cole was more generous and tolerant of her mood swings than anyone she had ever met.

The entire family treated August in the same kindly manner. Even Cole's remaining brother, Trevor, was gracious and friendly and constantly aware of her needs while she recuperated from the serious wound in her leg.

Dr. Steve and Cole's sister, Carrie, gave her a stick that they called a crutch. The instrument would enable August to move about the house, however slowly, when she finally felt up to it.

There was always a helping hand, a cool pitcher of water, or warm treats from the kitchen within her reach. August often mused about how she was left quietly to herself, or so it seemed; and then, magically, whatever she wished for turn up by her side.

Many times, those warm treats were delivered by an old black woman who lived in the house as a member of the family. August saw her for the first time shortly after Wolf's departure, when her body temperature had cooled to a near normal level. She thought she was dreaming again when the door opened and a woman with skin the color of night waddled through the opening. She balanced a tray with one hand and carried a buckskin shirt in the other. August had never seen a Negro before and could not help but stare at the other woman...

"I guess it be time for you an' me to be meetin' each other. Ma name is Mamie, and I be the one ta keep this here family from fallin' to the devil. Yessiree! It be a good thing to see ya up and not burnin' with the fires of hell."

Even though the old women shuffled slowly about the room, she somehow presented an appearance of moving quickly and efficiently. August simply tried to understand the torrent of words that tumbled from the old woman's mouth and could not help but stare with wide eyes.

"I was cookin' up some bread and mendin' your shirt, and Mamie, I thoughts to ma sef', how 'bout you go up and meet that little Injun girl now that she be better. Yessiree, that be what I thought." The odd looking woman stopped at the foot of the bed, folded her beefy arms across massive breasts, and puffed out her cheeks. "An' here I am!"

August's eyes bulged at the sight of Mamie's expanded face, and she sank deeper into the soft bed.

"What you starin' at, Injun girl? Ha! I knows! You never seen a woman like me, I bet!" Mamie let out a loud hoot from thick, smiling lips and, when she did, the body beneath her perfectly pressed gingham dress jiggled like nothing August had ever seen before. "I bet you be thinkin' that the good Lord, he just overdone me to a crisp, but I'm what you call a Negra. Yessiree, Negras are black, just like Injuns are red."

August lay stunned under the coverlet, hardly daring to breath.

Mamie placed the tray on the table and proceeded to lather a fresh slice of bread with marmalade. "Here now, sit up and let's be gettin' some meat on those puny little bones of yours."

Still awestruck, August did not dare disobey. She wiggled to a sitting position and reached for the bread with trembling hands. A wide, toothy smile spread across Mamie's dark cheeks.

From that time on, the wonderful old woman visited the patient daily with some sweet treat designed to entice August to eat. Slowly but surely, the Indian girl began to understand the strange dialect that Mamie spoke and the kindness in the black woman's heart...

The excited chatter of a squirrel brought August back to the present. She adjusted her position on the swing to ease the ache in her thigh, but refused to give in to the pain. Somewhere inside the house, Cole's sister-in-law, Emma, sang to the baby. A happy giggle of response followed a second later. August could not help the tiny smile that curved her lips as she listened to the child's delighted laughter.

Emma had also extended the hand of friendship and waited patiently for August to accept it. She did not push the young woman, however, but would spend the long days of convalescence entertaining August with stories of ranch life.

August came to adore Emma and Tyler's two older children, Janie and Thomas, who visited often while she was still bedridden. Emma would recognize the telltale signs of fatigue after a time, however, and shoo the children away. One or the other always managed to sneak back to her room though, for more of August's stories. She enjoyed their company and came to the realization that the children saw her not as an Indian, but simply as a woman being helped by their family during a time of need.

As August's strength returned slowly and she was finally able to leave the room, Emma replaced her guest's torn and bloodstained garments with articles from her own closet. August had never worn a white woman's clothes before and, though the garments felt odd against her skin, the strange material made her feel less conspicuous in the Wilkins' home. A strong bond was formed between the two women in the past weeks, and August would cherish Emma's offer of friendship for the rest of her life.

The front door opened to her left and interrupted August's thoughts. She turned her head and watched silently as Cole stepped onto the porch. An instant smile tugged at the corners of his lips when he spied her. He crossed the wooden planking to sit beside her and clasped her hands in his. *He is so powerful, his body so big, yet he is gentle at every turn.*

"I thought I'd check and see if you needed anything. You've been out here for quite awhile."

August glanced sidelong at Cole and, raising her chin a notch, the words erupted from her mouth before she could stop them. "Do you not have other things to do? It would seem that, as a man, you should have many jobs to take care of in a day. You spend too much time seeing to my needs. Do your brothers not mind when you act like an old woman?"

August was immediately apologetic—if only to herself. *Why do I speak to him this way? Why is it that I feel I must spar with him every time he opens his mouth? I should be ashamed; he has done many wonderful things for me.* She raised an eyebrow in surprise when his head fell back and a chuckle bubbled in his throat.

"Ah, August, you make my day. Are we always going to banter back and forth before we finally settle in and have a decent conversation?"

"You are doing it again." She frowned.

"Doing what?"

"What does *banter* mean? You always speak in riddles."

He took her hand and wrapped it within his large palm, and August's stomach jumped. She pushed the sensation away. Her gaze met his again and she saw no animosity in the hazel depths. Once again, her spiked words caused only a disarming grin that spread across his chiseled features—a grin that was fast becoming a cherished part of his personality.

"What I mean is that our conversations always start out like this—you snap at me, I laugh or blow it off, and once we get that out of the way, we move into what I like to think is a talk between two friends. If it offends you when I use words you can't understand, then I'm sorry. I'll try not to do that anymore." He tipped his head again, until he was able to look down at her. "Am I forgiven?"

August did not answer immediately; she withdrew her hand, crossed her arms over her midsection and stared across the yard with her nose in the air.

Finding her haughty actions amusing, Cole gently bumped her shoulder with his to get a response. "Am I?"

She ignored him.

He bumped her again.

A smile tugged at the corners of August's mouth.

"Is that forgiveness I see on your face?"

She gave in, nodded her head, and released a contrite sigh through her smile. "Do you not ever get angry, Cole Wilkins? It is I who should seek forgiveness from you. I do not know why I speak to you the way I do. I think it comes from the time you held me prisoner and played the word games. I remember being very annoyed with you." August shrugged her slim shoulders; her grin disappeared. "You and your family have been very kind. It makes me feel unworthy. I will try to do better and remember that kindness."

Cole held his silence as he watched August's yearning gaze return to the pines that edged the yard. Sadness replaced the remorse on her face before her mouth opened and soft words tumbled out.

"Where do you think they are?"

He knew exactly who she was talking about and, when her simple 'breath of fresh air' turned into hours alone on the porch, he assumed that she was thinking of Wolf and the others. She also dwelled on what the future would bring and, in his opinion, she dwelt on it too much. Hence, one of his reasons for interrupting her. The idea that August was lonesome for her own kind tore at Cole's heart; everything that was familiar to her was gone, and he only wanted to ease her time spent at the ranch.

The fact that she continually lived in his thoughts did not help matters, either. Cole was unable to concentrate on his daily routine any longer; frustration would finally cause him to simply forget the task at hand and seek her out. He was doing a lot of that lately...

"I'm sure we'll be hearing from Beau soon," Cole said, the realization that he was somewhat obsessed with August causing him to jump back to the present. "I would imagine that Wolf is being very careful. He'll make contact with my friend, and I know Beau will do everything in his power to help. Apparently, two prisoners were brought into the agency not long ago and sent south by rail. Beau thinks they might have been Fawn and Whitecloud. That's more information than Wolf would've had if he'd struck out on his own. We just have to wait and hope that they'll be found."

"I pray you are right. It is so hard to be here where it is safe, when Wolf and the others have put themselves in so much danger." Visions of the morning raid invaded her brain with a vengeance, and August pushed them away just as strongly. The waves of weariness that followed could not be ignored, however, and she suddenly felt the need to lie down. Sometimes, the blackness of sleep helped her to escape the horrific decimation of her family.

Cole gently clasped her hand again to lend comfort, then gave it a squeeze.

August's mind clamored for an excuse; *any* excuse that would allow her to escape the warm, tingling sensation his tender touch caused within her body. "I think I will rest for a time. I cannot seem to keep my eyes open."

She pulled her hand from beneath his and rose quickly, then fumbled to get the crutch positioned under her arm. The abrupt movement caused her head to swim with dizziness, however, and she swayed slightly. Cole bounded to his feet and, his hands on her upper arms, steadied her before she fell. Without so much as a word, he scooped her into his arms and the crutch clattered to the wooden planking.

August's earlier fatigue was suddenly forgotten when she found herself wrapped in his comforting embrace. The mere feel of his arms around her heated the blood in her veins. His face was only inches away; his warm breath fanned her ear. August's dark gaze scanned the firm lines of his stubbled jaw, and she fought the urge to reach up and caress the course hair—a fascinating phenomenon she had never witnessed on a man of her own race. Instead, she firmly grasped his shoulders in an attempt to keep her hands from following the same path as her eyes. The need to touch him was like nothing she had ever encountered in her life.

Cole experienced the same emotions and fought just as madly to hide them. Cradling her against his chest, his heart pounded with the same protectiveness he felt the night he gently tucked her feverish, wounded body into the wagon bed. His breath caught in his throat when he glanced down at the smoky brown eyes that peered deeply into his own.

A blazing aura of utter fulfillment stunned him; a sense that he was standing exactly where he should be combined with the knowledge that nothing would ever match the moment at hand. The color of their skin held no importance and circumstances meant nothing. It was just a small, perfect flicker in time, where there was only the two of them without the outside world and its biases intruding.

The fretful agitation he experienced before August came back into his life melted away—*and she's the cause*...The realization hit him so hard that he was amazed he did not discover it earlier. Since August re-entered his world, Cole greeted each morning with fervent anticipation of the day and a completeness he had never felt before. She was what he had searched for; it was this moment, it was this woman in his arms, it was as if he had finally come home.

How will she react if I tell her? She had spent her entire life hating the white man and what his kind did to hers; she detested the color of his skin and what it stood for. *Will she ever be able to get past that? And what if Wolf never returns for her?* The proud Sioux brave stated that August would never take a man to her side, but that was a lifetime ago. So many things had changed since then. The future did not look bright for the Sioux who were still on the run.

Cole blinked back to awareness and tightened his grasp on the woman in his arms. He needed to think through his emotions; to decide what he wanted and if it was right for both of them. He inhaled deeply and stared into the distance for a moment longer. He cleared his throat finally, breaking the uncomfortable silence, and muttered what he hoped was a plausible excuse as to why he held her in his arms.

"You scared me. I thought you were going to fall and hurt your leg again."

"But I did not." She stiffened in his arms. "I am well enough to walk to my room if you will simply help me with the crutch. I am not a child to be coddled."

She needed to be out of his arms, and she needed it now. Only then would she be in control of the sensations that coursed through her. August had no idea where the feelings came from; she knew only that she needed to be alone to sift through each one separately.

Cole was not yet ready to let her go. "Look, August, let's not start with the spiteful words again—the banter. I'll just carry you back upstairs, so you don't put any more strain on the leg. You can rest then; I saw how tired you looked a moment ago, so don't argue with me. Okay?"

She stared into his almost pleading gaze and, tossing caution to the wind, allowed a gentle smile to widen her mouth—one that was so close to his. "If 'okay' means 'yes', then I will let you carry me. Okay, Cole Wilkins, I will let you win the battle this one time."

Chapter Twelve

Wolf and his companions sat cross-legged around the perimeter of a small fire and listened to an old friend tell them of Beau McCabe. Little Fox now resided on the outskirts of the Pine Ridge Agency; the three travelers met the middle-aged brave at tribal council years before. Wolf had listened quietly up to this point, amazed at the change in the man. At one time, Little Fox was broad of chest, with flowing black hair. He was afraid of no one. Now, graying hair and bowed stature reminded Wolf of a frightened old man.

Out of respect for the former warrior, he did not interrupt when Little Fox expressed his reluctance to become involved. It was when he suggested that they enter the headquarters area and search for Cole's friend that Wolf leapt up from the circle of light.

"No!" His hand sliced through the cool night air. "We will not go in. McCabe must come to us! You must see to this, Little Fox. I will not be tricked into becoming a prisoner, because the soldiers think I am a hostile."

Little Fox shook his head at the other man's temper. "McCabe will not turn you in. He will help you. He is not like the others. He helps our people. I would not lie to you, Wolf. He and the white doctor have made our lives tolerable."

"Bring McCabe to us." Wolf stood firm.

"If it is discovered that I spoke to McCabe on your behalf, my family will be removed from our home. They will say I helped the others to escape." Little Fox stood and paced back and forth before the fire. "Life at the agency is much better than our existence when we were trying to outrun the soldiers."

Wolf scoffed at the idea. "Can you honestly say that you would miss being under the hand of the white man?"

"At least the government goods reach our hands at Pine Ridge. McCabe and the doctor have made it so. Food is not so plentiful at the other agencies. If you do not believe me, then travel to Standing Rock and speak with your cousin. Big Foot's people are slowly starving."

Wolf stomped from the fire with the image of his cousin imprinted in his mind. Chief Big Foot was once considered a great and powerful man. He watched over his tribe with the eye of a concerned father and welcomed any Sioux fugitives to his camp. *What has happened? It has been four winters since I last visited him. At that time, he spoke of overcoming the enemy and of how the Sioux would become strong again. Instead, they grow weaker and weaker as time passes.* He whirled and retraced his steps to the fire and the small group of men who huddled there. His fierce gaze fell on Little Fox.

"Why are you not fighting? Why have you all given up hope?"

"At one time, we were able to kill them." Little Fox sighed his defeat. "Now they are too many. They multiply as fast as the weeds in a garden. The white man is here to stay, Wolf, and that is a truth we must live by—even if it is hard to accept."

Little Fox did his best to maintain a semblance of the 'beaten Indian' when in the presence of the army. He would pick up the facade once more when he left Wolf and the others to return home. If any of the commanders knew he left the agency without permission, a severe reprimand would follow. It was only by chance that he happened upon Wolf when he did. If he did not return by the time the sun came up, not only he, but his wife and child, would pay for his indiscretion. Tensions were escalating between the two factions.

Little Fox rose to face Wolf. "You said McCabe knows of your coming. You said a white man assured you that he will help you, and this white man was right. Telling you this is all I can do. I must return to the agency soon or I will become one of the prisoners and be shipped away on the Iron Horse. I will not bring harm to my family by involving myself further—I cannot help you."

Wolf glared at Little Fox with disgust shining in his eyes. It was as if the man was afraid of the dark. The soldiers had done this to him, and Wolf vowed silently to never become the shadow of a man his old friend now was. "You are no more than a prisoner now, no matter what you choose to believe. What has happened to all of you?"

Little Fox clenched his fists. "You have not lived the life I have, Wolf.

You chose to run years ago and are still running. I chose to live in peace with my family. If I can do this only by the white man's dictates, then so be it. My family is tired and will not be pursued any longer. The food they give us is not good, but it is food. My wife and I surrendered in order that we may stay together and not see our child starve. There is not enough wild game to feed us." He spread his hands wide. "It is over, Wolf. It will be only a matter of time before you understand that."

"I will never give up! I will find my father and Two Feathers' wife. We will leave this land and travel far to the north, where there are no white dogs biting at our heels. Someday you will tell this story to your grandchildren and know that I never gave in, never let them defeat me. Our people will become strong in the north and no one will ever be able to take our land from us again!"

Wolf's impassioned speech caused Little Fox to wonder if the Sioux could regain their strength—if only momentarily. Their past life was a world away. His beaten gaze found the angry warrior once more. *Let him think what he must.*

"For our own kind, I hope your words come true. I will fight no longer. I have lost two children to the soldiers and will not allow my last to suffer the same fate." As Little Fox spoke the words, a small part of him wished he could gather the remnants of his family and ride north to freedom. Deep in his heart though, he knew he would never do it. They had endured too much already. Running now would only delay the inevitable. "The white man took our way of life from us, Wolf. For some reason, our gods have forsaken the people, never to return again—unless you are foolish enough to believe in the Ghost Dance. For me and my family, it is over."

"The Ghost Dance is not foolish! It is the only way we will ever reclaim what is ours!" Wolf raised a muscled arm and pointed across the flames. "There are those who say it is only a matter of time before the white pests disappear, never to be seen again. The plains will become brown again with the color of buffalo. It is the reason we must build our forces and become strong. When our call comes, we must be ready."

Little Fox only shook his head. "I will not fight the battle. I have my wife and child with me, and they are all I care about.

Two Feathers had listened quietly to the argument, but now raised his voice to be heard. "Little Fox, I will ask you one more time for your help. I ask you to do this so that I, too, may have the chance to find my wife. The soldiers took everything from me; they kidnapped my wife and killed my daughter. A life in the north is the only thing left for us. This is my decision, as it is your decision to remain at the agency. Will you help me, my brother, and tell McCabe that we wait for him? I have lost my only child; I do not wish to lose Fawn."

The mention of Two Feathers' daughter is what finally swayed Little Fox's thinking. He did what was required to save his last child; he gave up the freedom that his ancestors enjoyed. He could not expect Two Feathers to do less than was necessary to save his wife, no matter what direction the result might take him in. His gaze moved from Two Feathers to the very quiet Walking Bear before finally resting on Wolf's grim features again.

"I will do this for you. I will tell McCabe to meet you here and, hopefully, he will not ask how I know that you wait for him."

* * *

Anna set a serving dish mounded with scrambled eggs and thick chunks of smoked ham on the kitchen table.

Beau's eyebrows lifted in anticipation as he stared at the steaming platter. "You keep feeding me like this, Anna, and I'm not going to fit through the door much longer."

She laughed and took a seat beside her smiling husband as Beau scooped a hearty portion onto his plate. "You just eat and remember the times on the trail when a loaf of bread was the only thing you had."

Beau needed no convincing. He dug in and events at Pine Ridge became the main topic of the breakfast conversation at the Gatewoods.

Beau was filling his plate for a second time when a knock on the back door brought Anna to her feet.

"I'll get it." She crossed the kitchen, opened the door, and greeted the man on the porch with a welcoming smile. "Little Fox. I'm surprised to see you here this early. What can I do for you?"

The man's gaze darted nervously over her shoulder and into the kitchen. Seeing only Michael and Beau, his black eyes settled again on the woman in the doorway. Anna's brow wrinkled with apprehension when she sensed the Indian's discomfort.

"I was asked to bring a message. There are those who wait for Beau

McCabe. He is to go to Eagle Ridge and wait by a fire pit. That is all I know." Little Fox turned then, and hurried from the porch.

"Wait!" Anna called out to his retreating back. "Who is waiting for him?"

Little Fox glanced over his shoulder, shook his gray head, and continued down the dusty road. She watched after him for a moment, shut the door, and turned with a puzzled expression marring her brow.

"What do you think that was all about?"

"Sit down, Anna." Michael pulled out her chair. "Beau and I have been waiting for a message. I think we just received it."

Anna crossed back to the table and sat down with a wary stare. "What's going on, Michael? What kind of message have you been waiting for?"

"Michael hasn't been waiting for anything—I have." Beau leaned forward. "A friend of mine from Minnesota contacted me a few weeks back. Judging by the telegrams he sent, he's helping some friends search for two Sioux prisoners who might have come through here a while back—a woman and an old man."

Anna's eyes widened with recognition, and Beau realized at that moment that she knew exactly who he was talking about. "The day of Bingham's raid..." she breathed. "He brought in the only two survivors of a raid in Minnesota. It's them, isn't it?" She swiveled in the chair and looked at her husband with a fair amount of building exasperation. "Who's looking for them? Why has this been such a big secret?"

Michael set his mug of coffee on the table before him and met her questioning stare. "Because we're not sure who Beau is supposed to meet. His friend was very secretive. He sent three separate telegrams, and Beau had to read between the lines. For some reason—and we don't know what it is—his friend didn't want to give away the identity of exactly who he was supposed to meet. He said only that Beau would be contacted when they arrived. We didn't tell you because we weren't too sure of anything. He and I are going—"

"*I'm* going," Beau interjected.

"I'll ride with you, Beau."

"No, you won't. I don't want either you or Anna involved until I know exactly what's going on. Michael, you're still in the service and treason could become an issue if I'm reading everything right. For some reason, Cole didn't even want *me* to know all the facts. He seemed pretty hesitant to put all the details in a telegram that someone else might read."

"Who's Cole?" Anna asked through tight lips.

"He's the friend from Minnesota that I was telling you about. We grew up together. I lost contact with him though, when I left for West Point. I ran into him last month, when I was on the road. He and his brothers used to own a logging company north of Duluth."

"I remember you talking about running across an old friend, but you never said where he was from," Anna replied slowly, suddenly lost in conflicting thoughts of her own. "Was he the person who rode with you for a few days?" She rose from the chair to add wood to the cook stove as she waited for his answer.

"One and the same. I was surprised when I met up with him. Hell, it was like pulling teeth to get him off that damn ranch when we were younger. To come across him in a hotel dining room in the middle of nowhere—" Beau shook his head "—especially after all these years, was quite a coincidence. Cole and his brothers, Trevor and Tyler, sold the logging company and started breeding horses for sale as riding stock. He was delivering a couple out toward Fargo somewhere."

Suddenly, Beau's eyes lit with comprehension. "That's it! I told him about what I do for a living—told him if he ever needed to get a hold of me, to try here or in St. Paul. This whole thing must have to do with some Indians he ran into on the trail home. Somehow, he must be connected to the two prisoners Bingham hauled in." Beau rose from his chair, grabbed his near empty cup of coffee, and tossed the warm liquid down in one swallow. "I'm gonna head out there right now."

Anna moved to lay a hand on his forearm. "Do you think you should go alone? Wouldn't it be better to take Michael with you? Do you think this Cole will be waiting up on the Ridge?"

Beau heard the concern in her voice and patted her hand. "I don't know, Anna. It would be nice if he was here, too, to explain everything."

"Do you think it's wise to go by yourself, Beau?" Michael, too, was worried about his friend.

Beau did not offer Anna a response, but turned his gaze back to her husband. "I know you want to come with me, but I don't think it would be wise. Cole would never put me in physical danger, and I don't want either of you in trouble with the agency."

"I guess Beau's right, honey." Michael placed an arm around his troubled wife's shoulders. "He'll be fine."

"If your friend is here in South Dakota, will you bring him back with you?" Anna's face had paled to an ashen hue.

"Of course he will, Anna. You can't expect the man to stay out in the woods." Michael looked at her closely. "Are you trembling?"

Anna clasped her hands before her and took a deep breath. "I'll be fine...I'm simply concerned for Beau's safety." She lifted her eyes and looked at the other man. "Will you be long?"

"I don't know, Anna. We'll just have to see how this whole thing plays out."

The doctor looked at his friend. "We'll be waiting to hear from you, and be sure you watch your back. If there's anything we can do for your friend, just let us know."

* * *

Beau reached the end of the trail that led into a small clearing in the pines. His blue eyes settled on the remains of a small campfire; it was there that Little Fox told him to wait. The meeting would take place whenever Cole's people decided to present themselves. He was anxious to discover the entire story and the reason for all the secrecy. It had already been four hours since he left Michael and Anna's house and his curiosity was getting the best of him.

He reined in his horse, dismounted, and walked to the cold fire pit. Kicking aimlessly at a charred log, his eyes systematically searched the area around him. A bird's cry broke the eerie silence and, a second later, the hair rose on the back of his neck.

Someone watched him. A sixth sense honed from his years in the Cavalry and all the time spent on the trail alone, alerted him to another's presence. His intuition had never failed him, and he listened closely to it now. The person he waited for was just beyond the thick circle of pines.

He turned, and shielding his eyes from the bright sun, observed the majestic Black Hills set against a clear horizon. *Those hills are the Sioux's sacred ground. Somehow, they're tied to this whole thing.* The ground on which he stood belonged to the Indian; few white men dared to pass through the area. *A perfect place to have a secret meeting. Damn, I wish they'd show...*

* * *

Wolf's heart skipped a beat. He watched from the thick mantle of pines as the man dismounted and moved to the remains of the previous night's fire. His quiet observation brought back memories of a time spent within the confines of a white man's world.

He knew this man. It had been many years since their paths crossed and, even though McCabe was more filled out than the last time they were together, Wolf would never forget the face of the enemy.

Those were the times when the Sioux were hungry and beaten; their pride had been stolen from them. The memory returned as clearly as if it happened yesterday. Wolf would never forget the time spent at Camp Robinson and the awful days that followed; days when the Indians were driven eastward like cattle, farther from their home and farther from anything else familiar. McCabe never took part in stripping them of everything honorable, nor was he involved in the rape of their women or the death of their old ones, but he was still a soldier of the white man's government.

Wolf's faith in Cole faltered; his faith in Little Fox faltered. Suddenly, he was not so sure that he and his companions should make themselves known.

He motioned silently to his Sioux brothers, and they slithered quietly away from the edge of the trees. The three whispered softly once they were far enough away to speak and not be heard.

"What is it?" Walking Bear's brow furrowed in confusion. He had seen the change on Wolf's face. "Why have we not approached McCabe?"

"I know this man and cannot decide if we should trust him."

"How do you know him?" Two Feathers asked impatiently. "We must decide what to do. He will not wait much longer."

"Do neither of you not recognize him? He was at Camp Robinson. He was the lieutenant who led us east, just before we escaped many years ago."

"Cole said he is to be trusted." Two Feathers straightened to his full height. "I will meet with him and the two of you will stay behind. It is my wife we search for—"

"And my father," Wolf interrupted. A decision must be made. He wearily rubbed his forehead, confusion and uncertainty darkening his. His broad shoulders dropped with a sigh and his chin found his chest. A moment later, he raised his eyes. "We will do this together or we will not do it at all. I will abide by your decision." He waited as the other men exchanged surprised glances.

"We will meet with him," Two Feathers said, his tone filled with decisiveness. "We have trusted Cole enough to leave one of our own with him. Therefore, we must trust Cole's friend."

Wolf nodded, though uncertainty still clouded his eyes. He joined his companions as they crept back down the barely discernable path that led to the campsite.

* * *

Beau blinked when the warriors stepped into the sunlight; he had to assure himself that they were real. He had not detected a single sound—and he had listened closely. Though he knew he had been probably watched from the time he entered the clearing, the stealth with which the Indians moved still amazed him.

The four men stared at one another as each sized up his opponent. Beau was not foolish enough to make a move in their direction. He would wait until they decided to speak.

The tallest of the braves stepped forward. Beau eyed his powerful chest; he would not stand a chance if the man should decide to take him down. His eyes followed the movement of the brave's hand as it settled on the hilt of the knife that hung from his side.

"You are McCabe?"

"Yes. I'm Cole's friend. He's sent you to me for help. If I can, I promise to do that, but you need to explain what has happened and why you're here."

The large Indian before him was not convinced yet.

"You are alone?"

Beau lifted his arms to indicate the barren area around him. "It's just me."

"Sit then, and we will tell you our story."

* * *

Anna paced the confines of the small kitchen. She stopped often to peer through the window, wring her hands, and open the door to search the wide dusty landscape in search of Beau's return.

"Sit down, Anna. Beau will be fine. He knows what he's doing. He hasn't stayed alive this long by being stupid."

"But he's been gone all day. It'll be dark soon." She glanced out the window again. "Do you think his friend, Cole, is with him?" She turned to her husband with a pleading look in her troubled gaze. "Do you think we should get help and go looking for him?"

Michael rose from the settee and gathered his wife into his arms. "Anna, calm down. I don't know what's going on out there. Maybe his friend did come along and they're discussing the entire mess—whatever it is. Think about it. If we left now and were discovered, we'd put ourselves in jeopardy for not saying anything earlier—and when Beau comes back, he'd be fit to be tied that we took the chance of getting all of us in trouble. He's probably just waiting for the cover of darkness before returning. Let's give him some more time."

She laid her forehead against his hard chest, listened to the calming beat of his heart, and sighed audibly. The moment was the culmination of an exhausting and emotional twelve hours. Anna had been as nervous as a cat since Beau left for Eagle Ridge.

I wish this day could start over...

That morning before leaving for the clandestine meeting, Beau relayed tales of growing up in Minnesota—things he had never spoken of before. He went into more detail about his friendship with Cole Wilkins and about the man in general, but Anna did not need to imagine what Beau's friend was like. She knew of his strong character and the loyalty to family that this man carried within him at all times. The description of the area where Beau and Cole once lived was also not unknown to her.

She also knew details about the man that Michael, and even Beau, did not—intimate details; she knew what his sandy-colored hair looked like against a stark white pillow case; she knew how he could run his fingers lightly up and down her spine and coax a thrilled response from her body; she knew that his hazel eyes turned smoky after making love...

Yes, Anna knew Cole Wilkins. She knew him from another life. He knew her as 'Belle', Madam of her own 'house' in Duluth. Now, that other life, a life she had tried so desperately to keep in the past, had crept into the present to rear its ugly head once more.

Belle, or rather, Annabelle, was a person she had not thought of in a long time. She clung to her husband now in desperation, frightened of what the future would bring. Cole Wilkins was a part of her past; he had been her lover at one time, but that was all. In fact, he was the only man who ever treated her like a lady during those long forgotten years. He would visit her establishment, and they would spend glorious hours making love without the green head of jealousy hanging over them. They belonged to one another, yet they did not. Their times together were always happy, but each knew it would never be a permanent arrangement.

She was the one who finally ended their strange relationship. She added the money from the sale of her business to the cash she had saved through the years and left Duluth in search of something more. Cole begged her to tell him where she was going, but 'Belle' steadfastly refused. Cole was the one man she loved enough to leave.

Anna wished Cole only the best. Eventually, he would find a woman who was much more acceptable in the eyes of society and begin a life that excluded her. He did not understand his own destiny back then, but 'Belle' did. Cole had much to offer some lucky woman one day, and their attachment could have ended no other way.

Now, Cole Wilkins loomed on the horizon and, at any moment, he could follow Beau McCabe into her home. Would he understand that she loved Michael now, and that she had left her past life in Minnesota? Would he understand that 'Belle' died when Anna emerged? If not, did Michael love her enough to ignore her past?

Anna hoped she never had to find out—hopefully, Cole had remained in Minnesota. *It has to be...otherwise he would have come to the house to find Beau. Cole would have no reason to hide in the woods...* She felt beads of perspiration trickle between her shoulder blades as she swallowed back the fear of discovery and the urge to simply faint and never wake up. It was very well possible that this day would be the last happy one with her husband...

Enveloped within her husband's strong arms, Anna tightened her grasp around his waist. Fate had led her to Michael. She fell in love for the second and last time in her life, but did not have a clue how she could forestall the coming night. "Michael...I love you so much."

He gave Anna a quick hug, but peeled her arms from around his waist and peered closely into her white face. "What is going on? I've never seen you so upset, and we've been through far worse. You act like I'm the one who is in danger, not Beau—or his friend, Cole."

Anna's heart jumped crazily when her husband breathed her ex-lover's name. She needed to gather her wits about her before Michael became suspicious. "I just..." She glanced around the room before looking back up into his handsome face. "I just wish Beau would come back. I wish he wasn't involved in whatever he's doing up there."

Chapter Thirteen

August sat on the front porch swing and gazed out at the changing season around her. Since that first night three weeks earlier when she had finally found the strength to leave her room, the quiet spot had offered a foundation of solace. Green leaves had quickly turned to burnished reds, bright oranges, and numerous shades of yellow. Normally at this time of the year, the band would be on their way to their winter home in the mountains of what the white man called Canada. Not this year, though; possibly not even the next. *Who would I travel with? There is no one left.*

Despite her good health now, due to the concerned care given by Cole's family, a rush of despair raced its way through her heart. She could probably make the trek north by herself—if she left soon. When her mind was willing to meet the reality of her situation though, the thought of leaving these people she had come to respect struck another chord of sadness and loss. August covered her face with her hands and stifled the silent scream within her.

Wolf will never return in time for us to travel north; he would have to return sometime in the next week. No matter though; the time of year would not make a difference as far as her old friend was concerned. *Wolf will insist on leaving Cole's home immediately.*

We have no food or shelter to prepare us for winter. Where will we go when he does arrive–if he arrives? And if he does—do I really want to leave? I am caught between two worlds. One, which tugged at everything familiar to her and another that pulled at her heartstrings.

Cole...

August had never felt even a twinge of desire to share a man's life. She mapped out her future long ago—one that would help her people retain the old ways. She had continually fought for something her father believed in deeply. Her dedication to the Sioux was something she had firmly clung to since her vision on that long ago day.

Cole...

August rubbed her arms against the slight chill in the air and blinked back tears that suddenly appeared from nowhere. Now, her quest to hold tight to the Sioux world of old did not seem as important as it once did; because of a single white man, her life purpose was changing. *Living within your home and seeing you every day is pushing everything else away. I never thought our paths would cross again.*

August fought it daily, the feeling of...*what?* She had tried to capture the elusive sensation over the last few weeks; to identify it—an emotion that angered her; that brought the weight of shame to her shoulders; that made her forget what she had always believed in. *All thoughts race from my mind when I see him approach. He walks with an easy swing of his hips—the small line in his chin deepens when he smiles. He even invades my restless sleep in the dark of the night...*

August's thoughts spun backward to days earlier, when she and Cole sat by a meandering river a few miles from the ranch. They discussed his brother's children and their infatuation with August. Suddenly, Cole surprised her with words that August needed to forget...

"You know, August, you don't have to leave when Wolf returns. You'll always be welcome on the ranch. The children would miss you if you left."

She glanced at him with wide eyes. It was the first time he had said anything about the future, beyond the next few hours or days. Her stomach jumped. The thought of never leaving the safety of the ranch, of always being under the mantle of Cole's protection was inviting. He would make staying too easy—and she could not give him the opportunity. August's jumbled brain searched for a way to distance herself from the man who was becoming far too important in her life. The feminine line of her delicate jaw hardened in defense.

"I should stay because some white man's children would miss me?" She knew it was a cruel thing to say after the abounding generosity his entire family had shown her, but speaking the words somehow helped August to create the charm she sought; something that was more difficult to do with each day that passed.

Cole leaned back and stared down at her in amazement. A split-second later, the first dregs of anger sparked in his darkening hazel eyes. "Why do you constantly throw the color of my family's skin in my face? Dammit, August, they're the ones who nursed you when you were sick. They treat you with kindness and respect and make you feel comfortable in their home. What is it with you anyway?" Cole stood abruptly, shook his head when he glanced at her again, then marched to stand a few steps away. His face was red with agitation, and his fists clenched with ire.

The instant change in his temperament frightened her. Cole had never shown so much as a hint of anger since she arrived at his home and now, because she refused to stay and become a part of the white man's world, he chose to *remind* her of the generosity of his family—a fact that she was well aware of. A twinge of ungratefulness pricked at her conscience, and she fought the urge to slip her arms around his broad chest in apology. Somewhere in the back of her mind, she knew where it would lead.

August had been with a man before; all of the Indian women who were held prisoner by the enemy were forced to use their bodies to survive. She was innocent of real love though, and was hesitant to explore that realm with a white man—even if that white man was Cole Wilkins. She observed his stiff back and, steeling herself against the warring emotions in her heart, plunged forward—it was the only way to keep him at arm's length.

"I say the things that I do because it is true! We are too different. Even you must admit that, Cole. It would not be long before the soldiers came and took me away. I am what those stupid men call a hostile."

She bounded to her feet as fast as her injured leg would allow, felt the heat of passion trace its way through her veins, and gathered the confidence that kept her from apologizing—anything to keep her newfound emotions hidden. "What is a hostile, Cole? You tell me what you think the word means."

He kept his gaze trained on the trickling current before him and refused to answer. His rebuff spurred August on.

"I asked Emma to explain it to me, and I did not like what she said. I run from the soldiers, but does that make me a murderer? Does that make me someone to be frightened of? That is what the rest of your race thinks."

Cole still kept his rigid back to her. August became immediately incensed, grabbed his arm, and hauled him around to face her. The sudden hot anger born from her conflicting emotions overruled a cool head.

"Tell me, Cole, does the color of my skin frighten you? Am I less a person because of it?"

He closed his anguish-filled eyes and turned his head away, refusing to say something he would be unable to take back.

Seeing the pain in his averted gaze, August relented slightly. He had done nothing to cause her heartache. She stood firm in her resolve though, but gained control of her own anger before speaking aloud again. She drew a deep cleansing breath to clear her head.

"Do you not think I am grateful for the friendship you have all shown or for the many things you have done for me? I appreciated the gifts you gave to my family and the medicine to make me better when I was sick." The words rolled quickly off her tongue. "Do you not understand how much I have come to care for all of you?"

Cole's head snapped in her direction, and the look of yearning in his eyes was enough to make August stumble back. Her brain was a jumble of emotions again, but she drew in another deep breath and continued. She lifted her hand and rested the palm against her heaving chest.

"Do you know how hard the past years have been for me? My life is slowly being destroyed, and there is nothing I can do about it."

"Yes you can!" His silence was finally broken. "You can be proud of who you are and accept the difference in our colors for what it is. You can let me help you. We can figure this out, August. What if Wolf never returns? What will you do then? You have nothing to go back to!" He ran a hand through his sandy-colored hair before meeting her gaze once more. "I just wanted you to know that you'll always be welcome here. I'm sorry I got angry with you. I don't want to quarrel, August, but you need to understand that you have other options."

Cole's conflicted gaze darted about their surroundings—his internal struggle was evident. "Do you understand that I would protect you from those who would do you harm—that I would always watch over you?"

That was the exact moment when August became truly frightened. It was then that she realized how easy it would be to just let him take care of her and stop the constant running. She could give up her past life; she understood now that her people would never be strong like in the years before she was born, but that was not supposed to be her destiny. The vision had shown her that.

With chaotic emotions churning her insides, August turned and limped to her horse without another word...

August whirled from the porch. The swing no longer offered the comfort she sought and, ignoring the spasm of pain that shot up her thigh, she moved clumsily down the steps and strode out into the yard as quickly as her injured leg would allow.

"Grandmother," she muttered her desperation and clasped the oilskin bag with a shaking hand, "tell me what I am to do. Tell me what is right."

Overhead, wild geese flew in a 'V.' Their melancholy honks made her realize that time was running out. The grand birds had begun the long journey to their yearly wintering grounds, and she would be left behind to face an uncertain fate.

"Wolf, please come back..." The plea came from her very soul. "Come for me before it is too late. He takes my heart, holds it in his hand, and does not even realize it."

She hurried her pace to the edge of the trees, hoping to find comfort and strength within their towering silence.

* * *

Cole kneed Joe in the ribs and urged the animal from a trot into a canter. He was returning from Morrell, a small town an hour east of the ranch. A sun-browned hand patted the front pocket of his shirt in an effort to assure himself once more that the telegraph was still there.

Cole now knew for a fact that Wolf had made contact with Beau. The small group was already on their way to Fort Robinson and, with any luck, Two Feathers' wife and Wolf's father would soon be free. He was anxious to reach the ranch and inform August. Her spirits had been so low lately, and the telegram might be the one thing that would make her smile again.

He was aware, however, that, no matter how he looked at it, the end result would not be good—at least not for him. Whether Wolf found his father or not, he would return for August one day, and she would leave with him. It was a day he did not look forward to.

As each week passed, and she became more and more ensconced in his world, Cole became more certain of the fact that August was the one thing that had been missing in his life. He would enter a room and, if she was there, the light was suddenly brighter. It now felt completely natural to check in with her during the day, simply to see what she was doing. He had managed more than once to coax her into a ride across the endless acres that comprised the Wilkins' ranch, or to visit his sister's clinic a few miles away. The two of them had found a comfort level of familiarity he had never experienced with another.

Cole spent many hours a day scrutinizing their relationship. Their conversations always started out the same way; he somehow managed to anger her, she would respond in kind and then, suddenly, he would see the forgiveness in her eyes. That was the moment he liked best—when the deep brown depths turned smoky and her tawny lips curved upward ever so slightly. Cole's insides jumped just thinking about it.

I'm falling in love and there isn't a damn thing I can do about it—and the only thing I can foresee is misery. How in the hell can anything ever come of this?

August had slipped into his heart before he even realized he had opened the door. He also came to the realization that he had subconsciously tried to think of ways to keep her at the ranch. *Somehow, I have to figure out a way for her to stay—or figure out a way to fight the misery when she leaves...*

Wolf had told him in no uncertain terms that August would never accept a man in her life. *She'll leave the ranch with him, because Wolf can provide everything that's familiar to her. I'm only fooling myself if I think mere friendship could be enough to make her to say goodbye to the only life she's ever known.* He removed his hat and ran a shaky hand through his hair. *Christ, I don't want her to stay at the ranch simply as my friend...*

He wanted her. He wanted her as a man wants a woman; he wanted to feel the heat of her skin against his when he awoke in the morning; he wanted to grow old with her...

Cole jerked hard on the reins and Joe came to a prancing halt. He stared dumbstruck across the field and watched as the autumn wildflowers moved in waves, dancing in the wind.

The impact of his thoughts struck him like a powerful fist in the belly. It was true. He wanted to spend the rest of his life with August. The color of her beautiful skin did not matter; her past life did not matter. He would be proud to have her by his side, and to hell with what anyone might think.

Cole set his Stetson firmly on his head, adjusted the brim, and spurred the horse forward again. He had no doubt that his entire family would accept

August as his wife. *But how in the hell am I going to get her to believe it?* He would simply have to find a way; the alternative was unimaginable. He had finally found her, and he would do everything in his power to keep her. Somehow, they had connected across the barriers that separated their worlds, and they would continue to do so.

A sudden determination to meet each problem as it arose squared his shoulders. He would take the brunt of any difficulty; August had already endured enough pain in her lifetime.

With strength of mind and a steely determination to never let her go, Cole kicked Joe into a gallop. She would fight him the entire way, of that he was sure—she was too proud and committed to her people and their way of life to do otherwise. It mattered not that there was very little of that life left to fight for. He would tear down her defenses and make August see him in a new light. She needed to understand that their two worlds could come together, and that a love between them could be just as honorable as the life she had led thus far.

* * *

Cole pushed himself away from the table, only half-listening to Tyler and Emma's discussion about a new customer who would visit the ranch and select a few horses. At the moment, he could care less. All he could think about was August's reaction to the telegram.

Earlier, when he handed her the message and interpreted what it said, her eyes instantly lit with a happy glow. Before he knew it, she had hugged him tightly, then rushed from the front porch carrying the crumpled paper as if it were one of the greatest treasures she had ever owned. Her slim form practically skipped across the yard, and Cole's brow dipped with worry. He had to begin the battle immediately or, surely, Wolf would win. Her latest reaction proved it beyond a doubt.

August closeted herself in her room until late afternoon, and he was forced to wait to speak with her. She finally came downstairs to join the family for the evening meal, however, and he watched her closely, silently rehearsing the things he wanted to say. August, Emma, Tyler, and Cole were the only members present at the table that night, but, for the latter, the meal dragged on for an eternity. Now, with supper finished, he planned to ask August to accompany him outside, where he would create an opportunity to speak to her without interference.

Cole's plan would be put in motion shortly. He would explain his feelings—nothing so revealing as to frighten her away; just something for her to think about—something other than Wolf's return.

He pushed back his chair and stood. "August?"

She lifted her wary gaze to where he now towered over her.

"How would you like to take a little stroll before it gets too late?"

She did not respond immediately. Instead, she glanced down at the table as she rearranged her unused silverware.

"The air isn't too chilly yet—and it's a beautiful night." His gaze never left her questioning eyes when she looked up a second time.

August folded her napkin as Emma had shown her and placed the fine linen next to her empty plate. "A short walk would be fine." Her gaze scanned the room until it settled on Mamie, who stood in the doorway to the kitchen. A small smile meant only for the older woman touched her lips. "Thank you for the meal, Mamie. I will sleep well tonight." It was a ritual phrase; one she used every evening.

Mamie returned the smile. "You have a nice walk, Miss August.

She nodded at the couple across from them. "Goodnight, Emma—goodnight Tyler." August stood slowly, then crossed to her silent escort, who waited patiently near the door.

Cole placed his hand on the small of her back and guided her from the room. He lifted an eyebrow in surprise at the barely discernable jerk of her body that his touch elicited. She moved forward and out of his reach, breaking the intimate contact. It was something she had been doing a lot of late—assuring that they never physically touched.

Cole shook away his uncertainty. *You knew it would be one helluva long battle.* Without another word, the two continued across the living room and made their way outdoors.

* * *

Emma's eyes met Tyler's when the dining room door swung closed.

He shook his head in bewilderment. "What do you think is going on? I've never seen Cole so distracted."

"That's because you've never seen your brother in love." Emma rose from the chair, approached her husband from behind, and draped her arms over his broad shoulders. "My heart aches for them."

Tyler swiveled in the chair to search the green eyes above him. "Do you think she feels the same?"

"Yes, but she doesn't know it yet; or at least she hasn't admitted it." A sad smile touched her lips. "Think about it, Tyler. Life for August is so different here. I've never met such a proud woman, yet she's like a frightened child. She tries hard, but she can't hide her lack of confidence in our world. Nothing is familiar and there's no one here like her. I know she waits daily for Wolf to come, but I've also seen how she secretly watches Cole. He confuses her; in fact, he scares her to death, yet she is drawn to him...as he is to her. I think there'll be a lot of heartache for those two in the future." Emma pressed a light kiss to Tyler's rugged cheek. "Can I ask you something?"

He nodded.

"What do you think of the two of them together? Can you see August living here at the ranch with Cole? I think that's what he wants. I think he wants her no matter what the cost."

Tyler reflected on his wife's question for a few moments before reaching up to pull Emma down onto his lap. He settled her against his chest and sighed against the thick softness of her hair. "How could I not want for him to have what I have?"

Emma smiled softly at his words and placed a hand on his cheek.

"If Cole thinks it could work and he loves her, then I wish him all the happiness in the world. I think you're right though, Em. There'll be plenty of heartache to go around before this is all said and done...kind of like there was with us."

* * *

Cole watched August walk gracefully down the stairs before him and into the darkening night. His long legs easily caught up with her. He adjusted his steps to accommodate her slight limp and they fell into a leisurely, even pace that kept them side-by-side. His inner turmoil did not mirror the calm of the night and, just as he contemplated how to begin, August broke the silence. She glanced up at the starry sky and a contented sigh escaped her full lips.

"I was so frightened when Wolf first left me." She continued to walk as she spoke. She did not look at him, but was acutely aware of his every movement. "It does not seem so bad now that I know he is on his way to the

Fort to find the others."

"There was never anything to be scared of, August."

They walked on for a time in companionable silence, then Cole again spoke. "You've kept to yourself the last few weeks. It was nice seeing you smile at supper tonight. Is it just because of the telegram today, or have we finally managed to convince you that you're welcome here?"

August pondered his words as they walked. It was true that the telegram lifted her spirits tremendously, but she had not kept to herself because she was sad; she had not smiled tonight because of that single piece of paper. She enjoyed herself because, for a few short hours, she was able to put aside her panic-filled emotions—emotions that threatened to make her forget the past and allowed her to belong; to be a part of the Wilkins family.

The afterglow of those feelings still remained and, consequently, the fear of being alone with Cole retreated for a time. *I'm being as foolish and believing as a child.* August mentally shook her head at her earlier actions; not with condemnation, but more with simple admission to the comfort she had found tonight. She clasped her hands behind her back, enjoying the cool evening air on her skin.

"Your family has always been kind to me, no matter what. I will never forget that."

"And they'll never forget you. They've come to care for you deeply." He took a deep breath. "August, we need to speak of something."

She simply walked on and inhaled slowly in an attempt to retain some semblance of calm—until Cole gently captured her arm. He halted her beside him, and August stared warily into the face of her fear.

"Have you given any thought to what you'll do if Wolf doesn't return?" Cole was taken aback by the instant anger he saw in her brown eyes.

"He will return!" she cried. The tranquility of the night disappeared. "Why do you keep asking me that? He will come for me, and there will be no decision to make." August clung to the notion desperately. She had to. Once her friends returned, she would no longer have to battle conflicting emotions; needing to leave and wanting to stay. "We will go north and never come back to this place again." She yanked her arm free of his hold and turned to run.

Cole jerked her back against him, clasped her shoulders and turned her to face him. He forced her to meet his pleading gaze.

"August—"

"Release me, Cole." The determined line of her mouth tightened even further. "My friends will come for me. It will happen no other way, and then I will be gone. You and your family will not have to worry over one little red-skinned squaw any longer."

Even from her mouth, the term sounded insulting—just as she intended it to. The peaceful, friendly conversation had suddenly escalated into another battle between them.

"Why do you speak about yourself like that? Is that what you believe we think?" He fought the urge to shake her.

"I will say this only once more. Release me, or you will be sorry." Her body stiffened with the hissed ultimatum.

They were at a standoff and, finally, Cole's hands dropped to his sides. August retreated a step to hide the pounding of her heart. He reached out to gently clasp her arm again, but she deftly avoided the contact. It took every ounce of strength she possessed not to surrender to her passion. August clung to that strength now. She clawed at its surface. She prayed to the Great Spirit that he would not touch her again.

Unbridled emotions charged the air around them. Cole's fear cut him to the quick—he had just lost his chance to make her stay. He had to find some way to make her understand. His hands rose in appeal and she flinched. He took a calming breath and tried again.

"August—" he closed his eyes for a mere second to collect his thoughts "—I didn't ask you out here to battle."

"Then leave me be. I can walk by myself."

Cole clenched his teeth in an effort to maintain his patience. "I asked you out here to offer you choices for the future."

"I do not need choices. Are you white men so stupid that you cannot understand simple words?" *Do not give in!* her mind screamed.

"Goddammit, August!" The oath exploded from his lips and she jumped at the sound of his voice. "All right! Do you want to know why I asked you to come out here with me tonight? I asked you out here, because I wanted to tell you that I don't want you to leave! I can't bear the thought of never having you in my life again, August! I wasn't sure, but I hoped you might feel the same way; that maybe you thought life here with me could be acceptable to you. That's what I wanted to say!" He hollered the last mere inches from her face.

"I will not be a white man's conquest!" August yelled back. She cared not if anyone heard. "You could not possibly want me for admirable reasons! I do not believe you!"

"Then believe this."

He yanked her to his chest and his lips crashed against hers. August struggled in his arms, but he refused to let her go. Strong arms pulled her even closer and his mouth tore at her defenses; first with anger, and then with a slow pleading appeal to allow him into her life.

August could fight the war he waged no longer. The battle was lost somewhere after the first touch of his firm lips and before he drew her against his hard chest. It was August who now clung tightly to the man before her; a man who held her lovingly in his arms. It was August who returned the heated kiss with a passion that surprised them both. Clutching his broad shoulders, she pressed herself closer and gave herself fully to his firm, moist lips.

He gave—and she received. Her swollen lips searched for more—and he consented to her need. Calloused hands followed the curve of her body and pressed her closer still. Silently, they communicated their desire. They both needed this one moment, where the outside world did not intrude. They were simply a man and a woman; no past, no future—just the present...

August felt Cole's desire, hard and insistent against her hips, and reason returned with a vengeance. She tried to stall it, to make sensibility go away, but it came at her full force and, with a sob, she tore herself from his arms. Breathing heavily, her wild eyes searched for somewhere to run.

Cole took a faltering step forward, frightened that she had retreated to her past; terrified that he would be unable to reclaim the single moment of utter trust he had sensed. "August, please—"

"No!" She forced the single word from her mouth as she backed away. Her dark eyes continued to frantically search for an escape. He took one more step to close the distance between them, and August spun away. She fled then, without looking back.

Chapter Fourteen

Late the next morning, Cole halted the buckboard before Carrie and Steve's clinic, which was attached to the front of their home. He jumped from the high wooden seat just as his sister rounded the corner of the tidy, whitewashed building. She waved a greeting and crossed the yard to where Cole stood at the rear of the wagon.

"Hi, Cole!" Carrie stood on tiptoe and planted a sisterly kiss on his bronzed cheek. "I didn't realize you were stopping by today."

"Emma had some linen donations for the clinic. She was going to bring them herself, but Sara is a little under the weather today. I volunteered, since no one else was around and she didn't want to haul the kids out. She asked me to bring back something for Sara's soar throat." Cole dragged a heavy trunk from the back of the wagon and hoisted it onto one shoulder with a grunt.

"Come on in, and I'll put a package together for her. How long has Sara been sick?" Carrie opened the clinic door for her brother and watched him muscle the chest through the opening, and then drop it with a loud thud just inside the clinic waiting room.

Cole rubbed his shoulder. "She awoke this morning, owly as hell and complaining up a storm. Emma doesn't want her to get worse." Cole's gaze swept the waiting room. "Is Steve around?"

"No," Carrie called over her shoulder as she entered the immaculate examination room with Cole following in her wake. "He had some calls to make this morning and took the kids with him. I think he planned to get in a little fishing, too. I don't think he'll be back until later this afternoon, but if you're willing to wait..." She left the statement hang as she reached into a cabinet and began to place small vials of medicine into a bag. She turned her head then, and raised a skeptical eyebrow in his direction. "I'm surprised August isn't with you. Is she not feeling well either?"

Normally, August was to be found tagging along with Cole when he delivered supplies from the ranch. Carrie and August had become great friends and it was strange that the Wilkins' houseguest chose not to accompany him on this trip. She caught her brother's vague shrug in response to her question and pondered it momentarily before setting the medicinal supplies on the counter. She turned, placed her hands on slim hips, and gave Cole her full attention.

"What's wrong?"

"What makes you think something's wrong?" His guilty gaze scanned the sterile room.

"Come on, Cole. You always bring August with you—she loves to come along." Carrie waited patiently for an answer.

Cole winced inwardly. He would not escape without appeasing her curiosity. His gaze found the wooden floor beneath him. "You're like a mule at times."

"I'm sure Steven would agree with you," she stated indifferently. "I'm waiting."

Cole placed his hands behind his back and braced himself against the counter. "All right. We had a disagreement last night, and she's doing her best to avoid me today."

"A disagreement about what?"

"Christ, Carrie, you're as bad as Emma."

Carrie simply crossed her arms and waited patiently. When Cole did not offer any more information, she pursed her lips. "Okay, since you're acting like a seven-year-old, I'll ask you point blank. What's going on between the two of you?"

The question hung heavily in the air. Cole let his head fall back and closed his eyes for a moment. Finally, he met his sister's gaze again and sighed wearily.

"I don't know. I never thought I'd see her again after I came back from Fargo." He wandered about the room, touching various objects, gathering his thoughts, and feeling his sister's eyes bore into his back. At last, he stopped and turned to face Carrie. "When Wolf brought August to the ranch and she was so close to death, all I could think of was getting her well. After her recovery, she became a part of the family. Everyone cares for her deeply."

"Yourself included?"

Cole recognized the dawning compassion in his sister's eyes and took a deep breath. "Let's just say that she's changed my outlook on life. I see things differently now. I didn't want to scare her away last night, but when I told her she was welcome to stay at the ranch if Wolf doesn't return, she turned it around and said she wouldn't be a white man's conquest. That's not what this is, Carrie."

"I know, Cole."

"I understand that August is a Sioux Indian on the run and that we're totally different, but I care for her deeply. Does that seem strange to you?"

Carrie simply shook her head in sympathy. "Did you tell her that? Do you think she might feel the same?"

"She refuses to hear it." Cole was not going to kiss and tell, but he was all too aware of the fact that, when he held her in his arms for that few short moments the night before, August responded to him—before she became frightened. *She must feel something.*

Cole leaned against the examining table, crossed his arms, then reached up to rub his chin. His mood became pensive. "I think August is fighting an internal battle. I've thought about nothing else since our argument. She's caught between what she's known all her life and what I hope is a strange new future." He raised his troubled gaze to his sister's once more. "Can I ask you something?"

She nodded.

"What would you think if I tried to get her to stay on permanently at the ranch?"

"In what capacity, Cole? Let's be clear on what you're talking about."

"As someone I want to spend the rest of my life with." *There, it's out in the open.*

"I hope you're talking marriage someday; but, if you are, you've got to realize what the two of you will have to face. Marriage is tough enough without the added problems you two will surely encounter." Carrie crossed the length between them and wrapped her arms around her brother. "Just be ready for a lot of heartache, Cole. I support you; don't forget that. I would hate to see her leave, but I don't know how you're going to sort this through."

Cole hugged her back. "I don't know either, but I've got to figure something out. I can't let her just walk away."

* * *

Cole returned to the ranch later that afternoon and immediately searched for Emma. He would deliver the medicine Carrie provided for little Sara, then find August to fix what happened between them the night before.

He had battled with himself during the entire ride home over how to make amends. He would not apologize for kissing her; for a moment, she had enjoyed the tender caress as much as he. He *would* plead for her forgiveness however, for anything he might have done to make August feel unworthy of him. To the best of his knowledge, Cole had never spoken ill of the Sioux people. She took his words out of context and that misguided notion was what he needed to fix first; he needed to assure August that the difference in their ancestries meant nothing to him or his family.

Cole's eyebrows rose in surprise when both Tyler and Emma jumped from their chairs when he entered the house through the kitchen door.

"Thank goodness you're home!"

Cole immediately detected the alarm in Emma's voice. "I've got the medicine. How's Sara? Is she worse?"

Emma's expression changed from worry to confusion in the space of a split-second, then she realized that Cole thought she was upset about her daughter.

"Oh, no, Sara's fine...it's August."

Cole's features paled at her words, and he looked from one to the other, fighting the panic that instantly rose inside him. "What happened?"

Emma wrung her hands and glanced at her husband. Tyler, in turn, squeezed her shoulder before moving his gaze back to his brother.

"Did something happen between you and August? She left—"

"What do you mean *she left*?" Cole's stomach lurched. *I've lost my chance.*

"August came downstairs this morning dressed in the deerskin clothes she arrived in. She returned all of Emma's items; the dresses, the shoes, everything, and thanked her for the loan. Emma argued that the dresses were a gift. August just shook her head and said she had forgotten she was a Sioux Indian and it would be best for all of us to remember that. According to Clancy, she took Joe from his stall an hour later and left the ranch."

"You let her go?" Cole exploded. "You should've stopped her!"

"August is not our prisoner," Emma stated gently. "She's always been welcome to ride any horse on the ranch and to come and go as she pleases. She was gone before we knew it."

Cole turned on booted heel and headed for the closed door.

"Cole, wait!" Emma ran after her retreating brother-in-law and grasped his arm. "It wasn't until after she left the ranch that I realized she might not be coming back. Why else would she return all the things we gave her?"

Cole ignored his sister-in-law's last statement. In his mind, he pictured the numerous spots they had visited since her arrival and calculated silently how long it would take for him to reach the farthest one out. "I'm going to look for her. How long has she been gone?"

"About four hours," Emma and Tyler answered in unison.

Cole paused to nod in their direction. Their worried expressions told him that they were both more concerned than they portrayed.

"I don't think she left for good. August wouldn't steal my horse. I'll be back when I find her."

* * *

Cole saddled Spirit, refusing to let the knowledge of August's past stop him from seeking and claiming what he had wanted for so long. He was not sure where to search for her, or how long it would take to find her, but by the end of the day, he would take her in his arms and tell her of his love. He would bare his soul if that was what it took to make her stay. The mere fact that she took his horse showed that she intended to return at some point. After the weeks in his home and the trust built between them all, August would never steal from him or his family. In another life—yes; but, not now. She was somewhere close by, and he would find her.

* * *

Two hours later found Cole frustrated, weary, and beginning to doubt his earlier faith. Maybe he was wrong in assuming that she would not take what belonged to him. If she was desperate enough, she might run.

Where in hell is she?

Cole left the little-used road and turned Spirit onto a narrow, insignificant trail. He had not ridden this area in years and closely watched the landmarks for his return. The winding path snaked its way downward through a thick, shaded mass of Norway pines, and then suddenly sunlight broke through the branches. The horse stepped into a small field at the base of a hill, and the hair on the back of his neck stood on end with the wave of dark familiarity that washed over him. The treeless expanse that stretched before him was the same landscape he had seen in the twilight of his dreams. He kicked Spirit into a gallop.

Cole's blood pumped madly. He had ridden this hillside in the dream, with Spirit straining beneath him to reach the summit. This time, however, Cole unerringly sensed that he would reach the top and, when he did, she would be there waiting for him. August was the mysterious woman of his dreams, and she was waiting for him to arrive.

The land itself reached out to him and time stood still as man and horse crested the ridge. Cole hauled back on the reins, and Spirit reared up on hind legs as her master's eyes frantically searched the broad expanse for the woman he knew beyond a doubt would be standing in the field.

August was there—one with the backdrop of the approaching night. Cole slid from the horse's back and, never taking his eyes from the woman he wanted more than life itself, let the leather reins slip through his fingers. He strode purposely toward her.

August's face was unreadable. She stood proudly; frightened, yet defiant; wanting, but not asking. Not until Cole stopped before her and reached out a tentative hand did August's lids drop to hide the desire in her eyes. Her lips silently mouthed the word 'no.'

"August..." The single word was a quiet plea.

"We cannot—"

"You want this as much as I do, August. You kissed me back last night. You want me as much as I want you—I think I've always wanted you."

The whisper of his words brushed her soft cheek like gentle fingertips. He stepped closer and the air rushed from August's lungs. The feeling of betrayal toward her own kind was nothing compared to the treachery that her body yielded now. Every beat of her heart reached out to the man before her, but still August fought her need. She turned to run; if he touched her, all would be lost.

Cole's strong fingers grasped her arm. August would never know if it was his physical strength that pulled her back, or if her bursting heart demanded that she cling to the man she had struggled so desperately not to love. She was past caring when he pulled her into his embrace. The initial fear that fluttered in her chest passed quickly when his arms held her gently. There was no hint of force on his part, and no desire to flee on hers.

A small sigh of relief lifted Cole's chest. She was safe and, better yet, she was in his arms. Her petite form fit against the length of his, as though it was meant to be...

"August..." He breathed her name against her silky locks, squeezed his lids shut, and clutched her tighter. "I was out of my mind with worry when I found out you were gone."

August held her silence, reveling in the sudden bewildering sense of comfort she discovered in his embrace. He leaned back to cup her face and stare gently into her faltering gaze.

"Why did you leave the way you did? Were you coming back?"

August averted her gaze from the tender one before her; one that held a mixture of relief, the offer of a safe haven, and pain caused by her abrupt disappearance from his life. His actions and words over the past weeks held no conditions; only a promise of love. That knowledge weakened her resolve even further.

It would be so easy to just stay in your life...but, if I do, you will hurt even more. The security that was found in his strong arms though, pushed that fact away along with the troubled thoughts that had kept her awake the night before. *What am I to do?* She laid her head against his chest and listened to the rapid beat of his heart, again seeking the comfort that only he could offer.

"I...Cole...I have no answer. I just knew I had to get away." She tightened her arms around his waist, fighting the strange, yet exhilarating feeling that she was exactly where she was supposed to be. "I am so frightened. What will happen to me?"

"Stay with me, August. I'll take care of you. I told you last night that I want you with me forever. Why can't I get you to believe that?"

She tipped her head back, intending to tell him that she did accept his words as truth—that she did acknowledge her dawning emotions—but the words never left her mouth.

Cole's almost worshipful gaze took in the slim feminine line of her neck and the moist curve of her parted lips...lips that unknowingly begged to be kissed. August's eyes fluttered shut as his mouth brushed hers. "Do you know how I feel about you...?" he murmured.

The warm, gentle kisses continued, weakening her resolve. *This is where I want to be...even if it is for this day only...he is the one man I could—*

"Cole..." She moaned, then her lips met his with sudden, unbridled passion; not as a woman haunted by the life she had led thus far, but rather as a woman who had discovered the one person who could own her very soul. Everything was forgotten; the angry words, their different ways of life, the problems that were sure to plague their future. None of that mattered as his mouth tormented hers and he pulled her closer.

They dropped to the ground as one, each aware only of the feel of the other. Cole dragged August across his chest, and a moan escaped from somewhere deep within her when his hands pulled her even closer. She was finally in his arms, and never would he let her go again. His lips left hers momentarily as he rolled her onto her back, and his fiery gaze pinned her to the ground.

"I knew you would come," she breathed. "In some unspoken way, I knew, and I cannot fight you any longer."

"Then don't," he whispered. "Just love me, August. That's all I'll ever ask." His head dipped slightly and his lips trailed small kisses from her earlobe to the base of her throat, pausing at the rise of her breast and the frenzied beat of her heart.

Her head lolled on the fragrant grass beneath them. "It can never be."

"It can be all that we want it to be." Cole coaxed her mouth open once more, and August fought the searing kiss. She pulled her lips away to search the flaming depths of passion she found in his eyes.

"We can only live for now, Cole. There can never be anything more. You must understand that..."

"No, August. It can be forever. Just you and me, forever. I can never let you go now." His lips continued to leave a trail of fire wherever they touched.

A small, poignant sigh escaped her lips. He was wrong, but she could fight the battle he waged no longer. Her answer came in the form of a gentle kiss.

Cole slipped his hand beneath the ragged deerhide shirt to stroke the smooth velvety line of her back. Never in his life had he felt skin so silky—and never in her life had a man coaxed the breath from her body as he did now. The shirt lay next to her in the grass only moments later, beside the soft fringed leggings that were a symbol of her people.

Cole stood to stare down at her through eyes that were clouded with desire. His hands trembled as he quickly stripped, then his heart pounded in his chest as he dropped slowly to his knees. He reached out to touch the ivory medallion that lay in the valley between her breasts, next to the small leather pouch. It was the gift he gave her a lifetime ago.

August's skin burned with his touch.

Cole stretched out on his side and a strong, but gentle hand began a slow, torturous exploration of her supple body, building the heat as it began an erotic dance across her burnished skin. He worked his way downward from her shoulders, kneading his way across firm breasts, a flat stomach and smooth, silky thighs until he reached the creased scar—a reminder of the awful wound that almost took her life.

August lifted her head and watched in a dreamlike state as Cole leaned forward to press a soft kiss, and then another to the puckered mark. Her head fell to the carpet of russet colored grass beneath her again; this moment was destined to be. It was predetermined on the day she went to the mountain and her grandmother scooped the ashes from the fire. Cole; he was a part of her future even then. How could she not have know that? August embraced the passion and drew it close, along with the man whose arms made her feel safe in a cruel, unfair world.

Cole's mouth traveled the molten path to her swollen lips and, shifting his weight ever so slightly, he stared down at her with a smoldering flame in his eyes. He physically ached with need, but pushed his own fierce urges aside. "August—you are the one woman I have waited for my entire life. I want to love you, but not if you see me only as a white man. I want you to see me as a *man*— one that you trust because you know I'd never hurt you or take what is yours to give. I just want to love you, August, above all else."

Her heavy lidded eyes widened slightly, and she reached up to touch his mouth with a trailing finger. *Do not speak of love, Cole...the words will make it so hard for me to leave...*

She stared into his expectant eyes. In their depths she saw just a man— one who would not force her as the soldiers had done. Cole Wilkins was a generous, tender soul who searched for acceptance into her world. If she refused to grant it, he would honor her decision...no matter how difficult it may be.

August's fingers brushed past his mouth once more and trailed their way through thick hair to where the sandy-colored waves lay against the back of his neck. The pressure of her hand brought his warm lips to her own. Cole moaned against the slant of her mouth as he slipped into the warm depths that awaited him. The slow stroking rhythm carried August to the precipice, and lithe brown limbs entangled themselves in strong muscular thighs as she pulled him closer.

He responded by following her lead and, encouraged by her apparent willingness, Cole increased the depths and speed of his thrusts. He drew from the well of devotion within her heart and gave from the depths of love in his own until their passion became as wild as the earth upon which they laid. The tempest of emotions continued to build until the fever of desire cracked like thunder and released the pending storm. Moments later, as racing heartbeats slowed and Cole gathered August close, they settled into the silent calm that could be found only in each other's arms. Neither thought of where they were going, but only of the place they had just been.

Cole pushed himself up on an elbow, and his hand gently moved the thick strands of hair away from her damp cheek. August tilted her head to press a kiss against the callused fingertips that, only moments earlier, had burned her skin wherever they touched. Smoldering velvet brown eyes stared into cloudy blue ones as a trembling finger examined the small crease in his chin, the slant of his eyebrows, and the dark stubble that covered his cheeks. Small beads of perspiration gathered where his forehead met the line of thick tousled hair.

She would remember all of it. She would take it with her and would cherish the memories long after she departed his world. Loving Cole Wilkins from afar would be her penance for crossing the line.

She would not tell him that she was leaving. She had planned to run from his world earlier that day, but something brought her to the hilltop instead. As surely as day turns into night, she knew that he would find her...

Chapter Fifteen

"What's wrong?" Cole watched as August shrugged on the deerskin shirt, hiding the gentle curve of her back from his view. "Why are you so quiet?"

She did not answer, but just sat on the ground and continued to tug at the laces on her soft boots. Cole moved to sit on his haunches before her and raised her trembling chin with one finger.

August glanced at him, then quickly turned away with a guilty sigh. Her head shook slightly before she tackled the laces once more.

"August..." Cole's fingers stayed her hand as he dropped to one knee. "Look at me."

Still, she refused to meet his gaze. He drew her palm to his lips and gently kissed the soft center. His strong fingers traced the warm spot that his mouth had just touched. "What we did wasn't wrong. We've been headed for this day since the first time we met."

August opened her mouth to speak, then stubbornly tightened her jaw, jerked her hand from his grasp, and worked the laces of the remaining boot.

Cole was not about to give up. "When you left me that day I brought you the horses, your image stayed with me through the night. In fact, I kept picturing you all the way to Fargo. I was supposed to take the train home. I couldn't though—because I desperately hoped to find you again. August, we were meant to be together. Can't you see that?"

Her watery gaze lifted to meet his. Finding him was her destiny. Cole became a part of her future on the day of her vision so long ago. Somehow, he was meant to be in her life. There were too many obstacles, though—even if she had just willingly given her body to him. She remained silent as Cole clasped her hand and laid her palm against his chest.

"Do you feel this? My heart is yours, August. It has been since that first day. It wasn't until you showed up on my doorstep that I finally realized you were the one thing I've been searching for my entire life." He watched a tear slip down her cheek and reached out to brush it away with a gentle hand. "I love you."

"No..." Her head lolled in quiet panic when she finally met his gaze. "Don't say those words out loud."

"August, do you think I would have made love to you if it wasn't so? That's not the kind of man I am. I would never have taken from you what you weren't willing to give. What we shared was beautiful, and I don't want to just walk away—I *won't* walk away. Let me take care of you. We can be married and you'll never have to run again."

August tore her hand from his grasp and scrambled to her feet. "Married?" Her dark eyes widened in horror. "And what about my family? What do I tell Wolf when he comes for me? He expects me to leave with him."

"We'll figure it out when the time comes. Marry me now. Wolf is your friend—you don't need his permission. Wouldn't he be pleased that I could keep you safe—and happy?" Cole chose not to voice his true feelings. The thought of the Wolf returning scared the hell out of him. *She doesn't have a clue how he feels about her.*

"What about your family?" August blinked away her tears. Her shoulders drooped with defeat. "What do you think your friends are going to say?" The corners of her mouth dropped with disdain. "Here comes Cole with his little squaw wife."

"Stop that! It would never be that way." He said the words, but admitted to himself that she was right. There were too many people who would not look beyond the color of her skin. Cole was bound and determined to overcome it, though. "If two people love each other, that's all that matters."

His words hung in the air. They both understood that he waited for her to declare her love.

I will not say it out loud. If I do, I will never be able to take them back.

August shook her head in denial. "It is foolish to think that love will conquer all. You would end up hating me because you felt obligated to wed me because of...because we have been together as a man and woman." She was uncomfortable saying the words—even to him.

"August, I wanted nothing more today than to find you, make sure you were safe, and tell you how much I want you to share my life. I don't care about anyone else—to hell with their thoughts or their possible frowns of disapproval. Christ—why can't I make you see that? You and I are so..." Cole struggled momentarily to find the right word. "We are so connected—there's no other way to put it. You know it as well as I do. You proved it tonight with every kiss—with every touch of your hand."

August refused to acknowledge the truth of his words, turned with a raised chin, and stomped to the horses. She watched him from the corner of her eye as he gathered up his belongings. *How long will it be before he finally loses his patience?* She prayed that he would. It would make her leave-taking easier.

She hoisted herself across Joe's back and waited. Cole stared at her for a moment, his eyes unreadable, then walked to his horse. August turned away and focused on a distant point on the darkened landscape. Her brain reeled with jumbled emotions, but she would not speak—she dared not take the chance.

Suddenly she was plucked from Joe's back. Cole's strong arms easily positioned her in the saddle before him. He wrapped her in his embrace and kneed Spirit toward the path that led to the trees below. A soft whistle left Cole's lips a moment later, and Joe trotted along behind.

"Emma and Tyler will be happy to see that nothing happened to you." His voice whispered past her ear and an unexpected shiver ran down her spine.

August remained stubbornly sullen.

Two can play your game, August. You gave yourself willingly one short hour ago. He would never forget the joy of loving her so freely. Cole simply tightened his arms around her slender waist in response to her silence and whispered in her ear. "I'm a patient man, August."

* * *

August was hardly aware of the distant call of a wolf as they entered the ranch through the front gates. Only the hard steel of Cole's chest garnered her warring thoughts.

She had stepped over the cultural line by finally giving into her desire. Now, it would be her responsibility to fix the inevitable consequences. Separation was the only answer, but, as the gentle darkness of night surrounded them, August did not have a clue as to how she would accomplish her goal. Cole would press her more fervently now—he had seen into her heart and would not rest until she declared her love.

He remained, for the most part, quiet on the entire ride back to the ranch. His only words were those of concern for her comfort and warmth. August shook her head with each query. She had almost tossed away her mute resolve when, feeling her shiver with the drop in temperature, Cole tugged loose a warm jacket tied to the back of his saddle. He shrugged it on, then pulled her slight form within the confines of its warmth. His hard chest against her back and strong arms around her waist comforted her like nothing ever before. It would be so easy to just let him take care of her forever.

Cole reined Spirit in the direction of the ranch house when the heavy front door was flung wide open. Tyler and Emma rushed out onto the porch, and the shaft of light that spilled through the opening lit their relieved expressions.

August stiffened in the saddle and steeled herself for their reaction.

"Thank God you're home!" Emma hurried to Cole's side as he dismounted at the end of the wooden walkway. The sight of August's stoic features stopped her dead in her tracks. She bit back her next words, drew her shawl tighter around her shoulders, and watched her brother-in-law help the obviously sullen woman from the saddle. As soon as August's feet touched the soft ground, she spun away from the strong hands that gently held her arms and, bounding up the steps to the porch, raced past Tyler and through the open doorway.

Cole's disheartened sigh brought Emma's gaze back to him. Her brow dipped with concern. "We've been so worried. Where was she?"

"It's a long story, Em."

"Why did she run into the house like that just now?"

Cole's shoulders lifted in a helpless shrug and the formerly determined line of his whiskered jaw softened as the light in his hazel eyes dimmed. "Go talk to her. She won't say a word to me. Tell her how we all feel. Goddammit, tell her she can't leave." The impassioned plea was enough to sag his shoulders in the defeat he had staved off, but could no more. "Tell her I love her—she refuses to believe that she could be a part of my life."

Tyler stepped down from the porch, crossed the small distance to the horses, and patted his brother's shoulder. "Come on, Cole," he said as he grabbed up the reins of the animal closest to him. "I'll help you settle Joe and

Spirit in for the night."

With one last hesitant but hopeful glance at Emma, Cole followed his brother to the barn.

* * *

August slammed the door to her room, sagged against it and swallowed down the lump in her throat as she stared at the beautiful furniture within the confines of the four walls. Refusing to give into her emotions, she crossed the candlelit room to the window and settled her gaze on the retreating back of the man she loved, but could never have.

With a heavy heart, August finally forced her eyes away. She yanked a comforter from the end of the bed and wrapped its warmth around her slim shoulders. A regretful sigh escaped her lips as she sank to the floor in stubborn determination and leaned against the fabric-covered wall. She would not sleep in the white man's bed again.

August's dark eyes darted around the dimply-lit room once more. Her tired mind compared the trappings of Cole's world to another, almost forgotten life; that of sleeping within a skin-covered lodge half the size of the room she was now in, using tattered blankets or buffalo hides for warmth at night instead of the soft thick quilts, and of always wondering where her next meal would come from. Her trembling hand clutched at the small leather bag that lay against her breast. *I am sorry, Grandmother. I am sorry to have been so foolish as to think I could live this life—to forget my vision—to give myself to him...* August swallowed her sorrow and dropped her face into her shaking palms.

* * *

Emma jostled the tray of food in her hands and reached up to knock softly on August's bedroom door. There was no response. A second quiet rap brought the same result, and she turned the brass knob and entered the candlelit room.

"August?"

Another tentative step brought her completely through the doorway and her searching eyes found the young woman who sat against the far wall with her face turned away. Emma elbowed the door closed and moved to place the tray on a small table in the corner. August kept her gaze averted and tightened the blanket around her shoulders.

Without a word, Emma lifted another quilt from the back of a wing chair, laid it on the floor beside her friend, and took up the tray once more. She settled herself and the food next to August.

"You must be hungry. I've got some warm chicken and bread—I'm not leaving until you eat it."

She waited patiently for a response. August simply pulled the blanket tighter around her body. Emma reached out to lay her hand on the slender shoulder next to her. "We were worried about you today, August. I'm glad you came back. You know you're always welcome here."

August's chin snapped up, and Emma was surprised at the visible fear she saw in the velvet eyes before her.

"That is what frightens me." Her voice trembled.

"There's nothing to be afraid of."

"No?" August cried miserably. "Could you leave the life you have here and all the ones you love? Would you forsake everything you believe in because someone tells you that you have no choice?"

Emma clutched August's hand. "Cole would never force you to do anything. You have a choice. You're not a prisoner in this house."

"I am more a prisoner than you can understand."

"Why, August—tell me."

"Because I love him!" August jerked her arm from Emma's gentle touch, and the blanket slipped to the wooden floor. She was weary of the battle. She was tired of the constant strain of hidden emotions. A trembling hand raked through her long hair. "Because he is everything that my people have fought against my entire life." She breathed the last.

A lone tear trickled down August's smooth, brown cheek. Her heartfelt gaze pleaded for understanding when she tipped her chin to look at Emma. "For one short moment today, I forgot my promises to my father and grandmother. For one moment, I let myself believe that Cole and I could have a life together." She gathered strength with a deep breath. "When he found me today, I threw my past away to be held in his arms—I let him love me because I was not strong enough to fight my heart any longer. My people would be ashamed to know how weak I have become." August hugged her knees to her chest and dropped her forehead to the soft leggings.

Emma stared incredulously at the woman beside her. *That's where they were—they made love...* Cole and August had created an unbreakable bond. She closed her eyes and sought to find comforting words before carefully gathering the heartbroken woman in her arms. "We'll figure this out, August. We'll take it one day at a time."

"That is what Cole keeps saying." Her head shook slowly. "There is no resolution."

"Love does not make you weak, August—it makes you strong. If you stay, you'll be safe here. Cole will see to that—we all will. Your family will also be welcome. Honey, the times are changing. Your life as you know it is changing. Tyler has connections. He'll do whatever it takes to bring your family to the ranch and keep them here." Emma cupped August's tear-stained face. "You have to believe what I'm telling you. Cole loves you, and you love him. Don't let the fact that you've led different lives cause you to throw that away. Cole's friend, Beau, will find the others, and we'll all work together to bring them here."

Hopelessness pierced August's heart. Wolf would never stand for it. He would never take a white man's handout and, for the first time, she realized that he would never allow her to stay at the ranch. He would kill Cole for treating her as his woman—for taking her body when she was unable to find the will to say no. Her proud friend would declare the love he had for her—the love she always suspected was hidden beneath his gruff, but teasing words. He would drag her to the farthest reaches of the north—and her simple claim that she loved Cole would mean nothing.

Emma pulled August into the circle of her arms, but the Indian woman found little solace in the comforting embrace. *I will leave as soon as possible. When he least suspects it, I will be gone.*

* * *

August kept her eyes closed and listened to the sound of chickadees outside her window. The return of the tiny black and white birds signaled that winter was near. She still lay on the hard floor, sleeping periodically, fretfully; and solemnly planning her escape.

I'll need food, a horse, and warm clothes... Gathering those things could easily be done; fooling Cole and the rest of his family would be the hard part. She would reach into the deepest part of her soul to find the strength to actually walk away.

August tossed away the blanket, heaved herself from the hard floor, and moved stiffly to the window. Her keen eyes followed an eagle as it soared above the far off, pine-covered hillside. Her lids fluttered shut and her father's long ago words filtered through her troubled mind.

"A very great vision is needed, and the man who has it must follow it as the eagle seeks the deepest blue of the sky."

Watching the eagle once more, August's shoulders squared with determination. The majestic bird would never have to play at being anything other than what it was—*and neither will I.*

He needs to think I will never leave. The only way to fool him is to let him love me... She paced the confines of the bedroom, afraid of the future, and afraid to face Cole and the fact that their ill-fated love could not keep them together.

* * *

Cole paused by a stand of pine trees and watched the simple graceful turn of August's back as she sat near the river's edge. He had not spoken to her since they made love the night before. He had searched for her earlier in the day, only to have Emma inform him that their houseguest stated she was going for a walk.

August had again donned the clothes of the white man's world. Her silky dark hair hung nearly to the ground she sat upon. He paused for a moment longer, closed his eyes, and controlled the rapid beating of his heart. Cole was now acquainted with the fresh smell of the glossy strands—and the satiny texture as he ran his fingers through their length. He had also discovered the complete joy associated with holding the woman he loved in his arms.

Be patient with her, he coached himself. Not knowing how she would receive him, he reiterated the simple sentence over and over in his head as he approached the riverbed.

August tilted her head upright when he approached; a sixth sense warned her that he was suddenly near. She expertly controlled her erratic heartbeat and maintained an appearance of total calm.

"August—"

Her hand rose to stop further words, then she silently invited him to sit by resting her palm on the ground beside her. *You must not let him know that you will someday be gone from his life. Find the courage—it will be your only salvation.* She breathed in deeply.

"Did Emma tell you where I would be?" She watched him drop to the leaf-covered grass and rest his forearms on raised knees.

"Yeah—she said you spoke with her."

Another heavy sigh escaped her lips. "I did not want to see you again until we were alone. Your family hovers like hummingbirds."

He could not help the small twitch of a smile that played at the corners of his lips. "Yeah—they're like that sometimes." She melted his heart with the small observation.

Taking a gamble, Cole grasped her hand gently. When she did not pull it away, he brought her slender fingers to his lips and softly kissed one, then placed their clasped palms on the brown grass between them—and waited. He was aware of her inner struggle and would not push her.

The realization that the silence between them was comfortable, not strained or charged with emotion, suddenly hit him. The moment was as it should be—two people who loved each other deeply, simply enjoying each other's presence. August shifted to look directly into his eyes.

"How can this work—"

"Don't, August."

"You did not let me finish what I was going to say. I want you to know that I will try. I have never felt about a man as I feel about you. But it will be hard for me."

Cole placed a muscled arm across her shoulders and pulled her close until her smooth cheek rested against his chest. She did not see him squeeze his eyes shut to keep the tears of joy at bay. "We'll get it all figured out, August. I promise you that. I swear I'll never let anything hurt you. I love you more than I ever thought possible."

August fought the guilt that burned in her stomach. *This is just for now—it will never be forever—you must remember that.*

Cole tipped her chin until their teary gazes locked. Time stood still once more until his lips dropped to gently caress the tawny lips, then he coaxed her on to a more passionate kiss that bared his soul.

August's lids dropped as she returned the embrace with even more fervor than the man who held her. Cole eased her to the ground and moved to hold her tighter; she could respond in only one way.

Forgive me, Grandmother.

Chapter Sixteen

Camp Robinson,
Nebraska

Beau let the door of Fort Robinson's Processing office slam behind him, stepped into the abnormally warm October night, and headed for his tent erected near the outer west side of the stronghold.

A part of him was elated by the fact he was given permission, after a fair amount of persuasion on his part, to visit the fort's Indian holding areas in the morning. Groups of what were called 'subversive hostiles' were being held at the military post's detention center to be shipped south to a Florida jail. He had three days before that happened; three days to figure out how to get Wolf's father and Two Feather's wife released—if they were even there.

Another part of him held his optimism in check. If he found Fawn and Whitecloud and returned north with them, there was every possibility that, as a last resort, Beau would have to assist in their escape.

He reached his campsite, which was isolated from the other travelers passing through the fort, and dropped his pack, then quickly gathered wood to build a small fire. Wolf and the others were somewhere in the darkness, waiting for the signal that Beau had returned. It was not long before the three apprehensive braves moved stealthily into the fire's spreading light.

Beau hauled his pack closer, pulled out a wrapped package, and quickly distributed smoked venison and bread to his three companions. Two Feathers ignored the outstretched hand. Instead, the Indian dropped to the ground.

"Do you come with good news?" The man's calm demeanor belied the fear Beau read in his eyes. "Have you found them?"

Beau rested his hand on Two Feather's shoulder. "I received permission to enter the holding compound in the morning. We can only hope that they're there. When I spoke to the post clerk, he stated that a man and a woman were brought in from up north a few weeks back. He wasn't sure from what agency." He squeezed the Indian's shoulder in support. "We can only hope, friend. If they are here, then we have to find a way to get them released into my custody—a difficult thing to get accomplished."

"If they are here," the Indian returned with a determined gaze, "they will leave with us—one way or another. I will not leave Fawn if she is still alive."

"We can't do anything rash. We need to remain calm and think this through."

Two Feathers breathed in deeply to settle his conflicting emotions. He did not want to wait until morning. He wanted to find his wife this very moment. His dark unwavering eyes met the white man's once again. "I will wait only one day. If you cannot get them released, then I will find a way myself."

Wolf stepped forward to stand beside his friend of many years. "I am with Two Feathers. We will give you until tomorrow when the sun sets. You have helped us this far, and we will hold our patience one more day. After that, I cannot promise what will happen."

Beau knew it was useless to discuss it further. The men had made their decision known. He only hoped that he could accomplish the release in that short of a time or all hell would break loose.

* * *

Beau crawled from his tent the following morning. Small tendrils of smoke emanated from the charred wood in the fire pit. There was no sign of Wolf or the others. Beau had slept restlessly the entire night, but still did not hear the men slip into the trees at morning's light.

He splattered water on his face from a nearby stream and stowed his gear inside the canvas tent. Grabbing Wolf's beaded necklace from where it lay on a rock, he took one last glance at the brave's possession, and then slipped it into his jacket pocket. It was the one, single article Beau figured he could use to get the prisoners to identify themselves. Wolf suggested that he hold it in his hand. If the captives recognized it, the chance of finding them increased.

Glancing at his pocket watch, he hurried to the fort's large spiked gates to meet Sergeant Miller, who would take him to the holding area.

* * *

Beau had been through many detention centers in the past, but at first glance, was instantly appalled by the temporary living conditions the Sioux were forced to endure. Sergeant Miller spoke to three of the guards by the open front gate, but Beau heard nothing. His head reeled at the sight of the gaunt detainees in the semi-lit arena. Permission was finally granted for him to enter through the first locked gate. The captives' lackluster eyes met Beau's as he peered through iron bars.

The stench of human feces and unwashed bodies inflamed his nostrils. It was the first time that Beau wanted to turn tail and run. The conditions were horrible. Small children clung to their mothers, who looked too weak to hold them in their arms. Old men sat on the cool ground, their bodies wracked by hacking coughs. Only a few younger braves stood upright in a show of bravery.

Beau turned angrily on his heel and met Sergeant Miller's eyes. The man was busy placing a handkerchief over his nose. "I thought this was supposed to be a detention center for hostiles? All I see are sick leftover's from raids that managed to kill most of the younger men."

"They all got papers stating they're hostiles—gonna be sent south to keep 'em out of trouble." Miller shrugged. "You still want to go through here? If you do, you gotta hand over your pistol. Watch them Injuns though—they're quick and will be on you before you know it."

Beau checked his temper and reached for his sidearm. "I don't think old men and small children pose that big of a threat. Are you coming with me?" He plopped the gun in the sergeant's outstretched palm.

Miller adjusted the bandanna across his nose. "Don't think so. I'll stand in the fresh air and wait for you to come out. You got fifteen minutes before I send the troops in after you."

Relief ran down Beau's spine. Being alone with the detainees would give him an opportunity to speak with Fawn and Whitecloud—if he could find them.

The sergeant pulled a second ring of keys from a back pocket, clicked the lock open and waited for Beau to pass through the gate. "If something happens, give a holler. Like I said, don't trust these bastards." A second later, he slammed the gateway shut and stepped back through the first doorway. Suddenly, Beau was alone with the Sioux.

He reached in his pocket and drew out the necklace. He held it up for all to see, then began his search. "Do any of you speak English?" He walked on, holding Wolf's possession high in the air, turning his head from side to side. "Do any of you recognize this choker?" Black eyes watched him warily, but no one stepped forward.

"I'm looking for a young woman and an old brave. They are called Fawn and Whitecloud. They come from the north." Still, there was no response, except for slight murmurings among those he passed.

Beau walked on for another ten minutes. He stopped to show the necklace to more than one old man, but no one seemed to know the people he spoke of. He reached the far end of the arena and turned to retrace his steps. Defeat darkened his blue eyes.

The long journey to Fort Robinson was for nothing—they were too late. He hated to think of the report he would have to give to Wolf and Two Feathers when he returned to the tent.

He slipped the necklace back into his pocket and continued toward the gate. Before Beau reached the door, however, a small crowd of younger braves gathered to block his way. Beau automatically reached for his pistol. His hand met an empty holster. *Now you've done it, McCabe.* He raised his eyes as one of the braves stepped closer, then chanced a fleeting glimpse to the closed door behind the man.

"Why do you look for an Indian?" The man crossed his arms over what used to be a powerful chest and waited. No one spoke—the silence was deafening.

"I have a message from his son." Once more, Beau quickly pulled the necklace from his pocket and held it out. "Is there anyone here who recognizes this as belonging to a member of his family? It was made for his son by his own hands."

The crowd parted slowly, and Beau stood transfixed as a Sioux woman helped an old man rise from the cold dirt floor. When the elder gained his balance, she coaxed him slowly forward. The old warrior reached out with gnarled fingers and took the choker from the white man's hand. Rheumy, bloodshot eyes moved from the article in his palm to Beau's astonished face.

"Wolf?"

"Yes! Is Wolf your son?" Before the old man could answer, Beau addressed the woman. "Are you Fawn?"

She nodded hesitantly.

"Two Feathers is searching for you."

"You know of my husband?" Her shaking hand frantically clutched at Beau's forearm. Hope lit her tired eyes.

"He's with me. We're going to try and get you and Whitecloud released." At the sound of his name, the old man shook violently. The woman grabbed him with both arms to keep him from falling. Beau leapt forward to lend assistance.

"He is very ill, but he has waited for his son to come. Now that Wolf is close, it is too much for him," Fawn stated cautiously.

Beau helped the old man back to the wooden wall that he leaned against earlier. Propping him against the slats, the younger man quickly removed his rawhide jacket and wrapped it around the trembling, bony shoulders of the once proud warrior. Gently, he urged Wolf's father to the ground and patted his shoulder.

Fawn dropped to her knees and grabbed Beau's arm again. "You will see my husband?" Her round, doe-like eyes were hopeful for what Beau wagered to be the first time since being captured by the soldiers. He simply nodded his head. "Tell him we will be together again. We are this close, so it has to be."

Beau lowered his voice. "Listen, Fawn. Don't do or say anything about this. I'm going to meet with the post commander and try to get the two of you released. Don't mention your husband or Wolf. They're in hiding. I'll get you out of here, but you must not do anything foolish. Do you understand me?"

A soft smile spread across her face. "You do not have long to do this, do you?" Beau's forehead creased in confusion. "I will take care of Whitecloud. You must go quickly, then come back for us, or Two Feathers will come for me himself. Better that this thing is done without bloodshed; there will be blood if my husband attempts our release—and it will not be his."

Her self-assurance astounded Beau. *She must have been to hell and back, and yet she is confident.* "I can't believe you can smile in these conditions—even if you know that your husband is close by."

"He simply needed to find me—the rest is already done. Go now; they are opening the doors."

Sergeant Miller hollered his name, and Beau stood. With one last quick glance at the smiling Fawn and the old man who now held the necklace close to his heart, Beau departed quickly.

* * *

"The conditions are horrible!" Beau stated. "That old man won't make the trip to Florida, I can guarantee you that. Why not release him into my custody? As long as he knows he's going home, I'll get him back to Pine Ridge with no problems."

Beau's scathing eyes scanned the lush surroundings that comprised Colonel Forsythe's home, then his gaze moved to the Fort Robinson post commander as he poured another glass of fine bourbon and sat ceremoniously in a padded chair.

The man took a long drawn-out sip and crossed one knee over the other before turning his calculating gaze on the anxious man across from him. "I understand perfectly what the conditions are like in the detention center. I try to do everything I can, but the bottom line is that the government has had enough of the great Sioux."

"Enough of what, sir? There's plenty of room for everyone on the frontier. The government has already taken everything from them. What's left for them to do?"

"They won't stop until all hostiles are taken from their homeland and placed behind bars. According to Federal dictates, the other Indians must be dependent on the reservation style of living. With all the settlers moving west, the government feels this is the only way to stop the constant fear and complaints."

"Sir, you must realize that most of the Sioux being brought in now aren't hostile Indians. They're old men and woman, who are just trying to survive."

The colonel placed his near-empty glass on the oak table beside him with a sigh. "Beau, we've done everything possible to get the Indians to assimilate, but it's not working. With the threat of this Ghost Dance hanging out there, the government is even more determined to capture them all—even old men and women. The movement will be squashed no matter what it takes. I imagine you've heard of this new threat? Two months ago, it wouldn't have concerned me. Now, I'm not so sure."

Beau nodded. "It's all that was talked about at the St. Paul conference. It's a simple religious dance. Do you really think there'll be huge problems because of it?"

"The settler's are nervous as hell—they complain and the army must respond. The Sioux actually believe the dance will help the buffalo to reappear."

And the white monster to disappear, Beau thought. *If only it was that easy.* "I know the government officials have forbidden these gatherings, thinking the dance will incite the Indians to make war. I don't think they realize though, that forbidding them to practice their beliefs has more of a hand in pushing the Indians in that direction."

"Congress has decided to starve them out before the Sioux get that far. Withholding rations might break up the agency groups pushing the dance," Forsythe continued. "The government won't own up to it—they're afraid it will make them look weak in the papers out east. But, that's one of the reasons most of the shipments of beef were cut." He shrugged. "Blankets are even fewer. The best thing for these people is that they be sent to Florida or Omaha, Nebraska. At least it's warm there. There's nothing left for them out here." He picked up his drink and drained the contents. "Now, back to the two you want custody of. They came in on the hostile list, so they go south."

Beau checked his frustration and tried again. "Colonel Forsythe, do you really believe that one old man and a middle-aged squaw are going to change the outcome of the future? Let me take them. Let me take the old man home to die. He'll be placed on Pine Ridge to live out his last few days in whatever peace he can find. I could use the woman to help me care for him as we travel north."

Forsythe cocked an introspective eyebrow at Beau. "Why the eagerness to get ahold of these two?"

Beau withheld comment.

The Colonel settled back in his chair and pursed his lips. "I'll tell you what, McCabe. You give me a straight answer, and I might reconsider. What's going on?"

Beau stared straight into the colonel's eyes. "It's wrong to send them away. You know it, and so do I. I want to help the old man to go home and die. The woman's husband is now at Pine Ridge." *Forgive me for that one little mistruth.*

Beau sighed, leaned forward to rest his elbows on his knees, and clasped his hands before him as he continued. "Their entire band was killed when he was away from their hunting camp. They suffered the death of their daughter and were not even given time to grieve at each other's side. Bingham was in charge of the raid—they never had a chance." At the mention of the flamboyant Colonel, Forsythe's eyebrows lifted. Beau noted his reaction and was quick to continue.

"The colonel's methods are underhanded, and he labels those he picks up at will. This woman is not a hostile, sir. She was living quietly with her husband and child before their world was torn apart. Let me take them. They've done nothing wrong."

Forsythe stood and set his empty glass on the sideboard. He crossed to the window, clasped his hands behind his back, and stared out with a pensive gaze. A moment later, he turned to face a hopeful Beau. The liquor he had consumed softened the hard line of his jaw. "All right, McCabe. You've convinced me. The only reason though, that I'm rescinding the orders, is that you've never given me reason not to trust you. Don't start now."

* * *

The following morning, Beau was back at the office to process Fawn and Whitecloud's release papers. He filled out the required paperwork with thoughts of Wolf and the others as they paced through the second night of waiting. Two Feathers had not understood the need to wait, but Beau eventually convinced them all that everything would be fine if they would just hold their patience for one more night. It had not been an easy task. Now, he was just a walk across the length of the fort from getting Fawn and Whitecloud released.

The clerk stamped and initialed Beau's copy, then shook the hand of the rugged man across the length of the desk. "Good luck on your trip north, Mr. McCabe. If you stop at the canteen, you can purchase some supplies to hold you over for a few days."

"Thanks." With a quick flash of white teeth, Beau turned to leave the office, thankful that he had the foresight to purchase supplies the day before. He reached out to open the door, but paused when it was swung inward. Beau came face to face with Colonel Geoffrey Bingham. The hair immediately rose at the nape of his neck, and his lips thinned in immediate anger and loathing.

Bingham saw the instant dislike shoot from the Beau's eyes. "Mr. McCabe—" The Colonel nodded and waited for a reply.

Beau gave him none.

Bingham removed his hat and slapped the felt cap against his thigh, enjoying the puff of dust that wafted upward and into the face of the man before him. "Not talking these days? You had plenty to say the last time I saw you." His gray, impassive eyes scanned the length of Beau's tall, muscular body. "So…what may I ask are you doing down this far south? Not your usual stomping grounds, is it?" *Ah, now that got your attention,* he thought as he watched the tick in the other man's tanned cheek.

"Excuse me. I was just on my way out." Beau stepped around Bingham and proceeded to leave the office without any explanation.

Colonel Bingham's eyes narrowed. *What the hell is he doing down here?* He paused a second more, then turned to the clerk with a false smile set on his thin lips.

* * *

Beau shifted from one leg to the other in annoyance, raising small clouds of dust, as he held the reins of his own horse plus the two he had purchased. Finally, the bolt on the wooden inner gate clicked, and he saw Whitecloud shuffle through the opening with Fawn's help. They entered the yard through the outer door and both prisoners squinted and shielded their eyes momentarily from the brightness of the day.

"Here you go, McCabe." A rueful grin curved Sergeant Miller's lips as he shook his head and motioned in the prisoners' direction. "Don't know what the hell you want with a broken down old Injun. That squaw, though—" he hesitated with an appreciative lift of bushy eyebrows "—might have a few ideas for her." He cackled at his thoughts, then turned as if he had forgotten they were there.

Fawn heard his words, but met Beau's gaze with a proud tilt of her chin. Her savior moved to take issue with the Sergeant, but she halted him with a raised hand and a hushed voice.

"It is not worth it, friend. You will only delay our departure from this horrible place." Her features softened. "It has been too long a time from my husband. Please, let us go."

Her whispered words spurred Beau to help the old warrior onto the back of the smaller of the two waiting horses. Once settled, Whitecoud reined the animal around and, with a weak nudge of the elderly man's heals, the mare plodded toward the open gate of the fortress and toward the freedom beyond the walls. Beau and Fawn quickly mounted and prepared to follow suit.

"Halt!"

The single word was mind-numbing. Before Beau could turn in his saddle, six soldiers blocked the exit. Colonel Bingham strode with purpose from the main office and headed in their direction. "What's going on here, McCabe? Who gave you the authority to take these prisoners from the fort?"

Beau clenched his fists around the leather reins. His jaw squared. "My papers were processed by the order of Colonel Forsythe, *head* commander of this agency. I'll thank you kindly to remove your men—we need to be on our way."

Bingham's stance became languid as he crossed his arms and leaned forward. Beau longed to knock the lazy thin-lipped smile from his face.

"Sergeant Jones!" Bingham shot a quick glance at the uniformed soldier that sat astride the horse closest to him, then brought his gaze back to Beau's angry eyes. "Gather up these two prisoners and return them to the detention center."

"You've got no right—my papers are in order." Beau exploded. He dug in his heels and kicked his horse forward. The animal halted between Whitecloud and the oncoming soldiers. Beau whirled when Fawn suddenly screamed in terror as she was pulled from the saddle and thrown to the ground.

Beau's horse blocked Whitecloud from the soldiers' view. His steely gaze stopped the military men in their tracks. "You touch this old man, and I'll personally see you horsewhipped." He pulled his gun and pointed it at the man who now held the Indian woman in his clutches. He clicked back the hammer. "Let her go. Now!"

The sergeant released Fawn and quickly retreated. She scrambled back onto the waiting horse. Beau raised his gun menacingly. "Touch her again, and I'll shoot."

"Sir?" The unsettled man watched his commander's face redden in anger before Bingham pulled his sidearm from its holster and pointed the barrel at Whitecloud's chest.

"You just made a very stupid mistake, McCabe," the colonel

announced loudly. "I would think—"

A clatter of hooves pounded just outside the gates. Colonel Forsythe yanked on the reins of his horse and spun toward the opening. He and his small contingent of soldiers came to a spinning halt amid clouds of dust.

"What the hell is going on here?"

Bingham cleared his throat haughtily. "It's a good thing you showed up, Colonel Forsythe. This man, Beau McCabe, *was* going to take two prisoners from the fort. I arrived in time to stop him."

The post commander's calculating gaze moved from one man to the other to assess the situation, then rested on Beau in silent communication. Beau re-holstered his gun. "Mr. McCabe, do you have your papers with you?"

"Yes, sir, I do." Beau visibly relaxed in the saddle, but his heart still pounded against his ribcage.

"Then all should be in order. You may be on your way."

"I demand to know what's going on here! I captured these prisoners weeks ago. They're hostiles and need to be sent south! I signed the orders at Pine Ridge." The words spewed forth from the enraged Bingham's mouth. His arm shot out toward Beau. "And this man pulled a weapon on a United States Cavalry sergeant!"

"Well, Colonel Bingham," Forsythe said as his gaze swept the area, "the situation looks under control now. These two prisoners were transferred into my custody, and *I* have released them to Mr. McCabe. He'll be returning them to Pine Ridge." He glanced at Beau. "It's best that you leave now. There'll be no more disruptions."

With a wave to his men, the colonel urged his horse forward and left the small cluster of growing onlookers.

Beau met Bingham's fiery gaze and was acutely aware that the man wanted to tear him from the saddle. Instead of further fueling the man's ire though, he motioned for Fawn and Whitecloud to continue on.

Beau passed Colonel Bingham, where he stood in the dust of the plodding horses, and met the irate officer's gaze. Seething with pent-up frustration at having been outwitted by McCabe, the colonel hardened his jaw.

"This isn't over. You better watch your back, McCabe."

Beau's eyes returned to Whitecloud and Fawn, where they preceded him from the fort, but Bingham heard his quiet reply. "Kiss my ass, Colonel."

Once through the large wooden gates of Fort Robinson, Beau took the lead. His earlier turmoil was forgotten when he glanced at the woman and old man who rode with him. Neither seemed concerned about the confrontation. The unexpected freedom from the confines of the fort was enough to make them forget their ordeal.

Beau's horse walked alongside Fawn's and he turned to meet her contemplative gaze. "Is there something you need?"

She watched him a moment before responding. "Would you have shot that soldier?"

Beau moved with the calming rhythm of his mount, watched the landscape around him, and finally met her questioning gaze again. "I think I might have. No—" He shook his head and sent a smile in her direction. "I take that back—I *know* I would have."

"Dumb white man..." Whitecloud mumbled from atop his mount.

Beau's eyes widened at the insult, then instantly caught the hint of a smile on the old man's lips. His gaze turned to Fawn. He matched her grin a second later.

* * *

The small group traveled for a little more than an hour before they reached the agreed upon meeting spot.

Nothing could have prepared Beau for the emotions that raced through his blood at the sight of Two Feathers running across the meadow to drag his wife from the saddle and into his arms. To witness the joyful reunion between the two had been worth the long journey south.

Wolf held his excitement in check as long as it took to help the old man from the back of the horse. Once Whitecloud's feet touched the ground, the younger brave embraced his father tightly. There was no need for words.

Chapter Seventeen

August lay in the bed, curled her knees to her chest, and ignored the spasms in her abdomen. She eyed the tray of food on the table and swallowed convulsively at the sight of the congealed eggs. A weak roll of her body enabled August to stare out the curtained window at the low-hanging, ominous clouds that darkened the day. The turmoil in her stomach would end though, as it always did, through the course of the gray afternoon.

Once again, the medicinal plant made August ill—a small price to pay to ensure that she did not become pregnant with Cole's child. She ate the roots with numb determination after each beautiful session of lovemaking—a remedy her grandmother introduced her to years ago at the agency. All the woman of her tribe had done the same thing countless times when the white soldiers took what they wanted.

Cole's secret nightly trips to her room over the course of the last two weeks made it increasingly difficult for August to force the pungent tasting herbs down her throat—but it needed to be done. It also became harder and harder to imagine the day when she would no longer feel Cole's strong arms around her or hear his reverent whispered words of love.

Pushing aside the roiling sickness in her stomach, August concentrated on her escape. She would leave the ranch the moment the opportunity rose. Secreted food was stored beneath heavy blankets within the armoire and warm clothes lay in the drawers of the cherrywood dresser. She had even managed to stow an old canteen she found in Mamie's storehouse.

I have to be ready. August winced when another spasm tightened her stomach. *And I cannot travel and worry about a baby that might be on the way...*

Another, even more singular pain pierced her heart. *To have a child with the man you love is a wonderful thing—but not if that man is white; a man who will be gone from my life forever...*

August inhaled deeply, then let the air out of her lungs slowly in an attempt to ease another bout of the infernal nausea. The clatter of hooves racing up the front drive a moment later forced her into a sitting position. She tilted her head, listening, then heaved herself from the bed and consciously acknowledged the ache that shot from her thigh to her knee. The old injury reminded her once more of who she really was and a past she was forced to remember.

August trudged wearily across the thick carpet to the window and leaned into the pane of glass. A stranger leapt from his horse and raced up the steps to the front porch. He was lost from view beneath the overhanging roof. Excited voices drifted up the stairs and met August's ears a short time later. She returned to the bed, disinterest sagging her shoulders. *Someone will let me know what has happened.*

A sharp rap sounded on her door only moments later and, before she could give permission to enter, Cole bolted into the room. His worried gaze settled on her huddled form in the bed.

"August! A rider just came in from Carrie and Steven's. The clinic is on fire."

Her discomfort and the wave of queasiness were quickly forgotten as she bolted to an upright position. "The children are there!"

Her first instinct was to leap from the bed. She had no doubt that the rest of the family would rush to help put out the flames. The welfare of Tyler and Emma's children was also at stake.

"Everyone is safe," Cole assured her. "Tyler and Emma already left."

August threw back the covers, and it was then that it hit her. This was the opportunity she had waited for.

Cole watched as August dropped back down onto the mattress. He ran to her side and helped her lay back against the fluffy pillow. "Look, why don't you just stay here. You've been sick all day. I don't want to be worrying about something happening to you, too."

Cole...I love you. Please forgive me... "But—"

"No buts—you rest, and I'll see you when I get back." He quickly tucked the covers around her shoulders, dropped a quick peck on her lips, and turned to leave the room.

I'll never see you again! "Cole!"

His name hung in the air, and he turned back with a questioning gaze. August lifted her arms and welcomed him into her embrace. He returned to her and clasped her tightly against his chest. She breathed in the masculine scent of his skin, the fresh smell of his sandy-colored hair, and committed to memory the feel of his broad shoulders where they lay beneath her arms. "Kiss me."

"August, I really have to go..."

"Kiss me, Cole. Kiss me and tell me you will be safe—always."

Their lips met in a passionate show of desperation on her part and devotion on his. Finally, Cole set her back from him, then tenderly cupped her face in his rough palms. August placed her hands over his, mesmerized by the gentle look in his eyes.

"I have to go. I'll be fine, August. Have no fears on that account. I don't know when I'll be back, but I *will* be back."

He stood after another quick kiss, and she forced herself to let go of his arm. A tremulous smile curved her lips.

"I will be here waiting for you."

* * *

August stood in the upstairs window and waited until Mamie and Katy left in the buckboard. Until that moment, the three women were the only people left at the ranch. The rest of the inhabitants and all of the hired help had hurried to the Adams' in an effort to save the clinic and adjoining home from the hungry flames that consumed them. August watched Mamie store baskets of food in the wooden wagon box, then Katy helped the older woman up onto the high seat before climbing up herself to take the reins. The buckboard headed down the drive at a swift pace.

August leaned her forehead against the glass pane and closed her eyes, gathering courage for her departure. Knowing she was putting off the inevitable, she finally turned from the window and eyed the tray of food that Katy brought a few minutes earlier to replace the earlier uneaten meal. Little did the other woman know that she had unwittingly prepared food for August to eat on the run.

The time to leave had arrived. August ignored her melancholy, her still rolling stomach, her breaking heart and hurried to the armoire to pull out a canvas sack. Racing to the dresser, she yanked out a woolen jacket, a blanket, and the deerskin outfit she arrived in weeks earlier. She tossed them on the bed and rushed to undress.

Her hands suddenly stilled and, clad in Emma's dress, she moved to the full-length mirror to stare at the woman who, in a few short minutes, would disappear forever. Slender brown fingers caressed the beautiful blue cotton dress, then moved to gently touch the delicate lace at her throat and the three buttons that held the bodice closed. *I will never wear clothes such as these again...* She blinked back tears of misery.

August's jaw hardened with determination then, and she carefully undressed, folded the garment neatly, and placed it on the bed. Her hands rushed to pull on the buckskin leggings, then she threaded her arms into the fringed shirt. She moved to the foot of the bed then, and, dropping to her knees before a large cedar chest, heaved open the heavy lid. She rummaged through the sheets until she found the pair of moose-skin boots she had hidden in the trunk a week earlier. She dropped them into the pack.

Forgive me, Emma, for stealing from you... It would be winter soon, and she needed to be prepared for the cold.

August's gaze strayed to the open bag on the bed and her body trembled with shame. She had no choice but to take such measures in order to protect herself, yet the theft went against the sense of honor that had been ingrained in her soul since birth. To steal from those she loved; those who had opened their home to her, was unforgivable, but it could not be helped. She was forced to do whatever was necessary to survive the wintry miles ahead—miles that would deliver her to Pine Ridge.

She wrapped the food on the tray inside a bandana and stuffed it into the pack. August tied the bag closed then, and slipping her arms through the straps, balanced it on her back and crossed to the door. She paused to turn back though, and her wavering gaze scanned the room, from the chintz curtains to the overstuffed chair. Her mind screamed in outrage as images of Cole presented themselves. In her mind's eye, he moved the curtain aside with a disarming smile in her direction, then dropped into the cushiony softness of a chair, patted his lap, and beckoned her nearer for a quick kiss.

She fought the urge to gaze longingly at the huge, four-poster bed, with its beautiful quilt and feather pillows, and lost. He was lying there in the flickering candlelight, his eyes filled with promise and a smoldering grin curving his lips. He had slipped into her room on many occasions, when the house was quiet and darkness cloaked their passion. They had forged a bond of love over the last two weeks. They spoke of a shared future and lost themselves in each other's arms...

August had accomplished what she set out to do. She had managed to convince Cole that she would never be far from his embrace. She had heartlessly deceived the man she loved and, for that, she would never forgive herself.

The tears were instantaneous. August clasped a shaky hand over her mouth and raced from the room.

* * *

A tired and dirty group returned to the Wilkins ranch in the middle of the night. They had been gone nearly fifteen hours. The clinic was a total loss, but with the help of the Wilkins ranch hands, a good portion of the adjoining house was saved. Mamie and Katy stayed behind in the small guest cottage with Carrie, Steven, and their children. The two women would help organize the many donations that were already arriving for the new clinic.

Cole pulled the buckboard to a halt and waited for Tyler to help Emma to the ground. The latter man lifted a sleeping Sara into his wife's arms. Thomas sat up in the back of the wagon, with the help of his sister Janie, and rubbed his sleepy eyes.

"Come on, Tom. Time to head for your room." Tyler lifted the boy out and patted him on the shoulder, then gently pushed his son in Emma's direction. A second later, he swung his oldest daughter to the ground.

"Good night, Dad." Janie's tired smile lightened his heart. Tyler hugged her slight form and gave thanks one more time that his children were safe.

"Help your mom with the little ones." With a final kiss to the top of her blonde head, Tyler sent her on her way. He moved to jump back onto the wagon seat, but Cole shook his head.

"Go clean up, Ty. I can get the team unhitched. Help Em with the kids. Just leave some water on the stove so I can clean up before hitting the hay."

Tyler's shoulders slumped, but, when he looked up, a grateful smile tugged at his lips. "I'll take you up on that offer. I'm feeling my years tonight. Christ—I can't believe they lost the clinic."

"It could've been worse. Thank God no one was hurt and that the house was saved." Cole gathered up the reins and glanced at his brother one more time. His own features, too, sagged with exhaustion. "If August is awake, tell her I'll be in shortly."

"Will do." Tyler smacked the nearest horse on the rump, then plodded up the wooden walkway to the porch where Emma waited with the children. They disappeared into the house as the wagon bumped its way to the barn.

* * *

Cole trudged up the stairs to the upper floor an hour later, the overworked muscles in his legs protesting with each step he took. He reached the landing and a tired smile lifted the corners of his mouth. Someone had left a lamp burning for him.

He turned to the left and approached August's room. His hand approached the brass knob, then he hesitated. *Maybe I'll just let her sleep and talk to her in the morning. Hopefully she'll be feeling better.* He stepped away from the door and paused once more when, for some unknown reason, goose bumps rose on his arms. He retraced his steps and carefully turned the knob, then pushed the door open with the palm of his hand.

It took a moment for his eyes to acclimate to the darkness, and he breathed a quiet sigh of relief when his gaze settled on the feminine shape that lay beneath the covers. August's tiny form was outlined by a shaft of moonlight that streamed through the nearby window. Cole stood for a moment longer, waiting to see if she would awaken and turn in his direction. His wish did not come true and, not wanting to disturb her slumber, he slowly backed from the room and closed the door behind him.

* * *

Emma placed a platter of flapjacks and bacon on the kitchen table. With a gaping yawn, she returned to the stove and retrieved the tin pot of coffee to fill the men's cups. They had all slept in that morning, but still suffered the effects of the long hours the night before. Tyler and Cole discussed the events of the previous day as they dug into their breakfasts.

"I'm going to speak to Jack first thing this morning, but if I know him, he's already loading a wagon with lumber to haul out to Steve and Carrie's. We've got to get a building up and enclosed before the first snows." Although he spoke to Cole, Tyler's smile was aimed at his wife as she refilled his coffee cup. She responded with a small peck on his whiskered cheek before flitting out of his reach.

Cole watched the intimate exchange and, as usual at times such as these, his thoughts turned to August. *If she doesn't show soon, I'm gonna make a little visit to her bedroom—and to hell with what anyone might think.* He forced himself to look at to his brother again, but failed miserably in his attempt to listen as his gaze returned once more to the door that adjoined the kitchen to the living room.

"There's a keg of nails in the storage building," Tyler continued, "so I guess we've got just about anything Steve might need as far as building materials to get the clinic up and running again." He glanced at his brother and noticed his inattentiveness. His dark eyebrows furrowed in a frown. "Cole?"

"Hmmm?" His brother's hazel eyes were still riveted to the swinging door as he chewed thoughtfully on a strip of bacon.

"We could hitch a rooster to the wagon—or maybe we should just wrap a chain around a big tree and haul it over there. Hell, they could just live in a hollowed-out tree for the winter."

Emma spun from the stove with an incredulous look on her face when she heard her husband's words. Tyler met her gaze, rolled his eyes in the direction of his brother, and tapped his forehead.

Cole picked at the food on his plate and nodded. "Whatever, just as long as they have a warm place to live." His gaze moved back to the door before laughter burst from Tyler's throat.

"Jesus Christ, Cole. Just go find out what's keeping her. I can see that I'm not pretty enough to keep your attention."

"What?" Cole's disinterested gaze met his brother's twinkling one.

"I've been sitting here talking to you about Steve and Carrie's new clinic, and you haven't heard a word I said. I just told you to go up and find August."

Emma wiped her hands on a towel and crossed to the door. "I'll go up and get her. You two eat. Besides, Cole, August might not be dressed for the day."

"That's how he likes her!" Tyler called over his shoulder toward his retreating wife's back. Cole glared at his brother, then the scolding rebuke eased into a wide grin.

* * *

"August?" Emma knocked a third time. Receiving no response, she opened the door and stepped into the room. Her cautious gaze moved from the lump on the right side of the bed, one she assumed was August, to the blankets that were bunched over her head and, finally, to the folded dress that lay at the foot of the feather mattress. *Strange*, she thought. *August always hangs up her clothes...* Bumps of foreboding rose on her arms this time. Something was wrong.

She approached the bed slowly and was within three steps of the piece of furniture when she realized that August did not lay under the soft coverlet. Emma grabbed the bedspread and whipped it back, only to find a second quilt molded into the shape of a person. On the pillow lay a leather strap that bore the carving of an ivory horse.

Snatching up the piece of jewelry, Emma spun toward the dresser and frantically pulled out the drawers in search of the clothing the injured August had arrived in. Her frantic gaze settled on neither the leggings nor the shirt, and she raced to the tall oak armoire and yanked open the heavy doors.

By this time, her heart pounded frantically against her ribcage. *August! Why would you leave? Cole—I've got to get Cole!*

Emma spun and raced back to the kitchen.

* * *

Cole and Tyler jumped when the swinging door slammed against the kitchen sidebar. Emma appeared in the open doorway a split-second later. Her pale face and heaving shoulders were enough to let them know that something was horribly wrong. They leapt from their chairs to stare at the distraught woman. Slowly, and without a word, Emma held out the leather thong.

"Where did you find that?" Cole stepped forward.

"On August's pillow. She's gone. There was a rolled-up quilt under her covers to make it look like someone was sleeping in the bed. Her clothes are gone."

Stunned and confused, Cole could do nothing but stare back at his sister-in-law in slack-jawed amazement. He and August had spent countless hours whispering to one another about the future they would share and of the children they might have someday.

It was all a lie.

Yesterday, before he left for Carrie's, she had called him back to the bed and begged him to kiss her. *She was saying goodbye...*

Mechanically, he placed one foot in front of the other until he stood before Emma, then he reached out to take the gift he had given August so long ago. He turned the ivory disk slowly in the palm of his hand, but could not find the words to express his sorrow.

Tyler moved to place a hand on his brother's shoulder. "She must've left as soon as we were all out of the house. Cole...I don't know what to say." He glanced at his wife's ashen face. "Emma, why don't you check around and see if anything else is missing. Maybe we can piece this together."

It was happening again. This time though, Cole was not so sure he would find her. Her exit from his life was too well planned.

"I'm going after her," he stated resolutely.

"I figured as much," Tyler returned. "Let's think this thing through, though. She's got nearly a day on us." Suddenly it hit him that most likely, August had taken a mount. "Let's go down to the stable and see if any of the horses are gone."

* * *

Clancy met Tyler and Cole halfway to the barn. "Tyler, Cole—I was just on my way up to see you. One of the mares is missing. It's the little pinto that you purchased last year in Minneapolis. When I got back from your sister's last night, I did a quick check and noticed that the gate to her stall was open. Someone must've forgot to lock it with all the hullabaloo going on. Checked around this morning, just in case she was loose in the yard." He shook his head. "Can't find her anywhere. You want me to put a group together and go lookin' a little further out?"

"No," Cole shook his head. "We think August took her." The words tasted bitter in his mouth.

"August? What the hell would she be doing out at that time of night for? And she ain't back yet—"

Clancy's question caused Cole's stomach to churn, but he took a deep breath to calm his jangled and bruised emotions. "We think she's headed to Pine Ridge to try and find her people. I'll most likely be headed in that same direction in a few hours. Get a packhorse set up for me, would you?"

The hired hand glanced from one man to the other. "Sure...sure thing, Cole." He peered closely at the younger of his two employers. "You really gonna be leavin' today? My knees are achin' somethin' fierce. Sure as hell, it's gonna start snowing, and I think Joe pulled a muscle in his leg. That horse ain't in no shape to be takin' a long trip in bad weather."

"Then get Spirit ready." Without another word, Cole turned on booted heel and marched back to the house, with Tyler following in his wake.

* * *

"Which way are you headed?" Emma wrung her hands as she asked the question. She sat with her brother-in-law at the kitchen table. Tyler stood behind her with a comforting hand on her shoulder. Cole's pack sat ready on the floor next to the back door.

"I've been thinking about this for the last two hours. I'm going to travel through the same area I did last summer. It makes sense that August would do her best not to call attention to herself. I'd bet any amount of money that she's going to Pine Ridge and will take that same route. She knows that Wolf left there two weeks ago, with Beau. What she doesn't know is this." He tossed a folded telegram on the table before them. "I had one of the hands go into Morrell and send off a wire to Beau. I wanted it to be waiting for him when he got back from Nebraska, so he would know to be on the lookout for August. This was sitting at the telegraph office, waiting for me."

Emma picked up the paper and held it out so both she and Tyler could read the words.

"It's a message from Beau, sent from Fort Robinson," Cole explained. "They found Wolf's father and Two Feathers' wife. As we speak, he's on his way back to Pine Ridge." Cole rubbed his face with both hands and stared momentarily at the ceiling.

"That's good news, isn't it, Cole?" Emma's voice was filled with confusion. Her brother-in-law did not look happy about the turn of events at all.

"I have a feeling that this whole thing is going to blow up in my face. As horrible as it sounds, if I would've gone to the telegraph office myself, instead of sending someone else, I never would've sent the message to Beau."

"I'm not following you," his sister-in-law stated her continued bewilderment.

"When Beau gets back to Pine Ridge, he'll find out that August might be on her way south. He'll tell Wolf—who will most likely wait there until she arrives, instead of coming here immediately to collect her. *That* is what he would've done if it wasn't for my damned notification."

His eyes held a haunted look when he glanced up from the table. "I might've had a chance to find her if Wolf wasn't in South Dakota. Now, he'll wait there for her and, most likely, he'll take her to Canada when she arrives—if she arrives at all."

"I'm so sorry, Cole." Emma leaned across the table and took his hand. "But you have to listen to me. And, please, don't be angry with me. We all love August, and I'm sure she feels something akin to the same thing for us. Maybe this is as it should be, though. Maybe you should rethink your trip south. Look at the sky out there! You can smell snow in the air, Cole," she urged. "It's the first week of November. It will be so cold out there. At least consider taking the train as far as it goes."

"Yeah, and what about August? She'll be cold, too. And if you're right about there being snow in the air, she could be caught in a damned blizzard! What if something happens to her?" He shook his head in stubborn determination. "She's only a day ahead of me. I have to try and find her before she gets too far. If I go by rail, I may miss her. I know the only reason she's running is because she thinks she won't be accepted. She's also talked a lot about a dream she had and about seeing it through to its finish." He covered Emma's hand with his and his voice lowered to a near whisper. "I love her, and she loves me. You might think that August fooled us over the last few weeks by making us think she was happy here, but I know her words and actions were true emotions. It wasn't all a lie. I have to believe that—and I have to find her."

Chapter Eighteen

August raced across eight hundred miles to reach the sacred land of her people and, all the while, the urge to separate herself from the white world intensified. Surely, Cole was following. The need to escape the hold he had on her heart pushed her across the snowy miles, the first blizzards of winter, the treacherous crossing at the Missouri River—and even the need to stop and refresh both herself and the horse beneath her.

Her anxious flight was a journey to find her people—a journey to rediscover her father's dream. She needed to find Wolf and leave for their home in the huge mountains to the north. *He must be waiting for me. What will I do—where will I go if he is not at Pine Ridge?*

The exhausting trip wore on. August found it more difficult as each day passed to cling with frozen fingers to the pinto's shaggy mane; the basic instinct to survive was the only thing that kept her atop the horse.

Her weary mount crested a snow-covered butte. August's frozen eyelashes fluttered open. Her blurry mind took in the still barren terrain that was cut by a frozen river winding its way through the drifted snow. The pinto stumbled, and the freezing woman nearly pitched to the snow-covered ground. August buried her wind burnt face against the drooping neck of the pony, finally giving in to the cold and the seemingly unattainable end to her crossing.

Memories of her dreams; of her family refusing her access to the warmth of their fires, flitted through her mind. *Will they deny me again because of Cole? Will they chase me from their lives? Wolf—you must be waiting for me...I will find you, and you will keep me warm...*

The tired mare stumbled again and came to a trembling halt. August lay motionless atop the animal as the Dakota winds cut through the wool blanket around her shoulders. Her near-frozen lids opened slowly, and she stared numbly at the white ground. August summoned a last, thin thread of strength and clutched the ice-covered mane to keep herself from falling into the frigid, fluffy softness.

"August Moon..."

August slowly pushed herself upright, fighting the urge to separate herself from what little warmth the animal offered. Her mindless gaze scanned the snow-drifted landscape around her and cold, stiff fingers reached up to rub her bloodshot eyes. A woman stood in the swirling snow on the frozen trail before her. August blinked. The woman was still there.

"Please, help me..." August's words were barely a croak as she tightened the blanket around her.

The woman pushed back the buffalo robe that cloaked her gray strands, then lifted an arm. August squinted against the driving wind and, slowly, the cherished features of a life long past appeared across the wintry expanse.

"Grandmother?"

"Child, you do not have much farther to go."

August's body shivered. "I...I am cold...I do not have the strength to continue."

"You have more strength than you know."

August swiped at the tears that appeared from nowhere—the wet droplets froze against her chafed skin. "Take me with you...take me from this world. If I cannot have him, I do not want to go on. I thought I could be strong."

"Remember the ashes, child. That is your strength."

August slumped against the horse once more. She lay quietly, the frozen hide scraping against her cheek. The wintry world around her began to change...

How strange—the cold is leaving...ashes...Cole? Her skin warmed suddenly, and she forced her wide, confused eyes upward once more to see if the sun had chosen that moment to free itself of the heavy cloud cover.

"August Moon—"

She tilted her head slightly in search of the person who spoke to her.

"Follow me—I will lead you home."

"To Cole? Is he looking for me?"

"Follow me." The old woman turned and stepped through the thick blanket of snow.

August watched her grandmother's retreating back and suddenly she was frightened at the thought of being alone. She called out weakly. "Please stay with me...I've been so lonely. I'm afraid."

The vision before her turned slightly and raised a hand once more. "Then follow, child. We must be on our way."

August's bewildered stare skimmed the silent clearing and, lost in confusion, fatigue and fear, she kneed the pony in the ribs and urged the tired beast on through the deepening snow.

* * *

Someone pounded frantically on the door. Anna hung the pot of soup on a hook above the flickering flames in the fireplace and rushed to greet the unexpected visitor. Her blue eyes widened when they settled on one of the reservation Indians. He stood on the small porch, the frigid winds and pelting snow whipping around him and, miraculously, he carried an unconscious Indian woman in his arms. Without hesitation, Anna opened the door wider and urged the man over the threshold and into the warmth of the house.

Anna quickly shut the door behind them, then turned to place a warm, steady hand on the woman's frozen cheek before she moved to retrieve a cot from a nearby storage closet and place it before the roaring fire. "Put her here. We need to get her warm."

The Indian crossed the floor to place the unconscious woman on the makeshift bed.

After a cursory, yet expert medical check, Anna began to strip the frozen buckskin jacket from the woman's lifeless body. "What in God's name happened? Where did you find her? I can't believe she's still alive after being caught out in this storm."

"My son and I found her by the river. She was clinging to the neck of her dead pony."

"Dead?" Anna questioned, her voice rising with astonishment.

The Indian nodded. "The horse stumbled—the legs were folded beneath its body. But she still lay on top of the animal, with her arms wrapped around its neck. It was all my son and I could do to pull her free of the animal."

"She's not from the agency?" The question hung in the air as Anna pried off a second moose-skin boot and vigorously rubbed the frozen limb.

"I do not recognize her."

Anna grabbed a blanket from the sofa, warmed it before the fire, then laid it gently over the woman's body. She worked to remove the buckskin shirt beneath its folds as she continued. "Has she been unconscious the entire time?"

Realizing that the doctor's wife was undressing the near-dead woman, the Indian brave rose to leave. "She awakened slightly when I lifted her from the dead pony. She was aware of the cold—she kept murmuring something about coal."

Anna listened to the Indian's words as she removed a cold arm from the thawing shirt. Her hands stilled abruptly, however, when the implication of his words hit home. She brought warm palms to her suddenly flushed cheeks and her voice wavered when she met the gaze of the man standing next to her. Anna swallowed. "She asked for Cole?" Her words were the barest of whispers.

The Indian nodded again and could not help but wonder why Dr. Michael's wife's features had paled before his eyes.

"Go to the office." Anna quickly instructed. "Tell my husband to hurry home—and tell him to bring Beau McCabe."

* * *

"It has to be her. I sent someone to Rosebud with a message for Wolf. He should be here by morning." Beau crossed Anna and Michaels's bedroom and stooped to add more wood to the fire. He rose, turned, and studied the young Indian woman lying in the bed. Michael sat near her on a padded stool, and Anna worked at her knitting in a corner rocking chair. They all waited for her to awaken.

Beau brushed bits of bark from his hands, leaned silently against the fireplace, and thought back to the telegram he had received from his friend weeks earlier. Cole told him that an injured young woman from Wolf's band had snuck away from the ranch, and he was fairly certain that she would make her way to Pine Ridge. Cole also stated that he would travel to South Dakota himself in search of her.

Beau studied the woman's frail body beneath the blankets. His blue eyes narrowed. *So, what's going on between those two? Cole could easily sit next to a warm hearth and wait for me to send him a telegram. Instead, he's fighting the cold and snow to head west and find her.*

His mind wandered back to the day he, Wolf, and the others returned from Nebraska. Michael handed him the telegram, and Beau was back in the saddle, racing across the reservation to catch up with Wolf, who was on his way to Rosebud. The man had planned to settle his father with relatives, then immediately leave for Minnesota to collect a woman named August Moon. Once he had her in his possession, he planned to leave for the winter camp in Canada.

Wolf was furious when Beau told him that the woman had left the ranch in secret. Now, all the frustrated man could do was await her arrival. It would be useless to travel and chance missing her on the trail. Beau reflected now on the Indian's heightened anger when he was informed that Cole would also travel to South Dakota in the hope of finding the woman.

Beau turned once more to stare at the petite form lying in the bed. His brow furrowed with his frown. *Wolf never spoke of a wife. She must be his woman—he was adamant about leaving for Minnesota to retrieve her, then furious when he found out he would have to wait. Somehow though, Cole's got a stake in this, too...*

There was no way Beau could contact Cole on the trail. His only hope was that his friend would travel safely and arrive at Pine Ridge within the next week.

His gaze settled on the relaxed set of Michael's shoulders, then Beau stiffened when the doctor leaned forward suddenly to check on the patient. Michael quickly motioned his wife and friend to the bedside. The patient was stirring.

* * *

August's body trembled violently before her mind registered the blessed heat that encompassed her. *Cole's arms are so warm...where has grandmother gone? Cole? Did you speak to grandmother...?*

Swollen lids fluttered, then finally opened to a foggy world—a world that produced no memories. Her gaze traveled slowly from the unfamiliar faces above her to the furnished space that she and the strangers occupied. August was too weak and too tired to be frightened. She was warm—and that was the only thing her hazy mind deemed important at the moment.

Beau dropped to one knee beside the bed and smiled gently. "Don't be frightened. You were found clinging to your horse in a snowstorm and brought to my friend's home. He's a doctor. You're safe and warm now." He cocked his head slightly. "Can you understand what I'm saying?"

He watched her lips move, but no sound escaped.

Finally, she found her voice. "Where am I?" The hoarsely spoken words were a mere whisper.

"You're at the Pine Ridge Agency. Is this where you were headed? Where are you from?"

His questions confused her. *Where was I traveling to—why was I out in the cold? Pine Ridge...Cole...Wolf?* August's thoughts slowly cleared. She glanced warily at the other two people in the room before speaking.

"I...I was searching for my family. I remember. My friend came here to find help. Do you know a man named Beau?" August tucked the blankets more securely around her chin and melted into the pillow. Her question was asked with a mixture of hope and trepidation.

"It *is* you! August Moon—I'm so glad you made it here safely. I've been waiting for you. I'm Beau."

"How do you know my name?"

"Cole sent me a telegram asking that I watch for you. He thought you might travel this way, looking for your family. Just now, when you were waking, I thought I heard you say his name. I was hoping it was you."

Despite August's weakened state, she battled the spinning room and managed to push herself up to sit against the headboard. "He...Cole is not here...is he?"

Beau and Anna saw the immediate panic in her bloodshot eyes, and their wondering gazes met.

"No, not yet. He's on his way, though. He was pretty concerned that you wouldn't make it all the way here and was going to try to follow your trail." Beau shook his head, and both he and Anna could not help but see the transparent yearning in August Moon's eyes—yearning that was quickly replaced by determination.

"Wolf and the others. I must find them. Do they know I am here?"

"Your friend is probably on his way from the Rosebud agency by now. He refused to stay here at Pine Ridge and await your arrival when his father was so ill. I sent a rider for him last night."

August sank beneath the warm covers again when another shiver wracked her body. She had found her family. Now she had to get them to leave this place before Cole came back into her life. Her mind raced with dread.

He would come—of that she was sure. *Wolf will help me find the strength to fight him. We will leave and never be found again.* She clung to that hope—her disappearance from Pine Ridge would be the only thing to save her.

* * *

Wolf waited for darkness to shroud the snow-covered landscape before entering the Pine Ridge Agency and making his stealthy way through the rickety gate that led to the doctor's home. He had met Beau's messenger on the trail. Wolf was already on his way back to Pine Ridge. The forced inactivity and nagging worry had finally forced him west again in the hope of finding August before anyone discovered her.

The white man, Cole Wilkins, was on his way from Minnesota. Their paths would cross once again. A sudden desperate need to find August; to take her away from the reservation and from the man who caused fear in his heart, enveloped Wolf in a death grip—a building terror that ripped through his soul.

The messenger told him that a young Indian woman had been found nearly frozen to death just miles out from the Pine Ridge agency headquarters. Beau sheltered her in the doctor's home and now awaited his arrival. Wolf rode hard through the night and part of the next day, only to bide his time in the cold until dusk settled. Now, as he passed silently through the darkness and the wooden gate, his heart beat madly. *Let it be her.*

He stepped across the porch and gently rapped his knuckles against the hard surface. The door was wrenched opened a moment later, and Beau ushered him in from the cold. The two men eyed each other silently.

"Tell me, McCabe. Is she here?"

With a simple nod of his head, Beau led the stoic brave to the waiting August. The two men stepped through the open doorway, and both Anna and Michael immediately rose from the wooden chairs and left the room. Beau watched as August's eyes fluttered open and her gaze focused on the proud man standing beside him.

The bed was bathed in the soft radiance of firelight, making her skin glow a honeyed brown. Wolf's hungry eyes devoured the woman and a tender love shone brightly in the dark depths.

Instantly, Beau felt like an intruder and he, too, quickly exited the room. When the door latch clicked shut behind him, Wolf raced across the short distance to the bed, dropped to his knees, and was gathered into August Moon's trembling arms.

"Little One..." His words were a whisper against the satiny softness of her long dark hair, and he fought the lump of joy that formed in his throat when he felt her warm body against his. "You are safe."

"I...I did not think I would ever find you again." She leaned back slightly and reached up to touch the firm, muscular line of his masculine jaw. "I could not stay any longer at the ranch. I needed to find you." *For reasons I will never let you know...*

"I will never leave you again, Little One. I have worried over you, but I had to find the others. They are safe now—as you will be with me. I will protect you always."

Her expectant gaze moved toward the door. "Are Fawn and Whitecloud with you?"

"My father is with relatives." His joyful black-eyed gaze drank in her slight features, and he rejoiced in the fact that they were together again. "He is very ill, but maybe your safe arrival will help him become less sick. Fawn and Two Feathers left for the mountains to the north. They have gone to the winter camp and will never come back to this land again. Our friends have lost too much and will not take the chance of being separated again. August Moon—as soon as you have recovered from your long journey, and my father is able to travel, we will leave as they have done." *We will leave before Cole finds you.* "You will not fight me on this matter. The Sioux life has changed—we are welcome only as prisoners in our own land now."

The thought of traveling in the lonely cold again sent another shiver up August Moon's spine. Wolf was right though; they had to journey as far from this place as possible—but not for the reasons he deemed important. *If I do not leave now, Cole will find me. He will beg me to stay, and I cannot give him that chance...*

She reached for Wolf again and pulled him close. "Take me from here now—tonight. Let us leave this white man's world. Take me with you, Wolf, and protect me always."

Wolf rested his chin on the top of her head and closed his eyes. He had assumed she would fight him. Instead, August held him as one would a long lost lover. He gathered her closer to his broad chest, vowing to declare his love in the days that followed. "We will go now," he whispered. "I do not think I could bear to be separated from you again. Big Foot resides to the north at Standing Rock. He will take us in until we are ready to travel." Rosebud, he decided, was too close. Cole might find them there.

He helped her to rise from the bed and scoffed inwardly at the cotton nightdress that covered her body. Soon they would be far from this world, and the soft material would only be a memory of the white man who forced them apart. "I will ask the doctor's wife for your clothes."

He backed from the room, bereft at having her once more lost from his sight, and committed to memory the sight of August standing so scantily clad beside the bed. *Soon,* he vowed, *we will be as one. You have come back to me, and I will never let you go again.*

* * *

"August Moon? I have your belongings." Anna stood outside the bedroom door and waited. The sound of her patient's voice ushered her in.

The doctor's wife found August standing before the fireplace with her hands stretched out before her, seeking the warmth. The young woman turned to watch silently as her few possessions were placed on the bed.

Anna clasped her hands nervously before her and turned to meet the Indian woman's gaze. "Do you really think you should leave so soon? Wolf says you will go tonight. You're more than welcome to rest here for a few days."

"Why would you offer help to a complete stranger? You do not even know me. I am just another Indian squaw. If I leave too soon and become ill, who would really care?" August's cold stare unnerved Anna, as did the unexpected harsh words.

"I...it doesn't bother me that I don't know you. Michael and I welcome everyone who is in need of aid. My husband is a doctor. We are simply concerned about your health. You've been through a great deal these past weeks." *How am I going to get her to listen to reason?*

Anna watched the proud set of August's shoulders and tried another tactic. "Why don't you rethink this? You're welcome here, and so is Wolf. The weather is awful out there. For heaven's sake, we're in the middle of a blizzard! Stay and have a nice dinner, rest some more, and leave in the morning. The weather might clear before then. I could fix you a nice pack and find you some warmer clothes—"

"I do not need handouts." August squared her shoulders and lifted her chin. "My people have taken care of themselves for many years. We will continue to do so now. It should not matter to you or your husband what might happen to me."

Anna's brows furrowed slightly in anger, but she swallowed the rising ire and chose her words with care. "It might matter to a man named Cole."

The simple statement caused August to stumble back, then drop weakly into a padded chair.

Anna could not stop the self-indulgent smile that curved her lips. *I was right. There is some connection between you and Cole.*

"How do you know Cole?" August ran a shaky hand across her brow in a meager attempt to control her emotions.

"He's a friend of Beau's."

The Indian woman's shoulders stiffened again, this time in defiance. "And why would it matter to Cole if I am here or not? I am just another Indian squaw—as I told you earlier."

Anna's shoulders dropped with a sigh as she moved to another chair, sat down, and crossed her arms before her chest. "You stayed at Cole's ranch when you were injured. I know this, because he told Beau everything that happened to you and your family. He was the person who contacted Beau about him helping Wolf to find the others. When you disappeared, he immediately sent us a telegram asking that we watch for you." Anna tilted her head and peered at August curiously. "Why would you leave the warmth and security of his home when you knew that your friends would return for you? Why is Cole on his way here now?"

Suddenly, Anna needed to know. Something pushed her. Though she was happily married, she needed to find out if Cole loved this woman—and if August loved him back. Perhaps it was a hidden fear that drove her. A man from her past—one her husband knew nothing about—would soon enter her life again because of his connection to the woman who trembled before her. Anna could lose everything if Michael discovered the truth.

August bolted from the chair, fought the nausea that built in her throat, and ran to the bed to collect her clothes. Clasping them against her chest, she turned and raised her chin. "If Cole decided to make the long trip out here simply to see if I arrived safely, that is his own business—and his own foolishness. It does not mean that I must be here to greet him. I am leaving with Wolf tonight—" she hesitated "—to be with my own kind."

"You mean to *hide* with your own kind—to hide from Cole. What are you afraid of? That he's coming for you and you won't be able to send him away?"

"I am not afraid!" The terror in August's eyes belied her words.

"What happened between the two of you?" Anna pressed.

"Stop it!" August dropped the clothes and, as they fell to the wooden floor, she covered her ears. Anna's eyes widened in surprise at the other woman's reaction, but she could not stop now—her own fear drove her on.

"Is he coming here because he loves you?"

"No!"

"Is he searching for you so he can bring you back to Minnesota?"

"Why are you doing this!"

"Because I have to know if you're in love with him, and if he's in love with you! You're desperate to be gone, August, and I think it's because you know Cole is coming for you. It has nothing to do with your family!"

"My family means everything to me!"

"Then why did you ask for Cole when you were found, and not for them?"

The air in the room was suddenly suffocating, and August sank to the surface of the bed. Clasping her arms around her midsection, she rocked like a frightened child until the tears could no longer be held at bay. Anna rushed to her side, instantly ashamed by her words and actions. She sat beside the distraught woman and slipped an arm around her heaving shoulders.

"My, God...you do love him, don't you?"

August simply covered her face with shaking hands and let Anna pull her closer. Her head found a comforting shoulder.

"Forgive me, August. I'm sorry for upsetting you." She held the Indian woman for a moment longer before making a decision. She spoke in a quiet voice. "I know what you're going through. I know what it's like to love him, then leave him because it can never be. When I left Cole, I never thought I would find happiness again."

August's head jerked upright and she stared in amazement at the other woman through a teary gaze.

"It's true." Anna nodded her head and a wistful smile touched her lips. "It's a long story, but I was in love with him, too—a lifetime ago. All you need to know is that I wasn't the right person for him. I told him that, which I suspect you have also. Then I left. He never followed me. He's following you though, August. He must love you deeply."

"It can never be. We are too different."

"Why? Because you're Sioux? There are many white men who have taken Indian wives."

"They are mountain men—men who look only for someone to warm their beds. Cole wants more than that." August's dark eyes immediately widened when she realized the truth of her own words—and the extent of what she had just revealed.

Anna battled a sudden bout of jealousy and the image that materialized in her mind—an image of Cole and August making love. She left him years earlier because she loved him. Now though, because of those past feelings, she would tuck her possessiveness away in a hidden vault in her heart and try to help Cole regain the one thing that he apparently wanted more than any other in his life; and hopefully, her interference would not affect her marriage to Michael.

"Do you love him?"

A slight nod of the head revealed August's answer. "That is why I must leave tonight. Wolf will take me away before Cole arrives. This thing between us can never be."

"Why? Why not wait for him? If he loves you, and you feel the same, stay here. Talk to him."

"I cannot. I will go with Wolf and become his woman if he will have me. He will protect me and take me far from here. I will try to forget that I was ever in this white man's world, where I do not belong."

"But you love Cole! How can you give yourself to another man?"

"I have given myself to many white men in order to survive. All of the Sioux women have."

"But it wasn't like that with Cole, was it?"

"It does not matter." August's shoulder slumped. "Wolf will have me. I have known him all my life—he has always been good to me. We will make a life together, and Cole will be forgotten."

"Don't do this, August. I beg you. Just wait until Cole gets here, then make your decision."

August stood to gather her clothing from the floor, wiped the tears from her cheeks with the back of a hand, and reached for the top row of buttons on the nightgown that still covered her body. "The decision has already been made."

Chapter Nineteen

"Wolf, there are military troops everywhere. How are you going to reach Rosebud, then turn north without being detected?"

"I had no trouble when I traveled here."

"You were just lucky," Beau spouted back. "The War Department has moved hundreds of soldiers into the area since the beginning of November. Colonel Bingham is dead set on throwing every Sioux he finds traveling—whether it's across the reservations or not—right into prison. He suspects every Indian he comes across as being a follower of the Ghost Dance."

"Most are."

"Dammit, Wolf! Even if you do make it up to Standing Rock, that's the worst possible place for you to bring August. Both Sitting Bull and Big Foot are considered agitators of the Dance—they're being watched closely."

"We will stay away from the main trails. We need to be with my cousin."

Beau's chest heaved in a frustrated sigh, and he dropped onto a chair in Anna's kitchen and sent a silent plea to Michael for help. The doctor had sat quietly until now, letting his friend attempt to convince Wolf that leaving Pine Ridge—especially in the dead of night—was not a good idea. Now, though, he rose to face the proud Indian.

"Listen to reason, Wolf. Beau knows what he's talking about. The settlers are spreading malicious lies because of their fear. If you're found, the troops will most likely shoot and ask questions later. They won't care what your real intentions are." He held out his hands in a gesture of appeal. "Think, Wolf. What will happen to August Moon if they kill you?"

Doubt grew heavy in Wolf's chest. *Am I risking her life with my wish to finally make her mine?*

Michael saw the indecision flash in the other man's eyes. "Look, Wolf, wait until Cole arrives. Then, if you still want to head north, the three of us can accompany you and see that you get there safely."

The mere mention of Cole's name was all it took to make Wolf square his shoulders and stand firm. "We leave tonight."

The door to the bedroom opened and an anxious August staggered down the hall and into the kitchen. A resigned Anna followed behind, carrying a heavy coat in her arms. The doctor's wife draped the garment on the back of a chair, shared a dubious shake of the head with her husband, and went about collecting foodstuffs for the travelers.

"I am ready to go, Wolf." August swayed slightly and the brave rushed to steady her.

Beau jumped from his chair with anger blazing in his eyes. "Look at her, Wolf! She can hardly stand on her own, let alone sit a horse!"

August gripped Wolf's arm. "I can travel. I have been through much worse than this." She glanced at the man who steadied her. "Let us go."

"Come, Little One." Wolf picked up the thick robe he had arrived in, led August through the living room, and urged her toward the door.

"Wait!" Beau bellowed as he rushed across the room. August stood in the shelter of Wolf's arms and looked at him. "Wait for Cole. Please."

Wolf's strong jaw clenched in anger. "It is time for you to step aside, McCabe. You have helped me when no other would, but the decision is done. We will leave tonight. Unless you wish to bring the soldiers upon us, there is nothing you can do to keep us here."

Anna appeared with her coat draped across her arm once more, crossed to August, and handed her the garment along with a small sack of food. "Take this, August. If you must leave, then at least be warm. The food should get you to Standing Rock." The two stared quietly at one another. "I hope you know what you're doing."

August reached for the offerings, then dropped her gaze, refusing to meet Anna's questioning eyes. Wolf helped her to shrug on the jacket and opened the door.

Against everyone's wishes, he led August from the safety of the Gatewood home and into the blizzard. She gasped when they stepped onto the porch and buried her face against Wolf's chest when the cold wind stole their breath. He lifted her into his arms and carried her down the steps and through the deep snow, then resolutely helped her onto the back of his waiting horse. A moment later, they disappeared into the frigid darkness.

* * *

August's head slumped against the wide span of Wolf's chest. A second later, she snapped awake when his grip tightened around her slim waist in order to steady her on the horse's back.

"Do not fight it, Little One." His warm breath fanned her ear in the frosty afternoon. "Sleep—I'll keep you safe."

"If you can stay awake, then so can I..." The words were barely out of her mouth when her head lolled in slumber once more.

This time, her breathing changed and she did not move from the arms that held her securely. Wolf adjusted the blanket about her shoulders, reveling in the feel of her slight body nestled in his arms. He had done the right thing by taking her from Pine Ridge when he did. To stay would have meant Cole finding them—something Wolf was determined would not happen.

Instinct pushed him to stay one step ahead of the white man—if he did not, he might lose August forever. Wolf suspected Cole's emotions for what they were, and that meant that the man would fight for her just as fiercely as he.

* * *

August opened her eyes to the late afternoon sun. She remained motionless in Wolf's arms, taking a few moments to gather her thoughts; to rehearse her responses to the questions she knew he would ask, and to contemplate Wolf's comforting presence in her life.

Her brown eyes observed the snowy countryside now, and August's mind returned to her initial feelings when she stepped into the frigid night air the evening before. The cold had immediately curled its tendrils around her quaking body. She had wanted to race back through the door and into the white world and wait for the man she loved.

Before she knew it, however, Wolf lifted her high onto the horse's back, climbed up quickly behind her, pulled her against his warm body, and wrapped a thick woolen blanket around their lengths. The shared body heat quickly enveloped her and, somehow, she had managed to stay comfortable for the entire trip.

Now, she reflected on the journey through the night. Wolf's attitude had suddenly changed. He was no longer simply a lifelong friend; his actions and words were those of a man in love—a man protecting his woman.

August closed her eyes against the sun that glinted off the snowcapped landscape and leaned back. Wolf's arms automatically tightened protectively around her. *It is for the best...I will find the courage to become his woman and he will protect me from my own foolishness. My dear friend, I will make you happy. We will continue the dream together—something that I could never have shared with Cole.*

A deep sadness settled in her chest as she firmly pushed thoughts of the white man from her mind.

* * *

Another day of grueling, overland travel passed. August woke once more to the gentle sway of the horse's gait. Blinking her tired eyes against the cold, she spotted fires dancing in the distance. Sitting straighter, she strained to see the small log homes and hide-covered lodges that dotted the dark wintry countryside. She turned to speak to Wolf, but before she could mouth any words, he squeezed her gently and lightly kissed the cool cheek presented to him.

"We have reached Sitting Bull's camp. Soon, Little One, you will be off this plodding horse and next to a warm fire. We will rest for a short time and continue north to Big Foot."

A young brave ran through the snow to greet the weary travelers, and a shrill howl pierced the night air. Immediately, those who stood around the small fires turned to run in their direction. The doors of shoddy log homes were flung open to the cold and bodies spilled from the lighted interiors.

Within seconds, wild cries of joy were heard across the encampment. Village dogs yapped loudly in the melee. August was taken aback by the welcome. She quickly adjusted her seating once more and swiveled to peer incredulously to Wolf.

"Why are they acting like this?"

Wolf hailed the throng of happy onlookers. Women clapped their hands and patted the traveler's legs before he answered August's question. A wide grin spread across his handsome face in the firelight's glow.

"You are here—that is the reason for the excitement."

"Me?"

"Yes, you—Crazy Horse's daughter. Most have never seen you; a few only remember you as a child. The great one's daughter has returned to them, and they will spend the rest of their days thanking the Great Spirit for bringing you safely back to the Paha Sapas. Sitting Bull has awaited your coming. His wish was to speak with you as soon as we arrive."

"They knew I was coming?"

Wolf nodded. "When McCabe read from the paper and told me you were coming home, it was a tale to bring joy to our people."

August faced the teeming mass, who waved and shouted their welcome. Despite the darkness, their drawn and thin faces shone with renewed hope. They reached for her with happiness that could not be hidden. The simple joy was overwhelming, but it mingled with a sense of finality and sadness. *These are my people. It was right to come here—to give them hope. It was right to leave before Cole could take me away from everything that is familiar.*

The vision from years ago wound its way through her brain and, even with the heat of Wolf's body against her back, she shivered in the night. *I will give them hope, help them the best that I can, until the day of my death is upon me.*

Wolf reined their mount to a halt before a small log cabin that overlooked the banks of the Grand River. He helped August down, letting her body slide against his as her feet settled on the ground. Though she had shared his body heat during the last days, the intimate contact shocked her, and she immediately stepped from his embrace. Wolf was indifferent to her actions and clasped her elbow to lead her inside.

Once through the door, August removed the blanket from her head, shook the snow from her shoulders, and was immediately awestruck at the sight of the man who sat at a small unsteady table before her.

Sitting Bull looked older than his fifty-eight years, but he still sat regally upon the wooden chair as his two wives quickly cleaned the carved dishes from the table. The Chief swept his arm in August's direction and never took his gaze from her face.

"Come, child. Come into the light so I may rest my old eyes on your face."

After a tentative glance at Wolf, she moved closer to the gray-haired man and dropped onto the indicated chair. With a deep breath to settle the rapid heartbeat in her chest, August raised her chin and forced a greeting from her throat.

"Chief Sitting Bull, it is with great joy that I meet you tonight. I remember you—my band stayed with yours at winter camp many years ago."

"The joy is mine." He cocked his head and stared openly at her. "You have the look of your father about you. I heard that you and he met before his death. It is something he and I never spoke of during our time in Canada. You were a child then—now you are a woman."

August dipped her head and clasped her hands tightly. "That is true. My only wish since that last meeting with my father is to have had more time with him."

"He was a great leader. The white men, because of their fear of us, often take honorable Sioux warriors before their time. My day will come, also." The simple statement assured those standing in the room that Sitting Bull also considered himself a great man.

One of the chief's wives placed a bowl of fried meat before August on the table. The woman motioned for her husband's guest to eat. She waited for permission from Sitting Bull, which came in the form of a nod, then delicately picked up a chunk and ate daintily—even though her belly growled to be quickly filled. The old man watched her closely.

"I am happy to have you here, but not content to receive you in such surroundings." His clear eyes darted about the small one-room cabin with loathing. "We must take what the white man's government gives. The times are changing for us and for our children." Sitting Bull's gaze encompassed those in the room, and he sat straighter in the chair. "I ask you all to leave. I would like to speak with August Moon in private."

Wolf's eyes widened. If it were not for the chief's status among the Sioux, he would have protested vehemently. As it was, he trailed behind the wives as they exited the dwelling. He paused near the open door and turned back. "I will wait for you outside." With one last hesitant glance in August's direction, he walked into the night.

Suddenly, she was alone with the great man. August clasped her trembling hands tighter in her lap and waited for the chief to speak. *What does he want with me? I am a mere woman...*

The old man stood and moved to a blanket lying on the floor beside the fire. He settled himself comfortably, crossed his legs, and motioned to August. "Come, sit and enjoy the warmth.

She did his bidding and watched as he reached for an old pipe, lit the end of a branch in the flames, and puffed until the scent of the tobacco filled the small cabin. August waited patiently for him to speak. The fire warmed her body and she finally relaxed enough to enjoy the quiet solitude.

"Your arrival at Standing Rock has excited the people." Sitting Bull puffed once more, laid the beautifully handmade pipe across his knees, and stared into the flames. "It is like having your father in their midst. They have danced since Wolf told us of your coming. Do you know why they dance?"

August swallowed, and then darted a quick glance in the Chief's direction. "My friend has told me about the Ghost Dance. He said it is a ceremony to bring back the dead to this holy land. I am not my father—he is long since departed from this world. How can they believe that my presence will make a difference?"

"They believe because they have no other way to turn. If there is a chance that this land will be clean again—free again to belong to the people, they snatch at hope. Those who believe have said the buffalo will appear in great herds and our friends and ancestors will come to be happy with us once more." His gray head shook slowly. "Having Crazy Horse's daughter with them after years of hopelessness has only reaffirmed their beliefs."

August listened to his speech. *He speaks of the people's hope, and yet...his words do not convince even himself.* She remained silent to consider that strange observance. The fire crackled as Sitting Bull smoked his pipe again.

"Child, let me ask you something." He paused, deep in thought, then looked directly at her. "What have you seen?"

August's head jerked up to meet his steady gaze. "I do not understand." She had never told anyone of her vision, except for her grandmother many years earlier.

Sitting Bull peered at her closely. She saw the skepticism in his dark, wise eyes and turned away to add another piece of wood to the fire.

"I have heard that, over the years, you gained the heart of a warrior." He lifted his pipe to smoke and became lost in his thoughts once again. She waited for him to continue.

"Our women do not remain alone. Most take a husband early, raise children, and let their men crusade for them. You have not done that. You have become a part of the struggle."

"As you said, times have changed. I do what I must to assure survival on our own. My band has taken care of themselves for many years."

He puffed contentedly on the pipe and absorbed her answer. Taking the object from his lips, he stared down at the intricate carvings for a moment before looking up to watch the bright flames of the fire. He closed his eyes then, and nodded his head slowly. "Long ago, two young Lakota braves went in search of a buffalo herd. It was a fine day. Our friend, Sun, spread his light over the plains. Our Mother opened herself to his heat and, once more, reproduced the grass to provide food."

August sat transfixed.

"The two men met a woman walking up a slope of a hill. She was beautiful and carried a gift, hidden from their eyes. One man wanted her for his wife because of her beauty. But, when he touched her, a mist fell to the earth and the other man could not see them. When the fog disappeared, it was only the woman left to stand by herself."

August hardly blinked as she listened to his tale.

"The woman told the man she was on a journey to the people with a special gift. It was a magical small pipe made of red stone. It could be used to bring peace between all those who lived by Mother Earth's blessing. She followed the man to his home and spoke to his family. She reminded them to be good. She taught them prayers. She asked them for their help. She said that as long as the pipe is used, the people will live and will be happy. As soon as it is forgotten, the people will perish."

He looked at his own pipe once more, placed it between his dry lips, and drew the smoke into his lungs. August watched it leave his mouth in small, billowy puffs.

Sitting Bull leaned forward, intent on watching August's every nuance, and contemplated her nervousness. His eyes eventually turned back to the flames. "I enjoy a good fire. My old bones warm, and I find contentment for a short time." He hesitated slightly and turned back to meet her gaze. "I see things—events that others do not. Those dreams help me live my life by my own rules here at the reservation. By doing so, it unnerves the soldiers. I say my morning prayers and thank Mother Earth for the good things I still possess. I will not send one of my wives from me because the government states I may wed only one woman. My children go to the white man's schools. I do not want them to forget their proud heritage, but it is my belief our sons and daughters and all the generations that continue after will need to follow another way to get on in this world."

Sitting Bull placed the pipe reverently by his side and crossed his arms before his chest. "It is hard times that have befallen our kind. But, not all of the whites would wish this world on us. There are those who try to do their best for us. There are some that do not see the color of our skin. There are some that would share the pipe and find peace with each other. That is the real moral of the story."

August Moon's heart jumped in her chest and her eyes widened in surprise. *He knows...but how?*

"You must follow your own path, August Moon, as your father did his. He was taken early in his life. I think of him often—I imagine a time when we were both young. I remember our fearless effort to retain the land and the great battles we shared. Those days have since passed. I am happy for him now that he is not here to see our people's slow death—it will surely come to pass if we cannot find another way. Your father's great strength of spirit would have found him in a prison far from the hills he loved—he would have suffered a slow demise. Crazy Horse was privileged to die still fighting the cause." The old man adjusted his position on the floor and sighed. "But we must simply find another way to survive."

"Why are you telling me these things?"

"I tell you because your father was my good friend. You have decisions to make. The dark of the night is close, August Moon. There are dreams to conquer—and dreams to let go."

* * *

August closed the door quietly behind her and stepped from Sitting Bull's home. She glanced up to see Wolf patiently waiting for her in the falling snow. He motioned her to follow, turned without a word, and they walked a slippery path to the borrowed lodge she would sleep in.

Wolf opened the flap and preceded her inside the tent. August followed silently and noted that someone had kept a fire going for her comfort. She sank to the old buffalo hide on the ground next to the pit and held out her palms to the heat of the flames.

"The Chief's wives fixed this lodge for you to stay in. I will stay with my cousin not far away." He heard the tired sigh from her lips, hesitated, then sat down beside her. "Sitting Bull kept you long."

August drew her knees to her chest, encircled them with her arms, and continued to stare into the flames. "He spoke of the people and the hope I have brought them."

"You saw yourself how joyful they were when we arrived."

Her eyes continued to stare into the flames as if she had not heard his words. "He spoke of the Ghost Dance." She tipped her head to finally meet his gaze. "Have you danced? Do you believe these things can happen?" She instantly saw the fire of conviction in his eyes.

"I have not said much to you about it." He neglected to inform her why he had remained secretive. August believed in the people—and she believed in the Sioux's way of life—but would she participate in the wild, undulating dance? Would she beg their Gods to wipe the white man from the face of the earth? He did not think so. Not after her time spent with Cole Wilkins and his family.

"Let me ask you something, Little One. The missionaries have preached to the people about one God. They have told us his son will come back to earth to redeem lost souls. Is it so hard to imagine that he would rid the land of those who seek to own it—to do away with those who sin against others?"

August's thoughts spun in her head. She thought of Sitting Bull's words—a man who had fought long hard battles to retain his freedom—a man who now scoffed at his so called independence within the confines of a world gone mad. Now, the old man looked to another way. She had no answer for Wolf.

"We have always lived as one with the land," Wolf continued. "The Sioux have never sought to own the ground we sleep on—only to thank Mother Earth for the bounty she has provided. We would share when the white man steals all that he sees. Only a Messiah could right all the wrongs we have endured. Only a holy man can realize our struggle and understand who the true survivors will be in the end. Our families will return—that is the truth of the Ghost Dance."

August contemplated his strong belief—and found fault with his words.

It was the first time that she doubted her dream—a dream that would help the people. *Grandmother was wrong...* How could she, one lone woman, right the terrible wrong?

She closed her eyes and pictured Cole the last time she saw him. He continually told her, while in Minnesota, that she needed to realize her people were at the end of their lives as they knew it. He pleaded with her to let him help, but to do it the white man's way. Cole sympathized with the Sioux. He went out of his way to help her and her family when their 'hostile' life threatened to banish their very existence. He and his family would do their best. And, if their best was not enough, they would still protect her and those she chose to bring with her. They would welcome all into their home. August found it hard to separate the reality from the dream.

Sitting Bull knew. He understood her confusion. *Was he telling me it is over? What do I conquer—what do I let go?* August placed Wolf's strong hand in hers, hoping his touch would help her discover the answer.

"How can you believe that this thing called the Ghost Dance will rid the land of those who strive every day to take it from us? Tell me, Wolf. I am sorry, but I see it as foolishness."

He leapt up and instant anger sparked in his dark eyes. "Foolishness? Is that what your time with the white man has caused you to think? You are a Sioux, August Moon! Your father was a great man, who would have fought longer for all of us if his life had not been taken so callously. He would not have given up because he thought the fight was too difficult."

"The times then were not what they are now. Even Sitting Bull has concluded that the next generations will need to learn the ways of those who seek to enslave us."

"He has grown soft in his old age."

"He has grown wiser," she snapped back.

They were at a stalemate. Wolf stifled the heated words that sat on his lips and swallowed his anger. Arguments would not endear him to August. His broad shoulders lifted with a deep breath before he dropped quietly to sit beside her. He reached out to gently grasp her hand and August longed to pull away from him, but knew it would hurt him if she did.

"Little One. I do not want to argue with you. I am sorry for my angry words. You were gone from this madness for many months—you have not seen what I have. That is still no reason for my actions." His thumb rubbed the soft knuckles of her small hand. "Especially when my heart was filled with pain every day we were apart."

"Mine also was filled with sadness when I thought of you." She was being honest with him. Even though she had fallen in love with Cole, she had thought about Wolf most of her waking hours. The two men were the most important people in her life.

"When I saw you again at Pine Ridge, nothing seemed so bad because you were safe and we were together again. For a moment, I forgot the ache of what the soldiers did." He lightly squeezed her fingers. "Now we must decide the course of our future. At first, I felt a burning need to leave, to go north to find Fawn and Two Feathers—" *And put greater distance between you and the white man who searches for you.* "Now I am not so sure we should do this."

August leaned forward to better read his face in the fire's light. "I thought that is what you wanted. That we would leave and never come back."

"But how would we leave? Would we go as friends...or something more?"

"What are you saying?" August's heart pounded. She had always suspected that he felt more than friendship for her, but now she would know for sure.

"I have known you since you were a small child, Little One. At one time, I was certain you would never take a man to your side."

She gently slipped her hand from his and rose to put distance between them, suddenly afraid of what he would reveal. Wolf bounded to his feet.

"I do not believe that is the way it should be now. Even you understand we are like one at times. We have always shared the same dream, Little One. Could we not share it as man and wife?"

August's brain raced to find an answer. At Pine Ridge, the decision had seemed so easy. Now, when she was faced with his intentions, she was unsure if she could become his wife in the true sense. She needed more time to convince herself.

"Why do you want to stay here and not travel north?"

She purposely avoids my question. I have waited this long for you, August Moon—a while more will not matter. "I saw faces aglow with hope when we arrived. I am torn, Little One, but I do not think I could leave with you and forsake these people."

"You make it sound as if I am your possession already." Her voice rumbled with sudden, unconcealed anger.

Wolf stepped forward and rested his palms on her shoulders. August flung her gaze from his.

"Look at me." He retained his composure and refused to be pushed away. "I speak this way because of the excitement I feel at spending the rest of my life with you. We have only each other. Do not throw that away because I fumble with my words."

She lifted her eyes as he continued with words that came from his heart.

"I have loved you for many years, Little One. I kept it hidden because you stated you would never take a man to your side. I hope that has changed. Let us be happy together with our own kind." He saw the softening of her jaw and dropped his head to kiss her—a slow, tender touching of lips so as not to frighten her away.

Instant pain pierced her heart. August longed to feel warmth; to feel *anything* as a result of the kiss. His mouth moved gently across her cheek and, still, she could not find the desire she searched for.

I have no choice. Remember, he will always be gentle—he will be a good husband.

She tried to respond to his gentle ministrations.

But, he will never be Cole...

She pulled from his embrace and a tremulous smile curved her lips. Wolf took her actions as those of a woman frightened by the first stirrings of love.

"I will be patient with you, Little One." He bent to grasp his robe, wrapped the hide around his shoulders to ward off the outside cold, and left her to return to his own tent.

The flap dropped to keep out the chill, and August sank weakly to the ground. She buried her face in her arms and wept for the man who would never be hers.

Chapter Twenty

Beau pounded his fist on the surface of the scuffed oak desk. "Come on, Landers. Its not that damn difficult. Either the shipment of beef is here or it isn't. I saw supply wagons come in yesterday. These people need meat. What the hell are you hiding anyway?" He paced before the clerk, trying to maintain his patience with the reticent man.

Harold Landers mopped his face, even though the cold Dakota winds whistled around the building. He nervously stuffed the dirty hanky in a ripped front pocket of his shirt and shuffled through the endless stack of papers on the desk's surface. "I told you, Beau. The shipment wasn't beef. Those damn Sioux and their dance," he muttered. "They're ready for the warpath." He looked up. "Do you really think we should be feeding them right now?"

Beau placed his palms flat on the surface of the desk, narrowed his eyes suspiciously, and ground out his next words. "So what the hell was in that shipment?"

Landers sank back against the chair and eyed the irate man on the other side of the desk. He rolled his eyes and heaved a sigh. "Shit—you're going to find out anyway. All right, I'll tell you, but you gotta keep your damn mouth shut. Some Hotchkiss guns were shipped in from out east."

"What!" The word exploded from Beau's mouth.

"You know what's been going on, Beau. The settlers are getting nervous. They're afraid there's gonna to be an uprising."

"That's bullshit and you know it! Christ almighty—if the agency Indians get wind of this..." Beau crossed to the woodstove, unable to utter out loud what would happen in the future if the big guns were brought into the open.

The Sioux were already nervous. Over the last month, troop movement had escalated and Beau constantly watched the strained and continually thinning faces of the local Indians for any reaction. Tensions were running high as one finger pointed at the other. Beau turned slowly and glared angrily at Landers, which was enough to make the man to drop his gaze to the ground.

"Who's behind this?"

"Come on, Beau. Shit, I should never have told you. You know I can't—"

"It's Bingham, isn't it?" The reddening face of the office clerk told Beau all he needed to know. "That son of a bitch. He's instigated a lot of what's written about these people. He's got everyone out east in an uproar, because he demanded the influx of troops. Christ—the Indians are starving, Harold. They're less ready for an uprising now than they were six months ago." His eyes narrowed further and Landers nearly disappeared beneath the desk in the face of Beau's commitment to the Sioux. "Is Bingham here? I heard troops come in early this morning."

Harold immediately began to stack the papers on the desk into a pile, refusing to answer. "I got work to do—"

Beau pounded a fist on the flat surface again. "Fine! I'll find him on my own." He turned, and stalked toward the door.

"Now, don't go off half cocked, McCabe. You don't need to be buttin' heads with the Colonel." Landers hauled himself up from the chair and started around the desk.

Beau ignored the clerk, angrily yanked the heavy door open, and stopped dead in his tracks. He could not help but stare at the heavily clothed man who stood with his arm out, ready to turn the knob. Beau's jaw dropped open.

"Cole!"

"Well, I didn't expect to find you so easily." A tired grin tugged at the corner of Cole's lips.

Beau took one look at the heavily frosted mustache and beard and ushered his friend quickly through the doorway and into the office. His anger was forgotten for the moment.

Cole stamped the snow from his boots, crossed to the potbelly stove placed in the middle of the room, and held out his gloved hands. "I didn't think I was this close to the headquarters. As much as I'd like to sit next to this fire for the rest of the night, I've got to get my horse taken care of. It's been a long trip."

He turned back. Instant fear jumped into the hazel depths of his eyes. "Is she here?"

The simple nod of his friend's head caused Cole's shoulders to drop in relief.

"She showed up last week—almost didn't make it," Beau informed him. Noticing Lander's sudden interest in the conversation, Beau tipped his head in the direction of the door. "We can continue this conversation after we take care of bedding down your mount. Let's go."

Cole recognized his evasiveness and followed the other man back into the cold.

* * *

"She must've had one helluva trip out here," Cole said when Beau finished the story of August's near escape from the wintry cold. "I pushed it pretty hard and, still, she arrived here almost a week before I did."

Cole leaned against the last stall inside Michael's small wooden barn. Spirit was fed and now rested her large head wearily against his chest. The Minnesotan scratched the drooping ears.

Cole shifted his weight and tipped his pensive gaze in Beau's direction. "For some reason, you're skirting the crux of the conversation. She's not here anymore, is she?"

"Sorry, Cole." Beau shook his head. "She left with Wolf the same night he got here. They headed for the Standing Rock Agency, to the north."

Cole continued to scratch Spirit's ears silently, but his thoughts spun. *She's gone...* He glanced up. "Did she know I was coming after her?"

"Yeah. Cole...I've got to ask. What's going on between the two of you? As soon as she found out that you'd sent me a telegram and hit the trail yourself, she couldn't leave fast enough."

And I bet Wolf couldn't get her out of here fast enough either. Cole shrugged tiredly and rubbed his whiskered chin with a gloved hand. "It's a long story."

Beau noted his friend's agitation and sudden weariness. "Let's get you set up in a warm cabin, then we'll head over to Michael and Anna's so you can meet them. If I know the Gatewoods, there'll be hell to pay if we don't stay for a good home-cooked meal. By the look of it—you need some hot food. I've got plenty of time to hear the rest of the tale."

* * *

"You're really going to like Anna and Mike," Beau informed Cole as they leaned into the icy wind and walked down the snow-covered path that led to the Gatewood's front door. "The two of them are about the closest thing I have to a family. I know you'd prefer heading north, but it's pretty late in the day. How about we get in a good meal, hit the hay early, and start out first thing in the morning."

"I know that's the reasonable thing to do, but it doesn't make things any easier." Cole shrugged his shoulders beneath the heavy jacket and stepped up onto the porch. "I had hoped to speak to Wolf and August tonight—"

Before he could continue, Beau was hailed from behind. Both men turned, and Cole's gaze settled on a large man who crossed the road and headed toward the house, waving a welcome in their direction.

"That's the doc." Beau waved back and the two men waited for Michael to join them.

"Hi, Mike. I'd like you to meet Cole Wilkins. He finally made it out here from Minnesota. Just arrived."

Michael removed his glove and extended an arm to accept Cole's handshake. "It's good to finally meet you. We were wondering how much longer you'd be. Pretty tough trip out here?"

"It's not something I'd like to do every winter."

"Well, come on in and get out of the cold. I'll introduce you to my wife, then, if you wouldn't mind, I'd like to steal Beau for a bit."

"What's going on?" Beau asked.

"Nothing much—I just need help with some supplies that arrived for the clinic. I was just coming to look for you. I'll need them in the morning, and the crates are too heavy for an old man like me."

"I could help out, too," Cole offered.

"Absolutely not." Michael reached for the doorknob. "Tonight you're the guest—but I'll probably take you up on the offer another time. No arguing. Just sit and have a cup of hot coffee until we get back for dinner. There's no way Anna will let the two of you leave without a full belly." He stepped through the doorway at the front of the house. "Anna? We've got company!"

Anna smiled from where she stood in the kitchen beside the fire, stirring a bubbling pot of stew. It was just like Michael to bring someone home for a warm meal. *Good—it'll get my mind off of Cole.*

Her stomach churned with the thought. She had not slept well since August's departure a week earlier, and Cole's arrival loomed on the horizon like a thunderstorm promising to wreak havoc. She had spent agonizingly long days worrying that her world would turn upside down. What would he say? Would he give away her former life? Would Michael toss her aside, hurt and angry because she was living a lie?

Anna shook off her fear of the unknown. *I'll have to figure it out. Somehow, I'll keep my horrible secret from Michael. If I lose him, I'll be alone for the rest of my days.* She could not even contemplate what life would be like without him.

Squaring her shoulders, Anna dropped the ladle on the counter and turned to greet her husband as he entered the kitchen with his guests. The whipcord of her emotions nearly buckled her knees when she saw the man who stood between her husband and Beau.

Cole stood in the unfamiliar surroundings—stunned beyond belief. *Belle...*

"Anna," Michael smiled, "this is Beau's friend from Minnesota. Cole Wilkins, I'd like you to meet my wife."

Cole was speechless. What the hell could he say? Belle stood across the room—no more than a dozen feet from him—and she looked no older than she did the last time he saw her. Even more unbelievable? She was Doctor Michael Gatewood's wife—*Anna.* His eyes moved to the few strands of graying hair that laced their way through her russet-colored curls—the only clue that eight years had passed since that day she came to warn him that the devil himself had come in search of Emma.

Anna rushed forward with a sickly smile pasted on her white face. "Mr...Mr. Wilkins, it's so nice to finally meet you." She reached out to shake his hand, and Cole slipped off a glove and clasped her fingers. Her palm was cold and clammy.

She called me Mr. Wilkins. Think, Cole!

"It's nice to meet you, also." He continued to grasp her trembling hand, finding it hard to force out any other words.

Michael leaned forward and planted a quick kiss on her pale cheek.

"Honey, I hate to do this to you, but I asked Beau to help me with the medical supplies. If I leave them too long, everything will disappear. Would you mind seeing that Cole gets some hot coffee? The man needs to warm up after his long trip. We won't be long." After another quick kiss, he and Beau left for the storage shed.

The clock ticked away and, still, the former lovers could only stare at each other. Suddenly, Anna regained her shaken composure and motioned to a wooden chair at the far end of the oak table.

"Please...ah, sit down, Cole. I'll get you a cup of coffee." She walked with measured steps to the cupboard, retrieved a dainty cup, and filled it from the tin pot that warmed on the range top. She drank in the sight of him as he silently took a seat, then averted her gaze from his when he looked up.

"Belle—"

"I'm sure you're surprised to see me here," she interrupted quickly.

"You could've knocked me over with a feather."

Anna crossed back to the table and set the cup before him. She stepped back and nervously brushed away imaginary wrinkles on the white apron wrapped around her slim waist. Cole continued to stare in confused amazement as she moved hesitantly to the chair opposite where he sat. She sank down onto the hard surface and folded shaking hands before her on the table.

"Belle, how—"

"How did I get here?" She finally found the nerve to meet his gaze unswervingly. "I've been dreading this moment. Beau talked about you. It didn't take me long to realize who his friend from Minnesota was."

"You're still not telling me how you got out here."

Ignoring his question, Anna flattened her palms on the wooden surface of the table and sent a beseeching look in his direction. "Cole, I'm begging you. Please don't tell Michael about us. I've finally settled into the life I used to dream about. He's kind and gentle and doesn't deserve to be hurt. Finding out about my past would kill him."

"Is this where you've been the whole time? I was worried about you when you left without a word." Cole reached across the table and squeezed her hand. "Get that look of fear off your face. I'm not going to say anything, if that's what you want. I would never do that to you. Now, how did you ever find your way here?"

Her shoulders sagged with the reprieve he had just granted and a tremulous smile appeared on her face. "It's a long story, but first I want to thank you for keeping silent. I love Michael, Cole. He's the most important thing in my life now."

"I'm happy for you, Belle...Anna." His eyebrows lifted and he shook his head slightly. "I'll have to get used to calling you that. Why did you change your name?"

"I didn't—I'm just using a different version of it. I was born Annabelle Adams. I've really left my old life, Cole. Belle died on the trail out here—when Anna met Dr. Michael Gatewood."

Cole simply smiled and squeezed her palm once more before dragging his hand to the mug of coffee. He leaned back in the chair. "Alright, *Anna*. I can't wait to hear your story."

She left the table to gather a bowl, and then filled it from the bubbling pot hanging over the fire. She spoke to him over her shoulder as he stared at her slim back. Cole was still in awe that their paths had crossed after all these years.

"I decided to travel to San Francisco. I thought that, on the other side of the country—" her hands hesitated, "—I could start a new life without the threat of my past life finding me. I managed to obtain a spot with a wagon train traveling the Oregon Trail to the Pacific. From there, I planned to move south along the coast. It was going to be the adventure of my life before settling into a quiet spinsterhood."

A chuckle escaped from Cole's throat. "You? A spinster? I hardly think so." In his mind, Anna would never be a spinster. It was too hard to forget her dynamic personality.

She set the bowl of stew and a spoon before him with a wry smile. "Eat. The trip through the Dakotas was uneventful. It wasn't until the wagon train reached Montana Territory that my plans went awry. Cholera struck the entire wagon train with a vengeance. I didn't get sick, so I helped care for the others. Six people died the third week out. Everyday, more and more people were struck down and the wagon master finally had no choice but to stop the train so we could take care of those who were ill."

She sat at the table once more, propped her elbows on the surface, and rested her chin in the palms of her hands as she watched Cole consume his meal. He continued to listen attentively.

"A Cavalry troop showed up one day. Dr. Michael Gatewood rode with them and immediately shot orders to those of us who were not afflicted. I followed him from patient to patient, forcing salt water down parched throats to combat dehydration. The nasty task of dumping waste pails far from the train also fell within my job duties. It was the most grueling thirteen days of my life but, with so many sick, I didn't dare whine about the forced recruitment."

"I'm sorry, but—" Cole could not hide his smile "—this doesn't sound like a love story to me."

"Stranger things have happened—which I plan to speak to you about in a minute." Cole pondered her statement, but forgot about it a moment later when she began her tale once more.

"I was with Michael constantly. We worked together and ate together. The only time we were apart was when he coaxed me back to the wagon and made me lay down for a few short minutes every day. At the end of that second week, I was tending to a small child. Michael found me, and I'll never forget the tired smile of joy on his face when he proclaimed we were finally at the end of the outbreak. I stood to accept his handshake of congratulations, but before our fingers ever touched, everything went fuzzy. That's the last thing I remember until I woke at Fort Benton, Montana, with Michael by my side."

"How did you get there?"

"I don't remember, but he explained afterwards that the wagon master refused to wait for me to recover after having lost so many days on the trail already. My few personal belongings were dumped out of the wagon and they left me without another thought. Michael took me to the Fort, not knowing what else to do—and the rest is history. Within a month, he proposed, and I accepted." She raised her teary gaze up to meet Cole's. "It was the best thing I've ever done in my life."

Anna rose from the table, grabbed another cup along with the pot of coffee, and retraced her steps. She silently poured them both a cup and settled herself in the chair once more.

"Michael had enough years in the army to be able to transfer anywhere he wanted to go. We moved down to Camp Robinson—that's where he met Beau. When Beau mustered out of the service and told him about the Indian's plight here at Pine Ridge, Michael didn't hesitate to follow."

"How do you feel about this place?"

She looked up with love shining in her eyes. "As long as I'm with Michael, it doesn't matter where we are or what we have to put up with. I would follow him anywhere. I'll admit, this life was hard at first, but I've become as determined as my husband, and Beau, to make things easier for the Sioux—if we can. I imagine we'll grow old here."

Cole noticed Anna's face glow with happiness every time she mentioned her husband's name. "Well, I guess that's not such a bad tradeoff when you're doing what you want and with the person you want."

A swift jolt of sadness crossed his features, then disappeared quickly. Anna crossed her arms and stared quietly at him for a moment. "Can I ask you something?"

"Go ahead."

"Why are you here? What does August Moon mean to you?"

His eyebrows rose in surprise. "You know her? You've met August?"

"One of the agency Indians brought her here after he found her half frozen by the river. Michael took care of her. That girl went through hell to get back to South Dakota, and she fought even harder to stay ahead of you on the trail." Anna leaned her elbows on the table again, clasped her fingers beneath her rounded chin, and gazed thoughtfully at him. "I had a conversation with her before Wolf took her away. She loves you."

Cole's heart clamored in his chest, and Anna watched the color drain from his face. "She said that?"

"No—I beat her up emotionally, and then she *screamed* that at me. I was so distraught myself, what with worrying about you showing up and Michael leaving me, that I wasn't very nice at first. August Moon knows about us—I told her. I also told her that, when I left Minnesota, you never followed me."

Cole's guilty gaze dropped to the table.

Anna reached to take his hand. "Don't feel bad, Cole. You and I were never meant to be. I'm glad I was smart enough to figure that out when I did. I told August that you *were* following her, however—and it was most likely because you loved her very much." Her blue eyes softened as she stared across the table. "Do you?" His hazel eyes reminded her of a child who had lost his most prized possession and she continued softly. "You don't have to answer. I can see it on your face."

"I never intended to fall in love with her, but something just happened between us. She knows how I feel—and bolted because of it. I'm not leaving until I find her again and have a chance to get her to see reason. I don't give a damn that we're different. She has nothing here anymore—nothing except the face of something remotely recognizable."

"You've got a tough fight in front of you, Cole. These people are having a hard time letting go. They're very proud."

"Where did Wolf take her?"

"North to Big Foot's camp at Standing Rock. I don't know if they were going to continue on to Canada to meet Two Feathers and his wife or not."

Cole's hope deflated. The trip to South Dakota had taken so long—and now August was running from him again.

"I'm sure Beau will ride north with you if that's what you want to do." Anna leaned forward and rested her other hand on his forearm. "Go after her, Cole."

His eyebrows rose in surprise.

"I'm serious. I know her true feelings. She loves you, but life with her own kind pulls at her. It's a life that will soon be gone. She knows it—most of the Indians know it—at least the ones that are not like Wolf."

"Why do you say that?"

"Because Wolf is from the old guard. He will never accept reservation life. He will fight until the battle kills him. Don't let August Moon go through that misery. Take her away—make a life with her before she becomes another casualty."

Cole listened to her impassioned speech and could not help but wonder where her staunch emotions came from. "Why are you so intent on me finding her?"

"Because I remember telling your sister-in-law once that you deserved better than me."

"Belle—"

"Belle is dead. At one time, she was jealous of the woman who would enter your life one day and turn it upside down. Belle never would have guessed though, that it would be a courageous Sioux woman who would hold your heart in her hand."

Chapter Twenty-One

Cole and Beau traveled three long days though the winter cold to reach Standing Rock. They entered the Sioux encampment amidst barking dogs and small children who huddled along the compacted path. Beau insisted on a quick visit to Sitting Bull's camp in order to find out if Wolf and August had stopped to rest on their way north. He could not imagine the pair traveling all the way to Big Foot without some relief from the cold in the form of rest and food.

Sioux mothers yanked their children into the weather beaten log homes or buffalo hide teepees as the two white men passed by. Most recognized Beau, but with the strain of distrust always at the forefront, the stranger with him could not be disregarded.

Cole ignored the cold wind that blew snowflakes in a frenzied flurry about his horse and thought instead about the heat in the pit of his stomach every time he pictured August. *Has she been here?* His troubled gaze took in the disheveled camp, and he wondered what was hidden beneath the snow. Ragged shirts, chunks of buffalo hide, and threadbare blankets flapped in the wind through open windows with no glass—a meager attempt to keep winter from entering the Indians' living quarters.

Beau observed his friend's gaze travel from one squalid log home to the next. "Pretty sad, isn't it? This is what the Sioux have been reduced to on the reservations."

"Christ almighty—" Cole was appalled.

"Yup—that's who I blame."

Cole swiveled atop Spirit in surprise. "What do you mean by that?"

"Supposedly, He's one of the reasons they have to live like this. The missionaries don't allow them to worship their own Gods—only the one true

Christian deity. In my mind, it all ties together. If the natives had been allowed to worship who they please, then the white government wouldn't be so adamant about them conforming. In short, the white man wouldn't feel so threatened, and we may have been able to live in peace together."

"As much as I hate to agree with you, you've got a great point." Cole's gaze darted around the perimeter of the squalid camp. "Do you think she's here?"

"We'll find out soon. Someone will come out to greet us."

The words were barely out of Beau's mouth when a man wrapped in a thick buffalo hide exited one of the dwellings and headed in their direction.

"What the hell?" Beau whistled between his teeth. "That's Big Foot's right hand man, Spotted Eagle. They must've come south for some reason. Maybe we're in luck. If Wolf and August met up with him here, maybe they haven't left yet."

The two white men waited for the aging brave to approach them. The Sioux's high cheekbones only accentuated the thinness of his face, but he moved regally down the path, his unforgotten dignity acknowledged by those who stood and watched. He came to a stop and waited patiently as Cole and Beau dismounted before him.

"McCabe—much time has passed since we last met." Spotted Eagle reached out a hand in greeting.

Beau nodded his head, removed his glove, and grasped the Indian's hand with his own. "I've traveled to Nebraska and just recently returned."

"Wolf told me."

At the mention of Wolf's name, Cole tensed and waited to hear what the old man would say next.

Beau withdrew his palm and replaced his glove. "Wolf is here? That's good news. I had hoped he might stop at Sitting Bull's village before going north to Chief Big Foot's camp."

"Big Foot is here to acquire supplies. We will leave for our home in the morning. Wolf came here for the same reason and will travel north with us." Spotted Eagle's suspicious dark gaze rested on Cole, then moved back to Beau. "He says you helped to free his father. As I see it, Whitecloud simply exchanged one prison for another by returning to Rosebud."

"It was his choice. But, as we speak, Two Feathers and his wife are on their way to the winter camp in the mountains."

Spotted Eagle's eyes narrowed in response to Beau's comment. "It is a good man who holds his ego in check, yet lets those around him know of good deeds accomplished." The old man's gaze rested on Cole again. "You have brought a visitor."

"This is my friend, Cole Wilkins. He's traveled from Minnesota to see Wolf and the woman who rides with him. Can you tell us where they are?"

Spotted Eagle ignored the question and continued to stare at the Minnesotan. Securing the buffalo robe around his shoulders, he stood a bit straighter. "I have heard about you. When Wolf could find no other to aid him, you opened your home to August Moon when she was injured. You also asked McCabe to help Wolf find his father. Why would you do this?"

"I became friends with both of them." Cole wanted to be done with the inquisition, but held his frustration in check. Because of past experiences with the Sioux nature, he knew the man would get around to answering Beau's question in his own good time. "They needed horses, so I got them. August Moon was gravely injured soon after. I could do nothing else but try to make her well."

"And the color of their skin means nothing to you?"

"They were people in need. I would've done the same for anyone—no matter what color their skin was."

Spotted Eagle nodded, apparently happy with Cole's response. "So, you are here to see them?"

"It would make me happy to know they are settled."

Spotted Eagle turned to the brave who stood behind him. Words were exchanged before the younger man loped back in the direction they came from.

"Wolf is here, but it will be his choice to visit with you. Until then, you are welcome in my lodge. My fire is warm." Spotted Eagle turned abruptly and walked away, expecting the white men to follow.

Cole glanced at Beau and received a nod of accent. He gathered up Spirit's reins, and the two men fell into step behind the old warrior as they headed down the path.

* * *

The fire crackled, throwing out its heat to warm the inside of the teepee. Cole sat in awe—he was at Standing Rock, conversing with an old

Indian who, at one time, was a great warrior and instrumental in the demise of Colonel George Armstrong Custer. Chief Big Foot sat cross-legged next to the white man, relating the tale as he puffed slowly on a makeshift pipe after finishing a lengthy conversation with Beau regarding the welfare of his band.

Another thirty minutes passed before the occupants of the tent heard the telltale crunch of footfalls in the snow. The steps stopped just outside the heavy flap. Cole looked up, hoping against hope that August would step through the opening.

The flap was moved aside and Wolf entered into the warmth. He stood before them, and anger blazed in his eyes when his gaze settled on Cole. The white man was the first to scramble to his feet.

"Wolf—it's good to see you."

"Why have you come?" Rage now pinched his face.

Cole was aware of Beau rising to his feet beside him. Before the Minnesotan could answer the abrupt question, his friend reached out to grasp Wolf's hand and diffuse the suddenly tense atmosphere.

"We weren't sure you would be at Standing Rock. Cole wanted to be certain both you and August Moon made it here safely. We would have traveled on to Big Foot's camp if you hadn't been here."

Wolf's jaw hardened even more and his black eyes narrowed further, but the querulous look belied the fear that coursed through his veins. "We have both survived," he returned stiffly. Wolf's stony gaze did not even flicker as he watched the relief spread across Cole's rugged features. The fact that August Moon had lived because of a white man's generosity when Wolf could do nothing for her angered the reticent Indian. He took a deep breath to control his raging emotions. Cole's kindness in a time of need could not be overlooked. He swallowed his pride—and his frustration. "I thank you for all that you have done. My father is with his relatives. Two Feathers and Fawn will start a new life far from here, and—" Cole noted his slight hesitation "—August Moon has recovered from her injuries. I will tell her of your well wishes."

The flash of stubbornness in the black eyes did not discourage Cole. *If I don't push this, he'll never let me see her...* "I would like to talk to August myself, if you'll let me know where she is."

Wolf was trapped. He could hardly turn this man's request down in the presence of Spotted Eagle and Chief Big Foot. To do so would be inhospitable after all that Cole had done for them, and his old friend and cousin would not let it pass. Wolf hid his annoyance with a defeated sigh. "Come. I will bring you to her."

* * *

The frozen snow cracked loudly beneath the horses' hooves in the cold, dark night as Cole followed Wolf along the mile-long trail at the south end of the encampment. The man riding before him remained silent, stiff, and foreboding. Cole's stomach churned. He would know within the next hour if August would willingly alter her life in exchange for what he had to offer her.

He was so deep in thought that his mount almost bumped into Wolf's before he realized the Indian had reined his horse to stop. The stoic brave turned with tight lips and finally acknowledged the visitor with a nod of the head. He pointed to a tent pitched a short distance from the last cabin. Wood smoke filtered from the open hole at the top.

"She is there."

Cole was acutely aware of the fact that Wolf struggled with his own emotions as he stared in the direction of the lodge.

"She will be surprised to see you. August Moon does not know you are here." Wolf closed his eyes and gathered strength. The time had finally arrived for the two men to speak the truth to one another. His lids opened slowly, and he faced Cole. "What are your intentions?"

"I just want to see her."

"But you will not only see her, will you? We have never spoken of our true feelings."

Cole opened his mouth to speak, but was interrupted when Wolf lifted his hand, requesting silence.

"When I first met you, White Man, I knew you would forever follow my path. I felt that in my heart. I understood that you and I would have a great tie between us." His gaze returned to August's temporary lodge. "I think that tie is August Moon. I have wondered many times why she will not speak of you."

"Wolf—I didn't come here to cause you pain. But, if you must know, I care for her deeply."

"Enough to walk away and allow her to be her true self?"

"Enough to take her away and keep her safe."

Wolf's shoulders fell in sudden defeat. Visions of the years spent with

August Moon, of her smile when happy, of her determination when her mettle was tested, rested sadly in his head. She would leave with this man—the knowledge was something he had been aware of and fought against since their paths first crossed. That sixth sense was something he had battled since their arrival at Standing Rock—the night he first kissed her. Even then, he had sworn to be patient; but she had not returned the kiss as would a woman in love—at least not a woman in love with *him*. From that moment on, August had done everything possible to avoid physical contact. Pain sliced through his chest, but he clawed past it.

"Will she be your wife, or will she become the plaything of a white man?"

"I would never do that to her, Wolf. When I look at August, I see a woman I want to share my life with. If she feels the same, then I would ask her to be my wife."

Wolf turned his head to stare at the far horizon with brave acceptance. His chin dropped, and he ignored the continued pain that pierced his chest. The fight left him by degrees. He could not make the decision—he could not rule August Moon's emotions. Only she could decide. He turned back to Cole.

"Go. I ask only that you let the choice be hers. She has followed a dream her entire life. Not you, not me, can change that fact." His head shook slightly. "I will leave you alone to speak with her."

Wolf reined his mount away, dug his heels into the horse's flanks, and galloped back down the path. A few moments later, he disappeared into the darkness.

* * *

Cole sat atop his horse as the animal shuffled its feet in the snow. He was uncertain as to how to approach August. The decision was made for him when, a moment later, he saw a woman's petite, ghostly figure emerge from the shadow of the trees. She pulled the heavy flap back and entered the light cast from the fire within. A second later, she disappeared from view.

His heart hammered even louder in his chest and, before the flap had closed completely, he dropped from Spirit's back, raced the last few steps to the teepee and tugged at the rawhide. The woman on the inside stepped back to let the visitor enter.

Cole ducked through the opening just as August shrugged a thick blanket from her shoulders.

"Wolf, I was wondering why you have been gone so long." Her slender back faced him.

He gathered his wits and stepped closer.

"August?"

She spun in his direction, her eyes wide with an emotion he could not read. She flung the blanket away and stumbled back. Her head shook slowly as her hand rose to cover her mouth. She could do nothing but stare in disbelief.

Cole removed his Stetson, but never took his eyes from the one person he had searched for his entire life. "I had to come. I couldn't let what we had just disappear, simply because you decided to run."

August breathed in deeply to clear her frazzled mind. Her brown eyes took in the length of him, and her heart pounded all the harder. Recovering from the initial shock, she realized that simply having him within an arm's length provided enough happiness to last her a lifetime.

"I could not stay," she managed.

"Why?"

Her shoulders straightened with determination. "I have made my decision."

"Yeah, and you made it without knowing the whole story." Cole sensed her sudden confusion and pushed on. "Why do you think I followed you all the way out here?"

She refused to answer him.

Cole took a step closer; he was close enough now to touch. August watched him with cautious eyes.

"I was worried sick about you, but that wasn't the only reason I came after you. I came because, when you ran, I had nothing." He raised his hands slightly, palms up in appeal. "I was totally alone—no one could fill the void you left behind. Every time I closed my eyes, all I could see was you. I told myself that, if I was given only one chance in my life to do something right, it would be to make sure you didn't slip through my fingers. I love you, August."

He advanced with each word, and August retreated—until she felt a crooked tent pole against her back. There was nowhere else to run.

He stared down into her tear-filled eyes. "Did you hear me? I said that I love you, August. I want you for my wife. If you won't come back to Minnesota with me, then I'll stay here with you. I'll give up everything I've ever known just to see your smile every morning." Her gaze softened, however slightly, and he continued quickly. "I'll learn your way of life—I'll protect you when you need protecting and care for you when you're sick."

She lifted her arm, intending to push him away, but Cole grasped her wrist and imprisoned her hand against his chest. "I'll share your dream, no matter what it is. All I ask is that you give me a chance. All I want is for you to admit that you love me—I want to hear those words come from your lips. I need to hear it, August—you've never said it, but I know you do."

He stood before her, begging her to accept him; praying that she would take him into her world. He had finally found her again, and he could not walk away—even if she demanded it.

August stared up at him, her eyes wide with amazement at the depth of her own emotions. A moment ago, her life was jumbled. Even simple decisions were something she was incapable of making. She did not care about the future—a future that would not include the man she loved. Now, her turmoil was gone. The worries of the day had been lifted from her shoulders, and it was all because of this one beautiful man who stood before her and declared his love.

"Cole..."

The whispered name brushed his face as August gathered him gently into her arms and laid her head against the wide span of his chest. Cole lifted his arms tentatively, then wrapped her in his embrace. He rested his chin against the soft waves on top of her head. He had come home.

"Say it, August," he whispered.

"Just hold me. I've waited so long for you."

"Say it."

She tightened her arms about his shoulders, but remained silent. *If I say the words out loud, I will be lost forever...*

Cole leaned back and, gently placing a roughened palm on either side of her face, looked directly into her eyes. Slowly, he dipped his head and brushed moist lips against her open mouth. Before she could return the kiss, however, his mouth slipped away and began a slow, sensuous journey across the smooth expanse of her cheek. Cole retraced the path with languid kisses, reveled in the change in her breathing, and skipped past her seeking mouth again.

His hands slid downward to gently grasp her trembling shoulders, then he began a lazy, but determined assault of her earlobe, the base of her neck, and the exposed skin of her breastbone.

"Cole..." August breathed.

"Say it..." He pulled her close again and, with insistent hands, urged her body to respond to his heat.

"I'm sorry..." August's head lolled weakly to one side as he pulled the shirt away from her slim neck and bared a tempting shoulder. His lips burned a path across the exposed flesh, then sought her mouth again.

August moaned.

His hands traveled slowly, sensuously down the length of her doeskin-covered back until they gripped firm buttocks. Again, August groaned her need as he pulled her hips tightly against his.

He released her mouth and his hot breath whispered close to her ear again. "Say it..."

"I...Cole..."

His nimble fingers found the hem of the rawhide shirt, and August jumped when his gentle hands slid beneath the soft material to caress the silky skin of her lower back, then began another assent to her shoulders. His hands slid lower again then and, in one liquid movement, he lifted her into his arms and cradled her against his chest. "Look at me."

She was helpless to do otherwise.

"I won't give up. I'll win this battle, August. You're my life now, and I can't live without you. Say it."

Her lids fluttered mere inches from the heated gaze before her. The weight of her fears disappeared, to be replaced by a trust deeper than she had ever known. Cole watched her face closely and witnessed the exact moment she conceded to her desires.

"I love you..." August wrapped her arms around his neck and pulled his head down to hers. She kissed him passionately, all the while murmuring heartfelt words against his hot lips. "I love you..."

* * *

The periodic crackle of the fire was the only sound in the tent. Cole released a contented sigh as he watched the gray smoke curl its way upward toward the small hole at the apex of the support poles and disappear into the night. He pulled August closer beneath the blanket and ran a palm slowly across the gentle slope of her hip.

She clasped his hand, brought it to her lips, and nestled her face against the warmth. "You are here—I find that hard to believe. I think that, even as I ran, somewhere deep in my heart, I wished you back into my life."

Cole nuzzled the soft feminine spot beneath her ear. "Don't ever leave me again, August. This last week has been the worst of my life."

August turned in his arms and fitted herself against the length of his body. She reached up to caress his whiskered cheek. "Never fear. You are a part of me, and I will never fight my feelings again. I do not know what the future will bring, but we will meet it together. You must give me some time here though, before we leave."

His eyebrows rose at her statement and puzzlement widened his eyes. "You don't want to stay here?"

She shook her head and smiled tenderly at his total willingness to change his life for her.

"Don't feel you have to leave, August. We'll do whatever is best for you and, if that means finding our way in the Dakotas, then so be it. As long as we're together, we'll figure it out. I promised you that—and I meant it."

"We cannot stay here. I see that now."

"What changed your mind?"

August sat up, bereft at leaving his comforting heat, and reached for her shirt. Shrugging it on, she stood and picked up her leggings. Cole raised himself on an elbow and watched the slim length of her thigh disappear from his view— and nearly forgot that he waited for her to answer his question.

"I have to talk to you about something." August worried her bottom lip with straight, even white teeth. "I need to spend some time with Wolf before we leave."

Cole bolted to an upright position and grabbed his pants. Stuffing his legs into the trousers, he stood and looked at her with an apprehensive frown as he buttoned the fly. "What are you talking about? I thought we just agreed that we'd never be apart again. Now, you want to spend time with Wolf?"

She moved to stand before him, stood on tiptoe, and drew his mouth to hers. Cole felt her small hand on his cheek again when she ended the kiss.

"We will be together. There can be no other way for us. I need to tell Wolf this. I need to make him understand, but I do not think it will be an easy task. Can you give me that time?"

Cole sighed his relief and nodded.

August added wood to the fire, sank to the blanket, and patted the area beside her. Cole dropped quickly, settled her head on his shoulder, and waited for her to continue.

"I was going to go north with him."

"As his wife?" The mere thought of August in another man's arms sickened him. He had come close to losing her so many times...

She watched the flames lick at the small pieces of wood and contemplated Cole's words. *Would I have gone that far in order to be lost forever in the mountains to the north?* Enveloped now within Cole's warm embrace, she did not know if she could have seen her way to that end—or endured it if she had. "It would not have mattered. I saw only one thing in my mind—to be as far from you as I could. I knew what was in my heart, but I refused to acknowledge it. Poor Wolf was my escape. I see now how unfair that would have been to him."

August turned, pressed a soft kiss to his lips, and searched for the love she knew she would find in his eyes. It was there—shining brightly with a promise to never be dimmed. "I love you, Cole, but even this great happiness I have found with you does not take away the ache when I think of my dear friend. Wolf will not understand why I must leave with you, but to stay here would be even harder on him."

Cole reflected on his earlier conversation with the man. *Wolf will let her go easier than she thinks, but she doesn't realize it, and he won't tell her.* He sighed. *She will have to say goodbye in her own way.* Wolf loved her enough to let her fly free if that is what she chose. *Could I be that generous?* He looked down into her beautiful face—the face that had never once left his dreams the entire time he searched for her. *I don't think so—I would never have given up. I would have fought like hell until my death.*

* * *

August searched for Wolf again the following morning. He had vanished the night before, and she finally returned to the lodge and Cole's warmth to spend the night in his arms. Earlier though, he again urged her to find her friend, promising to give her the necessary time to say goodbye.

August trudged down the packed trail that led to the river. Wolf sat by the frozen water, and she paused for a moment to observe his noble profile as he stared out across the white landscape. Finally, she recovered her courage and forced one foot in front of the other. *My decision to leave with Cole will hurt you, my dear friend, but there is nothing I can do.* She could no longer ignore her future...or her dream.

Wolf glanced up from where he perched on a fallen tree trunk and moved slightly down the log in silent invitation. August dropped quietly onto the rotted bark and pulled the blanket tighter about her shoulders.

"It has taken you a long time to come to me. When do you leave?"

Wolf's astute observation of the situation surprised her. The words were the last thing she expected to come from his mouth. "How did you know?"

"I have known since the first time your white man came into our lives."

August clasped her hands in her lap and sifted through her own thoughts until a heavy sigh from Wolf's lips gained her attention once more. She glanced up again a moment later and found Wolf staring at the leafless trees on the opposite riverbank. Even from her vantage point, she could tell that he struggled with his own emotions.

"I have sat here this morning, trying to fix the pain in my heart."

"Wolf—"

"I have known you my entire life, Little One. I remember when the people ridiculed your grandmother for shouting out your heritage. And I remember you, with your fists high in the air, always ready to defend yourself."

August watched as the corners of his mouth turn upward in a wry smile that surprised her once more.

"Even then, when the others refused to believe, I thought her words must be true. You have always had your father's brave heart—one that beat true for the people and our beliefs."

August reached for his cold hand. "It still beats for the people, but I can no longer ignore my true feelings for Cole. I fought it, Wolf. I truly tried to do what I thought was right. When I left his home and came here to find you, I hoped that you would help me forget him." Her lips curved in a sad smile. "One cannot rule his or her emotions or their fate. I think, as you have said, that Cole was destined to come into my life. I felt it the first time we met. I just could not accept it—until now."

"I have also tried this morning to answer the question, 'Why?'" Wolf stated as he finally turned his head to look at her. "Why would the daughter of the great Crazy Horse forget her dream and abandon everything she has struggled for her entire life?"

"Please, Wolf—"

"But then, I remembered something that I once heard your father say. *When the legends die, the dreams end, and there is no more greatness.* We are the legend, August Moon. The Sioux have been one with Mother Earth since the beginning of time. Now, this new race of people, the white man, have come into our lives. They have killed the greatness that is the Sioux. We will always have the color of our skin; we will never be wiped from the earth, but the dream is dying." He tilted his head in deep thought as he continued to stare at her. "What right do I have to tell you to continue in the old way, when the old way will be lost as our bones turn to dust?"

"Our way does not have to disappear, Wolf. It only needs to be shaped differently. Cole and his family will help me—I will never give up completely. I will always fight to show those who would not believe that we bleed as they do—that we will always be a part of this land."

He shook his head. "Foolish thoughts, Little One."

His words frightened August beyond belief. Never in all the time she had known Wolf, did he ever lose sight of his heritage and the great Sioux tribe he was so proud of. "You talk like you have given up."

Wolf stood and stepped away from the log, and once more his dark eyes flitted from the barren trees to the ridge of snow banked against the far side of the river. "I hoped that you would become my wife—that we could leave for the north when the time was right and find what little of our life remains." He inhaled deeply and August watched his breath escape into the cold, clean air. "I promised your grandmother many years ago that I would always watch over you—she was assured that I would never let any harm touch your shoulders. You will leave with the white man now and my pledge will be broken—along with my heart."

August bounded up from the fallen log and grabbed his arm. "Stop it! We never spoke of love between us! Wolf, you have cared for me always, but never as a man loves a woman!"

"That perception is how you saw it." Suddenly, the yearning for something more blazed brightly in his eyes. "I have always loved you. I only kept silent because it was your wish, a *dream* that needed to be fulfilled, and I would not stand in your way. The white man has taken that from you."

"He has taken nothing—he only gives! Even Sitting Bull understands that not all white men are our enemies. He knows that some have tried to help us. He told me I would have decisions to make. He said—"

The words froze on August's lips when a gunshot reverberated across the frozen land. A terrified scream immediately followed. She and Wolf spun in unison and bolted up the trail in the direction of the camp.

Chapter Twenty-Two

Beau and Cole stepped from Big Foot's lodge and strolled down the path in the direction of August's tent. The two men had spent the morning with the great man, gathering what information they could about the needs of the Sioux at Standing Rock.

Cole was appalled at the squalid conditions the people were forced to endure. He shoved his hands into the front pockets of his heavy jacket and glanced at his surroundings. "I guess I can understand Wolf's desire to eventually leave for Canada and never come back."

"They don't have many options, do they?" Beau shook his head as he watched three young children scatter from the path before them and hide behind a large rock. Three pairs of black eyes peeked around the snow-covered stone. He reached in his pocket, lifted out a cloth sack, and dug to the bottom for pieces of rock candy.

Cole watched with a smile when the youngsters scampered from their hiding place and ran to Beau. His friend filled each outstretched palm with the remains of the bag amidst squeals of delight. He held up his hands to show the candy was gone, and the children skipped down the path and quickly disappeared behind the row of tents. The men continued on their way then, to collect August and leave for Pine Ridge.

Beau nodded to three braves they passed on the trail, and his shoulders rose with a deep cleansing breath. "I'm glad things worked out the way they did. After everything you've told me about August, I would hate to see her caught up in the tensions around here. This morning seems so...normal around here." His eyes scanned the few Indians who were out and about, tending to their daily chores. "I can't help but think though, that this calm won't last long." He shook off the feeling and quickly switched to another topic. "Are you going to go look for Wolf if August doesn't find him?"

Cole's stomach jumped at the mention of the fierce brave, then he nodded. "I'll give August the chance to convince him to leave with us first—or at least leave for Canada real soon. She told me he had planned to stay on for a while and that makes me nervous. Everything you've told me about the troop movements bodes an ill wind. If he doesn't listen to her, then I'll give it a try."

They approached August's tent, discussing the different choices Wolf had once they left Standing Rock behind them. Cole reached to pull the flap aside, but paused when the thunder of racing horses, rattling sabers, and the creak of leather saddles reached his ears. He met Beau's concerned gaze and, without conscious thought, both men barreled down the path leading toward a small cabin in the clearing. The sound of excited voices through the trees spurred Beau into a dead run, and Cole followed close behind.

They slipped down a small incline and reached the bottom of the trail. Close to forty mounted Federal Indian police rode past, with Colonel Bingham and an entire armed garrison in the lead.

"What the hell's going on? Why are Sioux riding with the army?" Cole panted as he jumped out of the path of the oncoming horses.

"They're not your regular reservation Indians. They've sold their loyalty to the army in exchange for a meager paycheck—and all the liquor they can drink. Shit! This isn't good."

The two raced after the mounted contingent, then skidded to a halt when the group of soldiers stopped before Sitting Bull's cabin. Beau's labored breathing filtered back to Cole's ears as he watched the other man stumble through the snow to where Bingham shouted orders to the dismounting soldiers. Dogs yapped wildly and skirted the flailing hooves that struck out at them in panic. The horses' frenzied whinny's combined with the chaotic shouts of Indian and soldier alike lodged a fear in Cole's chest greater than he had ever known. He held his breath as ten of the armed Indian police entered the cabin.

Beau pushed angrily at a riderless horse that blocked his path to the colonel. Bingham's face registered surprise when his nemesis stood before him, then he quickly replaced the astonishment with a cunning smile.

"You seem to be everywhere, McCabe."

"What the hell's going on here?"

The outward crash of the cabin door interrupted the colonel's reply.

Sitting Bull was dragged through the opening, across the snow, and thrown to the hard ground. The elderly man calmly regained his footing and glared at the soldiers gathered nearby.

Reservation families entered the clearing from all directions. They stumbled closer, and Bingham issued an order.

"Stand tall, men. Do not fire your weapons!"

Colonel Bingham raised his pistol in the air and fired one warning shot to forestall the agitated Sioux. The unarmed Indians halted their flight across the snow and could do nothing but stare helplessly at their great chief. A moment later, Sitting Bull's son was pulled from the cabin, his arms held tightly behind his back by two members of his own race. The chief's sobbing wives followed. One of them lunged at her son's captor, and the other screamed when she was knocked to the ground.

"I demand to know what you're doing here, Bingham! Your actions are outrageous! What has the chief done?" Beau's eyes reflected his panic.

"He's been convicted of conspiracy and listed as an agitator. I have a warrant for his arrest and will take him south. Now, step aside McCabe. You're outnumbered here."

"He's done nothing!"

"Nothing but incite these redskins," Bingham returned smugly.

Beau paled when two Federal soldiers grasped Sitting Bull's arms and wrenched them behind his back. His wary gaze then fell on the group of reservation braves who restlessly circled the perimeter of the clearing to better view their chief. The situation could easily turn sour at a moment's notice—and it would be the Sioux who suffered the consequences.

Beau gathered his inherent discipline, breathed deeply to control the erratic beat of his heart, and raised his hands in the direction of the agency Indians who stood by with mutinous expressions.

"Let's all stay calm. We can talk this through."

The hostility in their eyes revealed the potential explosiveness of the situation.

Bingham's horse jumped forward at his master's urging and nearly knocked Beau to the ground. "I'll thank you to leave the area immediately, McCabe—I'm in charge here."

Beau recovered his balance with Cole's help and spun back to face the man on the horse. "You're making a big mistake here, Colonel." His voice lowered. "Look around you. You're seriously outnumbered here. One blunder and you'll never be able to take back what happens."

* * *

August raced to keep pace with Wolf's long strides, but still the distance between them lengthened. Her feet continually slipped beneath her on the icy path, but somehow she managed to stay upright. The exertion of her headlong flight was not the only reason her heart beat wildly in her chest. The initial shock of hearing the gunshot was now replaced by a deep-seeded fear. She could not shake the feeling that something horrible was about to happen.

Wolf reached the top of the small hill and faltered a moment when he spied the mounted soldiers. Seeing his chief held in the grasp of the Indian police, he rushed from the forest and into the clearing.

Cole caught the movement from the corner of his eye. He turned as Wolf exploded from the bordering pine trees and barreled across the clearing. The Indian's flight across the snow caused more than one army recruit to raise his rifle high with anticipation.

"Halt!" someone shouted from the amassed group of soldiers.

Wolf never faltered, but just continued his fevered pace toward the chief.

Cole flinched upon the second report from Bingham's pistol and watched in wide-eyed disbelief as Wolf's body was lifted into the air, and then thrown backward into the snow. A thick blanket of red immediately covered the fallen man's chest.

Cole bounded toward August's friend, but froze when another shot rang out across the frozen land. He spun just in time to see another member of the Sioux tribe pitch to the ground. This man, too, had broken from the line of Indians to rush in Sitting Bull's direction. Cole's stunned gaze shifted to where the chief himself struggled to escape the instant chaos. A split-second later, three soldiers tackled him to his knees. More gunshots rang through the trees as additional braves left the ranks of Sioux in defense of their chief. The world seemed to slow, and Cole watched in wide-eyed horror as one of the Indian police pressed the barrel of a rifle against the back of Sitting Bull's head. He fired a single shot. The great Sioux Chief pitched to the ground and, in a flash, he was dead.

A mortified, shriek reached through the cloud of shock that held Cole spellbound, and he whirled. August dropped to her knees beside Wolf in the blood-splattered snow and wept into her hands.

Cole hunkered his body close to the ground in an attempt to escape the array of bullets that peppered the white powder around him as he ran to August's side. Upon reaching her, he unceremoniously shoved her onto her stomach and flattened his body across her quaking length.

August struggled against his weight. "Let me go!" she sobbed. "I must help Wolf!"

"Stay down!" Cole hissed against her ear. His anxious gaze found the staring, lifeless one beside them. "There's nothing you can do for him, August."

A bullet whizzed past his head and plummeted into the drift of snow next to them. He forced August deeper into the white powder, then clenched his eyes shut in prayer. *Please, God, don't let one of those bullets find her.*

It was an eternity later before the gunshots were silenced and Cole found the courage to raise his head and look over his shoulder at the carnage. Twelve Sioux Indians lay scattered in various grotesque positions in the trodden snow. The mounted Indian police and uniformed military sat at the ready with rifles aimed at the rest of the tribe, who stood motionless on the outskirts of the clearing. Beau also clasped a bleeding shoulder where he knelt beside the dead chief and his son.

August squirmed beneath him once more, and Cole rolled to one side, freeing her of his protective weight. A frantic crawl across the snow brought her to Wolf's side again. With suppressed pain, she raised a shaking hand to his sightless eyes, then closed the lids with a brush of a palm. August rested her tear-stained cheek against his and breathed a quiet prayer that he be allowed to join the others who had gone before him. A sob escaped her throat then, as the horror of the moment hit her square in the stomach.

Cole's own hand trembled as he reached out to touch August's heaving shoulders. There was nothing he could do to ease her pain; all he could do was be there...

Beau's heated words interrupted Cole's thoughts and August's grief.

"What the hell were you thinking! You killed one of the greatest chiefs who ever lived!" Beau's horrified anger overtook his good sense and he launched himself though the air in an attempt to pull Bingham from the saddle. Immediately, six uniformed soldiers surrounded the former lieutenant and, none-to-gently, hauled his struggling body away from their commander. Bingham regained his balance atop the horse, pointed his pistol dead center at Beau's head, and pulled back the hammer.

"You're the twitch of a finger away from joining your friends in the snow, McCabe."

"Go ahead," Beau seethed, "because if you don't kill me, I'll live to see you stripped of your command."

"You won't have the chance—not if I arrest you. I have the authority of the United States government behind me, McCabe. I've had just about enough of your interference over the past two years. You and your God-damned Indians can all rot in hell."

"Beau!" Cole raced away from the grieving August to intervene. When he reached his friend's side, he hauled the still struggling Beau from the restraining arms of the soldiers, who backed away with pistols raised. "Beau," he hissed next to the other man's ear, "shut your damned mouth or we'll never get out of here alive."

Another muscled attempt finally quieted the man, then eyes that were wide with disbelief moved from his friend's bloody shoulder to the second gunshot wound in the side of his abdomen. He spun with the voice of reason and faced Colonel Bingham.

"Sir, please. Leave Mr. McCabe in my custody. He needs medical attention badly. I can tend his injuries here, then escort him back to Pine Ridge." His hazel eyes darted to the slaughter around him, and he swallowed the acid in his throat. "His job is to see to the Indian's welfare. He works for the same government you do and reacted without thinking."

"The hell I did—" Beau raged quietly, then he swayed slightly and sank to his knees.

Cole ignored the angry whisper behind him and continued his plea to Bingham. "Please, sir. Just grant me this one request. Let me take my friend and leave." He dropped to one knee in the snow, then slipped an arm around Beau's shoulders. The other man now found it hard to sit upright.

"Who the hell are you?" the Colonel questioned.

"I...met Mr. McCabe on the trail a few days ago. We've been traveling together. We'll leave quietly, I assure you. Please, sir, this man needs medical attention."

A sudden, high-pitched warble caused the entire group to jump. Cole's head jerked to one side and, before his stunned mind could even comprehend what was happening, one of the Indian police ran to where August kneeled in the snow, cradling Wolf's dead body in her arms. It was not until the excited man yanked the keening woman to her feet that Cole bolted from his crouching position next to Beau. Anger and fear shot from the depths of his eyes.

The Sioux waved his gun in the air as he dragged August's struggling body closer to where the commander sat atop his horse. Cole leaped across a fallen body, rage roiling in his veins, but stopped short when Bingham fired a shot into the snow just in front of him.

The Colonel kneed his horse forward and kept the gun trained on Cole. "You stop right there or the next bullet will be in the back of your head!" He swiveled in the saddle as the paid Indian policeman approached with the struggling woman.

"It is she!" he hollered excitedly.

"Who?" Bingham asked as he motioned for his sergeant to stand guard over Cole. The man moved into position and shouldered his rifle.

"It is the Great One's daughter!" He forced August down onto her knees, but kept a tight grip on her upper arm. "She is part of the reason the Sioux dance. She is Crazy Horse's daughter. She has returned to the people and will bring false salvation to those who refuse to conform. She is one of your problems, Colonel."

Cole heard the declaration, but did not realize the implication of the words until Bingham's voice echoed in the clearing.

"Then truss her up for the ride south. We can use her as a bargaining tool."

The man wrenched August's arm behind her back and hauled her upright. A pained gasp escaped her throat and exploded into the cold afternoon.

Cole leapt forward, unmindful of the gun pointed in his direction. "No! August! Leave her be!"

He took another step, but his advance was thwarted when three soldiers jumped into his path and knocked him to the ground—but not before his blazing eyes saw the Sioux policeman strike August across the face as two others yanked her arms behind her back to tie her hands.

Through a red haze of anger, Cole bounded to his feet, used a closed fist to punch the man closest to him, and knocked over a second soldier in another attempt to reach August. He was tackled from behind by four other soldiers and dragged to the cold, hard earth. His struggles never ceased though, until he was pinned to the ground.

August fought desperately to flee the arms that held her, and flailing feet connected with the shin of the uniformed man before her. The soldier raised his arm menacingly, and the hatred for her kind blazed in his eyes.

"You're going to regret that, squaw."

She turned her face away from the open hand, but felt the sting of another brutal slap a moment later. August gasped in pain, gasped to clear her head, then raised her tear-filled eyes to Cole's raging ones when he bellowed his anger and struggled anew to free himself from the arms that held him prisoner. He managed to untangle his clenched fist, but before he could make good the threat, the gloved knuckles of the man next to him connected with his chin. His head snapped back and he pitched backward to the ground again, momentarily stunned.

"No!" August screamed. "Cole!"

"Shut the hell up." The uniformed man before her wrapped his fingers into the long length of her dark hair, then shoved her forward and into the arms of his troop members. She was manhandled into the saddle then, and her struggling body pinned between the legs of yet another soldier. "Gibson, make sure her squaw ass stays on that horse."

August's riding companion yanked on the cord to assure that her hands would stay tied and, instantly, a burning sensation blazed across her back.

"You and I are gonna have a nice long ride, squaw lady," he mumbled near her ear. "You be real quiet and don't wiggle more than I'll be likin', and you just might live till you're dumped in a cell somewhere." Gibson glanced toward the stunned Cole just as the other man shook his head to clear it. He kneed the horse forward to where his cronies held the now struggling Minnesotan. He dipped his head close to August's ear again. "Let's see if this gets your boyfriend goin' again." His hand snaked around her waist, traveled up a flat midriff, and crudely cupped a succulent breast.

August's strangled cry left her mouth at the same moment Cole's roar split the air. "You son of a bitch!" His renewed struggle brought him to his feet with the help of those who held him captive. "So help me God, I'll kill you if you touch her again."

August squirmed, but Gibson's brute strength kept her pinned against his chest. His fetid breath warmed the hollow of her neck. "This ain't nothing compared to what I'm gonna do with her a little later."

Cole's deep snarl rang in August's ears as he lunged toward the horse. He fought like a madman to free himself until one of the soldiers lifted his rifle and rammed the stock against his forehead. August screamed as Cole crumpled to the ground, a trail of blood crossing the bridge of his nose.

August fought the bile that rose in her throat and the hopelessness that beat in her heart. She could do nothing but watch as the men dragged both Cole and Beau to the back of a wagon, dumped their limp bodies into the bed, and prepared for the march south.

George Gibson urged his horse into line with the rest of the mounted soldiers. The animal plodded past Wolf's fallen body, and August's tearing eyes scanned the blood-spattered snow for the final time. She dropped her head to the side, and it was not until the man behind her realized that she was going to be sick that he let her bend forward to empty her stomach onto the white earth.

* * *

The entire garrison rode together for the next four hours. Reaching a crook in the Cheyenne River, Colonel Bingham led half the regiment further south. A numb August had no choice but to accompany them. She had closed her mind to the death of her people and the bruising hands of the man behind her on the horse. When the wagon that carried Cole and Beau headed east, however, a lone tear of despair trickled down her cheek.

* * *

That same night found Bingham's group camped in a small valley. August was yanked from the saddle, and her legs buckled beneath her when her feet touched the frozen ground. Sergeant George Gibson, her tormenter over the long miles, poked at her back with the toe of his boot.

"Little Squaw's not so full of herself anymore, is she?" He bent down and, pulling a knife from its sheath, waved it before August's face. Her eyes widened at the sight of the gleaming blade, and she could not help but cringe when George rolled her onto her stomach. She held her breath and waited for the knife to plunge between her shoulders. Instead, the sergeant slit the cord around her wrists in one swift motion.

George picked his teeth with the shiny blade and a feral smile curled his lips. "Don't think you'll be runnin' too far." He glanced up to see four privates enjoying the trembling of August's body. "You guys come over here and watch this little squaw. Make sure she don't run. I'll be settin' up a tent. Chester, you light a fire, then this little gal and me gonna get even closer than we was on the trail. Hell, she's been teasin' me all the way down from the Rock. You guys do a good job, and you can have a poke at her when I'm finished." The younger men elbowed one another eagerly and immediately took up their posts.

August's anxiety-filled eyes watched Chester closely as he lit a small fire, then crossed to his horse to pull a pack from behind the saddle. She shivered, then crawled closer to the warmth that already emanated from the burning logs. She huddled there, sickened by the thought of the coming night, and rubbed the feeling back into her upper arms.

August glanced up to find the men standing close around her, their eyes bright with anticipation at the thought of what would transpire later that evening. *How am I to escape?* Her head dropped forward. *I will steal a knife—I will kill myself before I let them take me...*

* * *

Nearly an hour had passed before the army privates became bored with only looking at their captive. She heard their whispered sniggers and stiffened when one of the men approached her. She sat ready to leap and run when a man with a dirty, curling mustache crouched before her. She would have backed away, but another soldier moved into position directly behind her.

"You don't have to be scared, honey. My name's Farley. You must be hungry." He held out a strip of smoked meat. "Go ahead—it's yours if you want it."

Uncertainty manifested itself as a wary gleam in August's eyes. Her gaze darted about the area, then back to the chunk of meat he waved in her face.

"Take it." He smiled.

August tentatively reached for the food, only to have it whisked from her reach with a malicious grin.

"So, you're hungry, huh? Hmmm. Well, little lady, how about you and me make a bargain." He wiggled the strip of meat before her eyes and his smile turned salacious. "I'll let you have this, but first you gotta give me a little sugar." Farley reached out to pull her closer, but August bounded to her feet, jumped the small fire, and was off. Immediately, the four men charged after her through the two feet of snow.

Moonlight lit the night as August plowed through the deep snow. The soldiers were gaining on her. One of them reached out a long arm and, with a fierce growl, grasped her flowing shirt, halting her flight. August screamed.

A moment later, she was surrounded by the leering group of soldiers, with nowhere to run. She frantically spun in a circle, and her arms goose bumped when she realized that her escape had been cut off.

Farley jumped in her direction, and August stumbled back. A pair of unseen hands found her back, however, and she was shoved forward again and into her pursuer's arms.

Her responding shriek was cut off by wet, seeking lips. Several pairs of groping hands pawed at her body. They were everywhere—covering her breasts, wrapped around her waist, probing between her legs. Heavy panting reverberated next to her ear. She kicked ferociously, trying to make contact with anything solid—anything that would award her an escape.

August ripped her mouth from slobbering lips that held hers prisoner and another piercing scream left her own. The cry was immediately stifled when a beefy hand covered her mouth. She yanked her arm free and clawed at the unknown. Her heart pumped madly. The laughing rumbles, the taunting remarks burned her ears, yet still she fought on.

Suddenly, she found herself on the cold, wet ground and cruel hands groped at the rawhide leggings in an attempt to slide the buckskin over her hips. Her brain also registered another hand—the cold one that worked its way beneath her shirt to squeeze a naked breast. Another panic-stricken scream ripped its way from her throat.

"That's enough!"

The fumbling hands left her body in an instant. August scrambled backward in the snow, putting distance between herself and her tormenters. She frantically yanked the leggings back into place, then gasped for air.

Colonel Bingham eyed her heaving shoulders and snow-matted hair and turned a murderous glare on the sheepish men who stood before him. He stepped closer, his lips drawn in a tight line.

"I don't have to ask what in the hell is going on—I can see clearly what your intentions were," he ground out. "If this squaw were any other, I would turn and walk away. But these stupid Indian savages believe her to be the daughter of Crazy Horse, which means she is the one card I have up my sleeve to finally bend the Sioux to my will. You will return to your tents, take up your weapons, and patrol through the night. Come morning, if one hair on her head is harmed, the four of you will pay dearly—so you'd better make sure that no one touches her. I suggest you leave my sight immediately before I shoot each and every one of you on the spot."

August sat shaking in the snow and watched with a measure of satisfaction as the men scuttled to do the colonel's bidding. She dropped her chin and breathed deeply again to clear her head.

"Get up, woman."

She rose tentatively, aware of little that went on around her. All of her energies were focused on regaining control. She had lived to see another day, and for that she would be eternally grateful. She felt the colonel's gaze bore into her, and she looked up through tear-filled eyes.

He glared at her for a moment before speaking. "I'll have one of the men find some blankets to keep you warm tonight. You can sleep by the fire. You won't be of any use to me if you're dead." He turned, took three steps, and paused to send a withering glance over his caped shoulder. "Don't tempt me, squaw. You will follow me now."

August stared back at him, her mind racing, then her chin lifted a notch in defiance. "I will not ride with that man when the sun comes up. You will give me my own horse."

"I'll drag you behind me in the snow before you're given your own mount. Now move!"

She stood taller—and stayed where she was.

The Colonel had had enough. "I don't think you're in any position to make demands. I'll shoot you if you disobey me. Or maybe you'd like me to call those men back." Bingham relished the flicker of fear that flashed in her eyes before being replaced by a look of reproach—a look intended for him. Her attitude momentarily unnerved him.

"I will ride alone or I will walk. If I die on the trail, it will be better than being groped until we reach Pine Ridge." She stood her ground and her gaze bore into the man before her. "I saw you that day."

August read the confusion in Bingham's eyes. Regardless, he unsnapped the holster at his side as she continued.

"I watched you come into my camp and kill my family. I still carry the scar from a soldier's bullet. What more can you do to me, but send me to them." Her defiant gaze darted to his hand. "Do it. I am not afraid of you."

He pulled the gun, stepped forward, pointed the weapon directly at her forehead, and pulled back the hammer.

August never flinched.

Bingham ground his teeth and stared at her silently before his eyes narrowed. "If you weren't Crazy Horse's daughter, you would be lying at my feet right now with your blood seeping into the snow."

"Do it. Show me how brave a white man can be when it comes to shooting a mere woman."

She saw the indecision in his gaze and the clenching of his jaw. A moment later, he lowered his arm, stepped aside, and waited for her to pass...

* * *

Cole winced in pain when the wagon wheel dropped into a rut and jarred him from nothingness. Rolling his head slightly to the side, he was jolted even further into consciousness when a piercing shaft of pain ran a jagged course across the top of his head and down into his right temple. A moment later, he shivered with a bone-numbing cold.

Thick lashes fluttered open to darkness. Cole's eyes adjusted to the shadows, while his brain comprehended the fact that he lay in the bed of a wagon next to another body. His confused gaze traveled down the length of a blood-soaked, jacketed arm, paused at the blood that also pooled near his side, then retraced its path until it reached the face of an unconscious Beau. Even in the dim moonlight, he could see that the both wounds still bled. His friend's lips were blue. He attempted to reach out and gently shake the other man, but paused when he realized that both their hands were bound with thick cords.

Cole closed his eyes against the pain in his forehead and attempted to organize his muddled thoughts. *What in the hell happened?* He could hear the telltale sounds of creaking leather, muted conversations, sabers rustling softly against stirrups...

Suddenly, it all came together in his mind.

August...

The horrible events of that afternoon rushed back with gut-wrenching clarity. The vision of August's tear-streaked face as she held Wolf's dead body; her valiant struggle to free herself when they realized who she was; the soldier slapping her across the face and another groping her breast, while others bound her hands behind her back. Cole inhaled the cold air one breath after another until the churning in his stomach eased and he knew he would not be sick.

Where is she? The revelation that she was Crazy Horse's daughter stunned him. She had managed to hide that truth from him throughout the weeks she was convalescing at the ranch. It was of little matter now, however. The important thing was that Bingham also knew her identity, and it put her in grave danger. *Christ—I need to find out where she is.*

A shiver of cold wracked his body, but Cole forced himself to ignore the icy discomfort, as well as the throbbing ache in his head and his blurred vision, as he inched his way across the wooden slats and closer to Beau. The shared blanket had fallen away from the other man's body, revealing a tattered shirt that fluttered in the wintry air. Cole groaned at the sight of the bloody opening in Beau's side and the suddenly clear memory of how it happened. He managed to clumsily pull his friend's jacket closed over the wound in his side, then reached with trembling, bound hands for the blanket. Rolling closer in order to share his body heat with the injured man, Cole pulled the scratchy wool across both their bodies and over their heads.

He could hear Beau's shallow breathing beneath the cover and rested a bit easier. He had no idea where they were going or how long it would take to get there. Settling his aching head against a sack filled with grain, thoughts of August rushed back to haunt him. He had no idea where Bingham's men had taken her; frustration and helplessness combined to bring on the unmanly tears. He had promised to care for her, to protect her and now, only hours after making the declaration, she was lost from him.

Hang on, August. I'll find you. I promise that, if it's the last thing I ever do, I'll come for you.

Cole closed his eyes against the burning sensation beneath his lids and found release in the blackness once more.

* * *

August swallowed down a sob of fear as she huddled atop an old mattress and leaned back against the wall of the locked prison cell. Her frightened gaze took in the bleak surroundings; then, with frigid fingers clamped across her mouth, she stifled a scream and stamped her foot to scare away the large gray rat that crept ever closer. She breathed a small sigh of relief when the rodent disappeared through a crack in the rock wall.

Cole. Please be alive—please find me...I'm here waiting for you. She squeezed her eyelids shut in an attempt to stop the ever-present tears; the effort was futile. They rolled down her cheeks, forming runnels through the filth that covered her face, and attested to the level of her terror.

Two days had passed since she watched the soldiers callously load Beau and Cole's inert bodies into the back of a wagon. Wolf was dead. So were Sitting Bull and countless others. The evening before, she dreamed of the vision from years ago. How many more times would she cheat death before she rode the black horse to her final resting place?

August leaned away from the cold, damp wall and trembled like a frightened child. She had escaped her own demise so many times—for so many different reasons. At other times, it was either her grandmother, Wolf, or Cole that helped her to see another day. *But they are all gone.*

No! Cole is out there somewhere.

August's limp body slid back onto the filthy mattress. She pulled her knees up to her chest and sobbed into the rawhide that covered her legs. *Cole, please...find me one last time.*

Chapter Twenty-Three

Cole crossed the small cell to check on Beau and was relieved to see that the blood flow from both wounds had finally stopped. The fact that Beau had not received the required medical care rankled him to no end. He glanced up and was surprised to see the other man's eyes open and watching him closely. Cole shook his head as he nodded toward the other man's blood-soaked shirt. "There's no damn reason that someone hasn't taken care of your wounds yet."

"You're hovering over me as if I was a three-year old."

Despite their rather precarious position, Beau's words caused a slight grin to curve Cole's lips.

"When you act like one, what do you expect?"

Beau winced as he repositioned himself on the cot. "I take it you're referring to my actions at Standing Rock?"

Cole simply shrugged his shoulders.

"I was so goddamn angry, Cole. I just couldn't believe they so callously shot and killed the chief." The image of Sitting Bull pitching backward into the snow still sickened him. "We gotta find a way to get the hell out of here. All hell's gonna break loose."

Cole crossed to the barred window and looked out at the Rosebud headquarters. He rested his forehead against the damp sill for a moment before turning back to face Beau.

"Where do you think she is? It's been three days and no one here seems to know anything."

"I don't know. My guess is Pine Ridge. I'm sure Bingham will keep her close now that he knows she's Crazy Horse's daughter."

"So, why are we here? Why did he split us up?"

"Because he wants me out of the way. He knows I've been out here since the end of summer and managed to become involved with a lot of the people at the Ridge. It was the luck of the draw that you ended up in here with me."

Beau sent Cole a wry smile, then winced in pain when he adjusted his position again. Once he was settled, he turned his bloodshot eyes toward the concrete ceiling. "I've gotta get some sleep, Cole. At least when I'm out, I don't hurt so goddamn bad." His gaze took in the large discolored area on Cole's forehead, and the clotted cut that sat in the middle of the bruise. "How's your head."

"I'll live. I just wished I didn't feel like I was half drunk. It takes awhile to focus."

"Shit," Beau mumbled from the cot. "Right about now, I'd give anything to get drunk off my ass." A few moments later, his breathing changed to an even rhythm.

Cole turned back to stare out the window and watched the comings and goings of the reservation personnel as they moved about the snow-covered compound in the bright sunshine.

How in hell are we going to get out of here? He shook his head slowly, then grasped the window sill when a sudden wave of dizziness overtook him. *I need to find a way to get a message to Michael and Anna. Beau's only going to get worse if he doesn't get that bullet out of his shoulder.* If contacting the Gatewoods did not work, he would try and persuade someone to send a telegram to Tyler. *Maybe with his connections at the State level, he can get us released. Whatever it takes, I've got to find August.*

The lightheadedness finally passed, and he opened his eyes again. His gaze continued to scan the compound and paused to rest on an old Indian brave who stood in the snow. The elderly man stared at the barred window in which the white man stood. Cole's body tensed, and he leaned forward for a better look.

Beau moaned in his sleep, and Cole turned in quick concern. Seeing that his friend still slept, he returned his gaze to the casement.

He blinked, then scanned the perimeter in both directions. The old man had disappeared.

* * *

A tapping sound outside the window brought both men in the enclosed cell to a sitting position. Their eyes met before Cole moved silently to the window that had been shuttered from the outside earlier by the jailer. He froze, however, when another succession of taps met his ears.

"Who's out there?" Cole placed his ear close to the bars and listened for an answer. The silence in the cell ticked away.

"Can you hear anything?" Beau whispered from his bed.

Cole raised a hand for silence and listened again. His eyes widened in surprise a moment later. "I'll get him..."

He hurried back across the cell and reached out to help the injured Beau stand. "Whoever the hell's out there just asked for you by name."

Beau pulled himself up with Cole's aid and leaned heavily on his friend as they shuffled back to the window. Halfway across the cell, the injured man's body dipped slightly and the room began to spin around him.

Cole tightened his grip. "Christ, we gotta get you some help. You've lost a lot of blood."

The pale Beau only flashed a tremulous smile and concentrated on keeping his balance. "Just get me to that damn window—and don't let go."

They hobbled closer. Cole propped Beau against the wall, waited for him to regain his balance, and nodded his head.

Beau took a deep breath and whispered. "Who's out there?"

"Beau McCabe?" A voice filtered through the slats of wood.

"Yeah, it's me. Who are you?"

"You don't know me, but I have someone with me that you know well. His name is Whitecloud."

"Whitecloud?" Beau rested his head against the wall and smiled at Cole as his lids fluttered shut along with a deep sigh of relief. "How did you know we were here?"

"He watched the soldiers bring you in."

"Tell him to get a message to Dr. Gatewood at Pine Ridge."

The two men listened attentively, and whispered Sioux words filtered back to their ears. Another voice responded in the foreign dialect.

"Whitecloud says a runner left this morning to notify the doctor. When he saw you, it was just a matter of when the man could leave without being found out."

"Can the runner be trusted? We've got to get out of here."

"Oh yes—do not fear. Walking Bear will finish the job. He said he would reach the doctor by tomorrow. We must go now before we are discovered."

"Tell Whitecloud thank you!" Beau waited for a response, but none was forthcoming. The voice was gone in the night.

He silently thanked God for granting him friendship with the small group from Wolf's tribe. His smile widened in Cole's direction, despite his wobbly stance. "Looks like we just found our way out of here. Mike's gonna ride to the rescue."

Cole took one look at the newly blood-soaked bandage on Beau's upper arm and placed the other, uninjured limb over his shoulder. "Well, he can't get here quick enough. Hopefully, he'll have some news about August, too."

He helped Beau across the cell again, settled the weakened man back on the cot, and pulled a blanket over his quaking body. He turned away then, but Beau grabbed his arm.

"We'll find her, I promise. She'll be alive, Cole. I know that's what you're afraid of right now, but Bingham would've finished her off up at Standing Rock if he was going to do it."

"I know—" Cole dropped his chin for a moment in despair. "I keep telling myself that, but what has she gone through, Beau? What has she suffered at the hands of those animals? Not knowing is killing me."

Beau simply patted his friend's arm in support before his eyes closed and his sweat-soaked head rolled to the side.

* * *

Anna smiled as she watched the children playing in the snow. She stopped to enjoy their antics, but tempered her humor momentarily when she thought of their future. They accepted their world, because it was the only world they knew. These Sioux offspring had always lived on the reservation and understood their heritage only as it was told to them. *Will this new way of life be easier because of their ignorance of the past?*

Anna did not think so.

She continued on to the clerk's office, basking in the warm rays of sunshine that had been absent since the beginning of the week, and adjusted the basket of food in her arms. She walked up the stairs to the office and thanked a uniformed man as he quickly opened the door for her and tipped his hat in unveiled respect.

She entered into the warmth of the building, crossed to the desk, and set her load on the scuffed oak surface.

"Good afternoon, Harold. I baked you a treat this morning." Anna pulled a package from the center of the large basket and placed it before the clerk. "It's your favorite—fresh peach pie."

Harold stood, his mouth instantly watering at the thought of the delicacy. His gaze followed Anna's hands as she unwrapped the tin, then swallowed back the drool when the aroma of fresh baked pie crust reached his nostrils. "Miz Gatewood, you're too kind, but I can't take it." He tried not to look at the slits in the golden crust where warm peach filling still bubbled from the inside.

"Now, why can't you accept this? I made it especially for you. All I ask in return is to have a little visit with the prisoner you have in back. I surely didn't expect you to do that for me without a little gift in return." Anna kept the smile pasted on her lips and stared back with wide, innocent eyes.

Harold pulled at his collar nervously as his gaze darted to the pie, then back to Anna. "I can't let you in the back cell. Your husband stopped in here earlier, too, when he heard Colonel Bingham had brought in a special prisoner. I told him the same thing."

Anna widened her eyes in a perfect guise of surprise. She already knew that Michael had visited the office, and she also knew that he was upset when the locals told him of a young woman who was being held separate from the other prisoners in the camp. Anna asked Michael to let her try to gain entrance and, though they fought about it, in the end Anna won the argument. Neither of them had reason to trust Bingham, and they were equally worried about the welfare of the most recent detainee.

"But, Harold, I just have a few items in the basket. I heard your new prisoner is a woman. She might require a few things. Has she eaten well? Wait one moment." The forced smile began to hurt the muscles in Anna's face. *You fat idiot—I'm going to get into that cell whether you want me to or not.* "Your prisoner *is* a woman, correct? I would hate to go back there alone if it was a big, frightening man..."

"No, it's a woman—only a squaw woman, but I'm sorry, Ma'am. I can't let you in—Bingham's orders. No one is to visit the prisoner."

Anna slowly unbuttoned her coat and slid the garment from her shoulders. Beneath the cover of her winter jacket, the low-cut neckline of her dress was enough to cause the clerk's eyes to widen. His cheeks flushed as the womanly bosom was offered to his gaze. Anna had specifically donned the garb as a last ditch weapon to seek entrance to the prisoner's cell.

"My goodness, but it's warm in here. Such a relief from the cold outside." She released an exaggerated, heart-felt sigh, ballooning her chest along with Harold's eyes. "Well, regardless, you may as well enjoy the fruits of my labor." She pulled a small knife from the basket and sliced into the pie with deliberate slowness, all the while watching Harold from beneath lowered lashes. His gaze continually darted between the rise of her succulent breasts and the slice of pie that now lay on a plate on the desk.

Anna shook her curly head of hair, planted a cheeky grin on her lips, and leaned forward to further expose her chest as she pushed the plate toward Harold with one finger.

Harold plopped into his chair, grabbed the ever-present hanky, and wiped his pate.

"Now, you wouldn't want me to have spent the afternoon baking you this pie for nothing, would you?"

Harold eyes widened in shock—he had never thought of the doctor's wife in a sexual way—as he was now. He lounged back in quiet astonishment, and Anna pushed her advantage.

"Come on, Harry. You know the good doctor and I always like to see the prisoners and look after their wellbeing. This woman has been here for three days. Why hasn't anyone been allowed in?" She leaned forward even more and watched Harold's eyes bulge even further out of their sockets. Anna purposely placed her palms flat on the desk, using the insides of her arms to lever her cleavage a little fuller. Landers swallowed convulsively. *Oh, God, Michael would die if he saw me in this dress and saw me acting this way...*

"Is it really true that this woman is supposedly Crazy Horse's daughter? I would love to meet her." Her eyes swept the desk before her. "Try some pie— it's my special recipe."

Harold's hand stopped in mid wipe at the view presented him. He quickly dropped his gaze, only to see the warm steam rising from the plate before him. He was near drooling now; Anna was not sure if it was the site of her breasts or the pie that had the sloppy man in such a state. She smiled inwardly though, when she realized he had just lost the battle. *Stupid man...*

"Well, I suppose a quick visit wouldn't hurt. If the Colonel hears about this though, he'll have my head."

"Oh, never fear!" Anna wrinkled her nose with an accompanying smile, then leaned even closer to whisper mere inches from his face. "The secret is ours."

She watched as the clerk grabbed the plate, then quickly pulled her coat back over her shoulders and picked up the basket. "I'm flattered that you're enjoying my bakery, but could you unlock the door? I want to hurry, so no one will find out. You're such a dear, sweet man to do this for me."

Harold heaved himself from the chair and licked the fingers of one hand as he dug in the open drawer with the other and grabbed a ring of keys.

Anna watched quietly as he crossed to the door that adjoined the office. The special security lock-up cells were located on the other side. The iron slab swung open, and she cast one last smile over her shoulder at the sweating clerk before she flitted past him and into the dark, cold hallway.

* * *

August jerked her head upright, sat up, and pulled the blanket tightly around her shoulders at the sound of keys turning in the lock at the end of the corridor. A cold hand pushed tangled hair from her eyes as her wary gaze riveted on the corridor outside the iron bars.

A woman entered the semi darkness and moved down the dank hall in the direction of the cell. She approached the chamber and called out softly.

"Hello? I came to see if you needed anything to make you more comfortable. I have some food and other things in my basket. Don't be frightened." Anna strained to see into the dark corner where the prisoner sat on an old mattress. "You'll have to come closer; I can't come into your cell."

Anna placed the basket on the floor and dug beneath the lid. *Maybe if I let her see what I have in the basket, the poor thing won't be so frightened.* She held up a small loaf of bread made earlier that day. "See, I have food for you." She held the staple between the bars and waited patiently.

"Anna?"

It was a voice from the past.

August stepped into the muted candlelight.

Anna gasped, quickly dropped the bread back into the open basket, and clutched at the steel bars that separated them. "Oh my God! August! How did you get here? Didn't Cole and Beau find you?"

August ran to the bars and wrapped her hands around Anna's fingers. "Anna, please! Help me. I cannot stay here." She pleaded through instantaneous sobs.

The doctor's wife reached through the bars and pulled the panicked young woman closer. "It's all right, August. What happened?"

"Cole found me. I was saying good-bye to Wolf...we heard a gunshot and ran up the hill. There were soldiers everywhere," the words caught in her throat, and tear-filled wide eyes stared from the interior of the cell. "They killed him...they shot him down for no reason!"

"Who was killed? August, you have to slow down and tell me what happened." For one heart stopping moment, Anna was certain it was Cole who was dead.

"Wolf. Colonel Bingham's soldiers shot him dead. Beau was also shot, and he and Cole were taken prisoner when they spoke against what the soldiers had done. I do not know where they are or even if they are alive!"

"Where did this happen?" Anna's mind raced as she tried to piece together the events.

"At Standing Rock."

Anna's thoughts finally crashed into one another and she dreaded asking the next question. "Were you there when Sitting Bull was killed?" August nodded mutely, and Anna squeezed her hand to lend comfort. "All right, let me think—I can't get you out of this horrid place until tonight. I'll find Michael immediately, and he'll come up with some sort of solution—I promise. He should also be able to find out where Beau and Cole are being held prisoner."

"They are both hurt."

"You didn't say anything about Cole being hurt. What happened?" Anna clutched August's hand as she waited breathlessly for the answer.

"One of the soldiers hit him in the head with a gun. They were both put in the back of a wagon before we headed south. That was the last time I saw them. The soldiers separated at the Cheyenne. I came here—I do not know where Cole and Beau were taken. Please, find Cole for me. He is the only thing I have left."

Anna gave the other woman's hand one final squeeze, then bent to pick up the basket. She passed the contents one by one through the bars. "Here's bread, water, meat, and some jelly. That should hold you until I come back."

"Please, take me with you. I cannot stand another minute of this place." Her gaze dropped to the dirt floor inside the cell. "I am sorry that I spoke to you so harshly when you helped me before."

"I can't take you with me now, August—and it has nothing to do with how either of us acted the last time we spoke. I'd never be able get you out of here without being detected. I promise, I'll come back with Michael. You have to believe me. We'll get you out of here as soon as we can."

She lifted the woven lid of the basket, pulled a thick knitted shirt from the bottom, and handed it to the trembling woman. She froze, however, when she met the dark, frightened eyes before her. "Word out in the compound is that the woman being held in this cell is Crazy Horse's daughter. Is it true? Was he your father?"

"Yes," replied August softly. "That is why I'm being held prisoner. Colonel Bingham has some purpose for me. I do not know what it is. I do know though, that if I become useless to him, he will kill me. Please, Anna, come back quickly before he decides."

"I will, but I have to find Michael first. It'll be just a little while longer. I promise."

"Find Cole—tell him where I am." August clutched at Anna's arm until the woman peeled her fingers away.

"I've got to go, August. The sooner I get out of here, the sooner I'll be back—I swear it!"

August watched as Anna turned with a final wave before she hurried through the exit at the end of the dark hallway. The heavy door that led to the outside world closed behind her.

* * *

"Michael! Michael, are you here?"

Anna rushed across the porch, fumbled with the knob, and nearly fell through the open doorway in her haste to find her husband.

He was there, sitting at the table, not in the least bit concerned about his wife's frenzied flight into the house. "Slow down, Anna. I'm not going anywhere. What's the matter?"

"It's August! *She's* Bingham's new prisoner!"

"What?" He jumped up from the chair.

"*She* is Crazy Horse's daughter, Michael. That bastard is holding her as a trump card. They were all there, Michel—August, Cole, Beau—they all saw Sitting Bull die!"

"So, where in hell are Cole and Beau now?"

"August doesn't know. She said that Beau had been shot, and one of Bingham's henchmen clubbed Cole over the head with his gun. They were loaded into the back of a wagon and, most likely, are riding with the group that split off and headed south."

"That son of a bitch." Michael ran a hand through his graying hair and paced the floor until he stood before the window. He looked out at the darkening afternoon. "Bingham can't keep it a secret for long. People will start to look for Beau. He's an investigator for the Bureau for chrissakes. I don't think they'll take his disappearance lightly." He turned to look at his wife. "I'm going to see Bingham, and I'm going to ask where Beau is. If he was at Standing Rock— which we know he was—they can't keep him hidden for long. Cole's got to be with him. If Bingham doesn't give me a straight answer, I'll tell him that I'm going to report Beau as missing."

"We also need to find a way to get August out of that horrible cell before she disappears. She's at her wits end."

The doctor shrugged his broad shoulders. "How in hell are we supposed to do that? Bingham will never release her. Christ, Beau told me what happened down in Nebraska when they tried to leave with Fawn and Whitecloud. With August's status as Crazy Horse's daughter, he'll keep her locked up tight."

Anna moved to a chair, pulled it away from the table, and indicated with a nod of her head that her husband should sit. "Come here, Michael. I thought of something on my way back from the jail."

He moved cautiously toward the seat and watched his wife's face as he sat. "I don't want you involved."

"I already am." She reached up to slide the heavy coat from her shoulders, forgetting the daring dress she wore beneath. Michael's eyes rounded under raised eyebrows and his mouth gaped open when the heavy wool material left her shoulders.

"What the *hell* do you have on?"

Anna immediately blushed at being found out and covered her scantily clad chest with both hands. "The pie wasn't enough to gain access to August. I figured I'd use everything at my disposal—and prepared myself appropriately."

Her husband's eyebrows lowered in a frown that was aimed in her direction.

"Don't give me that look, Michael. You tried, but couldn't get in. I figured that Landers would be simple-minded enough to be taken in by my...feminine wiles." She indicated the low-cut neckline and waited for his response. It was not long before a smile tugged at his lips.

"You are something, woman." He shook his head slowly in wonder. "All right—what do you have up your sleeve—since there's no room in that small piece of material covering your chest."

She ignored his humorous taunt with a wave of her hand and plopped down into another chair. "While you're trying to find Beau and Cole, I'll bring another basket of food over for August—along with a special treat for Harold."

Michael eyed her breasts, which threatened to spill onto the table. He frowned again. "What sort of *special treat*, Anna? And why will it be any different from your earlier visit?

"Because, this time, Harold's going to get real sleepy."

"What are you talking about?"

"I plan to bring him dinner. Let's just say that I'll add a few extra ingredients to the potatoes—like something from your medicine cabinet that will make him sleep like a baby. I'll slip back in when you think enough time has passed for the drug to take effect, get the keys out of the drawer, let August out, and put everything back as it was."

"Absolutely not!" Michael roared.

"Can you come up with anything better? It'll work—we'll just have to hide her somewhere."

"I can't let you take that chance."

She reached across the table and clasped his hand. "I've never disobeyed you on anything, Michael. I've listened to your advice, because you're always such a fair man. But, I'm going to do this, with or without your help. I'm not leaving August in that horrible place for another night. She's frightened, and they're not taking good care of her. No one can stay healthy in a place like that. If we wait, Bingham might have a chance to do something terrible to her." She sat back again and crossed her arms below her daring neckline. "Now, are you going to help me, or do I fumble along on my own?"

He sat back in his own chair and mimicked her determined stance. "I can't believe I'm going to say this—"

Anna bounded from her seat, ran around the table, and wrapped her arms around his neck. "Thank you! It'll go smoothly, I promise. I would never jeopardize your position, but I can't let Bingham get away with this, either. Thank you, Michael, for going along with my idea." She dropped a peck on his waiting lips, then straightened and moved to the counter to begin preparations for Harold's dinner. "Why don't you get whatever I need to make Landers fall asleep?"

Michael rose and grabbed his jacket from a peg by the door. "I'm going to find the colonel first and question him—"

A gentle rap echoed across the kitchen, and the doctor reached for the brass knob, pulled the door open, and took a step back in surprise. "Walking Bear!" he exclaimed. "I thought you went north with Fawn and her husband. Come in, quickly before someone sees you."

Anna quickly covered herself with one of her husband's shirt that hung on a peg close by.

The rugged Indian brave walked hesitantly through the open doorway and let Michael shut out the cold behind him. He tipped his head in deference to Anna before bringing his gaze back to the man standing before him. "I stayed with Whitecloud to watch over him. I have come with a message. I have not seen them myself, but Whitecloud has discovered McCabe and Cole Wilkins in the prison at Rosebud."

"Thank God they're alive," Anna exclaimed as she rushed to stand before the two men. "Do they know you came to tell us?"

"Whitecloud and a friend will try to see them sometime today." He looked at the doctor. "Only you can find a way to release them. I will ride back to Rosebud with you tonight."

Michael's thoughts spun as he put everything in order. First, he would need to insure August's escape and have her safely hidden. Then he would send a telegram to the Indian Bureau, demanding Beau's release on the premise that he was injured and that no formal charges had been made—they could not have been, because he suspected Bingham did not have enough to go on. Cole was simply a private citizen caught in the middle of a military battle—no need for anyone to know of his connection to August. Michael could have any response sent to Rosebud. He would leave for that location tonight and have an answer sometime tomorrow. At least he would be able to see Beau and attend his medical needs, if it was warranted.

"All right—I'll go gather up what you need, Anna, so you can do what we discussed. Walking Bear, sit and rest while I ready some medical supplies for our trip. Anna will give you something to eat." He paused to look at the two of them. "Christ—I hope this all works the way it's supposed to or there'll be hell to pay."

Chapter Twenty-Four

Anna shouldered her way through the open doorway of the headquarters' office. Harold glanced up from his usual position behind the scratched desk, and his eyes gleamed when he spied the wicker container in her hands.

Anna set the heavy basket on the desk before him and smiled. "Hello again, Harold. I thought I'd bring your prisoner some supper. I also made up a plate for you as a thank you for your generosity this afternoon."

"Well, that's awful nice of you, Missus Gatewood. I'm sorry though—I can't let you go in the back cell again. I took a big enough chance this afternoon."

Anna's hand fluttered in the air before his face. "Oh, don't you worry yourself about getting in trouble tonight. I didn't expect you to let me back there. It's just that you were so kind and caring this afternoon." She shrugged before her lips formed a cute pout. "I simply told Michael you needed to be rewarded one more time." She ceremoniously placed a covered tin plate in his hands. "I'll just wait right here while you deliver this to the prisoner. In fact, while you're gone, I'll set out your dish and get it ready for you."

She dipped her hand into the basket a second time and withdrew another covered platter. Anna lifted the edge of the linen and allowed Harold a peek at the contents.

The sight of the mashed potatoes smothered in a thick brown gravy and the aroma of the fried chicken was enough to make the fat man grab his keys, hurry around the edge of the battered desk, and almost race to unlock the door to the cell block.

* * *

Anna shivered in the darkness as she moved quietly in the shadows of various buildings that lined the main thoroughfare at Pine Ridge. She did her best to hug the rough-hewn walls at her back and made her way to the main office. Michael had kept his word and given her the sedative. Harold should now be sound asleep in his chair from the laudanum-laced chicken and potatoes.

She glanced up and down the street and, seeing no one, stepped lightly onto the wooden sidewalk and moved quickly to the window. Peeking through the pane of dirty glass, she spied the clerk. His head was angled against the back of the chair and his arms hung at his sides. Landers was sound asleep, slack-jawed, and oblivious to his surroundings.

Anna turned the knob and slipped into the office. Her heart pounded in her ears as she crossed to the desk, cautiously opened the drawer, and pilfered the cell keys from their hiding spot. She nearly jumped out of her skin when Landers snorted, then smacked flabby lips together in his sleep.

Anna hurried to the door that blocked her view of the cell block, then tried one key after another until the lock clicked open. She cringed at the noise, which seemed to echo across the office, and cast a cursory glance over her shoulder. August's jailer slept on.

Pulling the door open wide enough to slide into the semi-darkness, Anna raced down the length of the hall.

"August!" she whispered. "It's me—I'm going to get you out of here."

"Anna? Oh, Anna! You are here!" August flew across the cell and grabbed the bars as she watched her new friend pick through the keys to locate the correct one.

"Shhh! Harold is asleep—I don't want to take the chance of waking him."

"How did you manage this? Will we be able to escape?"

The cell door swung open and August flung herself into the other woman's welcoming embrace.

Anna grabbed the prisoner's arm and pulled her away from the swinging iron bars. "We'll get out of here—just follow me and don't say a word," she whispered over her shoulder as she closed the cell door and locked it again.

The two women tiptoed to the adjoining office door, checked to see if the clerk was still out, then moved quickly across the room to the outside exit.

"Wait!" Anna hissed. She pulled the keys from her pocket, tiptoed back to the desk, laid them gently back in their hiding spot, and pushed the drawer shut. She looked up to see August wringing her hands and flashed a quick smile. She crossed the room again then, and the two women slipped into the night.

* * *

Anna's breath refused to find a normal rhythm until she closed her own kitchen door behind her. August, in turn, dropped to the floor before the brightly burning flames in the fireplace in an attempt to heat her chilled bones.

"I cannot thank you enough," the Indian woman murmured as she held out her hands to the fire. "I was so frightened that we would be caught..." The words clogged in her throat.

Anna stripped off her coat and quickly went about gathering two mugs. She poured coffee into one and walked to the young woman who now wiped tears from her cheeks with a shaky hand. "Here, drink this—it'll warm you up."

August reached for the cup and her teary gaze met the other woman's as Anna seated herself in a chair. "If anyone finds out you helped me to escape—"

The doctor's wife waved a hand. "I don't want to hear another word about it. We just have to figure out where we're going to hide you until Michael gets back with Cole."

"Cole? You have found him?" Renewed hope burned in August's dark eyes.

"Walking Bear showed up here today. He's been with Whitecloud at the Rosebud Agency. They saw a regiment come in. They had Cole and Beau with them." Anna closed her eyes in a moment of thankfulness. "Thank God they're both still alive—but they're being held in the prison. Michael wired the Indian Bureau and is on his way to Rosebud now. He's certain he'll be able to secure their release and bring them back immediately. But, as I said, that's not our immediate problem. As soon as they discover that you escaped, I would bet we'll have a little visit from Bingham himself. We'll have to make sure he doesn't find you."

August dropped to her knees before Anna and grasped her hands. "I will do anything you say!" she pleaded. "Tell me what I must do and I will listen. I will kill myself before I let him take me again."

Anna's mind reeled with possible solutions to their problem. "How often did the clerk check on you? If he wakes up, do you think he'll check tonight?"

August shook her head. "He had already come in to bring me my last ration of water until morning."

"Good!" A wide smile split Anna's face. "Hopefully, that means they won't discover that you're gone until tomorrow—and it also allows more time for Michael to get back here with Cole and Beau. I've got some water heating. We'll set up the tub in my room, so you can bathe that prison smell off. In the meantime, let me work on where we're going to hide you. I think I have a plan."

* * *

Anna jumped when someone banged on the outside door. She glanced at the grandfather clock. It was nearing seven o'clock the night after she rescued August from the prison cell. Michael had been gone for over twenty-four hours.

"Open immediately!" An irritable voice called from outside.

Another loud aggravated rap sounded as she stood. Anna's gaze darted down the hall to the spare bedroom door. It silently shut, as if an invisible hand had guided it.

She stood, smoothed her white linen apron with damp palms, and crossed to the door. "Well, Colonel, I'm surprised it took you so long to pay a visit," she muttered to the empty room.

Anna opened the door and was greeted by a stern, disapproving look on the commander's face. "Colonel Bingham—why, this is a surprise. Is there something I can do for you?" A sweet smile touched her lips, but she did not offer entrance to her home.

"I would like to speak to your husband."

"I'm sorry, he's not here right now."

The officer looked over her shoulder, peered across the living room and into the kitchen. "Why then do you have your table set for two?"

"Because two people live in this house."

"But only one is here to eat their supper."

"I never eat alone, Colonel." Anna widened her eyes and smiled prettily once more. "I always wait for my husband no matter what the time of day. We see so little of each other with his busy schedule."

Bingham's lips tightened with exasperation. "Do you expect him soon?"

"I can't really say. One never knows what will keep him away. Being the only doctor at the agency, he's on call all the time."

"May I come in?" His question more closely resembled an order than an inquiry to Anna's ears. She hesitated slightly, then opened the door wider.

"Forgive my manners. Yes, do come in."

Bingham and two Indian police entered; none of them bothered to stamp the snow from their feet as they moved further into the room. The colonel turned with a deepening scowl and a glare that foretold trouble. Anna calmly closed the door.

"Are you aware that a hostile has escaped from my custody?"

"Oh, my goodness...no, no I wasn't."

"Harold Landers informed me that you visited my prisoner yesterday afternoon."

"I didn't visit a hostile, Colonel. I brought a meal to a young woman in need." Anna affected a surprised look. "Do you mean that poor young woman has escaped?"

"Have you visited any other prisoners?" Bingham ignored her question.

Anna merely shrugged her apparent ignorance, pressed a slim finger to her chin, and furrowed her brows in thought. "No, I can't say that I have."

"Let's cut to the chase, Mrs. Gatewood. You were the last person to visit that squaw. Where are you hiding her?"

"I beg your pardon. What gives you the idea that I would know of her whereabouts?"

His steely eyes bored into Anna's before he moved his gaze about the room. "I will ask you for permission to have my men search your home. If it isn't given willingly, then you will be removed from this house until a full inspection is completed."

Anna knew the request would come eventually—she had simply enjoyed playing the game—anything to rattle the pompous man before her. She smiled demurely and nodded her head. "There is no need to become...hostile, Colonel. You may look anywhere you like. All I ask is that your men do not leave a mess. I'll help however I can." She moved to a nearby chair and seated herself with the utmost composure.

Bingham never took his eyes from her smiling countenance as he issued a directive to his men. "Begin with the adjoining rooms on opposite sides of this house. Work your way to the center. Leave nothing untouched."

One of the Indian police walked down the hall and entered the spare guest room. Anna's outward appearance belied the fact that it was all she could do to breathe normally. "Quite the stretch of weather we're having for this time of the year, isn't it?"

The colonel paused for a moment in his perusal of the room, looked at the woman in the chair, and never answered. He turned his back to her. Anna's eyes immediately darted to the open doorway of the spare bedroom. She leaned slightly to the left in her chair to better see one of the Indian policemen as he searched beneath the bed. The man rose to his feet, then moved to check behind the curtains. A moment later, he disappeared from her view. A split second later, Ann heard the doors of the oak armoire yanked open.

Anna felt the beads of perspiration trickle down between her shoulder blades. *Michael—where are you?* She dropped her gaze as Bingham turned back to cast a glance in her direction. She reached for her knitting bag, sent him another unruffled smile and occupied herself with a half knitted sock.

Twenty minutes later, the two Indians finished their search. Anna had not spoken another word to the Colonel. She simply sat in her chair and clicked her knitting needles, hoping the noise drove the irritable colonel to distraction.

"Well, it seems we searched in vain." The commander's lips were drawn in a tight line again.

Anna glanced up and shrugged. "I could have told you that, sir, but I didn't want to stand in the army's way."

"I would appreciate it if you would ask your husband to see me immediately upon his return."

"Will you be at your command post tomorrow?"

"I'm speaking about tonight."

Anna stood, removed her apron, and dropped it across the back of a chair. *I have just about had enough of you, you pompous bastard.* She sent another smile, however, in his direction. "There's a very good chance he'll be in late if he hasn't returned yet, but I'll be sure to tell him."

Bingham pierced her with a long, accusatory stare. "You do that, Mrs. Gatewood."

Before she could reply, Anna heard the front door open behind her and spun to see a snow-covered Michael enter the house.

"Sorry, Anna, that I'm so late." He stamped the snow from his boots, then sat on a nearby wooden bench to remove the foot coverings. "You should have eaten without me. I was delivering a baby out at one of the settler's homes." His tired eyes showed no surprise when they settled on the Colonel who stood stiffly in the middle of the room. "Good evening, sir. Is there something I can do for you?"

"You know damn well what you can do for me, doctor," Bingham grumbled.

"On the contrary, I'm afraid I don't, Colonel. And, if you wouldn't mind, could we hold this conversation in front of the fire? I'm rather chilled after my long ride." Michael moved to the flames, clasped his hands behind his back, and turned to face the company commander.

Bingham's jaw clenched with indecision as he glanced from the doctor to his wife. "No conversation will be necessary. Your wife can inform you as to the reasons of my visit." He looked at the two Indian police with him, nodded to the door, and left without another word.

Anna's eyes met her husband's before her lids fluttered shut and the air rushed from her lungs. She waited until the sound of pounding hooves receded before flinging herself into Michael's outstretched arms.

"How long was that bastard here?" he asked as he hugged her close.

"I don't know—it seemed like forever. Thank goodness you're home." She leaned back to look up into his tired features. "You look exhausted."

"I am. I don't think I got more than an hour of sleep since I left yesterday."

"Did you bring them back with you?" She was hesitant to ask the question.

Anna watched the smile break across her husband's whiskered cheeks. "They're in the barn. We saw the horses out front when we came down the lane. We didn't want to deal with Bingham tonight. He won't get his copy of the release papers from the Bureau until tomorrow. Did you manage to get August? Is that why he was here?"

It was Anna's turn to smile. "She's hiding behind the false wall at the back of the armoire."

Michael's dark brow lifted. "What false wall?"

"The one August and I built yesterday. I couldn't think of anything else. Go get the men—I'll help her out. I'm not going to tell her that you brought Cole back. She needs a nice surprise after the last four days."

* * *

August helped Anna straighten the clothes in the wardrobe that had been her hiding place earlier that evening. She sat in the dark interior, shaking with fear and waiting for her host to call her out. With the thick boards between her and the room, and the clothes hanging inside, she could only hear muffled words.

She shut the wooden doors with a heavy sigh and turned to Anna. "When do you think they will return? I am worried that Michael will never be able to get them released—that I will never be with Cole again."

"Don't be."

August spun at the sound of his voice. "Cole!"

He stood with the light at his back, but his bruised forehead was still painfully visible. A heavy growth of beard darkened his jaw and his sandy-colored hair was still matted with dried blood even though the heavy waves were wet with a fresh washing. He was the most beautiful sight August had ever encountered.

She launched herself into his waiting arms with a sob. The reunited lovers never realized when Anna left the bedroom and closed the door softly behind her. They were aware only of the wild warmth between their shared bodies and the fervent need for each to touch the other. Passionate kisses were exchanged and words of love murmured as the outside world melted away. They were together again and nothing else mattered.

Cole hauled August up to meet his lips and crushed her breasts against his chest. His fingers tangled themselves in her long, silky hair and his mouth slanted across moist lips as he searched for a response.

August moaned against his searching mouth and his grip on her tightened. He clutched her to him, took two steps, turned, and fell across the bed, pulling August down with him. Her body covered his, and he reveled in her nearness and the soft, supple feel of her flesh. He needed her warmth, her devotion, her love, to erase the agony of not knowing where she was. A moment later, he peeled the shirt from her body, exposing her breasts, then reached up to caress the swollen mounds.

August's head fell back, basking in the renewed touch of the man she had loved forever. She groaned against his lips, then tugged his shirt from the waistband of his pants. They both sat up then, and struggled to relieve him of the garment. August dropped her head to kiss the muscular shoulders and furred chest, then ran her fingers across the downy length of his flat belly.

She rolled onto her side when Cole tugged at her leggings. A moment later, they lay on the braided rug near the bed. August's hands reached for the buttons of his trousers, only to be met by his own fingers as they rushed to help her pull them from his hips. An eternity later, the lovers fell back to the surface of the bed.

"August—" he ground out against her open lips "—I need you now..."

She opened to him and welcomed his length into her body. His passionate gasp heated her neck and the instant waves of fulfillment shook her body. She breathed his name against demanding lips as he stroked harder. The culmination of their love burned hot within her, and Cole answered her need with one final thrust and another bruising kiss.

Their mouths finally parted, but not yet willing to separate their bodies, they gazed at one another between gentler kisses. A roving hand still followed the slope of a satiny hip as another caressed the muscular line of a damp shoulder. They reacquainted themselves at a more languid pace, the speed of their passion slowing now that their untamed hunger had been spent.

Cole rose onto one elbow, followed the feminine line of her cheek with his gaze, and placed a gentle kiss of apology on her lips. "I didn't hurt you, did I? I'm sorry—once I felt your skin against mine..."

She placed a shaky finger against his mouth. "Shhh. I needed it to be that way, also. I needed to feel something other than the horrible nothingness." August reached up and gently touched the wound on his forehead. Her gaze followed her fingers as they traced a path down the side of his face and ended at his square jaw. She lovingly cupped his chin and pulled his lips to hers in another tender kiss. He responded by running his tongue sensuously along the seam of her lips until she opened her mouth and he gained entrance once more.

"I love you," he murmured a long time later. "I didn't know if I would ever feel you in my arms again." He rubbed his cheek against her silky shoulder and smiled to himself. "I thought of you every minute." He rose higher on his elbow and a quick flash of apology darkened his gaze. "I'm sorry I wasn't able to keep you from the soldiers. I promised to protect you always, and I broke my oath."

"There was nothing you could do, Cole. We were all powerless that day. But we lived when others did not." Instant tears burned behind her lids.

Cole rolled onto his back, tucked August's head into the crook of his neck, and hugged her close. He understood the pain in her voice. "I'm sorry about Wolf."

"I know you are." She nuzzled his neck tenderly. "Wolf did not deserve to die. I still do not understand why he ran into the clearing. Maybe it was because he saw the chief in the arms of the soldiers—maybe it was because you stood in their midst and he knew we belonged together. No matter what, I know Wolf would have done anything to bring me happiness if he had lived."

"He would also have done everything to assure you remembered who you were. Why, August," Cole whispered as he stared at the ceiling joists above him. "Why didn't you tell me you are Crazy Horse's daughter? Didn't you trust me?"

She sat up and stared at the hurt that sprang instantly into his hazel eyes and quickly reached out to stroke his cheek. "Trust has nothing to do with it. For years, I was ridiculed because my people refused to believe my grandmother when she told them of my heritage. Once they realized differently, I tucked that knowledge away." She slid across the short distance between them and laid her head back in the crook of his neck. Cole unconsciously wrapped his muscled arm around her shoulder and pulled her closer. "The only person I ever spoke to about it was Wolf—and not by my own choosing. He continually reminded me of my father and of my dream to help my people. I wonder now if he did that because he was frightened of losing me."

"We've never spoken about your dream, August."

She immediately tensed in his arms. "And we will not talk of it now. Wolf told me something that my father once said before he, too, was murdered—*the dream ends when the greatness is gone*. I believe that, Cole. The dream died with Wolf. I will remember him always for the great man he was, but to mourn him forever would be dishonorable. I had made my decision to be with you no matter the cost, and I know he would have approved in the end if given a chance. He loved me."

Cole wisely decided to drop the subject of her dream. August's stiff body, where she lay next to him, proved that she was upset with the turn in the conversation. She had been through enough.

"I know he loved you. We spoke of it." Cole rubbed a roughened palm down the soft length of her arm, lost in his own thoughts. Minutes passed before he raised himself on a bent elbow to better look at the woman beside him. "Our last conversation was about you."

Her slim eyebrows rose slightly in question, but she remained silent.

"He wanted to make sure that it was your decision to be with me. And, if so, that I would take you as my wife."

"What did you tell him?" She waited breathlessly for his answer.

Cole dipped his head to tease her full lips, then his hand trailed lower to cup her breast and the satiny softness of her belly. "I told him that I wanted you in my life forever, as my wife—" he dropped kisses along a path to her breast "—as my lover—"the hand continued to move downward "—and as the one person closest to my heart..."

Chapter Twenty-Five

The following morning, the two lovers still lay with limbs tangled beneath the warm coverlet on the bed. August slept on as Cole listened to Anna and Michael's muffled voices in the next room as they rose for the day. His eyes moved to the slumbering woman beside him and a gentle smile curved his mouth. Her head lay mere inches from his on the pillow.

He studied the slim arched brows above closed eyes. Dark lashes lay softly against the taut skin that covered her high cheekbones. His gaze followed the slim length of her nose to the full, slightly parted lips. Her warm breath caressed his own mouth and it was all he could do not to kiss her awake. He did reach out though, and gently brush thick strands of dark, wavy hair away from her exposed shoulder, then followed the gentle curve of her breastbone with a tentative finger.

You have been through so much in your short life... His thoughts moved to their conversation of the night before. She had not revealed much about her ancestry, nor would she talk about her dream in any depth. He stared at her in wonder, in awe of the many twists of fortune that had brought them together. *Do fate and dreams really end because we say it will be so?* He did not think so.

A quick shiver ran down his spine. He had also dreamed of her so many months ago. Night after night, the same vision returned to haunt him. It was only when he discovered her that day on the hill, standing against the beautiful backdrop of a clear blue autumn sky, did he realize in some small part of him that they were meant to be together. If August had decided to pass him by and not steal his horses that first day, he would have found her somewhere else.

But, it's not that simple. She speaks of her dream being finished. Wolf is dead, but I don't think fate is pleasant enough to leave it at that.

He watched her eyes flicker open and observed the gentle smile that creased her mouth when she looked into his eyes. "Good morning." A contented sigh left her lips. "You're still here."

"And where did you think I'd be?" He grinned back.

"I woke many times during the night to assure myself you were by my side. In my sleep, I kept seeing the arms of the soldiers taking you from my sight."

With one quick roll, Cole spread a muscular thigh across her own to pin her beneath him. He clasped her hands, drug them up to the pillow she lay on, and stared down into her smoky gaze. "They're not going to take me away. Michael assured that by order of the Bureau." He dipped his head to draw her mouth to his own. Moments later, Cole broke away, pushed a few unruly dark strands from her cheek, and sighed heavily. "We've got some decisions to make, August. And, we'll make them together. If you want to stay in the Dakotas—at least until spring arrives—just say so. We don't have to be in a hurry to do anything, except make sure you stay out of Bingham's sight."

She looked up at him through solemn eyes. "I have made a decision."

"You have? Let's hear it."

"I have decided that I am tired of your talking. You babble on like an old squaw. I can think of better ways to waste away our time."

A playful smile split his face and, as he lowered his mouth to hers, August put away her quandary for another time. She lived for the moment—she existed for this one small minute in time when Cole would make her feel safe and protected from the world.

* * *

Anna looked up as the happy couple emerged from the bedroom. Their cheeks were flushed from recent lovemaking, and a slim brow arched over her eye as she watched them move to the table.

"I was beginning to wonder if you two were ever going to come out." A teasing smile played about her lips.

August left Cole's side and crossed to where Anna stood before the stove. She spread her arms and pulled the other woman into a soft embrace. The doctor's wife could not hide her amazement as she looked over a slender shoulder at the smiling man across the room. She returned August's hug.

"Thank you, Anna, for everything you have done for me." August clasped her tighter.

"It was my pleasure, honey." She stepped back. "So, have you two decided what you're going to do now?"

Cole pulled out two chairs and indicated that the women sit. "August hasn't decided yet."

She tilted her head up to meet his gaze. "It needs to be a joint decision, Cole." She turned to Anna, and her features turned grim. "Have you heard what will happen now that Sitting Bull has been killed?"

Anna shook her head. "Michael and Beau left for the office. Beau is determined to meet with Colonel Bingham today. He says he's not going to sit idly by and let me become his nursemaid while that man decimates the countryside." Her eyes darted from August to Cole and back again. "You two really need to talk with them before making any kind of decision." She hesitated, then continued on. "You may as well know. Cavalry troops have started to arrive from Fort Robinson. I'm not talking a few hundred either. We'll find out why when Beau returns."

* * *

Beau sat outside Bingham's office, with Michael at his side. He tapped the chair with nervous fingers, and his anxious blue gaze darted about the room.

"That bastard is purposely making us wait."

"Be patient. We'll get our turn," Michael returned. "You know, he's not going to take the sight of you lightly. You're supposed to be locked up miles from here."

"He's too much of a coward to say anything about the last week. He won't want to be implicated in my sudden absence."

Beau heaved himself slowly from the chair, winced in pain, and looked out the large office window for the dozenth time. Hundreds of troops arrived by the hour. Something was afoot, and he wanted to know what it was. His gaze moved to a line of over two hundred Indians that stood waiting with their ration tickets in hand outside the agency storehouse. The cold Dakota wind swirled around their feet, picked up loose snow, and tossed it into the air around them. More than one woman shielded a child against the blustery weather.

They wait for the big white hand to feed them. Beau wondered how many would actually receive beef today. Two weeks earlier, Congress had issued orders to cut the portions to even less as a measure to control the Ghost Dancers. He shook his head and leaned against the wall. *Will it ever end?*

The door to Bingham's office opened and the man's aide stepped into the room. He looked around until his gaze rested on Beau. "Mr. McCabe. Colonel Bingham requests your presence."

Michael rose to follow and was stopped when the aid lifted a palm. "Sorry, sir. The colonel didn't say anything about you."

Beau stepped forward before the doctor could reply. "When I asked for this meeting, it was requested that the commander see both Dr. Gatewood and myself. The doctor has medical supply issues that need to be discussed."

Michael looked up in surprise at his friend's statement.

"But, sir..."

"I think we've had enough discussion. Dr. Gatewood is in charge of the hospital and has concerns. Please, move aside so we can get on with our meeting." Beau wanted to punch the little fop who stood before him.

The aide finally shrugged his shoulders, moved aside, and let the men pass. They entered the commander's office.

Colonel Bingham sat behind his desk. Opposite him was a familiar face; Colonel Joseph Forsyth from Fort Robinson—the man who had helped Beau with the release of August's family members. Seated in another chair was Chief Red Cloud. Bingham stared haughtily at the old warrior, even though he was considered a great man who had worked hard to keep peace between the two factions.

"Chief Red Cloud. It's been many months since we last spoke." Beau crossed to stand before the other man. The chief rose to extend a hand to his old acquaintance.

"I am glad you have arrived, old friend. We are discussing once again why my people at Pine Ridge go hungry."

"It's because they won't conform, Red Cloud." Bingham refused to give the honor due the warrior by addressing the chief by his elite status. "Tell them to stop this crazy dance and more food stores will be released."

The chief ignored the colonel and met Beau's gaze. "They only dance, McCabe. I do not believe in the supposed resurrection of our dead. Even if I did, the government's actions are still unwarranted. The food rations were promised as part of the treaty—and yet hunger still curls in our bellies. Our annuity money has been withheld. Those who do not dance are also suffering. There is no difference."

Beau bypassed any comment to Bingham and brought his gaze to Colonel Forsythe. "Have you brought reinforcements because of the Ghost Dance?"

The man nervously scratched his chin as he shrugged. "I've been sitting here giving this a lot of thought, Beau. The War Department ordered that my regiment help protect the settlers in this area. They fear that outbreaks against whites living at the Ridge might erupt. Our orders are to withhold supplies without preference. My feelings, however, are that we should let the Sioux dance—possibly even distribute supplies as a show of good will."

Bingham shot from his chair. "Don't let this Indian fool you, Colonel Forsythe. He plays at pretending to lead his people here—he shouts out against the dance only because he is afraid he will be the next chief to be arrested."

Chief Red Cloud glanced from one man to the other. "That is a mistruth, Colonel Bingham. I have been held captive before in my lifetime. Becoming a prisoner once again is not what frightens me. My fear stems from having to deal with those like you, who take all that they can from a people who can no longer fight for themselves. You feed on our demise as a jackal does on a dead animal. We are not dead—but will be if what has been promised does not come to pass."

"You are out of line, Red Cloud," Bingham sneered.

"My words hold more truth than you are willing to admit."

Colonel Forsythe stood and his gaze encompassed the men standing in the room. "We are all here for the same reason. That is to find a resolution we can live with—each and every one of us. Now, please, let us sit and discuss this in a mannerly fashion."

"There is only one resolution we can live with." Bingham's lips formed a thin line. "This crazy dancing must come to a halt immediately. Not only this agency, but the outlying frontier homesteads, are in a critical situation with the threat of an outbreak on the horizon. The frenzied leaders of this movement are whipping up emotions." He turned his glittering gaze on Chief Red Cloud. "If you can't talk any sense into those who would listen to your words, then the troops will continue to amass. And, I can guarantee you—their arrival will not just be a show of force. We will take measures if needed."

* * *

"I really thought that, with Forsythe in attendance, things would have gone better," Beau told those gathered at the table an hour later. "But, Bingham also managed to convince him that the Sioux will be on the warpath shortly because of Sitting Bull's death."

"How do you think the agency Indians are going to handle all these extra troops?" Cole leaned forward, his mind spinning with the implications— implications that could very well affect August. They needed to leave for Minnesota as soon as possible; he did not want her caught up in the tensions. They could do nothing at the moment to help the cause.

"They're nervous—and rightly so. Word has it that they believe their resurrection will come in some form by this spring. Seeing the mounting number of regiments arriving only heightens their belief that something needs to be done." Beau ran a hand through his wavy hair. "More troops are on their way. Forsythe came north with the entire Seventh Cavalry to assess the situation after Bingham notified Congress that there is major unrest. General Henry should be here in another day or two with the Ninth Cavalry. That's over one thousand soldiers!"

August's eyes widened with fear, and Cole slipped an arm around her shoulders to offer comfort.

Beau looked from one to the other. "I think you two should leave. I don't fear for our safety as whites living on the reservation. I do worry about August, however. If some edict comes down, we may not be able to keep her from the government's clutches. Plus, we now know—because of what happened up at Standing Rock—that there are those Sioux who would hand her over in a second."

"I agree," Cole nodded. He took August's hand in his. "Maybe we should listen to him. You haven't expressed one way or the other what you want to do. We could always return in the spring."

Up to that point, August had not made a decision. She did, however, reflect on the burning need within her to leave for Cole's home—to start a new life free from harassment and worry. Now though, after listening to Beau's story, she knew she could not leave. Something pushed her to stay on.

"I would like to stay. I know I need to keep hidden from the colonel. If he finds me, I will be used as a pawn. I'm sorry, Cole, but I can not leave yet."

He patted her hand and sent a hesitant smile in her direction. "I told you it would be your decision, August. I'm not sure if it's the correct one, but if you want to stay, then we'll see what happens over the next few weeks. Just promise me you'll give thought to leaving if tensions break."

She simply nodded her head as a shiver of foreboding crawled up her spine.

* * *

A lantern with the wick turned low bathed the Gatewood living room with a soft glow. The house was quiet until a loud pounding on the door awakened all those who slept.

Michael jumped from his bed, quickly pulled on a pair of pants and made his way through the house. Cole came through a bedroom door at the back of the house and followed his friend into the living room.

"Where's August?" Michael whispered before reaching for the door lock.

"She's ready to hide if needed." Cole's brow furrowed with worry. "Who would be pounding on the door at this time of the night?"

"Hopefully it's not someone who discovered August's whereabouts."

Michael clicked the lock and opened the door to find an army sergeant standing before him. "Can I help you?"

"We're in need of your services, sir. There was a battle."

"Where?"

"Out at the Strong Hold, sir. The Sioux secretly assembled and held a Ghost Dance. The South Dakota home guard took it upon themselves to set a trap. Managed to kill seventy-five of the Indians turned hostile. The army was called to intervene and now we've got some injuries."

Cole was stunned. "That doesn't sound like a battle to me—I'd call it a massacre."

The Sergeant shrugged with a lack of concern. "I was just sent to find the Doc—not analyze what happened." He glanced at Michael. "I'll ride with you, sir, whenever you're ready."

"I'll be set to leave shortly."

The sergeant turned to leave as Michael closed the door.

"Is there anything I can do?" Cole offered. If the "battle" was a sample of August's life, then he needed to see it firsthand. "I'm sure you could use help. Just tell me what I need to do, and it'll get done."

Michael's shoulders dropped with a heavy sigh. "It's not going to be pretty."

"And that's why I need to see it. It's August's world."

"No, Cole," August pleaded as she entered from the bedroom. "Please, do not go there. If something happened to you..."

Cole crossed to where she trembled in the doorway. He pulled her close, and she clung to him tightly. "It'll be okay, August. Michael's going to need help. I'll get Beau before I leave. He and Anna will be here with you." He turned and faced the doctor. "How long do you think we'll be gone?"

"It's anyone's guess—depends on the severity of the injuries. But, Cole, I think August is right. You should stay here with her. If things break open, the two of you might need to ride out of here as quickly as you can."

The doctor's words caused the fear in August's heart to mount—not only for her own kind, but for her newfound life with Cole. They were finally together after suffering so much. Bingham's incarceration was still fresh in her mind. She did not think she could bear it if it happened again. The next time, Cole might not find her.

"Please—stay with me."

Cole looked into her anxious eyes and surrendered easily now to her fear. "All right." He welcomed August back into his arms. "I won't leave."

* * *

Hours into the night, Cole was awakened when August's body jerked in her sleep. She flipped onto her back, and a small moan emitted from her throat. He moved closer across the length of the mattress and reached out to pull her back into her arms, but she fought the embrace.

"No...run!"

"August, it's Cole. Wake up." He shook her shoulder gently. "It's all right."

Her eyes snapped open, along with another gasp.

"It' me—Cole. You're having a bad dream."

August bolted upright with a frantic glance around the room. Recognizing the darkened space, she dropped her forehead into her palms and breathed deeply. Cole sat up beside her and touched a trembling shoulder.

"It was just a nightmare, honey. I'm here with you."

She shook her head, causing the silky dark strands of hair to swish across her back. Her continued silence frightened him.

"August?"

She turned to him, and he was taken aback by the tears that glistened on her cheeks. "Something will happen. We can not stay here."

Cole grasped her hand in support. "Okay. Then we'll leave in the morning. I'll send a telegram to Tyler telling him we're on our way north to the ranch."

"No." She shook her head.

"What do you mean, no? You just said we had to leave."

She heard the confusion in his voice. *How can I make him understand when the idea makes me tremble?*

Years of believing that some answer could be found—that some solution to the plight of the Sioux could be discovered, drove her to a decision. She had seen her people pleading for guidance in the ebony haze of her nightmare. They fell to the snow, but still clutched at her for help. August could do nothing for them, but her presence brought a calming effect to the many who had nowhere else to turn. A way to live peacefully among the many whites who pressed their way into the frontier had pushed her to a simple discovery of what she needed to do. She could not abandon them now.

August met Cole's questioning gaze. "I need to go back to Standing Rock. That is why we must leave here."

"Now, wait a minute, August." Cole's chest tightened suddenly with dread. "You know that going back would put you at risk. The Indian police know who you are. The same thing would just happen again, and this time they might kill you."

"It will not—"

"The hell it won't." Cole swung his longs legs over the edge of the bed, stuffed them into his pants, and stood to pace before her. He fought to keep his panic-born anger at bay. "Why have you decided to do this now? You admitted yesterday that you needed to stay hidden."

August lifted her chin in a show of defiance, and Cole could not help but wonder what was coming. "When you found me again, you said that where we go from here would be my decision—that you would do whatever I wanted as long as we stayed together."

"Goddammit, August, don't pull that shit on me. That was before Bingham had you thrown into prison."

"What of your words yesterday?" Her wide questioning eyes stared up at him. "You agreed to stay with me."

Cole ran a hand through his wavy hair, sighed deeply, and dropped his chin a moment to control the rapid beat of his heart. Once his anger had calmed to the point where he could speak again without hollering at her, he raised his eyes. "That was when I thought you would be out of harm's way—I meant what I said because I thought you would be here in the safety of this house. I didn't think you'd make a foolish decision to travel north again. That definitely changes how I feel."

"Is that what you think? That I am foolish?"

"Don't put words in my mouth." He looked at her and finally realized that she still trembled. "What's the real reason? When that soldier showed up a few short hours back, you begged me to stay with you tonight. Here—in this house. Now, suddenly, everything has changed. I don't understand."

August stared at her hands, where they rested on the quilt that covered her lap. Her body trembled uncontrollably. A tear found its way down the smooth skin of her cheek, and her despair nearly brought Cole to his knees. He climbed back beneath the covers and reached out to take her delicate fingers in his.

"I'm sorry. The thought of something happening to you makes me sick. Just tell me, August. What changed your mind? I need to understand."

She raised a tear-stained face. "I have to go back to them. For some reason, my presence gives them hope. If we leave for your home now, I will never know if I could have done something to help them."

"Dammit, you alone cannot change the future. You're one woman, August."

"I am one woman who had a vision years ago. That vision has driven me my entire life. Cole, this is my spirit journey, and I have no choice in the matter. I have to go. If you do not come with me, I will go to my people on my own."

"Is that what you have refused to tell me all this time?"

She nodded her head before resting a wet cheek against his bare chest. The calming beat of his heart eased her own inner turmoil. He was angry with her, yet still he loved her. "I have no control over this."

"Yes, you do." Cole grasped at any possibility that would get her to listen to reason. "We spoke once about how the life of the Sioux would change. That time is here, August. Traveling to be with them at Standing Rock will not change the outcome now. It will only put you in danger. Let's leave for Minnesota. We can do more with Tyler's help and connections."

"I cannot."

"August, please..."

She shook her head against his chest, and Cole closed his eyes against the pain that had rooted itself in his heart. He heaved a sigh against the silkiness of her hair. "All right," he conceded quietly, "but, I'm not letting you out of my sight. I'm coming with you."

Chapter Twenty-Six

The following night, Michael and Anna lingered on their front porch, shivering from the icy cold blast of winter wind, and watched as Cole and August disappeared into a shroud of darkness.

Earlier that day, Beau had managed to procure two mounts and a packhorse for their hurried departure, then left himself for the French Creek. Word had reached Pine Ridge that several wagons full of Sioux were massacred as they visited with non-Indian friends at Buffalo Gap to the west.

Anna pulled her woolen shawl tighter around her shoulders as she stared into the dark empty night. "Do you think they will ever come back?"

Michael tugged on her arm. "Come on, honey. No sense thinking about it out here in the cold."

Anna followed him into the house and headed for the kitchen where a tin pot of coffee sat heating on the range. A moment later, she had two filled steaming mugs on the table and she and her husband sat and stared blankly at one another across the wooden surface.

"They're making a mistake. We should have tried harder to get them to stay until tensions settled down." Anna pressed slender fingers to her temples and closed her eyes to keep the tears at bay.

Michael watched his wife closely as she struggled with her emotions. "It was August's choice. She felt she needed to be with her people." He hesitated a moment, then continued. "When a man loves a woman, the present—or her past—doesn't matter. I'm sure that's how Cole feels about August. He sees nothing but the woman he loves and will support her to whatever end."

Anna's head came up. "At the risk of getting them both killed? I just can't understand why Cole didn't put his foot down. He's got more sense than that. It's not like him to let his gentle heart rule a level head. What he should have done is dragged her back to the ranch."

Michael's eyebrows rose at her heated words. He hesitated again, made a decision, and charged on. "You talk as if you know the place personally—almost as much as the man."

Anna's startled gaze met his. She swallowed the instant fear that coursed through her veins. "I...I don't know what you mean." She rose quickly and hurried to busy herself about the kitchen.

Michael observed her agitated movements as she poured the grounds from the tin pot into a waste bucket, then silently prepared the coffee urn for the next day. He pondered her sudden quietness, breathed in deeply, and raked a big hand through the graying hair at his temples. "You were rather...upset today when they announced their departure."

Anna noted the tentative demeanor in his statement. *He can't know anything. It's impossible. Cole promised...* She brushed her hands across her apron and refused to meet her husband's eyes. "Of course I was upset. Who knows what will happen—I hate to see them become a casualty of either side."

"You sure there's not more to it than that?"

Anna's mind spun. Had she done something while the visitors stayed at their home? Had she inadvertently given away her past? She paled at the mere thought. *He'll send me away if he ever finds out...*

"Anna, come here and sit down."

She ignored his request. "I've got some things to attend to, Michael. Getting August and Cole ready to leave took up a big part of my day."

Michael pursed his lips, watched her continued bustling, and reached out to grab her arm as she passed by the table.

Though his face showed no anger or condemnation, Anna's heart sank. She knew instinctively what his next words were going to be even before he opened his mouth. She steeled herself against the whiplash of accusations that were sure to follow.

"You knew Cole from somewhere before, didn't you?" He looked up expectantly and waited.

Anna hung her head in shame and, when she did not answer him, Michael pulled her onto his lap. "It's okay, Anna. I shouldn't play with your emotions." A gentle hand pushed the wisps of hair back from her cheek. "I know about everything—I know about you and Cole in another life. It just took me a little time to put two and two together. I don't want this hanging between us anymore."

Her eyes snapped up to search his tender gaze. "You know about Cole?" Anna shook her head slowly. "I don't understand. How come you haven't said anything?"

"I figured—"

"Wait!" She breathed out, then pressed a palm against his chest to stall any further words. "You knew, yet you didn't asked me to leave." Anna was as puzzled as she was fearful.

"Are you going to let me talk now?"

She simply nodded her head, still bewildered by the conversation.

Michael pulled her closer. "I thought I would let it ride—and had planned to since we were first married."

"First married?"

"Anna?" One dark brow lifted over his right eye in warning.

She snapped her lips closed.

"Then Cole came out here. I figured he must be the other man in your life. I've watched you since he arrived. You've been as nervous as a cat. Anna, I don't want the past haunting you anymore—or haunting us. I want nothing between us."

Tears filled his wife's eyes before her gaze found the floor.

"Don't cry, honey."

"How did you know? Michael, I'm so ashamed." Her head jerked up and her eyes widened as the tears still flowed. "Do...do you know all of it?"

He nodded. "I think I have most of it figured out. Cole isn't the only thing you've hidden. Am I right?"

Anna closed her eyes in shame and found the fortitude to continue. "But how—how do you know?"

He pulled her head to his shoulder and gently stroked her back to calm her fear. "Do you remember when you woke at Fort Benton and you had been so sick? I was the only one to care for you—and because of your fever, you babbled constantly. It wasn't too hard to put your past life together—especially when a couple from the wagon train knew who you were and were only too happy to inform me when they pulled out and left you behind. That's probably one of the reasons the wagon master dumped you in the middle of nowhere. Before you awoke though, you continually asked for a man named Cole—more than once you cried that you loved him. Then Beau spoke of his old friend from Minnesota with the same name. I just knew it had to be him."

"But you still married me..."

"Of course I did. Anna—the life you led before we met was your own. I saw what kind of person you were when you worked so hard during the cholera outbreak. You pulled your own and never shrunk from any duties thrown your way. I think I started loving you even then."

"Michael," Anna whispered as she wrapped her arms around his neck and clung desperately to him. "I love you so much—" A moment later, she leaned back and stared into his eyes that were so near to her own. "You knew everything when you left me with him that first night. Why did you do that?"

"Because I watched you pace from the time Beau told us Cole was riding west. The night he arrived, I couldn't face the fact that, since the two of you had found each other again, it might mean the end to us. I left you alone with him so you could figure out what you wanted to do. I prayed you would choose me."

A sob sounded in her throat as she flung herself into his embrace once more. It took a few minutes before she was able to whisper again into the crook of his neck. "I love you, Michael. Cole came here to find August, not me—but, no matter, his appearance didn't change how I feel about you. Leaving you has never crossed my mind. I don't know what I did to deserve you, but I'm so lucky to have you in my life." She lowered her mouth to his and kissed him passionately.

Michael pulled back for the slightest moment and a grin touched his lips. "No, Anna, I'm the lucky one."

* * *

Cole and August reached Cherry Creek on the northern end of the Standing Rock reservation a week later. They had skirted the trails and the known Army and Cavalry camps, watching closely the entire time for any sign of Bingham's troops.

They rode into Big Foot's camp and immediately went in search of the chief's lodge. Cole could not help but notice that the squalor of the encampment was no different from the Sioux who had lived with Sitting Bull. If anything, the conditions were worse. Once more, he experienced the deep urge to take August and run as quickly and as far as they could.

Instead, a young man on the trail met them and, after a few quick words of introduction, Cole and August were led to the chief.

They entered the teepee to the sound of a hacking cough. Cole was flabbergasted by the sight of Big Foot lying weakly on a rug next to the fire. Gone was the grand man he had visited with only a short few weeks earlier. In his place was a feeble and weak leader, who was being eaten with sickness. The old man sat up slowly, was wracked by another round of coughing, then lifted his watery gaze to the two visitors. He motioned them closer to the warmth of the flames.

"Cole Wilkins. I did not think we would meet so soon again. My runner said you have brought the woman, August Moon, with you." He wiped the moisture from his eyes and focused on the woman sitting before him. "I would like to hear the tale of how you managed to free her from the colonel's clutches. It does my heart good to know that she was not one of the dead left to us after Sitting Bull's murder. You also became a prisoner. Is that not true?"

Cole nodded. "Beau McCabe and I were both taken that day. I'm glad you left or you probably would've been taken into custody, also. Beau's connections to the Indian Bureau helped to have the interference charges dropped. Colonel Bingham was none too pleased with our release or August's escape."

Chief Big Foot nodded his head in return. "McCabe has done much to help us, but I fear it is not enough. But you," his gaze moved to August, "will help the hearts of our people—it is the only thing left to do. Seeing Crazy Horse's daughter among us gives them hope."

Suddenly, his body contorted with another fit of coughing. Spittle oozed from his mouth, and Cole and August hurried to aid the man with a cooling sip of water. They waited until he caught his breath and helped him to lie back on the bed. His fevered hand gripped August's arm with surprising strength.

"You have risked much by coming here."

"I could not stay away."

"Before my friend's life was taken in such waste, he and I spoke about your father. He also spoke of a conversation he had with you."

"Sitting Bull was a very wise man."

"Heed his words, August Moon." The old man curled his body on the blanket as another round of coughing weakened him further. He spoke in a raspy voice. "Sitting Bull's followers, those who are left, have sought refuge with me since the murder. They have no other place to turn to. Most are widows and children brought in by only a handful of warriors. I have tried to care for them, but our food stores are almost gone. Child, this cannot be your battle alone."

August squeezed her eyes shut against the flood of emotions that assaulted her. *How can this not be my battle? I cannot just turn my back on them for an easier life, no matter how I long for it. The time has not yet come.* She sat back on her haunches until Big Foot fell into a restless sleep. The quiet minutes helped stall what was sure to follow. Cole would demand that they leave immediately.

He stooped beside her and placed a gentle hand on her shoulder. "He's finally sleeping. Let's leave here, August. Even the Chief sounded like he was urging you to go. We can't take anymore chances."

August raised her hand for silence. She stood with Cole's help, thanked Big Foot's wife for her warm fire, and followed her lover from the teepee.

Cole grabbed her arm as soon as they exited the rawhide dwelling and she made to go around him. He hauled her to his chest and searched her face with a pleading gaze. "August, we can't stay here. The chief already has enough mouths to feed. I just feel we need to get the hell out of here. I don't know what it is or why I've got this nagging feeling, but I want to take you back to Minnesota. I want to put you on that horse and go now."

Instant tears sprang from her dark eyes. "Please, don't make me leave. I love you and would do anything you asked, except that."

Cole's absent temper flared as he grabbed her shoulders. "Why in hell can't I get through to you? Dammit, August, there's nothing left for you here. Why can't you see that?"

A frigid look pulled her mouth tight as they stood in the moonlight and faced one another. "There is something left. It is my vision. It is the dream that haunts my waking hours." She remained in his arms, but Cole felt her body stiffen in his embrace. Her big eyes watched him sadly. "This is what I spoke to you of so many months ago, Cole."

"What?"

"The reason why I always felt we could never find a life together. We are still different—no matter how much we love each other. I have lived a life so foreign to you that you cannot understand why I will not desert my own kind."

Cole stared down at her. August was one of very few people who mattered to him, but this one tiny proud woman bore the weight of the world on her shoulders. Could he live without her? Could he leave now and go back to the ranch alone? No. All he wanted to do was protect her—to love her.

It was simply another test of how deeply they really cared for one another. He guessed there would be many more times in future where one of them would have to swallow their pride and feelings simply because of the different cultures. She had spent most of her life running, but now she stood her ground, prepared to face whatever the future held with unflagging courage. He would also.

Cole pulled her against him, embraced her tightly, and breathed in the scent that was simply August. He could do nothing but stand beside her.

"I'm sorry." He kissed her warm temple. "We'll get through this together and, when you're ready, we'll go back to Minnesota. You've got to understand that I feel so helpless here, August. I can't protect you the way I need to. My promise to you is that once we leave here, I'll spend the rest of my life making up for what the soldiers did to all of you."

* * *

"He gets sicker by the day. We must do something for him." August knelt near the fire and readied a bed for herself and Cole. They slept in a lodge that was quickly constructed with the help of some of the band members when she refused to leave Standing Rock. Earlier, they had visited with the failing chief once again.

Now, as she knelt before the fire, she fought the urge to simply run with the man she loved. Over the course of the last few nights, dreams had nagged at her in the dark restlessness of sleep. She continually envisioned the sunken, hungry look of her people, bloody battles, and the Sioux dying in the snow. She had not told Cole. August suspected he would remove her from Standing Rock in an instant if she informed him of her dreams—no matter what.

A nameless premonition caused her to shiver, even though the heat of the flames she tended warmed her skin. A sinking sensation deep in her soul forewarned that something horrible would happen—it was an awareness akin to the vision of that long ago day on the mountain—and she did not want Cole involved. *But I cannot send him away—not after I refused to leave and he promised to stay.* They were trapped between worlds.

August shook away her fear and brought her attention back to the sound of his voice.

"I told you. Let's go back to Pine Ridge and take Big Foot with us. Michael must have something that would relieve his suffering. The man has pneumonia—I'm sure of it. How in hell is he going to last the winter out here?"

She glanced up at him, then quickly stood and moved into his comforting embrace. August leaned her head against his chest and sighed. "He will not leave the people. He is their leader. I am frightened for his life, Cole. Big Foot will not live if he does not receive help—he becomes weaker every day."

The warm pressure of his hand rubbed her back with slow soothing circles. Suddenly, it came to her that there was a way to find help for the chief. August leaned back and reached up to touch Cole's whiskered cheek. "Listen to what I say. You go back to Pine Ridge and bring Michael here. I will stay and wait for you." Even as the words left her mouth, August wanted to swallow them back, but knew she could not.

"No way." He shook his head in adamant refusal. "I'm not leaving you here."

"What else can we do? If I travel with you, it will only slow down help for the chief. Besides, I do not want to tempt fate and give the soldiers a chance to find me."

Cole put his hands on August's shoulders, searched her beautiful features, and stared deeply into her eyes. "Listen to me. I am not going to be separated from you again."

"I feel the same way, Cole. But will we watch him die?" Her round brown eyes stared back. "I cannot go. There will be a council tomorrow night and my attendance has been requested."

"A council for what?"

Her gaze fell silently to the floor. She refused to look up.

Cole reached out to raise her chin until her edgy gaze met his once more. "What, August? What's going on?"

"The people have no more meat," she returned uncomfortably. "Some of the widows are already feeding strips of tanned hide to their children."

"Jesus Christ—why didn't you tell me this before now?"

"Because it is something the whites would never do."

Cole momentarily closed his eyes. A second later, he opened them and searched her wary features once more. Guilt shamed him to the core. He had eaten well every day from the food stores brought on the journey with them. Even though he had selflessly shared his staples with members of the tribe, he had still made sure that, if he and August left for Minnesota, they would have enough to eat until they reached the first few inns along the trail. "So, what is going to be done?"

She turned from him, dropped to her knees, and busied herself with a pack. "The braves will begin to kill ponies again—most of the animals are starving anyway. We need to eat."

Cole's stomach turned. She had said 'we', separating herself from him once more, and had not even realized it. He knelt beside her, pulled August back against his broad chest, and caressed her satiny hair with his stubbled cheek. "How can I leave you again? If I go for help, please come with me."

She shook her head firmly. "I cannot. I will stay with Big Foot and his family."

"August, don't do this to us again." He felt the hand of fate on his shoulder once more and shrugged it away.

She reached up to cover his fingers where they lay gently on her shoulder and closed her eyes for a second to relish his warm touch. "We seem destined to be parted. Cole, I will not leave, and you cannot stay. If I travel with you and the soldiers find us, we will never get back here to help. They will put me in their prisons once more. But, if you are alone, you can pass through their lines quickly. The chief needs care. It will only be this one last time. Be assured that I will be here when you return. I love you—do not ever forget that."

"Don't talk that way—it sounds like we're saying a permanent goodbye."

"Does this mean that you will seek Michael's help?"

He turned her in his embrace and she saw the fear in his hazel eyes. "I guess I have no choice."

August felt the gentle tug of his arms as he pulled her to his chest. She clung to him tightly. "I am so confused, Cole. My heart tells me to hold you tight, to be happy with what we have found together. But, I cannot watch this suffering without trying to make it better."

* * *

August's stomach rolled as she swallowed down the last of her dinner. The horsemeat was stringy—something she was no longer accustomed to—and possessed a flavor that brought back memories of being on the run with her small group only months earlier. Wolf had been alive then, ever busy with plans to travel to the winter camp. Even though the constant threat of soldiers was forever with them, at least she had been certain that her life was leading its destined course. They were all able to hang on to a slim thread of the Sioux's natural life.

How, in such a short time, has everything changed? August would never have guessed only a few short months ago that the end of life as she knew it was so near. In that short time, the Sioux's very existence had been snatched away before her eyes. Wolf had left her world, along with Sitting Bull and countless others. Hope for the Indians' continued survival was all but gone. The only thing left to do was to sit and watch the trail daily and wait for Cole's return.

Agitated, loud voices drew August's attention from her conflicting thoughts. She leapt up from her warm seat by the fire, pulled the flap aside, and frowned as she watched a young man run breathlessly from one lodge to another. Grabbing a blanket to wrap around her shoulders, she rushed toward two women who ranted excitedly as they frantically pulled the teepee hide from the support poles of their lodge.

"What is happening?" August clutched the arm of the squaw closest to her. The woman quickly shrugged loose and continued her frenzied packing.

"You have not heard? We are leaving. A runner has come in. The soldiers are on their way to arrest Big Foot."

August's heart slammed against her ribs as she stumbled behind the woman to the backside of the lodge.

"Are you certain of this?"

The other woman ignored August for a moment as her own panic took over. Deft hands expertly folded the buffalo hide that now lay in the snow. She finally looked up with fear blazing in her dark eyes.

"We will try to run to Pine Ridge and seek help. We need food and horses. Without these things, we will never escape to Canada. Red Cloud can help speak to the government and aid us in keeping Big Foot from becoming a prisoner."

"Pine Ridge..." August's words trailed away as she spun to see the entire camp being broken down in a flurry of motion. A sensation darker and more frightening than she had ever experienced settled on her shoulders. She whirled again and raced to Big Foot's tent. She reached the former location of the man's lodge—his wife and children already had the teepee down—and knelt before the chief, where he lay helpless on an old buffalo robe.

The youngest of the great man's children led a black horse forward, then backed the animal between the adjoining poles of a waiting travois. August's face registered shock when she recognized Cole's mount, Spirit. They had both thought the mare was lost to them after Colonel Bingham arrested Cole.

She moved to the horse, reached an arm out to encircle the wide neck, and laid her forehead against the dark, muscled neck. "Spirit," she breathed, "you are alive." The animal snorted softly and stamped its hooves in the snow. Somehow, August felt closer to Cole as she embraced the animal.

"August Moon?"

She tilted her head to see Big Foot motion her closer from where he lay shivering in the snow. With a last gentle pat to the animal's flank, she stepped a few paces and dropped to the ground beside the old man, who wheezed in the cold air.

"Chief Big Foot, why are we leaving?"

"We can stay no longer."

"Do you think it wise to travel to Pine Ridge?"

"If I stay, I will be arrested as a supporter of the Ghost Dance. Only Red Cloud can help me now. Our food is nearly gone, August Moon, and we will never be able to outrun the soldiers on the way north to our wintering grounds." The sickly man waved his hand and shook his head in despair. "Too many children starving. The winter has been hard. Our only hope is Red Cloud's promise to take us in."

An image of red snow flashed in August's brain. Her own blood curdled. "I...I do not think we should travel south." *Forgive me Cole—I will not be here if Big Foot heeds my words, but I will find you in the spring of the year.* "I know of Colonel Bingham. He will kill you before you have a chance to speak the truth. Let us leave for the north. I fear for your life—I fear for all our lives."

"The children will not make that long journey. I do not know what else to do. We need Red Cloud's protection and will have to avoid the soldiers on our way south." He was seized once more by the tightening in his chest. Blood-colored discharge from his lungs splattered against the buffalo robe as the Chief gasped for air. He clutched her arm weakly as the spasm passed. "He is our only hope. We will move through the Badlands in an effort to stay hidden."

How was she going to change his mind? Instinct forced her to try again, even though her plea would put more miles between her and the man she loved. "It is not right, Big Foot. I feel it deep in my heart. This is our last chance to move north to safety. If we are caught on the trail, our people will never stand on their own again—the soldiers will think we are trying to escape."

Big Foot's eyes clouded with uncertainty as he considered her words. For one hopeful moment, August thought he would change his mind. After another bout of coughing though, his watery gaze looked up and she saw the defeat return to rest in his glance. His head shook again where it was cradled against the back of a traveling pack. "The decision is made. We have no other choice."

* * *

The wind swept across the barren land as the cold, hungry, and weary band traversed the rugged terrain. August huddled against the frigid temperatures and once more, glanced at Big Foot where he lay on the travois behind Spirit. For five long days, the elder rested weakly on his moving bed as he was hauled mile after mile southward.

Somehow, the group had managed to stay clear of Bingham's troops, but in doing so, they missed Cole along the way. August was devastated time after time as each bend of the trail revealed his absence in her life. Each step took her farther from the safety of his arms; surely he had already reached Standing Rock and found them gone.

Mothers carried their weak children, who were wrapped in the scraps of old blankets—anything to keep the cold hand of winter away. It was an unbearable journey; a journey to seek assistance from an outside world that bore down on the Sioux nation. They trudged on.

A young mother stumbled in the snow, thrown off balance by the weight of the toddler in her arms and the baby that was cradled in a sling around her neck. August hurried to the exhausted woman's side.

"Let me help you," she stated softly as she reached out to take the older sibling. The child showed no reaction when August wrapped him within her own blanket, but only lay weakly in her arms.

She adjusted the child in her grasp as her exhausted gaze swept upward once more to the rock ledges above. Her dull eyes searched for the man she hoped would appear from nowhere. August moved on in a trance and concentrated only on placing one foot before the other in an effort to keep upright. The muscles of her once injured leg contracted, causing streaks of pain to shoot down past her knee and into her lower limb.

Cole! Find us...find me...

Chapter Twenty-Seven

Cole and Michael rode almost non-stop for three days in an effort to reach Standing Rock. Plumes of air whistled from the whiskered muzzles of their mounts as they trotted along the frozen riverbank. A line of four mules, weighted down with enormous packs of food stores and medicine, struggled against the lead ropes that pulled them ever onward.

Cole's brooding eyes darted across the white landscape, searching for any sign of troop movement, and his uneasiness mounted. He discovered upon his return to Pine Ridge, that Forsythe and Bingham ran daily forays in an increasingly wider area throughout the entire reservation. The Sioux on the run were easy targets; their extreme hunger combined with the frigid temperatures to make them more and more vulnerable. Those who could not surpass the awful conditions any longer came in from the hills to surrender. The beaten Indians begged without humility for food to feed their starving children.

A deep sigh escaped into the cold, garnering Michael's attention. The doctor glanced at his companion, understanding Cole's fear.

"How you holding up?"

The other man shook his head. "I just want to get there. I know that I had no choice but to go get you, but there's this...thing...nagging at me, and I don't know what it is. I won't feel comfortable until August is standing beside me again. Christ, I wish I would have insisted that she leave with me."

"You're spooking me, Cole, and frankly, I wish you'd knock it off. And, besides, we've made damn good time. We're already on Standing Rock reservation land. We'll be there by tonight."

Tonight won't be soon enough for me. Cole's thoughts returned to the last night he held August in his arms. The feel of her skin against his, the overwhelming need to protect her, and the promise to spend the rest of his life making up for everything his race had done to hers. If something had happened to her because he left her behind, he would never forgive himself.

* * *

Cole leapt from his horse in the eerie silence of twilight, hurried to one of the dilapidated log shanties, and steeled himself against the foreboding shiver that ran the length of his spine. He shouldered a battered door open and the echoing emptiness told him instantly there were no inhabitants. Michael entered the dwelling behind him.

Cole glanced over his shoulder as he battled his fear. "They're gone."

"It doesn't look like there's anyone in the other houses either. It's like a ghost camp."

"Son of a bitch!" Cole pounded his fist against the wall in a mixture of anger and frustration. "Where in hell is she?" He whirled and retraced his steps through the doorway. His frightened gaze searched the surrounding area.

"Do you think they left for their wintering grounds?" Michael asked.

Cole closed his eyes against the pain of the unknown. *She said she would be here waiting for me. She said that she loved me. I know it wasn't a hoax. We've come too far...* He dropped his head until his chin rested on his chest. *Think, Cole!* A moment passed before he turned to the man standing on the rickety porch.

"They must've headed south to Pine Ridge. I'd be amazed if they even get that far. There's no way they would travel north without supplies, especially with the chief being so sick. August's people are tired and starving. Maybe the chief's health worsened and they decided to come looking for us."

"You took the words right out of my mouth. I'd wager that Big Foot was afraid of discovery. They must've gone the long way around in order to hide from Bingham and Forsythe."

"Through the Badlands? At this time of the year?"

"They'll do anything to avoid conflict—especially if the old man is as sick as you said he was."

Cole removed his Stetson and ran a gloved hand through his thick, wavy hair. His weary gaze moved about the barren encampment. "Christ—I'd give anything for Beau to be riding with us. He knows the trails the Indians use.

We don't."

Sudden determination lit in his eyes. He fit the hat back on his head and grabbed the reins to his horse. "Let's go. We just need to ride around, pick up the trail, and follow it as fast as we can. There's no way three hundred and fifty people can cover up a move like that. August said she would be here when I got back. Something pushed them out of here. I just hope like hell it wasn't Bingham."

* * *

Colonel Forsythe raised his hand to halt the Seventh Cavalry. Pulling on the reins of his prancing horse, the senior officer watched and waited as three of his scouts galloped toward him from the top of the far rise. The contingent left the Pine Ridge headquarters only a few hours earlier, traveling steadily through the frosty morning in search of any hostiles who might be on the run. Still, he was surprised when it seemed that his reconnaissance team might already have discovered a group of malcontents.

The small scouting detail reined their mounts to a skidding halt before the long line of regimented soldiers. The sergeant saluted his commanding officer.

"Sir, we've come across tracks heading south not much more than a mile east of here. It looks to be quite a good sized group—possibly three to four hundred."

"And they were coming from the north?" Forsythe was already calculating what he would do with a band that size.

"Yes, sir. They're following the Porcupine Creek. The army has a base camp set up just south of here. We could hold them there."

Forsythe nodded his head; his brain worked furiously. "Send Corporal Jones back to headquarters. Have him inform Colonel Bingham of my request that he ride out with as many troops as he can muster. I want the added protection of his men. We need to make a show of strength in order to avoid bloodshed. I'll expect his arrival by nightfall."

"Yes, sir. I'll get them going immediately."

The sergeant spurred his horse and rode down the line of soldiers. Colonel Forsythe heard the man holler out the orders, saw Jones and another private break from the procession, and head back in the direction of Pine Ridge.

* * *

Later that morning, Forsythe's runners reached Pine Ridge headquarters. Corporal Jones dismounted before the clerk's office, wrapped his reins around a hitching post, and entered the building with a smart step.

Harold Landers looked up, his boredom reflected in the casual glance he gave the intruder before returning his gaze to a newspaper spread across the desk. "Can I help you?" he mumbled while flipping a page.

"I'm looking for Colonel Bingham. I see his detail is still in quarters. Can you tell me where I might find him?"

Landers looked up again and shrugged. "Try the artillery shed. I saw him walking that way this morning. That's about the best I can do for you."

Jones tipped his hat to the disinterested clerk and retraced his steps outside.

He and his companion approached the weapons area a short time later. The place bustled with activity and, in the middle of it, was the man he searched for. Jones approached the commanding officer and saluted smartly.

"Sir, my name is Corporal Jones of the Seventh Cavalry. Colonel Forsythe has asked me to deliver a message."

Bingham eyed the corporal with self-importance and raised an expectant eyebrow. "Well, get on with it man. I haven't got all day."

Jones cleared his throat at the officer's rudeness. "Sir, Colonel Forsythe's scouting party has come across the tracks of a large group of Sioux who are headed south. He would like you and your regiment to ride out to Porcupine Creek. The Colonel feels he needs a show of force in order to subdue the Indians and avoid a battle."

"You don't say?" Bingham nodded his head as his gaze searched the area around him. "Wants a show of force? Well, corporal, find yourselves fresh mounts and we'll be ready within the hour."

The colonel turned on booted heel and entered the shed. Four Hotchkiss guns sat at the ready against the wall. His gaze moved from one shiny metal barrel to the next. Bingham removed his military issued glove and ran a hand across the cold iron of the gun closest to him. The rapid-fire cannon block moved both horizontally and vertically at the touch of his hand and was capable of firing successive shrapnel rounds. His gaze moved to numerous crates of two-pound shells. His contemplating eyes narrowed. The guns would provide the ultimate supremacy in a battlefield.

"Private Duncan!" he barked.

The man hurried through the open doorway and to his side.

"Yes, sir?"

"We leave within the hour for Porcupine Creek to meet Colonel Forsythe and the Seventh. Prepare these guns for travel."

Private Duncan's eyes bulged in amazement. "We're taking all four?"

Bingham spun with anger shooting from the steely depths of his eyes. "Did you not hear what I ordered? I would suggest you move immediately!"

The man scuttled away to do his bidding. Bingham shook his head at what he considered to be the continued incompetence of the men around him. He jerked the glove back onto his hand and stepped with purpose into the sunlight.

* * *

August's shoulders burned from the weight of the small child she still carried. His mother beside her walked in a trance, her unblinking eyes never wavering from the trail before them. Palpable pain contorted her ashen features. That same morning, the Sioux woman's baby had finally succumbed to the cold hand of starvation and died in his mother's arms. August helped the woman to bury the child under a pile of rocks when the frozen ground refused to be disturbed by their rooting hands.

August's gaze swept the rough terrain around them for the hundredth time. A child wept weakly from somewhere behind her. The footfalls of her people, as they plodded on across the frozen grass sprouting through the snow, disappeared in the bitter wind. They trudged forward toward hopeful salvation at Red Cloud's camp.

How many more will die? August felt the pangs of hunger rip through her flat stomach. The small bit of food supplies they had left Standing Rock with were completely gone—no one had eaten in the last day and a half; still, Big Foot urged them on from the confines of the travois.

The remembered warmth of Cole's tender embrace kept August upright and moving. Her mind latched onto the vision of his smiling face as each mile was eaten up, and she swallowed her fear at never finding him again. *I am here, Cole,* her silent plea reached the heavens. *Find me before the bloodshed comes.*

Let me touch you one last time...

She trudged on until she realized that, one by one, the weary fugitives were stopping around her. Their haunted eyes scanned the bluffs that surrounded them and, like the approach of death itself, the dreaded echo of hooves and creaking leather were carried along on the winter wind.

August set the toddler on the ground beside his grieving mother, straightened slowly, and pulled the thin blanket from her head. She turned—and waited; trepidation trickled through her veins. Her dark eyes widened in horror when, a few minutes later, blue-clad soldiers lined the ridge around them. Over four hundred military men surrounded the Sioux, and each had a rifle pressed to his shoulder.

A commotion at the front of the group of Indians caught her attention; two braves hurried to tie a ragged piece of white cloth to a pole. They hoisted the obvious symbol of surrender and waved it high in the air. Big Foot lay near by. Six mounted members of the Cavalry picked their way down the bluff and trotted in the chief's direction. August covered her head with the blanket again to shield her face and moved closer to the chief's travois.

Colonel Forsythe's horse cantered closer, his men riding close behind him with weapons at the ready. The officer reined his mount to a halt when he reached the old man. He tipped his head in respect of the elder.

"Chief Big Foot. You are far from your home."

Big Foot raised himself weakly onto one elbow. "We travel to Red Cloud."

Forsythe's gaze followed the line of Sioux that stretched out against the white landscape for a quarter mile. "You expect me to believe this? You're far from the trail that would lead you there. Why would you take your people through such a desolate area when a shorter route was possible?"

Big Foot opened his mouth to answer, but gasped for air instead. He lay his head weakly against a bent arm until the spasm of coughing ended.

The colonel's gaze dropped to the bloody spittle that covered the snow beside the old man, then he dismounted quickly and stepped forward to assess the situation. His concern for the chief flashed in his eyes. Removing a glove, he reached out and touched the old man's heated brow. Forsythe straightened abruptly and turned to face his lieutenant.

"Mr. Ames. Bring up a wagon, along with my personal physician to attend Chief Big Foot. Prepare the men to move this group to the outpost for the evening."

The lieutenant's thin brows rose over brown eyes. "You've decided not to bring them back to Pine Ridge?"

"No," Colonel Forsythe stated with a shake of his head. "Red Cloud's group is already overflowing the boundaries of the agency—besides, the Chief needs immediate medical attention, and his people need relief from the cold." His determined gaze settled on the hundreds of Indians who waited in the snow for their fate.

August tightened the blanket around her head when his searching eyes rested a moment upon her, then moved on.

"It looks like they've brought most of their lodges with them. We'll head south now, set up on the banks of Wounded Knee Creek, and wait for Colonel Bingham."

* * *

A bitter wind whipped through and around the quiet encampment. August stayed with Big Foot and his family inside a tent that was provided by Colonel Forsythe. Along with the rations handed out by the military, the generous colonel had even provided a small stove in deference to the chief's illness. The troops patrolled the perimeter of the camp, but the Sioux ignored their presence. The limping, tired group had finally found succor from the cold. Their taut bellies were full after many days, and the enormous fatigue of their winter flight was forgotten as peacefulness settled upon their shoulders, despite the presence of the army.

August's head swiveled in the direction of the canvas flap when Colonel Forsythe's voice asked for entry. A moment later, the commander ducked through the opening with three men following in his wake; one was a Sioux member of the reservation police. August quickly sheltered her face from his prying eyes with a tattered blanket and turned to face the stove. She peeked around the ragged edge of the cover, however, when the colonel hunkered down near Big Foot's bed.

"I hope you're more comfortable, Chief."

The old man simply nodded his head and Forsythe continued.

"In the morning, I'd like you to gather whoever you feel should attend a meeting to discuss your band's future."

Big Foot raised his head from the pillow. "We will go to Red Cloud."

"I don't know if that's possible," the colonel returned. "Red Cloud has taken in many of the mountain Indians, plus retained his own followers. His camp is already bulging." He inhaled deeply. "Chief, you are now my prisoner. It needs to be decided where all of you will be sent."

August's heart fell as she listened to his declaration.

"We will not leave our homeland." Big Foot stated weakly in defense of his people.

"Old man, you have no choice. I'll do everything I can, but the decision will be left up to the War Department."

"We will—"

Colonel Forsythe raised his hand. "We'll meet tomorrow to discuss this. I wanted to let you know in advance—"

"Sir?" A soldier poked his head through the flap. "Colonel Bingham has arrived and requests a meeting with you."

August's head snapped up, and fear curled in her belly.

The commander straightened after a quick pat on the Chief's arm. "You rest easy tonight. We'll get this all figured out in the morning and try to find a compromise." He stood and exited the lodge.

August scuttled across the ground to sit near Big Foot. She clasped his fevered hand in hers. "This is not good for the people. Bingham was the commander at Standing Rock the day Sitting Bull was killed. He brings only evil with him."

Big Foot's bleary gaze settled on the woman before him. "We cannot fight. There are not enough braves to protect the many woman and children. My strength is gone, August Moon, but I will plead to have us placed in our land. We will ask McCabe and Cole Wilkins to help us."

The mention of Cole's name brought instant tears to August's eyes. Would he ever find her again? Would she ever feel the warm Dakota sun on her face again? Too many events would have to transpire before the end result of deliverance and salvation. Beau and Cole were only two men against an entire white government. And, now Bingham had arrived. August shivered at the mere thought and tried to shake off the cold hand of death that gripped her shoulder.

* * *

Colonel Forsythe strode in the direction of the soldier's compound. His bushy eyebrows dipped in consternation at what seemed to be an inordinate amount of commotion ahead of him. The light cast by small fires lit sporadically around the camp illuminated Bingham, where he stood on a knoll dolling out orders to the troops around him.

Two Hotchkiss guns were being dispatched up the side of the ravine. Already, one ominous metal barrel pointed toward the many teepees that dotted the sloped landscape. He moved more decisively with each angry step he took.

"Colonel Bingham!"

Bingham turned, lifted an arrogant eyebrow, and stepped down from his vantage point.

"What are you doing with these guns?" Forsythe continued as his eyes searched the hillside.

Bingham peeled off his gloves one finger at a time and swept a hand high in the direction of the ravine. "I have to say I was rather disgruntled when I heard you had not disarmed the Sioux. I'm simply safeguarding our troops by setting up the Hotchkiss guns in the event of a conflagration. As soon as the artillery is in place, we'll search their tents and collect the hostiles' weapons."

Forsythe's eyes widened incredulously as he fought to control his flaring temper and ignored the angry tick in his cheek. "At the risk of raising even more fear among the Indians? Colonel, we've taken a headcount of all the Sioux. There are only one hundred and twenty braves, and most of them are in a weakened state. Somehow I doubt that the two hundred and thirty women are going to pose much threat either, especially when we have close to eight hundred soldiers in our ranks."

Bingham's mouth drew tight with anger, and his back stiffened before meeting Colonel Forsythe's withering glare. "May I remind you that this is my campaign? The entire Pine Ridge reservation and the surrounding lands are *my* domain."

Forsythe breathed deeply and tried another tact. "I understand that, Colonel Bingham. But it's dark already. Do you really think you will find all the weapons they might have in their possession? Let's keep the peace throughout the night and quietly confiscate their arms in an orderly fashion come morning."

Bingham's gray eyes narrowed. "Are you going soft on these savages?"

The other man held his frustration in check. "I've set up a Pow Wow for tomorrow. I don't think it's advisable to take the chance of antagonizing them for no reason. These people realize they have nowhere else to turn. They'll meet with us calmly to discover their fate."

Bingham squared his shoulders. "You are here in South Dakota simply because Washington ordered extra troops in deference to the settlers' complaints. I will not risk my men's lives, because you have decided the Indians might take offense." Bingham stalked away.

"Colonel Bingham!"

The irate man hesitated and turned back.

"Do I have your word that you will let these people rest for tonight?"

Bingham slapped leather gloves angrily against his woolen-clad thigh. "I did not realize we were making adolescent promises to each other."

"I'm simply assuring a quiet night for all. There will be enough heartache tomorrow for everyone concerned."

Bingham stared silently, his gaze ominous. "Fine. We'll disarm them with the morning's light. I will not hear one word, however, from those savages until that deed is accomplished. Good evening, Colonel." Without waiting for a response from Forsythe, he whirled to continue up the ravine on foot, barking orders the entire time.

His back stiff, Colonel Forsythe spun and headed in the direction of his tent.

* * *

Thick gray clouds amassed on the western horizon as morning dawned. The dark haze cast an ominous shadow across the windswept ravine.

August lay wrapped in a thin blanket and gave thanks that one of the chief's wives invited her to sleep within their tent. The warmth of Colonel Forsythe's stove was a blessing after the many frigid days and nights during the journey south.

She forced herself into a sitting position, ignoring the burning sensation that ran from her hip down to her bent knee. A bugle call sounded morning reveille somewhere from within the soldier's encampment. The blasts were enough to wake the others who slept close by. Shortly afterward, a large group of soldiers arrived at the chief's tent.

"Chief Big Foot! We're here at Colonel Forsythe's request and are to accompany you and your speakers to the center of the camp. May we enter?"

The Chief's daughter-in-law opened the flap and stood back as the soldiers entered. Corporal Jones led the way. August's level of comfort sank as the uniformed men strategically placed themselves around the circular interior, guns in hand. Her gaze found the two widows who had shared the tent. Fear shot from their dark eyes.

Big Foot heaved himself up to a sitting position. His wizened stare moved from one man to another. "It is not necessary to have your guns ready for battle. We will meet you at the required place without trouble."

Muffled, querulous voices, then an outraged scream rang out suddenly in the encampment. The chief's eyes instantly narrowed with distrust. "What is happening out there?"

Jones first nodded to his men, then responded to the chief's inquiry. "Our orders are to gather up any weapons you might have in your possession. The other tents are also being searched."

Immediately, the regiment soldiers turned to the closed buffalo-hide packs that lay about the interior of the tent and began dumping the contents onto the ground.

The seeking eyes of a beefy soldier with greasy hair shifted to a small pack that lay on the floor behind August. She leaned back, instinctively shielding it with her body.

The man took a step in her direction, while his companions continued their rummaging. "What do ya got in there, squaw?"

August glared at him in silent refusal.

He raised his rifle in an effort to intimidate her, and an evil sneer appeared on his face. "I know you savages can understand English. You can either move of your own accord or be pushed out of the way, but I'm checkin' that pack whether you like it or not."

August started to move out of the way, but before she accomplished the task, his foot came up and the heel of his boot pushed against her shoulder and roughly shoved her sideways. He stepped over her sprawled body with one foot and dragged the pack back across her legs. The odor of his feted breath in the close surroundings assailed her nostrils. "Next time, squaw, my boot will be in your face."

His gaze pierced her along with another sneer as he tossed the bag at a private, who gleefully watched the interaction between the two.

August sat up slowly and rubbed her bruised shoulder.

"Check it out, Wilson, and keep an eye on her—she looks like a wildcat."

Big Foot wobbled to his feet. "There is no reason to abuse the women of my camp. We have agreed to meet with Colonel Forsythe."

Jones snorted. "Then tell your bitches to get out of the way. We're searching everything—can't take the chance of one of your bucks pulling a gun." He turned to his men. "Find anything?"

The private dug through August's pack, released a loud whoop, then spilled the contents onto the floor inside the tent. He pulled a small silver knife from the jumbled mess. "Looks like she was hiding this."

August's body jumped a moment later when the barrel of another soldier's gun pressed tightly against the back of her head. Her heart hammered in her chest, and she suppressed the sob in her throat and the quaking of her limbs.

"This little squaw would've cut your throat, Wilson, given the chance." The pressure of the barrel increased.

August squeezed her lids shut and ignored the instant beads of sweat that formed between her breasts.

"Want me to put a bullet in her head?"

"Knock it off, Sully. Pick on someone your own size." Corporal Jones stepped over the spilled possessions and stopped at the entrance of the tent. "Let's go, men. There's nothing here except the pig stabber Wilson found." His triumphant gaze fell on the chief. "Get yourself ready, old man. The colonels are waiting for your presence."

The last of the soldiers left the tent, and August inhaled deeply to help stop the shaking of her hands.

Chapter Twenty-Eight

Cole and Michael followed the Indians' trampled path along the winding edge of a frozen riverbed. Hardened lumps of packed snow skidded outward from the pounding hooves as mile after mile was eaten up. The two men had traveled throughout the dark hours of night, allowing their mounts to rest for only short periods of time. Now, as the morning sun tipped the horizon through a mass of building clouds, they rounded a small bend with the turn of the river.

Both men hauled back on their reins simultaneously when a contingent of soldiers headed north came into view. The horses pranced to a skidding halt as Michael brought a hand to his forehead in salute.

The sergeant who rode at the front of the thirty some odd men brought his hand up smartly in deference to the doctor's military station. "Sir! I'm surprised to see you way out here."

Michael brought his arm down, then acknowledged his traveling companion with a nod of the head. "You know Mr. Wilkins, I presume."

Sergeant Anderson sent a wide grin in Cole's direction. "Good to see you again, Mr. Wilkins." An awkward silence fell over the group before the man cleared his throat and brought his eyes back to Michael's. "You're pretty far out from headquarters, sir. The Sioux are growing more restless as each day passes. Would you care to ride with us?"

Michael sat relaxed in the saddle and answered along with a quick shake of his head. "No, thank you—we need to be getting home. We're on our way back from visiting some of the settlers to the north. I think we got slightly off course with the snow."

Cole swiveled his head in surprise, but kept his mouth shut when he realized that Michael had decided not to reveal the true reason for their trip. The doctor rested his forearm on the saddle horn and calmly addressed the man before him.

"Has there been much Indian movement in the last few days? Mr. Wilkins and I are slightly surprised at the wide swath we've been following. We haven't seen any Sioux in our travels."

"You're lucky, sir. This path was made by Big Foot's group just yesterday."

Cole tensed in the saddle.

Michael affected a look of surprise. "Big Foot's group? What are they doing this far south? Where are they now?"

"Colonels Forsythe and Bingham have them holed up out at Wounded Knee Creek. The old Chief said he was taking his people to Pine Ridge to find protection with Red Cloud. Big Foot must've heard there was a warrant for his arrest and was runnin'. The Colonels don't believe for a minute that's where the group planned to go. They were traveling this path, which is too far west to make the story believable."

That's the reason they left. They were trying to reach Red Cloud without any confrontations. Cole exchanged a guarded glance with Michael before the sergeant spoke again.

"Sir, if there's nothing more, we need to be on our way. Just keep a look out on your way back."

Michael nodded, and he and Cole waited as the group rounded another corner in the trail. Instantly, their gazes met again.

"Bingham's there," Cole ground out. "How far south do you think the encampment is?"

"We can't be more than about two hours out. I know exactly where they are."

"Then let's get the hell out of here. August has to be with them. If Bingham sees her, who knows what the hell he'll do."

* * *

August stood wearily in the snow with the same child clasped in her arms. Once again, the toddler's mother huddled beneath a wool blanket and stared blankly in a grief-born stupor. The entire band had tramped through the snow behind the slow moving Big Foot and paused in the center of the camp. The appointed Pow Wow would be held shortly. August's worried gaze rested on the pile of various weapons that had been taken from the tents that morning. Old guns, knives, and even tent poles were piled in disarray.

A handful of soldiers moved among the tired and hungry Sioux, distributing hardtack for the morning meal. A uniformed man stopped before August and cast a leering glance from her head to her toe, then back to her face.

Her eyes filled with instant panic when she realized he was the same soldier who had held the gun to her head in Big Foot's tent. August dropped her chin and refused to meet his gaze, her stomach revolting against the smell of his fetid whiskey breath as it fanned her face.

"You're the smart-assed squaw from the Chief's tent, ain't ya?" Eliciting no response from the woman, he held up a piece of the hardtack, cracked it in half, then shoved the smaller piece under her nose. August turned her head away. The grisly man forced the broken chunk into her hand. "Here ya go, squaw," he whispered close. "Sorry, there ain't nothing for your little savage to eat. He looks pretty starved already, so why waste anything on him. Maybe by the end of the day, this earth will be minus one more of your little bastards."

His arrogant strut carried him away, and August gritted her teeth in an attempt to keep the anger from tumbling from her mouth. She forgot about his crudeness a second later though, when the boy's mother took the child from her arms and coaxed his lips open to receive her share of the hardtack. Once the child realized he had food in his mouth, he made quick work of the entire piece. August immediately offered her tiny portion also, then watched as the child devoured that morsel, too. A comforting hand touched her arm, and she glanced up to meet the mother's gentle gaze.

"Thank you," she said quietly, then shook her head sadly, adjusted the tiny child on her hip, and joined the other tribeswomen, who moved back from the line of older braves that now surrounded the chief. The meeting was about to begin.

August's attention was drawn to Colonel Bingham when he stepped with self-importance through the doorway of a large tent, followed by a tight-lipped Forsythe. The arrogant colonel swaggered to stand before the chief, secure in the knowledge that his men would rescue him if something went awry. August melted into the crowd of women.

Bingham clasped his hands behind his back and studied the throng of sunken faces that stared back with defiant eyes. Except for the sound of an occasional wintering bird chattering in the sparse trees, total silence reigned across the ravine. His steely gaze finally settled on the Indian leader.

"Chief Big Foot, do you have an interpreter selected?" The colonel pierced the old man with a hateful stare.

Big Foot took a shallow, wheezing breath from where he sat on blanket spread across the top of the snow, then proudly raised his chin. "That is not necessary. My people will understand you." The old man crossed his arms and glared back. "We would like our weapons returned."

Bingham snorted, and Forsythe dropped his head forward in frustration.

"I don't think that will be likely," Bingham replied. His gaze scanned the blanket-wrapped Sioux, and he became acutely aware of the fact that more than one of them might still have weapons hidden beneath the covers. "In fact, we will complete one final search to assure that all weapons have been confiscated. I will give your braves one more opportunity to come forward on their own before we begin."

A low rumble of protest raced through the crowd, and a sudden, eerie premonition washed over August. Her throat tightened, and suddenly she was unable to breathe normally. She waited with fear roiling in her stomach as Bingham lingered to see if any of the Sioux would volunteer hidden weapons.

The seconds ticked by, and an impatient nod of his head was all it took to make a large group of armed soldiers enter the crowd. They yanked blankets from the Indian's shoulders or clawed beneath flowing deerskin garments. Women loudly protested the prodding hands of the white men. August slapped out at a young soldier who tried to raise her shirt.

Colonel Forsythe marched forward with an angry gaze, took in the actions of the regiment, and spun to face Bingham. "I've had just about enough of this," he roared. "All you're managing to do is upset what could be a peaceful meeting. Call your men off!"

The words were barely out of his mouth when a triumphant shout echoed through the large gathering. A gloating soldier thrust a corroded gun high into the air—one that had been yanked from the arms of an aged brave.

A smug grin curved Bingham's mouth. "You should learn, Colonel Forsythe, that you can't ever trust these red-skinned savages." The smirk left his face a second later though, when another high-pitched scream rang out from the center of the group.

A young brave, who stood only a few feet from August, held a shiny rifle high in the air. She whirled in panic as more soldiers entered their midst and, consequently, her vision was suddenly clouded—the same sensation she experienced on the mountain years earlier settled over her. Her frenzied heartbeat weakened her knees, and she resisted the urge to faint.

"No," she whispered to the man. "Put the weapon down...there will be blood—"

The metallic click of a gun hammer snapped behind her, and August whirled. An army recruit stood with legs spread and his pistol trained on the brave.

"Please..." she pleaded. She reached out a hand in supplication to the man, but, before she could take another step, a second soldier knocked her to the ground from behind. She rolled onto her side as the brave released a piercing war cry, then sprung to her knees and stared in horror as the irate Sioux challenged the white men around him.

"This is my weapon!" he shouted, shaking the rifle in the air. "I paid for this gun with the white man's money and will not release it."

Give up the gun! August mouthed silently.

She blinked once before the brave was grabbed from behind. The rifle was knocked from his upraised hands, and he was hurled from the arms of one soldier to another.

August flinched when a shot rang out—and chaos reigned. Another shot was heard, and another. The imprisoned Indian slumped in the soldiers' arms, and then pitched to the ground with blood pouring from his mouth.

August screamed, then scrambled on her hands and knees across the snow and into the throng of shrieking woman. Children screeched their terror when their mothers shoved them to the ground and dropped on top of them.

A shocked sob burst from August's throat as the Sioux braves leapt to snatch up the confiscated weapons, but their efforts were in vain. August's mouth gaped open in horror when the soldiers picked them off one by one. They fell to the ground in a bloody heap, one on top of the other as the sound of repeated gunfire thundered across the ravine.

Stunned senses spurred her to crawl frantically across the ground, her disbelieving brain assailed by the total confusion. She cringed, then screamed out a sob when rifle slugs spewed up the earth around her. Still, she kept moving. August froze in terror only seconds later when she came upon a young

Sioux mother, who wept loudly and pulled at her stringy hair with blood-soaked fingers. The woman's young daughter lay sprawled on the frozen ground before her, with sightless eyes staring skyward.

August swallowed the bile in her throat. Her vision of years ago was coming true...All around her, her people lay in grotesque positions, moaning in agony as their lifeblood seeped into the earth. The end had come.

"I do not want to die! Cole!" she sobbed into the pandemonium around her. Where could she run to? A bullet hit the ground mere inches from her hand, and August catapulted to the left. She landed on her back, then froze when an ear-splitting whistle originated on the ridge that surrounded the ravine. The whirring noise strengthened then, and an earth-shattering explosion thrust her people into the air along with mangled chunks of dirt. Bloody limbs splattered the ground, turning the muddy snow to varying shades of red. The rapid volleys of the Hotchkiss guns raked through the lodges and into the scattering Sioux, cutting down everything in their path.

* * *

At Michael's urging, Cole finally halted the frantic pace and let his mount slow to a restoring walk. They were only a half-mile from where the soldiers held one of the last bands of Sioux.

August never left his thoughts as they rode south. He prayed, negotiating deals with not only his God, but hers as well. He silently vowed to forcefully put her on a horse and travel east to Minnesota as fast as the wintry weather would allow—if only he were allowed to find her alive.

"How goddamn far is it, Michael?" His frustration laced the short, clipped words.

"Two more bends and we're there. I can't—" The doctor reined his horse in abruptly beside Cole's mount. "What the hell was that?"

"A gunshot. It came from the south..." Cole's words trailed off as his frightened gaze searched the far stretch before him. His features paled as the hair rose on his neck. The men exchanged worried glances, then swallowed lumps of fear when, only seconds later, more shots echoed in the distance. A ghostly silence followed—until a loud blast reverberated across the hills.

"Jesus Christ," Michael gasped out. "That's one of the Hotchkiss guns—"

Cole did not respond, but just pulled a knife from the sheath at his side, deftly slit the lead rope to the pack mules, and spurred his horse into a dead run.

* * *

Insanity reigned. August fought her way through the thick smoke, the destruction left by the big guns, and the clinging hands of those who lay on the ground with only moments to live. She ran for her life, joining others who sprinted across the bottom of the ravine.

Her headlong, frenzied flight was interrupted when she stumbled over an inert object that lay in her path. Her quaking body pitched into the snow; an unseen, seeking hand reached through the thick smoke and seized her foot. Pushing herself up onto her elbows, she kicked out in panic, then glanced back through wide eyes and into the pleading gaze of a young Sioux brave who was covered in blood.

"Help me...I cannot move..."

Her frightened gaze traveled from his clutching fingers to the bloody stumps that had formerly been his legs. The absolute horror of the moment sent a mind-numbing shudder through her body and, before she could respond, a deep gurgle rumbled in the man's chest. His body arched slightly before his chest dropped to the cold ground.

The menacing report of the Hotchkiss gun jolted her from her stupor. August flattened her body against the ground, covered her head with her arms, and waited for the deadly shrapnel to rip her back open and end her torture. Instead, terrified screams to her left caused her to jerk her head upright again. Three women, with children in their arms, raced in her direction. Fear contorted their faces just before they were mowed down by the crossfire.

August stifled yet another choked sob and scrambled up from the cold, blood-soaked earth. She sprinted for the line of trees at the top of the knoll as her vision of long ago arrived to wipe away not only her existence, but also that of the entire Sioux nation. Her great people would never walk the face of the earth again.

* * *

The smell of acrid gunpowder and sulfur burned August's nostrils, but still she staggered on. She chanted to herself as the screams of her people faded into nothingness behind her. She clung to a new vision now—one of a shared life with the man she loved; the man who fate had sent her way. She understood it now with a clarity she had never seen before. August stumbled, pitched to the frozen earth, then clawed her way across the snow, determination and absolute fear urging her on.

Cole...I will not die...

The thick smoke cleared and August bounded to her feet, continuing her race across the ravine. She ignored those who already lay dead in the field and those who dropped one by one before her. The huge guns on the hillside sent bullet after bullet whizzing past her head, and still she staggered on. She had to stay upright; she had to keep moving away from the carnage.

She was nearly to the base of the slope that led to the blessed tree cover, but whirled in fear when thundering hooves reverberated behind her. An overwhelming sense of foreboding quickly turned to a moment of sheer joy when she saw the dark horse, its eyes wide with fear, that galloped toward her.

"Spirit!" She raised her arms and flung herself into the path of the terrified animal, then lunged for the rope that trailed from the animal's neck. She swung herself up and across the wide back and dug her heels into its heaving sides. The wide-eyed animal shot forward.

* * *

Cole raced toward the gunfire and the thick haze of dark smoke that hugged the treetops at the edge of the ravine. He bent low over the straining horse, pushed the animal to its limit, and heard the pounding hooves of Michael's horse behind him.

August...August... Her name was a constant chant in his frightened mind.

He reached the northern end of the valley and was catapulted into a nightmare as the horse skidded to a stop. The insidious smell of death hung heavy in the air. His horrified gaze widened in disbelief at the sight of the ongoing massacre. Sioux families ran for their lives, and Cole's mount danced beneath him, straining against the bit as another volley was released from the Hotchkiss gun only yards from where he had crested the gulch. A shocked gasp left his lips when the cannonballs ripped through a group of Sioux who clawed their way up the opposite incline. An instant later, their dead bodies littered the hillside.

"Stop! Stop the goddamn firing!" Cole swung his leg over the back of the horse, jumped to the muddied ground, and raced across the short distance to the small group of soldiers who surrounded the cannon. He seized the gunner and flung him to the ground. The astonished man looked up and, before the enraged Cole could dive on top of him, another soldier balled his fist and knocked him to the ground. Three uniformed men stood above him with murderous glares a moment later. Cole spit blood from his mouth and eyed the men who towered over him.

"What the hell's the matter with you! Those redskins are getting away!" one of the soldiers bellered.

Cole bounded to his feet and tore in the direction of the gunner, who had also regained his footing and quickly readied the killing machine for another round. Michael appeared from nowhere and blocked his crazed friend's frenzied flight. Cole struggled against the strong arms that kept him from jumping the soldier once more.

"It's too late, Cole! Goddammit, listen to me! There's nothing you can do!" Michael shouted over the continued blasts from the big guns that sat on the opposite hill.

"They're killing them for no reason! She could be among those still alive down there!" Cole shook off the doctor's strong grip, raced to his horse, grabbed the saddle horn, and swung himself onto the animal's back. "I've got to find her!"

Michael was a step behind and up on his own horse just as quickly. "We'll work our way around the ravine. If we go down the middle, we'll get caught in the crossfire."

The two men spurred their mounts across the upper bluff, their anxious eyes taking in the slaughter that escalated below. Cole's gaze followed yet another volley as it sailed across the wide span, then he dragged back on the reins again when he spied a familiar black horse racing through the blood and smoke.

"Spirit..." he breathed. "Jesus Christ, Michael, it's my horse!" Another volley landed close to the animal, and suddenly time stood still as he waited for the mare to clear the smoky destruction. The men held their breath. They waited, each second seeming like an hour and, still, she did not appear.

The haze finally cleared, allowing the carnage to be seen once more. Cole stiffened in the saddle again, and dread burned in his chest as his gaze followed a familiar shape. It ran into the path of the racing animal with arms flung wide, then smoke clouded his vision once more.

"Cole! Did you see that?" Michael kneed his mount closer and kept his eyes glued on the scene below.

They watched, without words or breath, until Spirit suddenly broke through the cloud of dust and smoke again. This time, someone clung to her back.

"August! Jesus Christ, it's August, Michael—she's alive!"

Cole could only watch in horrified dread as the animal weaved its way across the frozen ground in search of the far side of the valley, where the land rose away from the killing. Spirit leaped across fallen bodies, raced through the fog of gunfire and, somehow, August managed to keep her seat atop the careening animal.

"Hold on...you're almost there," Cole whispered into the bedlam, willing his silent plea to reach her. In his terrified mind, he felt each stride of the horse as if it were beneath him. He rode with August, his fingers clasping the leather reins tightly each time it seemed she would be thrown from Spirit's back. Somehow, she and the horse managed to dodge the continued cannon shots and gunfire. Spirit's muscles bunched as the terrified animal fought to climb the far hill, with August urging her on.

"She's going to make it!" Michael hollered. "Go, August—run!"

"What the hell—?" Cole's heart sank into his stomach when two soldiers jumped from behind a large rock in the distance. Spirit ran past them just as one of the men raised a Winchester to his shoulder.

"Oh, God..." Cole breathed. His brow furrowed in pain and foreboding.

Despite the deafening gunfire all around him, the single report ripped through Cole's consciousness. August slumped forward, grasping frantically to Spirit's mane as the bullet tore into her soft flesh.

Cole's heels came down hard and the horse sprang forward and down the side of the hill.

"Cole! It's suicide! Cole—stop!" Michael screamed the words to his friend's retreating back, but to no avail.

Cole plunged on—downward through the scattered rocks; the fallen, misshapen bodies of the Sioux men, women, and children; and out across the bottom of the frozen riverbed. He squinted against the smoke and kept his eyes on August's slumped form; a form that somehow managed to cling to Spirit. Bullets whizzed by his head; they creased the ground before him, but still he kept going. Fear for his own life did not come into play—his only thought was to get to the woman he loved.

He reached the bottom of the incline where Spirit began her climb what seemed a lifetime ago. August and the horse were lost from his sight though, in the thickening smoke that billowed across the hillside. Cole's eyes burned from the stench of the small fires that dotted the path before him. His frustration whipped the horse into a frenetic pace. The animal stumbled, regained its footing, and continued upward, weaving a crooked course around the flames.

Another black cloud of smoke rolled across the hillside. Cole broke through the blur and an all-encompassing dread settled on his shoulders at the sight of the uniformed man who stood on the trail before him. The officer brought a rifle to his caped shoulder.

Even in the smoky haze, Cole recognized Colonel Bingham's pompous stance. His terrified gaze flew to the top of the hill. August still clung to Spirit's back as the horse neared the crest. His eyes darted back to the Pine Ridge commander. "Stop! Don't shoot!"

Bingham pivoted toward the shouted voice from behind. Surprise flashed in his eyes when he recognized the man who sat atop a large, lathered roan.

"What the hell?" Raging determination and the hint of a smile shot from the colonel's gaze when he turned, re-shouldered the weapon, and set the sights on the middle of August's back. "I hope you're watching, Wilkins," he muttered as he clicked back the hammer.

Cole's hand was as steady as a rock as he drew his sidearm and fired point blank at Bingham's back. The colonel gasped, surprise turned to pain, and sank motionless to the muddied snow.

Cole spurred his horse past Bingham's inert body. One cold glance showed lifeless eyes that stared into a smoky Dakota sky. His gaze returned to the hilltop then. August was gone.

Chapter Twenty-Nine

The memory of her vision from long ago burned a searing brand into August's back. The pain intensified with each loping stride of the horse beneath her. She clung to the flowing mane, weakly pressed her knees into Spirit's heaving sides, and urged the animal to press ever onward.

The icy wind bit at her exposed skin but, surprisingly, she no longer felt the cold—only the heartbreaking awareness of the death of her proud people. The years of running the plains freely, of greeting the day with laughter, of living the life of their ancestors, were gone. The dream was dead.

Spirit stumbled and came to a staggering halt. The animal trembled beneath her light, clawing load, and lowered her head to the frozen ground. White foam bubbled from her mouth and dripped into the snow. Sticky blood-covered flanks heaved with exhaustion.

August, weakened from the loss of blood, lay with her muddied cheek pressed against the course hair on Spirit's neck. Try as she might, she could not find the strength to urge the animal forward, nor could she force her eyes open. She simply remained frozen in time in the dreary light of morning, injured and bleeding. Warm tears burned beneath her lids at the sound of the muffled reports. The Hotchkiss gun continued its killing spree, sending the last of a glorious Indian nation to the hereafter and beyond.

Spirit shuddered beneath her, and August tightened her grip on the shaggy main with an agonized gasp. Her brow creased in pain from the gaping wound in her side, and she struggled to open her eyes. A puzzled gaze stared down at the continual drops of red that splattered to the ground around Spirit's hooves.

My blood...my life flows slowly back to my mother...Soon, I will be gone from this earth...I have no regrets, but one. Cole...

A raven's warning screech reverberated across the small clearing to those who would listen. Spirit jerked her head upright, shuddered again, then dropped her muzzle to the earth once more.

"They are coming for me..." August mumbled incoherently to the weary animal. Her injury though, would not allow more than a clenching of her fingers as they weaved themselves tighter into Spirit's mane. "We will die together, my friend..."

"August!"

She lay motionless and blinked back warm tears. A sad, weak smile touched her lips. "It is good to hear his voice...even though I imagine it..."

Unexpectedly, strong but gentle hands lifted her from Spirit's back and clutched her against a broad, familiar chest. She breathed in his scent and was content that she would die knowing his arms wrapped her in their warmth. It was a wonderful dream.

"August. Honey, I'm here—" The voice wavered somewhere above her in the darkness.

A warm, loving hand touched her face, but still August refused to open her eyes, knowing that if she looked into the real world one last time, the wonderful dream would disappear. "I love you, Cole... The soldiers have won— they have taken my dream..."

Cole listened to the mumbled words with growing fear in his heart. He had entered the clearing to find her draped across Spirit's back, her warm blood soaking the snow below her. He thought she was gone from him forever.

"August? Please open your eyes!" he hissed out in a shaking whisper, then kissed her cold brow. "It's your dream. We won't let them take it. You're going to be fine. I'll help you fight for the rest of your life."

Her lids fluttered open, and confused eyes met his frightened gaze. "It is too late..."

"No, it's not. We have each other." He continued to stroke her cheek with a roughened palm, then gently pushed away the strands of windblown hair lying against her smooth skin. "We're going home to Minnesota—you and me. We'll have a wonderful life at the ranch—I promise you. We'll have lots of babies, and I'll keep you safe, but you have to stay strong."

"I cannot...They shot me, Cole. My vision—it foretold my future so many years ago. I will die like the rest of them..." August gagged on the blood in her throat as her mind swam its way back to the massacre and death she had cheated for a short time. "I am sorry I did not love you more..."

He clasped her to him once more and battled terror-born tears when she shuddered in his arms. "You've always loved me enough. You'll have many years to prove it—you'll have many days of me loving you in the warm sunshine. You just have to stay with me, honey. We'll get you to Michael and he'll fix you up." As he spoke the many promises to her, Cole shrugged his free arm from the warm coat, then slid the jacket from his opposite shoulder and wrapped it around her quaking body. "I'm going to lay you down for only a moment."

"Do not leave me...for then surely I will be dead."

"I'm not going away. I need to get you a blanket."

The cold that emanated from the earth encased her body when the warmth of his arms disappeared. Frozen snow crunched beneath boots as they tramped away. Now, she would meet death face to face. August shivered uncontrollably. Tears flowed from beneath her lids.

Cole hurried to Spirit, grabbed the trailing rope from the tired horse's neck, quickly led her to his mount and secured the rein to his stirrup. He ripped off the bedroll attached to his saddle, yanked a woolen shirt and another jacket from his pack, and raced back to a trembling August.

His gentle fingers lifted the buckskin shirt up from her waist. The air rushed from his lungs at the sight of the ragged, bloody skin. It was when he carefully peeled the shredded material from the edge of her wound, however, that August's eyes flew open in pain and a scream that curdled his blood left her lips.

"I'm sorry, August," he gasped. His stomach churned at having to hurt her. "But I have to stop the bleeding." Deft hands flipped a knife from its sheath and cut a strip away from the blanket, then he quickly wadded the shirt in his shaking hands and placed it gently over the wound. Cole secured the homemade bandage with the ribbon of woolen material, then flinched when August's body arched in reaction to the pain that roared through her body.

"Goddammit, Michael! Where in hell are you when I need you!" he ground out through a clenched jaw while tying another knot.

His impassioned plea reached August's consciousness, and she struggled to open her eyes. "Cole?"

"I'm here, August. I love you. Stay with me, honey—I can't lose you now."

She felt more than saw the woolen blanket he hurriedly wrapped her in.

"Are you real? Am I dreaming? Cole, I hurt..." Her confused gaze focused on him.

"I know, honey." He shrugged his arms into the extra coat and lifted August's limp body into his arms. He fought the urge to lay her back in the snow then, when the pain brought on by moving her was evidenced by a low moan.

"Cole...please...I hurt. Leave me. It is done..."

"The hell it is," he returned with another light kiss to her cold brow. A determined Cole stomped through the snow with a worried glance at the treeline. "We gotta get the hell out of here, August. They'll be coming soon to find both of us." *Son of a bitch—I shot a Colonel in the United States Cavalry in front of witnesses!* "You just gotta hang on. I won't let them take you, but it's gonna be a long ride to Pine Ridge and we have to move quick."

By the time Cole settled her on his lap high atop his horse and kneed the animal into a run, August's body had wilted into unconsciousness.

* * *

Cole spurred the horses on, using instinct alone to guide him around the edge of the ravine. Thankfully, August had lapsed into a coma and did not feel the galloping ride. In order to reach Michael and Anna's home, he would have to skirt Wounded Knee, stay hidden, and keep as far from the killing as possible.

Cole's stomach rolled each time he forced the horses around the dead bodies of Sioux women and children lying on the trail. The animals crashed through the dense underbrush, their eyes wide and nostrils flaring from the scent of the bloodshed around them. Cole urged his mount on, knowing without a doubt that, if they were discovered, it would be the end for both he and August. She lay limp against his chest, and he prayed for her life.

The trail split in the distance. Cole hauled back on the reins, and his indecisive gaze darted from one path to the other. A quick choice to take the southerly, more trampled route was made. Going in the other direction would take precious time—time he did not feel August could afford. He urged the horses on again, then froze when a voice called out from the stillness around him.

"Cole!"

He jumped, tightened his hold on August, and reached for his gun. Cole spun the horse around—and breathed a sigh of relief. Michael barreled toward them, icy water spraying in all directions as his horse galloped across a small stream.

The doctor reined to a skidding halt beside his friend, and his features paled when he spied August. "Is she—"

"She's hurt bad, Mike. We have to get back to your place."

Michael was already digging into his saddlebag for medical supplies.

"As much as I want you to look at her injury, we gotta keep moving before the army finds us."

The doctor brushed aside the other man's concern with a simple wave of the hand. "They got their killing done, Cole. They won't bother with her if someone comes across us."

"No—but they'll sure as hell bother with me."

Michael glanced up, his hands suddenly still with his confusion. Cole's eyes were dark with worry. "Why would they want you?"

Cole's unflinching gaze met the doctor's. "I shot and killed Bingham."

Michael's jaw dropped in shock, but before he could respond, Cole rushed on.

"The son of a bitch had a bead on her when I got to the hill. He appeared from nowhere. It was him or August, and I chose August."

Michael swiped a trembling hand across his face before he met Cole's gaze again. "Jesus Christ." He quickly re-buckled his saddlebag strap. "Let's get the hell out of here or we'll both be shot for treason. Come on—I know a trail through this area that'll keep us hidden."

Michael led the way, and the small group melted into the trees a moment later.

* * *

Michael jumped from his horse before it even came to a stop, raced across the snow-covered path to the porch, and burst through the front doorway of his home. A startled Anna turned in his direction from where she stood before the fireplace.

"Michael!" She rushed to his waiting arms. "Where have you been? I thought you'd be home days ago."

The doctor closed his eyes above his wife's head, organized his thoughts, then leaned back to look into Anna's blue eyes. "Honey, listen now. Bingham's contingent massacred Big Foot's entire band out at Wounded Knee Creek."

His wife instantly shuddered in his arms and clasped a trembling hand across her mouth as her face turned a deathly shade of white. "Oh, my God." Her tear-filled eyes widened along with a shake of her head. "What were they doing that far south?"

Michael dropped his arms from her slender waist, grabbed a large canvas bag, and began to pile medical supplies into its depths. "I don't know the whole story, but—" he stopped his hurried packing and turned to face Anna "—August was with them."

His wife continued to stare across the room, steeling herself against the awful news. "Is...she...?"

"She's barely alive. Cole's hiding out with her a couple of miles from here. Anna, she's in serious shape—she was shot. We don't have any time to waste. We've got to get back to them."

"What do you mean 'hiding out'?" Anna swung open a door to a curio cabinet and snatched at supplies to add to her husband's medical pack. "What are you thinking? Why didn't you bring her back here? Michael, what's going on?"

Her husband straightened to his full height, then rubbed a weary hand through his hair. "Jesus Christ, Anna. It was horrible out there. When Cole and I got to Standing Rock, the Sioux were gone. We followed their trail south to Wounded Knee. By the time we got to the top of the riverbed, you could hardly see anything—Bingham had the Hotchkiss guns. The army mowed down everything in their path." He closed his eyes momentarily to help block out the awful images of death, then glanced at his wife again. Her face was white as a ghost.

Anna sank onto the surface of a wooden chair. "August—?"

"Somehow, she ended up on Spirit, outran the cannonballs, and got to the opposite side of the ravine. She was almost to the top of the bank and...was shot in the back."

Anna gasped. She bounded from the chair to again aid Michael in filling the pack. She kept her gaze down and drew a deep breath. "You're not telling me something. I can hear it in your voice—you haven't explained why Cole and August are hiding out."

Michael reached out to rest a hand on Anna's forearm. Instantly, she slammed her eyelids shut and waited apprehensively for the rest of the story. "When Cole saw her get hit by the bullet, he took off across the ravine. He was almost to August when Bingham appeared out of nowhere. She was trying to make it up the embankment, and he pointed his rifle at her."

Anna shook her head slowly and whispered into the room, "Please don't say it..."

"Cole shot and killed him without hesitation. There were witnesses."

Anna burst into tears. "They'll find them—both will hang!" She covered her face with her hands.

"No, they won't." Michael grasped his wife's shoulders and forced her to look him directly in the eye. "I'll be goddamned if we'll let that happen. You finish here with the supplies. I'm gonna hook up the buckboard. Anyone who sees us leave will think we're going out to Wounded Knee to help the injured. Once we get to Cole and August, I'll do what I can for her, then we're going to hide them under canvas covers in the back of the wagon and bring them back to the house—by that time it'll be close to dark."

Anna jerked her head up in disbelief. "I'll do anything for them, but our house is the first place they'll look for Cole. Hiding them here will be their death sentence!"

"Not if I tell those in command that Cole was killed in the crossfire— they won't even bother to check and see if August is alive. To them, she's just another dispensable Sioux. I'll head back to Wounded Knee as soon as we stabilize her. I know Beau will show up out there when he hears about this tragedy. He and I can pull it off."

Anna reached up to rest her palm against his whiskered cheek. "What you're talking about is treason, Michael. I'm behind you, but are you sure?"

He nodded, then bent to touch her lips lightly with his own. "I would expect no less from them if you and I were in trouble and, after what I witnessed today, I won't let the U.S. army take one more life if I can help it."

* * *

Anna wanted to slap the reins across the mules' backs, but simply swallowed her anxiety and tightened her grip on the leather straps. To race across the landscape and into Pine Ridge headquarters would only alert the soldiers. A cold foreboding wind and the darkness of a coming winter storm surrounded the buckboard as they traveled closer to the agency.

Cole sat in the back, shielding his body and August's with a canvas tarp. He would duck beneath the heavy covering when the agency buildings came into view.

The wagon bounced through a deep rut, and Anna glanced over her shoulder to see how August fared the jarring ride. Her anxious glance calmed when Cole sent a cautious smile in her direction, then cradled the unconscious woman even deeper into his arms.

Despite the grim situation, a grin tugged at her lips. "How can you smile, Cole?"

"Would it be unmanly for me to say that, if I didn't, I might start bawling like a baby?"

"Don't start—I'll be crying along with you. How's she doing?"

"She's not shivering anymore. I think she's finally starting to warm up." He adjusted the woolen blankets around August's shoulders, tightened his protective grip even more, and glanced up again. "I'll never be able to thank you and Michael for everything you're doing. Michael is risking a lot with his commission."

Anna shrugged off his gratitude. "We risk nothing as long as you're not discovered. It's going to be a long winter, cooped up in the house, but August won't be ready to travel for quite awhile."

"If she makes it..." Cole's stomach flipped with the mere thought, and queasiness set in when he thought back to Michael's impromptu surgery in the middle of the woods. Not knowing when he would return from Wounded Knee, he removed the slug imbedded in August's back and cauterized the wound to stop the bleeding, then left with the confidence that she had half a chance to cheat death again.

"She will, Cole. While she recuperates, we'll figure out a way to get the two of you back to Minnesota without being detected."

"I'll tell you what, Anna. Once we're back at the ranch, I'm never letting her out of my sight again. Although, neither of has much of a choice now, do we?" Michael explained his plan to Cole as he operated on August. As of tonight, he would be listed as an official casualty of the Battle of Wounded

Knee. It was the only thing to be done in order to assure that he would not hang from the neck at a military trial.

Anna's lips tightened in a hard line, and her gaze turned to stone. "I'm glad you killed him, Cole. That man deserved to die for his horrible actions over the last few years. He did his best to take and take from the Sioux—the more he could demean them, the more pompous he became—all in the name of taming the western frontier."

Cole leaned his head against the wooden side of the buckboard and let his lids flutter shut. He had killed two men in his lifetime and, try as he might, he could find no remorse regarding either of their deaths. Both possessed evil and heartless souls that were void of any conscience, and both had tried to take from him personally. He was done though—he was through with the killing. What he had experienced over the last four months and, especially the horrible events of the day, would scar his mind forever.

He shifted where he sat, opened his eyes, and stared into the silent features of the woman in his arms. *August.* His embrace tightened protectively. *You're going to make it. I'm going to take you home and we'll stay together forever...*

The ranch was a perfect place for them to hide out. Once they were away from South Dakota, the years would pass and the government officials at the reservation would forget his offense. *But, I'll never forget theirs...* He would never forget the sights, the sounds, the smells of the slaughter at Wounded Knee, but he would make it up to August over the course of their lives. He kissed her temple and listened to the simple cadence of her breathing.

"Cole! Get under the canvas—there's a contingent of soldiers coming up the trail! They must have spotted us coming in."

Without a word, Cole slipped beneath the cover, careful not to jostle August, and pulled the bulky material over them. He prayed that she would remain unconscious. If she moaned aloud, they would be lost.

The regiment approached the wagon, which had stopped now along the trail. Anna grasped the leather reins in her gloved hands and slowed her breathing. A light smile touched her lips in greeting as she met the eyes of the lieutenant.

"Ma'am," he tipped his head. "I'm glad to see you coming in. It feels like we're going to have quite a storm."

She dipped her chin in acknowledgement of his statement. "Yes, I think you may be right. I was going to go out to Wounded Knee with my husband, but we met another regiment who advised us that all these medical supplies would not be needed. When the weather became worse, Dr. Gatewood insisted I head for home before the storm hits."

"That was good thinking on his part. There's not much left out there. We were able to subdue the Sioux and rid ourselves of most of the hostiles."

Anna's stomach churned. *You weren't even there, yet you speak like it was your victory.* "I heard we didn't lose too many of our soldiers." The words tasted like sawdust in her mouth, but she needed to know if there would be a manhunt for Cole. If she could keep the man talking, it was sure to come out.

"Only thirty-three injured. The military did experience a great loss, though." Anna raised an expectant brow with his statement. "Colonel Bingham was killed."

She affected a look of sadness, however hard it was to accomplish. "Oh, my! I hadn't heard that. How awful."

"Missus Gatewood, please be aware that it is suspected your houseguest was the man who pulled the trigger."

Anna's heart thudded. "My houseguest? You mean Cole Wilkins?"

The lieutenant nodded.

"I find that hard to believe. He left for Minnesota nearly two weeks ago."

"It's true, ma'am. In fact, I find it hard to believe Dr. Gatewood didn't inform you of Wilkins attempt to stop the gunners at Wounded Knee. Your husband intervened so the shooting could continue."

"Well, that silly man," Anna laughed lightly and shook her head. "You know, I suppose if what you're telling me *is* true, that my husband was probably afraid of upsetting me—especially after the actions of today. To think we had a cold-blooded killer staying with us. Too bad Michael wasn't able to stop him." Anna gasped and her eyes widened. "Do you know where he is now?"

The lieutenant squared his shoulders. "Never fear, ma'am, if he's out there, the Cavalry is sure to find him. Hopefully, he will be among the dead when a full count is taken. If not, he will be found and stand trial. Beyond a doubt, he'll be hanged for his crime."

"Thank you, sir, for your comforting words. I really must be on my way now, before the weather worsens. It's nearly dark and I look forward to the comfort of my warm home." She smiled. "I will be sure to lock my doors tonight."

The frontline of the regiment tipped their hats when Anna clucked loudly, flicked the reins across the backs of the mules, and sent the wagon on down the trail.

The lieutenant's gaze took in the mound of supplies covered by a tarp in the back of the wagon and, with a yell to his men, kicked his horse into a trot and led the group down the trail.

Chapter Thirty

Anna assured that the kitchen curtains were drawn tightly against the fury of yet another Dakota blizzard. She would not take the chance—even with the storm that raged outside—that someone would see into her home.

Michael entered the house through the back door, shrugged off his heavy coat, and joined the chilled Beau who sat at the kitchen table. "Your horse is settled in for the night. I threw an extra blanket on him. He should be fine by morning."

Beau looked up. "Thanks, Mike. I don't think I could've taken one more minute in the cold." His fingers wrapped around a ceramic mug to heat the stiffness from his frozen hands. He had traveled through the mounting storm and finally arrived from Wounded Knee. Michael had urged him to travel back to Pine Ridge the evening before, but Beau, despite his weakened state, insisted on staying to sift through the bodies and record the many deaths. The massacre had left an enormously bitter taste in his mouth.

The door leading to the spare room off the kitchen opened with a creak, and Cole stepped into the brightly lit room. His bloodshot gaze settled on the small group assembled around the table. With a heavy sigh, he joined them, pulled out a chair, and sank tiredly onto the hard surface. Anna immediately handed him a mug of hot coffee and patted his shoulder.

He glanced up with a wan smile. "Thanks. I think this is the only thing keeping me awake."

"Nothing yet?"

A weary shake of his head preceded his answer. "No, but I'm not so scared anymore. She's resting a lot easier."

Anna lifted a plate of warm food from a shelf above the stove. She placed the full platter on the table before Cole and handed him a fork. "Eat. I'll go sit with August and give you a break."

"I'm not that hungry."

"Don't give me that, Cole. You've hardly had a thing to eat since yesterday. She's going to be okay. Michael gave you his promise." She waited until Cole lifted the fork and picked at the fried chicken on the plate. Satisfied, Anna left the kitchen on silent feet.

A quiet, introspective chuckle left Beau's throat. Cole glanced up, his hand stopped in mid air, and he arched an eyebrow in his friend's direction. "Welcome back. I heard you come in. You look like hell."

"Have you looked in the mirror?" Beau reached up to give Cole's shoulder a reassuring pat. "Michael told me the good news. I'm glad August will pull through this."

Cole dropped the fork next to his plate, rubbed his face with both hands, and sighed deeply. Resting an elbow on the edge of the table, he looked quietly at his friend. "Beau—"

The other man held up a warmed palm. "Don't say it. There's no need."

"The hell there isn't. If it wasn't for you and Michael, I'd probably be dangling from the end of some military rope. I'll never be able to thank you enough."

Michael listened to the exchange, and his thoughts turned to his earlier conversation with Cole. He arrived home that morning with bloodstained clothes and a haunted look in his eyes and explained to Cole what he and Beau had done to insure that the army thought he was dead. *It's a damn good thing I had the foresight to grab civilian clothes when I collected Anna and my medical supplies...*

As ghastly as the deed was, he and Beau found the body of a Sioux man with his face blown away after one of the many explosions. They chanced the opportunity to drag the dead man from the trail and into the pines where they quickly stripped him, then forced the non-military clothes onto his frozen limbs.

Both men identified the body as Cole Wilkins for the army death records, then quickly pushed the corpse into the mass grave of frozen Sioux bodies before anyone looked closer. Michael neglected to tell Cole how, only moments later, he turned to see Beau on his knees, retching into the snow.

Michael stood and stretched his arms over his head to help rid himself of the tiredness that would not disappear. "I'm going to join Anna. Take all the time you need, Cole." He, too, disappeared from the kitchen.

An old grandfather clocked ticked steadily in the adjoining living room. Cole cleared his throat in the quiet and brought his gaze to Beau, who now stared at his hands, deep in thought.

"It—" he cleared his throat once more "—it must have been horrible out there. I don't know what to say."

Beau shrugged to cover his true emotional state, then leaned back in the chair. His blue eyes, dark with frustration and pain, darted about the room before meeting the tired eyes of his friend. "I never thought it would end the way it did. I expected...skirmishes over the years, but not a full-blown massacre such as the one I walked through yesterday. Those bastards in Washington finally got their way. The Sioux are in their back pocket at last; the events of the past two days will be touted as a huge battle won by the whites." He picked up his coffee cup with a trembling hand, took a sip, set the cup down, and shook his head.

"Most of them are gone...all it took was thirty goddamn minutes and they were dead—except for a few lucky men, August, and four babies." Beau lifted a watery blue gaze. "Four babies, Cole, who somehow managed to survive the bullets and the freezing overnight temperatures." Unabashed tears trickled down Beau's whiskered cheeks, and his jaw clenched momentarily to control the grief that welled in his veins. "The army dug a huge hole to throw all the corpses in. One by one, their bodies were tossed into the grave as if their lives never had meaning. Michael and I dragged the body of the man we told the army was you and dumped him over the edge. We had no choice." His words were as much an apology to himself as they were to the Sioux people. "We both knew we had to get rid of the evidence before someone discovered our deceit. When we got to the edge of the grave, someone hollered. They had found the infants wrapped in...blankets... still alive." Beau's voice faltered and his eyes darted about the room as he blinked back tears and swallowed convulsively in an effort to gain his composure once again.

Cole swiped at his own tears, wondering what turn of fate had spared August. He would give thanks for the rest of his life that the cloak of death had overlooked her.

Beau swallowed again, and then sighed before continuing with his gruesome story. "I had a chance to say a private goodbye to Big Foot. It was the oddest thing." His eyes held the bewilderment he felt. "He was frozen in a half sitting position. It was if he still watched over his much-loved family." Beau dropped his face into upturned palms and rubbed his forehead in agonizing slow motion. He opened his mouth, but Cole heard no words—he witnessed only another sad shake of his friend's head.

Suddenly, the need to hold August in his arms forced Cole from the chair. He craved the smell of her hair; the touch of her satiny skin; the feel of her slim fingers within his.

Beau glanced up, understanding Cole's desire to reassure himself that August was alive. He nodded. "Don't ever let her go. Get her well and get her the hell out of here."

"I plan to do that as soon as she can travel."

"Just so you know, I'm going with you."

"What?"

Beau wiped the dampness from his cheeks. "Don't look so surprised."

Cole stood and looked at his friend. "I figured there would be no way to get you out of here after what happened. When did you decide?"

"When I said goodbye to Big Foot. I'm going home to Minnesota. Someone has to watch over you and August."

Cole dropped his chin and shook his head with just a hint of a smile on his lips. He reached out an arm and clasped Beau's hand that was already outstretched in his direction.

Beau nodded to the bedroom door. "Better go take care of that fine woman of yours. I'm not going anywhere until the two of you come with me."

* * *

August felt Cole's heat against her side and his comforting, protective arm draped across her midriff. Even in his sleep, the angle of his arm proved he was wary of disturbing the grievous wound inflicted by the soldiers.

She opened her eyes and stared at the dim light cast by a lantern on the dresser and thought back to the earlier hours of the day. Cole, Anna, and even Michael had thought she remained in a deep slumber from her injury. In truth, August had watched them from beneath dark lashes. She had listened to them speak of the horrifying events at Wounded Knee, but remained still, not willing to discuss the events with them until she was ready.

She mourned her people in the private recesses of her mind throughout the long day—those special souls whose wailing, grieving spirits would forever walk the land. August would never share those stolen hours of her grief with anyone—not even Cole. Firm resolve now ran through her blood. She was ready to meet the world and all its pain.

August's dark brown gaze moved about the dimly lit room and settled on a nearby table. On it was a pitcher she knew held cool water that would soothe her parched throat, but she could wait. She would never fear hunger or thirst again.

Tipping her head to the side, she studied the handsome features of the man lying beside her. Her eyes followed the defined line of his jaw, the straight contour of his nose, and the thick dark lashes that lay against his flushed skin. His warm breath fanned her face, bringing comfort to her soul as never before.

Cole was her man. He was the one person on earth whom she could trust completely. Fate had somehow placed her life in his hands when she was a young girl on the mountain. She had not known it then, but celebrated the fact in her mind now as she completed a slow perusal of his face. No one person from her past or anyone she would meet in the future would ever have such a profound impact on her life.

She moved slightly to press her lips against the warmth of his mouth. Cole stirred slightly, but slept on. His hand tightened automatically against the gentle curve of her hip.

A love deeper than August had ever experienced enveloped her like the sun on a hot summer day. She had survived the years of torment at the white man's hand and had remained strong during despondent times of hunger and death. Now, she would cherish each day, giving thanks always for the gift of life—and the gift of being given the chance to share that life with someone who was an intricate part of her spirit.

She pressed another gentle kiss to his mouth, and Cole's eyes flickered open to the shadows of the room.

"August..." A soft smile creased his face.

Never taking her eyes from his, August found his hand where it lay near her hip, brought it to her lips, and pressed a kiss to the inside of his palm. "I should have known you would be there to take me from the madness. I should have felt it in my heart." A quick flash of pain flared in her eyes, but she blinked it away. "I watched for you on the horizon everyday as we traveled south. You never left my thoughts, not even when I ran for my life. Even with so much death around me, I could only think of you."

The remembered pain pierced her heart, but she rose above it. "I thought I was dead when you found me. I thought they had won."

"They'll never win completely." Cole gathered her close, careful to let her find a comfortable position against him, and rested a whiskered cheek against her temple. The remembered smell of gunpowder, the screams of her people, and the flash of a charging Spirit with August on her back blazed across his brain. He would never forget the acute pain of watching the bullet tear into her soft flesh or of the murder of a proud people. He closed his eyes against the awful ache. Cole waited for the lump in his throat to disappear so he could speak without his voice breaking.

"The Black Hills will always be your land, August, but we can't stay. We can't fight for your dream or the rights of the Sioux—not from here. There are too many ghosts. This horrible thing that happened won't be fixed overnight." He mirrored her heavy sigh with one of his own. "I went back to Standing Rock and you weren't there. I swore that, when I did find you, I'd forcibly put you on a horse and take you back to Minnesota. I don't want to do it that way. I want you to leave of your own free will."

August simply rubbed her cheek against his shoulder and remained silent, understanding that Cole was not finished with what he needed to say.

"Leaving has to be something that you want deep in your heart. You won't have to do anything against your will ever again. You've lived that way most of your life." He rubbed a roughened palm across the smooth skin of her upper arm to sooth his own beating heart. "Will you come with me? Will you be my wife because it's what you want and not because it's something I desire?"

A lone tear found its way across her cheek. *He gives me so much...*She nuzzled closer, turned to breathe in the scent of his hair, and smiled a gentle smile to herself. "I will go."

An invisible weight lifted from Cole's shoulders.

She found his hand and laced her fingers through his. "I will leave my home, because if I were to stay without you, my life would mean nothing. We can go to the ranch, or we can find a new home in some other land. I do not care. As long as we are together, then I will be happy."

Cole slid his arm from beneath her shoulders and carefully turned so as not to jostle her injured body on the mattress. He raised himself up onto an elbow and stared down into her eyes. It suddenly came to him that he did not see the exotic looking woman of months ago—the woman with burnished skin and dark, wild eyes that seemed so different to him at that time, or the hazy apparition of his many dreams.

What Cole saw was a woman he loved deeply. The hidden waves of her shining hair, spread across the pillow, beckoned his fingers to run through its length. He could not help himself as he reached out to touch the satiny strands. Deep, abiding love rested calmly in her soft glance—a look that held no conditions—only a simple heartfelt promise of a life they would share.

He dipped his head to caress her lips, then dropped sweet, delicious kisses on a path to her neck and nuzzled her ear. Life with August would be wonderful and exciting, indeed.

"Cole?"

His name floated across the short span of air that separated their lips.

"I love you."

Epilogue

The intense heat of the South Dakota summer radiated skyward in dusty waves. Swooping, airborne ravens called out a raucous warning to a lone eagle that soared effortlessly above a flattened hilltop. The majestic bird dipped its body and hung suspended in the air for a small moment in time before the wind currents carried him aloft once more. He drifted higher into the turquoise sky and screeched loudly to those who would listen; the haunting call echoed across the barren landscape to the ghosts of the past.

The music was strangely out of place in the hot, desolate countryside. An antelope standing along the gravel road jerked its delicately pronged head upwards, listened to the odd noise, then bounded back across the brown expanse to disappear over a small butte.

Dust billowed into the air around the wheels of the nineteen fifty-seven Chevrolet, forming huge gray clouds in the hot afternoon sun. Thick sandy powder layered itself across what used to be shiny metal panels of red. The occupants of the car listened to melodies created by a big band's clarinets on the local AM radio station.

The raven-haired driver lifted his gaze from the desolate road ahead to the rear view mirror. His great uncle, Thomas Lakota Wilkins, still snoozed, his gray head bobbing against the back of the seat. A thin film of dust covered the older man's glasses as his head wobbled against the backrest.

John Wolf Wilkins smiled inwardly as his bright hazel eyes took in the sudden change in the landscape. The rolling brown hills slowly transformed themselves into pockets of green pines that sprouted on the rising countryside. He waited anxiously for the car to crest a small hill, knowing that the familiar sign would be there.

His family had made the trip to Thunderhead Mountain every year since he was sixteen. He was now twenty-eight and had just completed his medical internship at the University of Minnesota. When he was done visiting the mountain, John Wolf would spend the next three weeks with his family in the northern part of the state. The ensuing vacation was the first real break he had enjoyed in a long time.

As the first song ended and another took its place, John Wolf remembered his first trip to the Crazy Horse Memorial. It was a grand occasion; the entire family had traveled to see the dedication of a long-awaited dream come true for the Sioux nation.

"We're almost there, Grandmother." John Wolf tipped his head and settled his gaze on his great, great grandmother. Her petite form leaned forward a little more eagerly on the vinyl seat. Beads of perspiration clung to John Wolf's brow in the searing summer heat, but the elderly woman sat peacefully; her snow-white hair was pulled back in a tight bun, save for the few wispy wind-blown strands that batted her weathered cheeks. She appeared cool and comfortable, instead of wilted, after the two-hour drive from Rapid City. She had relayed a tale to him once about spending weeks on a horse and encountering blizzards and the stark, cold Dakota winds in order to reach the land they were driving through now. Since then, she had never complained about the heat or showed evidence that it even affected her.

His grandmother turned and observed him over the lenses of the tiny glasses that were forever perched on the end of her nose. "Do you remember the first time we traveled here to visit?"

"Funny you should ask. I was just thinking about that."

August's gaze turned back to the open window in order to catch a first glimpse of the mountain. "Your great, great grandfather journeyed with me that year. It was the first time we returned to my homeland after leaving so many years before. He would be so excited to see the progress as the years go by." Her clear gaze followed the passing landscape. "Even though I sense his presence around me everyday at the ranch, I somehow feel closer to him when I come here."

John Wolf reached across the length of the front seat and squeezed her tiny, wrinkled hand. "You still miss him, don't you?"

She turned with eyes brighter than of a moment earlier and blinked away the tears that burned her lids. August observed her great, great grandson and, once again, the realization hit her that, of all the children she and Cole shared, and of the many generations that followed, John Wolf was the one that took her breath away every time she looked at him. Except for the slightly darker hair, he could have been her loving Cole. "He was so frail when we visited that first time. I think I knew then that he would not return again."

John Wolf did a quick calculation in his head. Grandmother was ninety-four years old, so...Grandpa Cole would have been...ninety-two when he died. Now she spoke as if she was much younger than her age. "You had many fantastic years together, didn't you?"

The ever-present smile appeared on August's lips as she nodded. "Yes, dear, we certainly did. My Cole was always so careful to make my life nothing short of amazing. He felt a constant need to make up for those awful years, when my people were running from the soldiers."

Whenever she spoke of the past, John Wolf felt an eerie shiver run down his spine. The year was 1960. It was hard to imagine that this delightfully witty old woman who sat next to him had lived during a time when the last of the great Indian wars were fought in the United States. She had survived the horrible slaughter at Wounded Knee and lived to tell the story to her great, great grandchildren. It was even more amazing that she was the daughter of Crazy Horse, one of the greatest Indian Chiefs of that last forgotten era. No one who worked at the Memorial was even aware of it.

John Wolf lightly squeezed her hand again. "Will you tell them this year? Will you finally let them know that you're one of the benefactors who keep this project going?"

A soft smile touched her lips as, again, August reflected on the past. Her family had always respected her need to remain private, but that fact never stopped them from pressing the issue to let others know of her ancestry.

August rested her head against the window frame and relished the warm Dakota wind on her face. *My father would be so proud of my many family members...* She tilted her head and pondered a moment. The time spent with the great man encompassed only a few short hours of her life, yet her father had defined her values and her way of life from the time she was a small child.

Throughout her many years, she had watched her own children, and then their children, become United States citizens who pledged their lives to the Indian cause. They were teachers, doctors, and public officials with one common goal—that of making the Indians' lives more prolific throughout the country. Cole had always remained true to his promise.

She returned her gaze to John Wolf and sent a smile in his direction. "No, I will not say anything. I do not need praises sung to inflate my ego. Knowing that someday this great monument will be completed, that a stone figure of my father will look out over an Indian college—one built for the betterment of my people—is enough for me."

"I think you're nuts," a disregarding voice spouted from the back seat.

August turned slightly and grinned at Thomas. "Well, I see you have finally awakened from the dead."

Thomas removed his spectacles and blew the dust from the lenses with an embellished whoosh of his lips. He slid them back over his nose, adjusted the black frames, and looked at his aunt over the rims. "Uncle Cole would have loved for you to garner the respect that you deserve—and you know it, yet you do nothing about it."

August simply smiled wider. "Be quiet, old man. You always did talk too much."

"Look who's calling who old."

"Ho! I could still beat your decrepit old body in a footrace."

John Wolf shook his head at her tenacity. The two forever seemed to be harassing one another, but it was the nature of their relationship. *Uncle Thomas was eight years old when he met grandmother. I bet neither of them will ever admit that they possess a special relationship that excludes all others.*

John Wolf shook his long hair, which was tied back in a ponytail. His great uncle had never once missed the yearly sojourn to South Dakota. He would always stand by August's side, no matter what came out of his mouth. John Wolf figured out years ago that the bantering between them was simply a way to cover their true emotions.

Seeing the entrance sign come into view, he clicked on the blinker—although no other vehicles were on the road—slowed the car, and turned onto the lane that led to the Crazy Horse Memorial. His eyes darted to his grandmother's tightly clasped hands—the only indicator that being back at her birthplace churned her insides.

The car chugged around another turn and wound its way through a pine tree-lined avenue. Dairy cows plodded down the middle of the road, but a quick honk of the car horn spurred them to lumber their way into the nearby ditches. The Chevy then made its way into the gravel-covered visitor's parking lot a few minutes later.

John Wolf pulled the vehicle to a stop, but not before positioning it so his grandmother could catch her first real view of the mountain. He jumped from his seat to help Thomas from the back. It took three separate efforts and a lot of cursing from his uncle's lips to finally get the old man to a standing position. *Hmmm...Grandmother is right. He does seem older and more helpless than her.*

August used her own open door to lever herself from the car. Her heart beat just a little faster as she stared out across the valley and perused the progress that had been made on the Memorial in the past year. A painted outline of her father was now visible on the limestone mountain, where he sat proudly atop his horse. She adjusted her glasses to better view the rocky ledge that would one day be an arm pointed out over the valley.

"Missus Wilkins!" a voice called out her name.

August swiveled slowly to see her old friend, Charlie Morsett, hobble across the parking lot in her direction.

"Hello, Charlie! It's good to see you again."

The groundsman, a balding, short, rotund man clad in his usual bright red suspenders, smiled widely when he reached the car. Both Thomas and John Wolf shook hands with the elder before he turned to address August again.

"I bin waitin' for you, Missus Wilkins. Got your message last week that you were comin' and have watched for ya every day. Got a table set up on the viewin' deck. Give me a sec once you're there, and I'll have a pitcher of lemonade ready to go."

A soft laugh bubbled in August's throat as she shook her head. "Charlie—you're always so good to us when we come out."

"There's just somethin' about ya, Misses—can't quite put my finger on it. I love to see ya visit the mountain."

August, John Wolf, and Thomas exchanged secret glances.

"I see by the one vehicle that ya came with a small group this year."

She leaned heavily on Charlie's offered arm of support and walked slowly beside him across the gravel. "Everyone gets busier and busier as each year goes by." She nodded her head in John Wolf's direction, and then to Thomas, who grasped his nephew's arm. "These two never miss it, though. They enjoy the visit as much as I do."

"It's just that you bully us into coming out here with you. We've got no goddamn choice in the matter." Thomas' cranky, but untrue, observation went unnoticed as he shuffled along.

Before reaching the viewing deck, Charlie led the small group first to a huge rock with a marble inset. John Wolf and Thomas hung back with the groundsman and left August alone for a moment to read the words scribed in the granite. She placed her hands on the smooth exterior and tipped her chin slightly to peer through her bifocals.

"When the legends die, the dreams end, and there is no more greatness".

Arthritic fingers danced slowly across the surface, and her paper-thin eyelids dropped for a moment in a silent prayer as she remembered a time when she sat near a frozen river. The years seemed to melt away...

She saw Wolf as clearly as if she were sitting beside him again. She also saw the pain that clouded his eyes—a pain caused by the fact that she was leaving with Cole. Her loyal friend had stated the exact same words only minutes before the soldiers killed him. She shook her head sadly and glanced down at the rock one final time.

How strange that my father's words will be remembered into eternity because of this simple rock...

August's mind returned to another time, another place. She saw herself as a much younger woman, sitting on the front porch swing at the ranch, where Emma painstakingly taught her to read. *If it was not for her patience, I would not be able to enjoy this tribute...*

A deep breath cleared her mind and she turned with a bright smile to those who stood behind her. "Shall we continue?"

The group strolled to the viewing area that overlooked the valley, all the while listening to Charlie regale the ongoing progress atop the summit. Once they reached their destination, he quickly pulled a high-backed chair out from the table, waited for August to sit, then rushed to retrieve the promised lemonade. Their host returned a few minutes later with the tall, cool drinks.

Charlie waited until August set her glass back on the table, then approached the group again from inside the studio. "Missus Wilkins—I built ya a bench the other day when I knew ya were comin'."

"A bench?" Her brow furrowed above the tiny spectacles.

Charlie bobbed his head. "Ya always seem to have such a connection with the mountain. I wanted ya to have a special place to just sit and look at it. The bench is down the hill a little ways in a nice shady spot. The view is great and the walkin's not too hard. Slope's not too steep for ya, either. It's a nice quiet spot to reflect."

"Why, thank you Charlie. I think I'd like to see this bench of yours." She smiled in pleasant surprise, then glanced at her grandson when she rose. He followed suit quickly and took her arm. "John Wolf, would you mind staying here with Thomas? I would like to sit by myself for awhile."

"At least let me help you down the path, Grandmother."

"I'll be fine. Charlie said the walk is not bad."

"But, it's so hot—"

August cut his words short with a raised palm. "Please, Wolf, I can do this myself."

He arched skeptical eyebrows. "*John* Wolf."

"What?"

"You called me Wolf. I was simply correcting you."

"I did?" She tried to remember what she had just said, then shrugged her forgetfulness away. "I won't be gone overly long." She kissed him on the cheek, then reached up to place a gentle hand on the same. "You are so very handsome. You look so much like my Cole." She paused a bit longer to enjoy his features before casting a skeptical glance at her nephew. "Thomas—don't be cantankerous." Her eyes sparkled behind the glasses. "Just sit and be good for my wonderful boy."

Thomas rolled his eyes behind his own thick lenses. "You think I'm a baby? Christ—I'm so old I can't even pee well on my own anymore—and there you are telling me to behave."

August ignored his remark and John Wolf's chuckle before turning back to her host. "Which way, Charlie?"

He pointed to a cleared path to their left, which wound its way through the pines. "Just follow that down. You won't miss it. Enjoy your time, Missus."

August noticed John Wolf's lips tighten in indecision and touched his arm lightly. "I'll be fine—and I won't be long."

"Okay—I'll give you some time alone, but then I'm coming down to help you back up the hill."

"You are treating me like an old lady."

John Wolf threw his head back and belted out a laugh, then shook his wavy hair. "That's because you *are* an old lady."

"And only you could get away with saying that! I won't be long."

"Neither will I," he returned decisively. "Promise me you'll wait for me to come down and won't try the trail on your own."

August nodded her promise, strolled to the top of the hill, and took one cautious step after another as she made her way downward. Halfway to the bench in the distance, she paused to hold a tree limb and catch her breath. *August, you are getting old.* Her true age hit her and she flinched, but continued on.

She arrived at Charlie's bench a short time later and sank breathlessly onto the surface. "My dear," she muttered to herself, "you are going to feel your little walk tomorrow." Already, her calves were tightening with fatigue, and the old injury from a lifetime ago caused her thigh to ache.

She settled against the backrest, unconsciously rubbed the sore spot on her leg, and stared out at the mountain. *Even after all these years, I feel like I have come home...*

The massive hill's flat surface shimmered in the afternoon sun, and August gave thanks that no construction was in progress at the moment. The mountain was hers and hers alone, in the quiet afternoon. Being back in the sacred homeland of her birth lightened her heart immensely—as it always did—and she felt the silent strength of the hills surround her. The long-remembered smell of Dakota pines raised her spirits even more.

She closed her eyes and brought a hand to her chest. Her searching fingers found the familiar comfort of her grandmother's oilskin bag and the white horse Cole had gifted her with so many years ago. She had never taken the treasures from around her neck—even when the pouch turned stiff with age. The two keepsakes reminded her of all the conflicting events across the years.

August sat long and reflected on her life. She had experienced so much in her ninety-four years. Her crowning glory though, were the years spent with a beautiful man whose love for her grew stronger every day they were together. Once she stopped battling her own feelings for Cole, she had never regretted one day wrapped in the happiness of his arms.

She had mourned the death of all her family members, and Cole's, and now she was the last survivor of that first generation. Tyler, Emma, Beau, Trevor, Janie, and even little Sara were gone. They had all worked tirelessly over the years to lobby at not only the state level, but even in Washington DC for the Indian cause. Little by little, the government finally admitted the past wrongs inflicted against her people. Cole's family had given of themselves only because they loved her so much. They believed deeply in her dream that the

Sioux way of life would never be completely extinguished.

A lone tear followed the brown wrinkles on her face, trickling downward until, finally, the glistening drop splattered onto the light cotton of her shirt. Yes, she had grieved their deaths, all of them, but none so much as her Cole. He died peacefully in his sleep beside her one night, and August did not think she would ever get past the devastation of his absence in her life. *I guess I haven't, but I still go on day after day for my children and their children. But, I miss him so much...*

She closed her eyes again and let the sun's filtering rays caress her with their warmth. August envisioned Cole in her mind's eye; he was, once again, the handsome young man who stole her heart so many years ago. She pictured his smiling face as each of their five children was born. He insisted that each carry a Sioux name, so they would never forget their heritage or the proud people who were their ancestors.

One by one, they left the ranch to become fine adults, but they always returned. Try as their children might, they never completely understood why she and Cole were content to stay within the boundaries of their Minnesota home during those early years. Their parents never explained that they stayed hidden to keep the military from finding out that Cole did not die that fateful day at Wounded Knee. It was a penance August and her husband happily carried out.

She brought her gaze back to the mystical hill before her, lost in all the dreams of the past. Through all the heartache and pain, she had been blessed with a wonderful man in her life.

The whisper of a kiss against her cheek jolted August from her reflections and her surprised gaze darted upward. A wide smile spread across her face as she moved slightly on the bench to make room for him.

She waited for him to sit, then rested her head on Cole's shoulder and fought the joyful tears that threatened to spill onto her lined cheeks. "It is so good to finally see you again. I've missed you more than I can say."

"I've always been with you, August."

A playful grin tugged at the corners of her lips and she nudged his arm. "Why have you never called me by my entire name? I have never heard you say August Moon."

"I guess it's because I've never really known you as that other person. To me, you were always my August."

She caught his teasing smile when she peeked up at him and, again, her heart skipped a beat as she basked in his gentle gaze. Her eyes moved back to the mountain, accompanied by a small sigh. August watched in silent wonder as an eagle soared across the vastness of the valley.

"Will my children and all those that come after be able to tell the story of my life? Will they know that I tried to continue the dream even after that horrible day at Wounded Knee?"

Cole reached up to slip an arm around her frail shoulders, and his warmth encompassed her. "Look at the mountain, August. It's there—your children and their children and all those to follow will remember. The mountain will always remind them of your dream—that two people with different beliefs can come together as one. You taught them that." He turned her in his embrace and smiled gently into the eyes he loved so much. "Your life and the way you chose to lead it were the real dream, August. Now it's time to let them take over."

He pulled her closer and gently clasped her hand where it lay in her lap. August glanced down at his strong, masculine fingers and raised an eyebrow in surprise. The hand her beloved Cole now pulled close to his heart was that of a young woman. Gone were the gnarled fingers of the aged. Her stunned gaze followed the sleeve of a deerskin shirt to the intricately beaded cuff—a cuff she remembered working so hard to shape during a long cold winter in the mountains of Canada.

There would always be misunderstandings between the different cultures, but it was time for her to put the cause to rest. After reflecting a moment more on Cole's profound words, she tilted her head upward and allowed the Dakota sun to warm her cheeks, secure in the knowledge that now the dream would not die. Her family would carry on.

"You are right—they will do well."

"Then come with me. We have so much time to make up for."

He pulled her lithe, youthful body up from the hard bench and into his arms. Spirit cantered up behind them and, before he lifted her onto the mare's back, he dropped his mouth to hers and kissed her deeply. He lifted his head a moment later and, with the strength of youth, Cole set August atop the horse's wide shoulders, leapt up behind her, and they began the journey again.

Following is an excerpt from

Keeper of the Heart

Third book in the "Keeper" Trilogy
By Kim Mattson

Due for release by Port Town Publishing
In April, 2004

Keeper of the Heart
By Kim Mattson

Trevor Wilkins clicked the button on the silver stopwatch and, immediately, a wide smile creased his face. "Now, that's the sort of time we've been looking for. I think we've finally got ourselves a winner!"

Dougan O'Malley slapped Trevor on the back with a joyful grin of his own. "Way to go, boss. You were right to stick with this one."

Trevor slid the timepiece into his pocket and kept an eye on the magnificent black horse as the training jockey hauled on the reins to slow the animal's pace around the track. "Make sure Willy cools him down good and, by the way, tell him he's doing a great job. I'd tell him myself, but I have to get the hell out of here and get cleaned up. Tyler and Emma are coming down for a short visit. I'm meeting them at the St. Paul Hotel for an early dinner."

"Will do, Trevor. I plan to hit the road, too, just as soon as I settle The Ghost in." He shook his head; amazement still glowed in his eyes. "That horse is gonna be something, all right. Tell Missus Em I'll see her back at the ranch. If I don't get my Irish butt back up north soon, Katy will have my hide!"

A chuckle rumbled in Trevor's chest when he pushed himself away from the fence. "So, that woman of yours still has you jumping through hoops, huh?"

Dougan's curly red head bobbed in a nod. "Nothing wrong with havin' a good woman to keep you in line when you're needin' it, Trevor—and havin' her to warm your bed on a regular basis is just an added bonus."

Trevor lifted an eyebrow as he shook his dark head. "Well, I'll leave the 'jumping through hoops' to men like you and my brothers. It's definitely not for me. As far as warm beds, I'll leave that to your imagination. I never kiss and tell. " He reached out a hand. "Thanks for taking the time to bring The Ghost down. I just can't seem to get out of the city anymore. And make sure you tell Katy I'd give anything for one of her home cooked meals."

"You should tell her yourself. It's a bloody shame, Trevor, that you got a fine house in the making up north, yet you never get home to finish it."

Trevor's brain flashed to a year earlier when he decided to move out of the ranch house permanently and build his own place a mile away. The original homestead was filling up quickly; Cole and August had two children and another on the way. Combine that with Tyler and Emma's brood, and the place seemed to be turned upside down more of often than not. There was no longer room for him, at least to his way of thinking. He could not work up the enthusiasm required to complete his own home, either. It seemed senseless when he spent so much time in the city.

"Ah, someday, Dougan, things will calm down and maybe I'll get it finished. Doesn't seem that important right now. Besides, I like St. Paul and all it has to offer."

Trevor shook Dougan's hand, then turned toward the stable that sat adjacent to the racetrack. He sighed. Not only did his family continually badger him about his uncompleted home and unmarried status, but now it seemed they had enlisted the hired help to aid in their cause, as well. He shook his head again.

Why should I change my lifestyle to please them? I'm happy, and that's all that should matter—to anybody.

Trevor had long since given up on the idea of marriage. Instead, he found the excitement of breeding racehorses, the thrill of discovering a true winner, and the constant trips around the United States to be better bedmates than a woman who would constantly nag at him because he was never home. *Not that a few pretty fetching ladies haven't tried...and age doesn't seem to be a factor.* They flounced before him with their powdered faces, rouged cheeks, and expensive clothes, each doing their best to cajole him into a trip down the aisle. They offered not only themselves, but their homes as part of the deal. Trevor pursed his lips and shook his dark head again. Sometimes, the efforts to snag him into wedded bliss were downright embarrassing. *Nope...I'm right where I want to be. Thirty-nine years old and too goddamn set in my ways. I'll leave the contracted lovin' to Cole and Tyler and go on my merry way.*

The cool air inside the barn enveloped Trevor when he entered the massive structure and headed for the office to assure that The Ghost would have one of the better stalls during the training session. It had taken four years, but the Wilkins' had finally managed to breed the right combination of horseflesh. The result was a two-year old Thoroughbred that promised to tear up the track. Cole, Tyler and Emma were more than content to let Trevor handle the demanding details of track life as they added yet another dimension to their partnership. It was a perfect arrangement—and a perfect life for the middle Wilkins son.

Trevor finished up at the office, and then retraced his path past the long line of immaculate stalls. He stepped into the bright sunlight and froze when a whirling ball of flesh and ragged clothes nearly knocked him to the ground.

"Hey, slow down, you little ruffian!" Trevor bent, grabbed the straps of worn out bibs, and set a young tow-headed boy back on his feet again. The child immediately tried to scramble away from the tenuous hold, but Trevor tightened his grip and yanked him back. "Hold it right there. You gotta watch where you're going, or you're gonna get hurt. What's the hurry?"

"Let me go!" A pair of fearful watery gray eyes glanced up at the much larger man, then shifted to stare over his shoulder in the direction he had just come from. He lunged once more, but Trevor only twisted his fingers around the straps of the boy's bibs for a firmer grip.

Trevor followed the child's wide-eyed gaze to where a shopkeeper ran toward them, his white apron flapping in the wind and his fist waving in the air. His green eyes narrowed as he looked down at the boy. "That merchant isn't perhaps looking for you, is he?" He reached out a free hand and patted the bulging pocket at the boy's waist. "What do have in there?"

The fight left the lad, his shoulders slumped and, a split-second later, a single tear escaped down a tear-streaked cheek. "It's just a old apple. Mr. Timmons said he was gonna throw out a whole pile of rotten ones anyway."
"What's your name?"

The boy wiped at his runny nose with a ragged sleeve and shuffled his feet, but could not find the courage to look up. "Jonah," he muttered.

"So, Jonah, why did you steal that apple?"

Trevor leaned closer, but still missed the whispered response.
"I didn't hear you."

"I said I was hungry," he spouted back. "That old man wasn't gonna sell them old apples anyway."

Trevor heaved a sigh. The kid had a point. "That doesn't matter. If you're hungry, go home and eat. I'm sure your pa wouldn't be happy to hear that you stole that apple."

"I ain't got no pa."

"Hey—hold onto that kid!" an angry voice shouted.

Trevor and Jonah looked up at the same time—just as the shopkeeper crossed the street.

"I've had enough of you pilfering little brats helping yourselves to anything you want in my store!" Mr. Lucas Timmon skidded to a halt, his red face and the beads of perspiration that ran in rivulets down around his chin evidence of his wrath—and his lengthy chase. He lifted a beefy hand, ready to box Jonah's ears, but his downward swing was halted in mid-air by Trevor's restraining hand.

"I don't think stealing a rotten apple is reason enough to beat this boy." Trevor rose to his full height with a stern frown furrowing his brow.

"The hell it ain't. It's the only thing these urchins understand," the enraged man spewed. "Someone has to put the fear of God into him." He raised his palm again.

Jonah cringed, raced behind Trevor, and grabbed onto the leg of his newfound protector. Timmon jumped just as quickly to grab the boy, and Jonah released a high-pitched shriek and clutched even tighter to Trevor's leg.

"That's just about enough," Trevor ground out. He grabbed Timmons and muscled him against the barn wall, then held the shopkeeper in place with a bent elbow as he reached behind him to pick the clinging boy free of his leg. It was a useless endeavor. Every time he managed to loosen the boy's arm, the kid would wrap a leg around Trevor's longer limb. The older man shook the leg again and watched the boy's head bounce like a puppet; the death grip only tightened. Trevor's lips thinned into a straight line. "You know, I'm just about out of goddamned patience..."

"Jonah!"

Trevor swung his head to the right, toward the slender, middle-aged woman who stood on the curb. A toddler perched on her jutting hip, another held her hand, and two young girls—heavy burlap sacks in tow—stood behind her. The woman's gray eyes held a frazzled, rather desperate look, complimenting the wispy strands of sun-bleached hair that fluttered in the wind about her high cheekbones. She tipped her head upward, and the faded brim of her floppy hat flapped in the breeze. She squinted against the glaring sun, deepening the lines about her eyes.

"Ma!" Jonah let go of his savior's leg and ran to her side, then slipped behind the faded folds of her cotton dress. He peeked around the back of whom Trevor assumed to be his little brother, who straddled his mother's hip.

The woman glanced down at her son. "Jonah? Mr. Timmon ran out of his store hollering that you had stolen an apple from him? Did you steal an apple?"

"Ma..."

"Don't 'ma' me. Answer my question, young man." Her gentle, but firm voice brooked no obstinacy on her son's part.

Jonah trudged from behind her skirts, dug into his pocket, and pulled the rotten fruit into view. He held it out to his mother.

"Don't be giving that thing to me," she admonished. "Give it back to Mr. Timmon, along with an apology."

Trevor withdrew his arm from the shopkeeper's chest and let the man catch his breath. Lucas Timmon glared at him, straightened his collar, and lifted his nose to peer at Jonah through round spectacles for a moment before turning his gaze back to the boy's mother. "I don't want an apology, Mrs. Holcomb." He cleared his throat and stared into the eyes of the weary woman. "I want five cents, and you'd better be glad that's all I'll charge you. As for your son, I intend to call Sheriff Newton and have him handle the matter for me; so, you can march yourself and your passel of dirty little hooligans back to the store."

Her thick, dark lashes dropped shut upon the man's insult to her children, and the bodice of her worn dress swelled when she drew in a deep breath to control her anger. "Mr. Timmon, I will be more than happy to pay you double for the apple, but at the moment, I have no money on me. I'll go—"

"Wait a minute." Trevor stepped forward, dug into his pocket, and pulled out a silver coin. He dropped it into Timmon's outstretched palm. "There's no need to harass this woman over a nickel."

The woman bristled unexpectedly upon his interference into her personal matters. "Excuse me, sir." She eyed Trevor's expensive clothes, right down to his shiny black boots, and finally brought her condescending gaze back to his. "I don't need you to be a knight in shining armor, coming to my rescue."

"I just—"

"You just what?" She cut him off again as her gray eyes turned to steel. "Just because you have more money in your wallet at present than I'll probably have in a lifetime means nothing. I can take of my own—I've managed so far."

Trevor's jaw dropped in stunned amazement. The petite, feminine, and extremely needy person from a moment before was a sham. The current woman looked ready to chew him up and spit him out. "Now listen—"

"You listen! I don't know who you think you are, but you can take your shiny boots and mind your own business while I take care of mine." She raised her quivering chin another notch and looked at Mr. Timmons, but spoke to her son. "Jonah? You apologize this minute for stealing from the store."

Jonah shuffled his feet on the wooden walk, sighed heavily, and shoved his hands into the pockets of his bibs. "Sorry, Mr. Timmon. You won't have to worry about it happening again."

His mother pierced the shopkeeper with a darkened glare. "I hope that you won't bring the sheriff into this small matter. As soon as we get home, I'll send Jonah back with your nickel." She hiked the wiggling baby more securely onto her slender hip and glanced at her silent offspring. "Come, children. If Jonah needs to come back to town, we must be on our way or he'll be traveling in the dark." She turned then, and stomped away with her brood.

The tilt of her head and the scrambling children who trailed out behind her reminded Trevor of a mother duck and her babies, out for an afternoon stroll. He blinked, shook his head, and turned to the shopkeeper. "Who in the hell was that?"

The man adjusted his glasses on his nose. "That, sir, is Claire Holcomb; one of the toughest one-hundred pound bundles I've ever met. Normally, she's a soft-spoken woman, but you don't want to get her dander up—like I did today. I'd finally had enough of her brats, though. I have to keep an eye on them every time they come in the story, or they'd steal me blind."

Trevor eyed the rotten apple in the man's palm. "You would begrudge a small child a rotted piece of fruit when he's hungry? She doesn't look like she's got much money."

"Hell, they're always hungry. Claire's old man died two years ago— got drunker than a skunk one night, fell in the river and drowned. Wouldn't have blamed Claire if she pushed him in herself, though. He was mean as they come when on the liquor. She's trying to make a go of it at her small farm by selling milk and eggs to some of the restaurants in town. Hand to mouth, that one." He shook his head. "She'd be better off givin' those youngins away, but she refuses to do so." With a suddenly disinterested shrug, Timmon nonchalantly pitched the decaying piece of fruit into the street, turned, and headed for his store.

Trevor watched the apple roll to a stop in the middle of the busy lane. He turned, placed his hands in his pocket, and contemplated Jonah's mother as she hustled the children across the street only a half-block away. As though feeling his gaze upon her, she turned and the light breeze pressed her thin cotton dress against her slender body. Beneath the faded material, long legs and a flat stomach were outlined against the brightness of the day.

Claire brushed a wayward strand of hair back from her face and met his gaze again, no matter how hesitantly, then another deep breath left no doubt in his mind as to the fullness of Mrs. Claire Holcomb's breasts.

Trevor's stomach tightened at the sight, and his green eyes narrowed. How in the heck can a middle-aged widow with five scraggily urchins make me lust after her like a stud after a mare in heat?

Trevor shrugged the incident from his mind, mounted his horse, and headed in the other direction.